A sinister vampire offers Charon a choice he can't refuse: play a deadly game of winner takes all, losers die.

Charon relishes the competition and molds himself into a sexy vampire who defies vampire law, savoring his power and embracing the role of villain. He also loves surrounding himself with hot young men. But when an alluring vampire stalks him and threatens to turn him into the Vampire Council unless he helps with a seemingly impossible task, will Charon risk his perfectly narcissistic life on the challenge? Does he have any other choice?

THE VAMPIRE'S PROTÉGÉ

From the Vampire's Angel universe

universe

Damian Serbu

Published by
NineStar Press
PO Box 91792
Albuquerque, New Mexico, 87199
www.ninestarpress.com

Warning: This book contains sexually explicit content, which is only suitable for mature readers, and scenes of graphics violence, blood, and gore.

Print ISBN # 978-1-947139-71-8
Cover by Natasha Snow
Edited by Jason Bradley

To Jule
For a lifetime of friendship, loyalty, and love

Prologue

INTRODUCING CHARON

Everyone thinks they adore the Vampire Council with its rules and regulations that allegedly govern all vampires and thereby ensure the safety of virtuous humans. People want to lose themselves in the tales of the Council members: Xavier and Thomas and their love; Anthony and Jaret and their guarding of humanity; Catherine and Harriet and their whims within a righteous vampiric empire. Most of all, the Vampire Ethic provides comfort with its guarantee that goodness protects an individual from a vampire attack, with its promise that all vampires defend innocence.

Vampires accept this reality because it gives them a collective soul. The ethic protects them from the stereotype of evil incarnate preying upon humanity. Or, in the least, obedience to it keeps them alive, lest the Council hunt them down and murder them for transgressions against it.

Humans desire the Council's laws to maintain their fantasy of security from the supernatural realms. Who would dismiss a hidden force of vampire police that might swoop in at any sign of danger and annihilate the perpetrator?

Yet deep inside, so many long for something different, something that avoids this utopian trope and perfect world, all tied up in a pretty bow. Part of everyone, that piece so desperately stamped down and derided, seeks an alternative story.

To be sure, many will deny it. Fight against these words and honorably cast them out as the devil's temptations. Yet no proof of Satan or such demonic forces presents itself. Because even those thoughts really stem from the inner being in everyone, that secretly locked-up atom inside a person that pines for freedom and seeks release, even as the goodness scolds it.

Still people contest these words. Deny them.

Yet a fascination with villains thrives in America. Think of the great antiheroes of history and their legendary fame. The Wicked Witch of the West. Darth Vader. Hannibal Lecter. The Joker. The infamy of historic figures such as Adolf Hitler or Ted Bundy or the Son of Sam. The people who don the costumes at Halloween of Lord Voldemort, Dracula, or Vlad the Impaler because it empowers them for a night with beautiful wickedness. People laugh at Scar, Ursula, and even Mr. Potter. They read the tales of Lex Luther and Cujo, privately wishing they would eventually triumph over the heroes of the story and bring a bit of destruction to the globe.

Jack the Ripper lives through the ages because he successfully hid himself, true. But also because his perfect malevolence went unpunished. People want that for themselves. His legend draws them back again and again to that story with the hope of their own misdeeds going unchallenged.

Thus, whether admitted or not, people long to meet Charon. Yes, so many cry out for Charon and his story. People want him. Readers desire him, need him, really. The world will have no choice but to love him. All will embrace him as they have these other villains of history. They will celebrate his perfect treachery.

Unlike those obedient to the Vampire Council, Charon hardly worries about a bit of notoriety from time to time. Fear of retribution never enters his vocabulary. He need not concern himself with the Vampire Council and its regulations. Nor does Charon often fret over any other person or entity cracking down on his masterful empire.

ART HEIST

31 January 2015
New York City, New York

Charon walked briskly through the darkening night as soon as the moon called to him. His mission hurried him past several tasty-looking young men, despite the hunger for their blood that lurked in his belly. He hardly paused to admire the New York City skyline as he passed the Empire State Building.

He reached into his pocket and reviewed the instructions one more time. It still bothered him that the man demanded that so much money be transferred into a Swiss account before he would provide this information. Naturally, Charon killed him as soon as he handed over the plans, but he nonetheless lost those funds, which now went to the gent's family. Not that he needed the money with his otherwise vast wealth. It was the idea of the man somehow getting one up on him that disturbed him.

Charon crumpled the paper and threw it into a trash can, right before he turned down a darkened alley. Charon swiftly moved upon the security guard, twisted his neck, and shoved him aside. His vampire abilities recalled the instructions perfectly and shut down the museum's entire security system without alerting outside authorities.

Charon ripped off his black outer garments and brushed off the John Varvatos suit, making sure he looked completely impeccable. The suit fit his muscular body perfectly, framing him into the most desirable twenty-something-year-old man in the city. He glanced in a window at his reflection to fix a strand of his short sandy hair before moving toward the front door of the Museum of Modern Art.

Tricia waited, as expected, at the front door and began to unlock it as he approached. Her conservative blue business suit hardly fit the tight body underneath, though the hose showed off an alluring calf, or at least Charon imagined it would be for those so inclined.

As she opened the door, she peered around nervously and nodded to a nearby guard before looking at Charon. "Mr. Haden," she whispered, "I'm afraid we have to cancel our plans."

"Blade, please." Charon smiled brightly.

Tricia blushed. "Blade. Our security system went down. Or, at least it seems so from the front desk here. The guards are looking into it. But I don't think I can take you into the museum until we get it back online."

Charon's shoulders slumped, and he pouted. "I leave early in the morning. I so wanted this private viewing. I hate to try to blackmail you"—he grinned—"but my donation was contingent upon seeing it alone with you."

Tricia fidgeted with the keys in her hand. "Please, step inside so I can at least relock the outer door."

Charon walked inside and nonchalantly brushed against her, making sure their hands touched ever so slightly. He hovered close and spoke in a whisper. "Is there anything we can do to change this? I'm in a hurry. Though I might be able to get a bite to eat afterward, to further discuss the art and my gift to the museum. If any charming and intelligent curator would join me, that is."

"Let's see what we can work out," she whispered. Tricia giggled and looked around. "Come to my office." She said this loudly, so the two closest guards heard her.

They moved toward a hallway and went around a corner, toward the small office where Charon had first negotiated this deal with the single woman in her thirties. He plied her with stories of his love for art, true enough, and then added the insinuations of a single man's longing for a spouse and kids, all complete fabrications. She shared the same longing and flirted with him shamelessly. His initial check for a few thousand dollars, drawn from an untraceable account, convinced her of his trustworthiness, and here he sauntered, almost at his real goal.

While plenty of evidence revealed his first meeting, nothing would record his appearance here tonight.

Just before reaching Tricia's office, she dashed down a side hall and picked up her pace. "If they know I'm doing this, they'll stop me. Come on."

"Aren't you in charge tonight?"

Tricia pressed the elevator button three times. "Technically. But with this glitch in the system, not really. I'm too low on the totem pole, so to speak."

Inside the elevator, Charon held his tongue because Tricia wiggled around nervously, and sweat broke out on her brow.

He placed his hand gently on her back. "Relax." He patted her. "We'll just take a peek and get out of here."

She nodded, sighed, but then grinned at him. When the door slid open, she again scurried away with Charon in tow.

She smiled at the guard standing nearby. "Thomas, Bill wanted you to help him in the other wing with something because of the outage. I said that I'd watch over *The Starry Night* until you got back."

"Why didn't he call me on this thing?" Thomas tapped his walkie-talkie.

Tricia shrugged. "No idea."

Thomas shook his head and walked down the hall. When he turned the corner, Tricia raced the last few feet to the painting.

She screeched to a halt in front of *The Starry Night* and stepped aside, motioning for Charon to stand in front of it. Charon scanned the area, but no guards were in sight.

"Join me." He reached over, wrapped his arm around her waist, and pulled her close.

Just as Tricia began to resist, Charon latched tightly onto her, yanked her close, and leaned down and bit fiercely into her neck. Her warm blood flowed delightfully down his throat until her heart stopped and he dropped her to the floor. He hardly took notice as images of her innocent life passed through his mind because of the blood. Who cared about another lost and lonely soul?

"Aren't you beautiful?" Charon asked the painting as he took hold of it.

Time for some vampire speed. Charon clutched the painting close to him and ran with supernatural speed through the building. Even pausing to unlock the front door with Tricia's keys went so quickly that no one spotted him. He never slowed until safely back in his hidden lair, deep underground.

Charon placed the painting on a wall and sat back to admire it. "Exquisite!" He poured a Jack Daniel's and Coke, deciding to stay in for the rest of the night and enjoy his latest acquisition. The boys back at his palace would love it. And Tricia, after all, satisfied his hunger for the night. He lost count of how many times he'd visited the museum to visit this particular Van Gogh, perhaps his favorite painting in the entire world. How delightful to add it to his private collection.

DID THAT TALE gain everyone's attention? Good. Read on. Learn about Charon's origin, and find out why he went scot-free of any recrimination from that precious Vampire Council despite his caper at the Museum of Modern Art.

PART ONE: THE RIVER STYX

Chapter One: Loki

11 AUGUST 2011

Fort Lauderdale, Florida

Charon cheered again when Loki appeared on screen, as he and his old college buddies watched a pirated copy of *Thor* before they headed out for the night.

"Dude, I thought once we graduated you'd mature or something and quit being a complete ass." Bill tossed a handful of popcorn at Charon, who dodged most of it. "Still cheering for villains is so undergrad."

Charon raised an eyebrow. "Because you were so mature last night when you seduced that girl to get a little action?"

Bill shook his head. "Adults have sex. Children worry about pretend characters."

Charon paused the movie. "Shut the fuck up when Loki's on. He kicks ass. Perfect evil, though his little hurt act gets old. Just grow a set and embrace the evil."

"Come on." This time Ken threw popcorn at him. "Keep this going so we can get out of here and meet chicks."

Charon shook his head. "Not my style. Anyway, we're going to my bar tonight, so good luck getting laid there."

Gene laughed. "Right. Um, we'll go with you until you hit it off with some dude you want to deflower. Then you'll suck his face off in a corner while we quietly take our leave to a straighter climate and get our groove on."

Charon wiggled his eyebrows. "You should try it sometime. You may like it."

Ken grabbed his package. "Show me."

"Whip it out, big boy."

"Stop!" Bill held both hands in the air. "No one wants to see that. Start the fucking movie again."

The group watched the rest of the movie, all of them teasing Charon when Loki fell into oblivion at the end.

Ken punched Charon in the arm. "Poor Loki. Dead dude floating around in space."

"Just watch." Charon grabbed Ken's fingers and twisted until he cried out and yanked his hand away. "I bet we see him again. No way they let his lovely evil die away so easily. Let's go."

About twenty minutes later, the four men climbed into Ken's car. "I can't believe I have to fucking drive. Not cool. There are plenty of bars within walking distance, so I could drink, too."

"Poor, sober Ken." Gene mock cried. "Like you've never driven drunk before."

"Yeah, but it's not cool."

"Because you borrowed Mommy's Lexus?" Bill laughed.

"Fuck off." Ken pulled out of their rental property driveway and started toward the gay bars in nearby Wilton Manors. He cranked the music, prompting Gene and him in the front seats to belt out the lyrics.

Bill tilted his head and looked at Charon. "Seriously. Don't you think it's time to stop the act?"

"What act? Dude, not another heart-to-heart. We just did this last night." Charon loved these guys, at least as much as Charon loved anyone. But he loved them because, ever since being thrust together in a quad during their freshmen year of college, they partied hard, embraced the joys of life, and no one cared how it affected anyone else around them. Charon lived his whole life that way, never having dreamt that he could find soul mates that easily. "You getting soft now that you have a responsible job? Or is growing up with Daddy the pastor catching up with you?"

"Don't be an ass." Bill jerked his head slightly toward the two dancing fools in the front. "They can't hear us. You can let your guard down. I'm just saying, aren't you going to want more in life? How long can you keep up with the whole I'm-like-the-villains shtick? You're not really Loki, you know. Don't you want something more? Don't the one-night stands get old after a while?"

"This coming from the dude who has a girlfriend back home but got laid last night? The fiancée permits a fling here and there? Seriously?"

"It was a sloppy blow job. And I'm not proud of it. A little sick about it, actually. Hardly romantic. Stupid decision by a drunk."

"And hardly all mature and reformed, either. To answer your question, I'm not planning on any change of character. Been this way my whole life. I like it. It works for me. And just to set the record straight, if I ran into Loki, I'd bend him over a sink and fuck his brains out until he couldn't walk. Then I'd take over his empire. I'm a much more powerful bad guy than him."

Bill shook his head and laughed. "You're a twisted fuck."

"And that's why you love me."

"Well, some of us know you're alone, too. Always alone."

Charon glanced out the window and watched the streetlights pass by. "I like it that way. It keeps life simple."

Poor Bill. Dude grew up in an oppressive Christian environment and those religious scruples bit him in the ass from time to time. Of the four of them, Bill possessed the closest thing to a conscience. Thankfully, they parked outside the bar and hurried to get inside before Bill continued his interrogation.

Charon scoped the crowd of pretty guys, especially large for it being a weekday, and even winked at a hot little number as he twirled around on the dance floor. By the time he got to the bar, Gene already handed him a Jack and Coke and raised his glass in the air.

"To our night at the gay bar!" They clinked their plastic together and drank. "Don't know why you make us come here, though. You seem to find plenty of action at our places. A threesome two nights ago, if I remember."

Charon laughed. That hot jock blowing him as he got sucked off by his girlfriend ranked as one of the hottest hookups of the last three years. "Just lucky that night. Closet case. He'll never be the same again."

Bill and Ken joined them, and they chatted a bit before Charon saw a dude staring at him from across the room.

"Fuck."

"What?" Bill asked.

"Another love-at-first-sight idiot. No way I'd do him, even for a night. I totally don't want to deal with this."

"Where?" Gene looked around. "I don't see anyone. And how do you know that already? Maybe you're just too in to yourself."

"Trust me. Look at him pining away over there." Charon pointed to the average-looking guy, not hot, not ugly. Probably in college, waiting for Prince Charming to walk through the door and sweep him off his feet.

Hoping that Charon might be it. Ugh. "I'm going to put an end to it now." Charon hopped off his stool and started toward the other side of the bar.

Bill grabbed him by the arm. "Just leave him alone. He's harmless."

Charon jerked his arm away. "You're getting soft."

Charon walked straight across the bar and stared at the guy the whole time. The dude glanced into his drink, shifted from one foot to another, and cautiously looked back up at Charon with a nervous grin.

"Hey."

"Listen, neither one of us wants to waste our time tonight. I saw you ogling me, but you're so not my type. This is not happening. No way, no how. It creeps me out to think of you just undressing me with your eyes. So go troll for someone else. And try to stay in your league this time."

The guy almost spilled his drink as he set it on the nearest table without taking his eyes off the floor, and then walked toward the front doors.

Charon spun around and noticed a much hotter number eyeing him. Mid-twenties, short brown hair, pretty blue eyes, nice biceps exposed by his tank top. As he walked by, the guy held up his glass.

"Impressive asshole move." Despite his words, he grinned.

"Gotta do what you gotta do." Charon moved past him and returned to his friends.

Gene shook his head and handed him another drink. "You really are getting worse. That was wicked. That dude was never gonna approach you."

Charon threw back the rest of his drink and tapped the bar to order another one. "Better safe than sorry."

The silence unnerved Charon. Did they decide on some conspiracy against him? Was this heading toward some awkward and dumbass intervention? Fuck it.

"Hey, guys, so this isn't your scene. You can fire away. I'll find my way home. Eventually." Charon smiled, hoping to convince them that all was well and they could just get going.

Gene and Ken drank the rest of their liquor and nodded as they walked away.

Bill hesitated, setting down his half-full glass. "You sure?"

"Couldn't be more." Charon slapped Bill on the back. "Go get another pre-marriage blow job."

Bill half smiled—it seemed an attempt to appease Charon more than anything—and followed his friends out the door.

The alcohol relaxed Charon the minute his friends left. He dialed into his inner party boy, scanned the room, and headed right for the hot little twink in the tight jeans, dancing with his friends. He moved to the music himself, bumping into the guy a few times, making sure their eyes met as often as possible. Definitely mutual interest.

After a couple of songs, Charon let his arms fall to his side, feigning exhaustion, and walked back toward the bar, staring at the guy the whole time. He admired the dude's bright green eyes, his soft musculature, his light complexion.

No shock when about a minute later the guy stood next to him at the bar, ostensibly to order a drink. "Hey."

Charon smiled widely. "Hey. Nice dancing."

Twink grinned back. "You hitting on me?"

"What do you think?"

Twink shrugged. "Just wondering."

"Wondering, or hoping?"

He laughed this time. "How about both?"

"Good. Me too. Let me buy that." Charon slapped a twenty on the bar and waited for the bartender to finish the transaction.

"Ever been up there?" Twink casually motioned toward a dark balcony above, where a couple people stood alone and watched the dancers.

Charon shook his head.

"Too bad. Want a tour?"

Twink pushed away from the bar with his drink in hand and walked swiftly toward a set of stairs without waiting for a response. Charon liked his hubris. Confident little fuck. By the time Charon reached the top of the stairs, Twink was halfway down, beyond the two men leaning on the railing, and moving into a pitch-black corner. Charon sauntered along, barely noticing that one man had his pants around his knees with someone sucking him off right at the point where darkened shadows concealed the men's identities.

Charon slowed down, unable to see a thing, and a set of hands reached up and pulled him into a kiss. Charon reciprocated but took control, yanking the little guy toward him as their tongues intertwined. Charon felt the urgency of the other as he sucked at his tongue and clung to the back of his neck.

Charon slid his hands down the guy's back and then shoved his hands into his pants and grabbed his ass cheeks. No underwear. Totally hot.

The slight man pulled his hands down and grappled with Charon's belt, rubbing his now-hard cock once he got the zipper undone. Twink fell to his knees and in seconds had Charon's dick halfway down his throat. Charon moaned with pleasure as he cupped Twink's head in his hands and pushed himself even farther in, only holding tighter when he felt the first gag.

Charon savored the feeling for a minute or two before pulling the guy off and standing him up.

"Turn around and drop 'em, sweet thing." He spun the guy around and shoved his pants down.

"You got a condom?"

Charon licked his ear instead of answering. Twink turned his head and accepted the kiss and passion as Charon reached around and grabbed his penis in order to stroke him to more and more excitement.

"Oh. Do me. Will you do me?" the hotty begged Charon.

Charon shoved the dude against the wall, the invitation now open. He spit on his own hard shaft and shoved it in. He loved the pain he heard in the guy's voice as he planted himself all the way in, until his pubic hair tickled the guy's ass.

"I like that you shave," Charon whispered.

"Fuck me."

Soon enough, Charon gave one final thrust and shoved his face into the guy's hair as his semen spurted into his ass. They stayed in that position for a minute before Charon pulled out.

He reached down to pull up his pants and underwear.

"You wanna help me out?" Twink sounded desperate as he pushed his still-hard dick against Charon.

Charon stepped away but leaned down and kissed Twink on the forehead. "Gotta run. Take care of that, but close your eyes and think of me."

"You're just taking off?" There was hurt in Twink's voice. "We could hang for the night." Now desperation.

"Can't." Charon hurried away before it got even worse. Not that he minded dismissing someone when the time came. It just took energy Charon wanted to reserve for another, longer lay later in the night.

He dashed down the stairs and headed for the front door. Time for another bar, before Twink raced after him and begged for a second chance or regretted caving in to not using a condom and pleaded for Charon's status. Sure, he could ease the guy's mind since he was negative on his last test, but if Twink wanted to fuck strangers, he better get used to the anxiety.

He almost exited when someone reached over and grabbed his arm. "Going somewhere?"

Charon tried to jerk away, but the other one held tightly. Painfully so. "What the fuck? What's wrong with you?"

Charon turned to see the hot dude in the tank top from earlier in the night, who toasted his "asshole move" but now gripped him tightly.

"Let me go."

He released him. "We should talk."

Charon smirked. "And why would we do such a thing?"

"Because I have an offer you're going to want to hear."

Charon laughed. "Bad come-on, dude."

"It wasn't one. I'm straight."

Charon started to ask another question when Twink appeared at the bottom of the stairs. "Listen, I'm heading out. If this is such a great offer, why don't you come along?"

Charon hurried toward the door and pushed it open. He paused for but a second when he heard the guy following behind him. Why the fuck did he invite the guy along? Strange. But something about him intrigued Charon. No harm in hearing him out.

Chapter Two: Labels

11 AUGUST 2011

Wilton Manors, Florida

Charon walked briskly toward the traffic light, continuing on the path to the little wine bar across the street where he'd intended to go before his new straight pal delayed him. Without a word, the guy caught up to him.

"You care where we go?" Charon asked.

"Nope."

"You're weird." Part of this whole scenario absolutely creeped Charon out, like the time the dude approached him about getting into porn, but unlike that time, another part of him wanted to listen to this one's proposal or insanity or whatever. Like some fatal attraction drew him to this stranger.

The guy laughed softly. "You've no idea."

Even stranger. Whatever. Charon intended to keep this in public and safe. Might as well enjoy a freak session with a straight guy while he waited for his semen to build back up for another run at some hot little number. Might even spend the night with the next one.

Charon sat at a small table to the side, expecting the guy to take the opposite seat. Instead, he went over to the bar and ordered something. He returned with two empty red wineglasses and set them on the table.

"My treat."

"I don't let guys treat me. Leads to expectations and bullshit."

Again the dude laughed. "Typically, I suppose so. Drink anyway. This is a very expensive bottle, and I would hate to drink it alone."

"What's your name?" Charon asked.

Dude smiled. "In time."

This got more fucked up by the minute. Total mistake to engage the lunatic, no matter how good-looking or powerful his aura. "Don't you even want to know my name?"

"I don't need a formal introduction, Charon. Though in a minute, I'd like to learn your real name, and not the frat-boy image you portray."

"You know my name?" Charon's jaw dropped open, but he recovered quickly. "And I don't go for frat-boy covers. I am who I am."

The man nodded. "I stand corrected. You're quite right. It's not some façade but rather your true persona. That's why we're sitting together, actually. Though I still know it's not your given name."

The shop owner appeared with the bottle of wine, holding it out to the guy with a sweeping gesture. "Not many ask for this one. Rare. With a wonderful bouquet! Still, it usually sits there for quite a while."

"Because most can't afford it." He sounded like Charon with the snotty, dismissive answer.

The waiter attempted one more time to chat but gave up and uncorked the wine, poured it, and took his leave.

"He usually talks up a storm." Charon smelled the wine. Exquisite.

"Tiresome."

Charon laughed despite the guy unnerving him. "I enjoy his chatter. Nice enough."

"Nice doesn't usually appeal to you."

Charon tasted the wine. "That's the second time you claim to know something about me. And kind of got it right, but not quite. I like nice people. In small doses. And when I seek it. Before this gets any stranger and you reveal that you're a serial killer or whatever, would you explain what the fuck's going on? How did you know my name? What exactly do you want?"

This odd companion lifted an eyebrow and took a long drink of the wine, then held it in his mouth for several seconds before swallowing and closing his eyes. After a long moment, he opened them again. "That is wonderful. Perhaps you're right about him. He recommended it, so I should go lighter on him."

"That's not an answer to my question."

"I don't intend to answer it right now. Since you're so eager to get on with our business, allow me to cut to the chase. At this point, you're free to go as you choose. That freedom won't last long. The longer you persist with hearing my offer, the more entrapped you become in the game. I'll explain everything, on my time—not yours, but you'll have to be patient. When I finish this small monologue, I'll ask a few questions. More curiosities than anything, to fill in a few gaps in my knowledge. You may answer or refuse. Any refusal becomes an end to our conversation. That is, until you reach the point of no return. Understand?"

Charon swirled his wine and laughed. "You're even more fucking nuts than I thought. Whacked completely out of your mind. You somehow think you're the Phantom of the Opera."

"Yet still you sit here. You obviously sense that I offer something marvelous."

Charon raised his eyebrows. Kook.

The man leaned over the table toward Charon. "Even in your brilliance, with all your wealth, your complete control over all situations, and utter disregard for those around you in your quest for whatever you want, I possess something you would die for. It would rival the rather impressive art collection on your walls." Again Charon wondered how this guy learned so much. "Your furniture, the penthouse, none of that can measure up to this opportunity. But you have to play my game to get it or even find out what it is. First question. And I warn you, don't piss away this opportunity with your attitude."

He paused, but Charon said nothing. How did he know so much about Charon? Instinct told Charon to accept the offer to get away and leave at once. Nothing good could come from this impossibly weird conversation, could it? On the other hand, he taught himself that information about Charon for a reason. And the bottle of wine spoke of wealth, as did his Guess jeans and DKNY tank top. The Rolex, too.

Charon looked around. The owner of the shop chatted away with a couple of other patrons and four other customers sat around a table across the way. Perfectly safe. Might as well continue. If anything, this totally odd interaction could amuse Charon for a while.

"What's your question?" Charon lifted his glass and smelled the wine again.

"How did you get the nickname Charon?"

Charon shrugged. "In college, from my fraternity brothers. No big deal."

"Of course not. But you must admit it's intriguing. I already figured they labeled you with it. Let me rephrase the question. You seem more like an Eros, the way you convince anyone who sees you to fall in love. Or, at least they think they want to love you, until they meet the real you."

"Well, you just answered your own question, didn't you? I hardly act like Eros, pining for true love and offering it to those around me."

"Still, then what about Apollo? A beautiful and powerful God. Or Achilles? He'd even match your sexuality. But Charon? Have you seen the depictions of him? Snarled and ugly as he demands payment for crossing the river into death."

Charon laughed at the brief lesson in Greek mythology. He already knew it, of course. Truth be told, Charon fit his image much better than those dazzling names and personas. "They may match my appearance better. Yeah. That's true. But I got slapped with Charon because I paddle anyone who comes my way across the River Styx toward gloom, only humor them to get what I want. The name is about where I lead people."

"Charming." The man smiled and then tilted his head back and roared with laughter. "Especially that you so embrace the negative moniker given by those closest to you. Your truest friends even think you're a fiend."

"Yeah, well, speaking of charming, it's not like they're much better."

The man nodded. "To an extent. At least, they were. Yet since college, they returned to their given names. Reformed their behaviors quite a bit, this weekend notwithstanding. You, however"—he shook his finger at Charon—"still go by your Greek god's name to the point of using it anywhere you go, not just with them. You still party like a freshman. There's nothing mature in your life. Now, that could be the trust fund you stole and live off. No need for responsibility with you."

Fuck. How did he know about that? Nobody knew that. Nobody. "Can you read minds or something?"

"No, I can't. I like to toss you little tidbits from time to time to keep you interested. But it's not time for me to explain that yet. We're still learning about you."

"What else is there to tell?" Charon became uneasy again. "You nailed it. I don't intend to change. Charon suits me just fine. I like it."

"And being unencumbered by relatives or people close to you helps as well."

Charon nodded and took a big drink. "You got it."

"Though I learned a lot, I still haven't figured out if you mean that or have resigned yourself to it."

"I'm not lying to you."

"Perhaps to yourself? Anyway, I'm sorry I've frightened you to this point. I didn't know how else to get your attention."

Charon poured each of them more wine and gave in completely to the moment. Something held him here despite his initial fear and the general creepiness of what this guy knew. He either needed to bolt now or stick to it. No one ever intimidated him into fear or submission.

"Actually, you're lying to me for the first time. You've enjoyed this. You love the fear and control over me, as much as I do when I get it over other people. But you were at least right. It got my attention. So no more bullshit. What other questions do you need answered before you reveal this amazing game you want to play?"

The man smiled and leaned far across the table toward Charon, mere inches from his face. "That's the Charon I've grown to know and love. That's better. Good." He moved back into his own space. "Your real name?"

"Blade Haden. How on earth did you know everything else but that?"

He smiled. "Just making sure you were still compliant, despite the real you coming to the surface. Of course I knew it. You gave it to yourself."

"Well, I never knew any other name."

"I know. So, Blade Haden-cum-Charon. I think we've almost advanced to the next stage."

"Your point of no return?"

He nodded.

"Then let's cross it." Charon drained his glass.

"You don't want to ask any questions? Maybe I'm a cold-blooded killer and chose you as my next victim."

"Then I'm already dead. And I did wonder about that. But I hardly think that's your game because this took too long. You took too much care for something as pedestrian as that."

"Come now, humor me with a little something."

Charon thought for a minute. He really had nothing else but wanted to move to the next thing. "Okay. What's your name?"

"Good question. I'm afraid you don't need to know it."

"Seems like we might spend some time together, at least for the night. Am I supposed to just shout 'Dude' every time I want your attention?"

He laughed. "Fair enough. How about this? Call me Styx."

"Sticks? After all this buildup, you want Sticks?"

He shook his head. "S-t-y-x."

"Ah. I see. You like my nickname and want to be like me."

"I've no desire to take on someone else's persona. Give me more credit than that. But I do intend to be the river that transports you to where you long to go. Just as the River Styx provides our dear Charon with transportation."

Chapter Three: Kidnapped

11 AUGUST 2011

Venice, Florida

"That's totally weird." Charon laughed at this guy. "Seriously, Styx? Lame."

Styx glanced around the wine bar before he stood up and leaned close to Charon. "It was spur-of-the-moment to humor you. But if it annoys you, all the more reason to go with it. It's time. We've crossed the line. Come."

Charon hesitated as Styx walked toward the door, opened it, then turned around and motioned for Charon to follow him. Styx smiled. Well, if one must die at the hands of a deranged straight dude, at least pick an absolutely gorgeous one.

Charon followed him to the door. As he passed him, Charon leaned in and whispered in his ear, "I'm not dumb enough to go somewhere alone with you."

Charon walked several feet onto the sidewalk and turned around. One second, Styx closed the door; the next, he spun around and vanished completely. Before Charon could ask "What the fuck?" a force slammed into him and took his breath away. Charon struggled against it to no avail. His body moved with such speed and strength—through town, across roads, and even over a swamp—that he almost threw up.

A couple times, he thought he saw a human form carrying him, maybe even Styx's tank top, but no way could a person move this swiftly or bear Charon's six foot one, two-hundred-twenty-pound frame that easily.

Sore, bewildered, and totally pissed, Charon gasped for air when Styx threw him onto a sofa that faced a wall of windows through which a huge body of water was visible. Charon guessed it was the ocean but had no idea where exactly.

"What the fuck?" Charon sat up. Too late for fear, he let the anger consume him instead.

Styx casually sat opposite Charon and crossed his legs with his back to the water. "You crossed the line. I warned you."

"What fucking line? What's going on here?"

Styx sighed and rolled his eyes. "Would you like a drink to calm your nerves? The wine in my cellar is even better than what we had at the bar."

Charon launched out of his seat but halted two steps away, realizing this ass could overpower him again if he tried anything. He breathed heavily and glared at him.

"You're feisty. That's another reason I chose you." Styx motioned back to the sofa Charon had vacated a moment ago. "Please. Sit. I'll grab the wine, and we'll discuss this in more a civilized manner. You're angry, as I predicted. But you'll come to love this opportunity."

Charon eased back onto the couch as instructed, then waited as patiently as possible while Styx left the room.

Charon scanned the room, noticing the wealth for the first time. Though it was dark out, Charon could just see the waves that cascaded onto a sandy shore that served as the backyard. Furnished in a very contemporary and sparse style, everything stank of money, even more than Charon possessed, with white leather chairs and couch, glass tables, a seventy-inch television, and what looked to be original statues and paintings.

Styx returned a moment later with another bottle of wine. "A private reserve from a small winery in the hills of Italy." Styx opened it, poured two glasses, then swirled the wine as he crossed the room and handed one to Charon. "It'll taste better after it breathes." Styx returned to his chair.

"Listen, I appreciate the wine." Charon sat the glass on an end table without tasting it. "You've got a great view and all. Beautiful, stunning art. Decent hospitality. Except that you fucking kidnapped me." Charon's voice rose with each word of the last sentence. "And you've had some weird proposal and approach ever since we met. With all due respect, could we cut to the chase?"

Styx smiled and drank his wine. "All in good time."

"What ocean is that?"

"You're full of questions. I'll humor you on this one, just don't forget who's in charge. It's not an ocean. That's the Gulf of Mexico, off Florida. I bought this place for more than it was worth because I could renovate much of it to meet my special needs. It's not easy to find something this isolated in Florida, where you can also still build a home."

"You carried me here that fast?" Charon almost whispered the question as the reality of his captivity began to set in more and more.

Styx smiled and nodded.

"So what the fuck are you?"

This time he laughed. "All right, all right. You're impatient. But I knew that. And seemingly unafraid by the circumstances. I predicted that, too."

Charon decided to level with the dude and see where that got him. "Fear isn't something I tolerate. Frankly, I learned to conceal it. But you don't know me as well as you think. This is creeping me out. Then again, at some point, you just have to go with the situation and see where it leads, so you might as well suppress the fear because it won't change anything."

Styx threw his head back and laughed more heartily this time. "That's the spirit. That's why I chose you. Let's begin." He drained his wineglass, sat it down, and clapped his hands together before standing up and moving to hover over Charon.

Styx frowned, leaned over, and opened his mouth. Charon flinched at what he saw before pure fascination took hold as he watched the fangs smoothly descend. *Holy shit. A vampire. As in, they really exist? No way.*

"Impressed?" Styx asked as he stepped away and returned his mouth to a normal human one.

"You could say that." Charon again masked the range of emotion swimming through his head and sounded as casual as possible. "It certainly clarifies things. Either you want to convert me, get me to do some bidding as a human, or I'll be dead soon enough. Not a lot to worry about, really, until you explain yourself." Charon reached over and gulped down his wine, then held the glass up to Styx. "You're right. This is good shit. Shall we?"

"Indeed." Styx reached for the bottle and refilled their glasses.

"So spill it. You're a vampire?"

Styx nodded. "You accepted that rather well."

Charon contemplated a moment, especially marveling at the fact that his fear really had disappeared completely. "You know, the way you picked me up and sped here scared me, but at some point, I accepted death or fate or whatever. That alone introduced something extraordinary, right? I guess you being a vampire explained it. No need to piss my pants or anything. Like I said, only three choices from here, no matter how much I scream. Can't think that you'd let me just dash out of here and onto the beach to get away."

Charon left one thing unsaid, at least until he calculated the situation. Could this whole mess turn out in his favor? This guy alluded to it when they first met. If he just wanted to suck his blood out and leave him for dead, Charon would still be back in Fort Lauderdale or floating in the Atlantic Ocean. Play it cool, he figured, and see where it got him.

"That's true. As I mentioned a number of times, you've crossed the point of no return. You'll play my game, whether you want to or not. Death is the only way to opt out."

"Yeah, well, that won't happen voluntarily."

Styx smiled. "I'm counting on it."

"Let me get this straight. You obviously stalked me, learned all you could, then picked your moment to nab me. You targeted me specifically. You threaten to kill me, but it doesn't seem inevitable or I'd probably already be dead. What gives? Why me?"

"Why you, indeed. That's precisely the question we should start with. It began with your appearance. The muscular body because you work out. I'd say about 6'1", not too short, not too tall. The glowing green eyes, the short coifed hair in a faux-Mohawk. It's a fabulous look. But you already know that, don't you?"

"I'm pleased with my look. Do you like my hairless chest, too? Or is it the trail of trimmed belly hair down to my junk? I thought you weren't gay."

"I'm not. This has nothing to do with sex. Still, for the end game, I want the perfect specimen."

"So you picked me for my beauty?" Charon laughed. "This is getting stranger instead of clearer. I mean, of all the hot guys in the world, me? Don't get me wrong, I'm flattered and all. Just seems random."

"To the contrary. There's nothing random about your selection. It took centuries for me to arrive at this point. Before I could select people, I needed to perfect the plan and all it required. Once I finished that, I spent the last five years choosing my contestants, including you. It started with your appearance, but I rejected at least a hundred others who fit the bill after further investigation. You can probably guess the personality traits that added to my wish for you. You're callous. A fiend. You care for no one but yourself, or at least put your needs and desires before all others. My background investigation confirmed it all the more. No, there's nothing random about the study I did of you for the last five months."

Charon sipped his wine, starting to enjoy the game. Why not go down with a little entertainment, at least? More and more he sensed an opportunity lurking here, one that he could seize. Perhaps become a vampire himself? That would not suck, no pun intended.

"Well, you're chatting me up now. That's good. Still not really any closer to the big reveal. What's going on? You said contestant? What, is this a vampire version of *The Price Is Right*?"

Styx laughed again. "See! It's just that moxie that called me to you."

"I'm just being myself."

"Of course. And right now, you want to learn more so you can use the situation to your advantage. See? I know you better than you realize." Styx pointed at Charon. "You want to become like me. You want what I have. And you've already figured out that you may just get it. That's why you became so casual so quickly. That's why you put aside any fear. And that's why I wanted you in the game."

Styx jumped out of his chair and rushed toward Charon. He cupped Charon's face in his cold hands and wiggled it back and forth. "Too bad I'm not gay, because this would be the perfect time to plant a kiss right on those luscious red lips. I do believe that you're already in the lead." Styx released him but remained nearby.

"You'd make a shitty producer if we're going with the game show theme. Because here I sit, well into the episode, with no idea how to play it or what I might win. What kind of contestant did I become? What am I leading?"

Styx plopped to the floor and stretched out his legs in front of him. "You've entered my competition! There will be three of you. You'll meet in a bit. And the games will begin at once."

"What's the prize?"

Styx reached over and patted Charon on the knee. "Exactly the spirit. Exactly. I'll tell all of you at once. The others have waited a tad longer than you. They're even more anxious. In fact, I think we should get them, don't you?"

"Where are they?"

"Locked in rooms downstairs." Styx stood up. "Not to worry. They have similar views of the channel and all the amenities one could ask for. But I've magically held them here. One for two years, the other for just over a year."

"What took so long? Aren't they pissed? I'd be."

"I imagine they are. But I don't care. And what took so long was finding each of you. I needed the perfect three contestants. You round out the panel, so to speak. So let's begin."

With that, Styx reached over and pulled Charon out of the chair. He let go of Charon's hand and spun around toward the stairway he had descended earlier to get wine. Styx motioned to follow, so Charon grinned and headed toward him.

Chapter Four: The Contestants

11 AUGUST 2011

Venice, Florida

Charon followed Styx down the stairs, which emptied into a level just beneath the living room with the same glass wall and view of the water. A full bar stood along another wall with glass shelves, liquor bottle after liquor bottle, and contemporary steel barstools underneath a lacquered counter. The wall opposite the windows was all racks of wine bottles, one on top of another, from floor to ceiling. The furniture down here was more masculine, black leather and dark woods. Three lounge chairs faced the water, like three people sat there for hours, drinking and admiring the setting sun in their retirement.

Except that no retired people lived here and it appeared completely staged for something else entirely.

Styx smiled as he opened more wine, carried the bottle and one glass to the far left chair, and sat both on an end table next to it.

"Please." He motioned toward the chair and wine. "That's all yours. Sit. Josh will prefer straight-up bourbon, and Grady doesn't drink. I'll put out some apple juice, just to piss him off. Relax a moment while I fetch them."

"Is this competition with a couple dogs or something?"

Styx answered as he disappeared down a hallway. "I imagine that's what you'll think of them."

Charon tasted the wine, another excellent vintage. If he survived this event, he decided to take up learning more about wine. Maybe buy a winery or something. He had mastered the arts and other refinements, but his college buddies and nightlife always kept his drinking tastes simple. Jack and Coke. Shots. Something quick and easy.

Maybe Bill was right. Maybe Charon needed something new in his life, a major change, and becoming a wine snob just fit the bill.

A moment later, Styx appeared with an African-American hotty, a couple inches taller than Charon, with carefully sculpted hair, incredibly hot muscles clearly evident since he only wore a pair of basketball shorts, and glistening white teeth.

"Who's he?" He jerked his head toward Charon.

"Josh, meet Charon. Charon, Josh. He's the final contestant. We begin soon. Josh, you're in the middle there, with your bourbon. Please let Charon know about yourself, since you and Grady already met. Charon can introduce himself once you're all together. I'll fetch Grady."

Styx spun around and left Josh and Charon in an awkward silence. After a second, Josh jerked his head toward Charon and came around in front of him. He held out his fist for a fist bump, then flopped into the chair next to Charon.

"Better obey, or he freaks." He sipped his drink. "What do you want to know?"

Charon arched a brow. "What do I need to know? Seems like you know what he wants better than I. So, are you the one who's been here one or two years?"

"One. And I don't mind it. Once I figured out what I'll get at the end. Grady's the one who can't get over his anger. That's why it'll take longer to get him. Because Vamp has to control him first."

"You call him Vamp? He told me his name was Styx."

"What the fuck? Actually, to be honest with you, you know, he never gave a name. That's just what we call him."

Charon nodded and fell silent.

"I think he just wants us to know each other's backgrounds, you know?" Josh leaned back and itched his crotch. Great, Charon had landed in some college locker room. "We really just know the basics about each other. Mostly because Grady's a shithead. So I'll fill you in. You probably haven't been punished yet, but if Vamp gets pissed, it's not pretty. To be honest, there's not much to tell. My dad was a judge; Mom stayed home and spoiled me. Got to college, hated it, so partied hard and flunked out. Dad cut me off, but fuck that, you know? Mom slipped me money and I sold drugs until I got my own little empire going, see? That's it, to be honest with you."

"He picked you because you're a drug dealer?" Charon stifled a laugh.

"So you're an ass like Grady, huh? That's cool. Fuck you, too. And, no, it's not the drug dealing. You should see what I built. How much I'm worth. The women who flock to touch this body and experience me. I drive a camouflage Hummer, and I just pull up and women climb in to suck me off. Bet you don't have the ladies all over you like that, even if you are kinda pretty."

Charon smirked. "If I wanted women hanging on me, they would. But conquering guys is a lot hotter."

Josh slapped his hand on the arm of the chair. "Guess I nailed it with pretty. Pretty boy."

Great. A homophobe, too. Charon supposed that fit the locker room analogy. "Is that it about you? Seems rather mundane."

"Guess I forgot to mention that I killed people to get most of my money." Josh leaned over the arm of his chair and stuck his face inches from Charon's. The light humor and carefree demeanor evaporated, and he stared into Charon's eyes. "By the end of this, I'll have you sucking my dick right before I twist your neck and kill you."

Charon reached up and calculatingly pushed Josh back into his seat. "So my sexuality unnerved you and forced you to prove your masculinity? Charming."

Josh and Charon jerked their attention toward the hall when they heard Styx speak. "I'm glad to see you two getting along so splendidly." He reached behind him and shoved Grady into the room. "He actually complied rather quickly this time. Grady, this is Charon. You already know your dear friend, Josh. I assumed a bit of apple juice would appease you, while the rest of us drink like adults."

"Fuck off." Grady, every bit as hot as Josh, walked across the room, with that strange jock walk that Charon could never figure out. No one would naturally swing their arms that way and puff out their chest just to walk. Still, beneath the Indians T-shirt, Charon spied a hard chest and luscious biceps. Grady had especially pretty, plump red lips. He scowled, though, putting a dent in any allure.

"What's going on tonight, Chief?" Grady yanked his arm away from Styx's hand.

Styx walked in front of them after ushering Grady to his seat and slamming him into it.

"Chief?" Styx crossed his arms and stared hard at Grady, then scanned toward the other two. Charon thought Josh looked indifferent, and the entire scene made him smile with the shear absurdity of the experience. "And what are you smiling about?"

"Life." Charon lifted his glass to Styx in a toast.

Though Styx persisted with his closed posture, Charon saw the hint of amusement in his eyes. "I've had enough with the names and nonsense. What's up, you ask? It begins tonight. Do you understand? Tonight the contest commences. No more pouting and attitude, Grady. Josh, you're not as special as you think. And Charon, you're not as clever as you think. I'm in charge here, and will be until the end. I think you already surmised the game. One of you will become a vampire. The other two will die. It will all occur on my terms. Anyone gets any funny ideas, and you just elected to exit the competition early."

Charon stifled a laugh, still utterly amused by the cheap Hollywood horror movie he found himself in. Styx glanced at him again, but Charon kept his cool and smiled. The news kept the other two quiet for what felt like several minutes as each pondered the information.

"I trust you introduced yourself, Josh?"

"Yeah." Josh nodded.

"So he knows that you constructed your own little empire? That you killed without remorse to do it? That you lust for women and power."

"Got it covered." Josh spun a finger in the air.

"Good boy."

"I'm not your boy." Josh clenched his teeth.

"Ah, but you are. You're all three my boys."

Josh scratched his crotch again. "Is that why you brought a fag on board?"

"That had nothing to do with it. Now, Grady, tell Charon about yourself."

"What's he need to know? Nothing." Grady scratched his head and then played with the string on his sweatpants.

Styx silently crossed the room, reached over, and twisted Grady's ear until he shouted in pain.

"You ass. Stop it. I can't be a vampire with one ear."

"Then talk."

Grady jumped out of his chair. "Dammit. Don't fucking touch me. I'll talk. I'll talk." He stared out the window and spoke to it. *Strange bird with some intimacy issues.* Perhaps Styx missed on including this one in the competition. Josh presented a legitimate foe, but Grady appeared beatable without much effort.

"I was born on a farm in Wyoming. Grew up angry, pissed at the world, hated the shitheads around me. My only release was playing baseball. Got drafted by Cleveland." He pointed to his chest. "But went for an education instead. So I played ball in college until I got kicked off the team for a bar fight. Actually, it was about the tenth one, and coach claimed he couldn't cover for me anymore. Tenth bar fight. Lost count long ago of how many people I pummeled. Been in and out of trouble since, until this fuck captured me. Lucky him, he didn't want me as a sex slave."

Grady fell silent but kept his back to everyone else.

"And tell them why I chose you. It wasn't just the fighting. That's rather mundane. Macho bullshit, really."

Grady shrugged. "Don't know. Maybe the dude I killed in the alley fight. Maybe just my strength. Probably that."

Styx looked at Charon. "You probably ascertained that it had nothing to do with his intelligence. It was how he likes to control other people. To lord his strength over them, no matter the situation or innocence of the other party. And he has no regrets about any of it."

Grady finally turned around. "Why should I?"

Styx smiled and patted him on the shoulder. "You shouldn't. Please, sit."

Grady complied without the recalcitrance.

"Good. Good. But Josh and Grady need to know something of Charon, here. After all, he's the only one untainted by a murder. Why on earth would I choose him? Charon, will you tell us? You didn't come from the happy little families of the other two, did you?"

Did Styx mean to intimidate him with the reference to murder? Charon almost laughed again. No, he never killed anyone, but not from any moral qualm or ethic. The need or opportunity just never presented itself to the point of risking it. Truth be told, he would love to murder the two Neanderthals in the room with him right now. They hardly interested him and stood in the way of what he wanted. Styx stood waiting for Charon this time, so he decided to tell as little as the other two shared with him.

"Nope. No family. Mother gave me up at birth. Probably some cracked-out whore or slut or something. In and out of foster homes and the like, until I survived to go it on my own. I didn't like being controlled by asshole adults, even as a little tyke. Then, probably like you two, had to figure out how to provide for myself. Perfect solution, really, was the old lady who cared for me a few months when I was like seven or eight, between homes. Rich bitch. When I got old enough, I just went back and cared for her in her old age, thinking to get my hands on all her money. Her husband left her with a fortune and no kids. I got lucky, really. Lived with her for about five months, acted like the dutiful son, and she died. Left it all to me. She put it in a trust that just leaks it out until I'm thirty, but it gives me plenty a year. Speaking of killing, though. I thought I'd off her, was figuring out how to do it, when the bitch's heart gave out and did it for me. Anyway, from there, off to college, then just partying and having fun." Charon told the story as if recounting a movie he recently viewed, mostly because he felt no emotion about it whatsoever. Life did him wrong from birth, so he figured out a way on his own to correct it. As simple as that.

Josh half laughed next to Charon. "Must be nice not to have to fuck around with a family. Irritates me. Or, it did."

"Growing up, I never imagined a family. It was just never my reality. Then, yeah, once I got my hands on the money, it made life easier. Made choices easier. I get to buy lots of cool stuff, fancy stuff, and no one ever nags me about anything."

"What's up with your name?" Grady laughed. "Karen. How'd you get a girl's name?"

Styx looked at Charon and smiled. "I told you. Not smart." He tapped his head.

"Right. It's C-h-a-r-o-n. Charon. A Greek mythology thing, you wouldn't understand."

"Cool." Josh grinned in approval. "Now I get why he named himself Styx for you. The river."

"I'm impressed you know the reference." Charon took a drink of wine.

"What, stupid black kid can't learn?"

Charon frowned. "Growing up with a judge for a dad hardly sets you up to be a stupid black kid. Chill. Just that not many people worry about Greek mythology. Lurch over there certainly doesn't."

"Who you calling Lurch?" Grady launched out of his chair at Charon. Charon sat immobile just to see what Grady would do, but Styx grabbed him by the shirt collar and effortlessly threw him back into the chair before anything else could develop.

"Fucker."

Charon laughed at Grady's rejoinder. "Clever." What a caveman. Sizing up the competition, he hardly worried about Grady, unless Styx imagined an Ultimate Fight Club event to the death. But Charon surmised that Styx imagined something much more intricate than mere fisticuffs. Josh, on the other hand, continued to worry him. Strong, intelligent, and indifferent. Not unlike Charon himself.

"That should do it for introductions." Styx interrupted Charon's thoughts. "You know each other well enough now and why I chose you."

"You mean we're starting?" Josh again handled his cock. Why did straight dudes love to play with their junk so much? "To be honest with you, I lived in this prison for a year, Grady here for two, and he gets to go free from the first?"

"Relax." Styx held up his hands to Josh. "It was just happenstance, in terms of when I found each of you. I found Grady first, then you, and it took time with each person to watch and learn. I needed the perfect specimens. It was impossible to do all at once. At any rate, the timing will have no bearing on the competition. He'll be in his room from time to time, just like you. Be happy that it's almost over."

Grady stretched his arms in the air. "Josh is just an impatient little bitch. So, why we out here this time?"

Styx clapped his hands three times. "I wish I could express my excitement. We begin now. One month from today, we'll reconvene right here. Let me explain this test. On that night, I'll give each of you one million dollars in a new bank account. From now until that time, you should contemplate what to do with the money. Because I'm going to release you for a weekend, to do what you wish. Whatever your heart desires. Oh, Josh and Grady already know this, but Charon, I froze all your previous accounts. I effectively made all three of you penniless."

Charon wondered how Styx could access the trust and deplete it but knew the truth of the words. *Interesting game.* After all the talk of muscle and killing and morality, the first test would focus on financial acumen. Almost humorous, the ease of this test before it even began.

"So, again, when we come back together, you'll have three days to do what you please with one million dollars. What and how you do it will determine your grades on the first test. Think as if you have my power and resources. That's why you have a month to ponder the challenge. Now, to your rooms."

Grady and Josh jumped out of their chairs and raced down the hall.

"You trained them like hunting dogs," Charon observed.

"They know the consequences of disobedience. Let me show you to your room."

Styx led Charon down the hall, then stopped at the third door and opened it with a flourish. "Please, enjoy your stay. I'll see you in a month."

Styx then shoved Charon into a large room and slammed the door behind him.

Chapter Five: First Test

11 SEPTEMBER 2011

Venice, Florida

Charon marveled at how quickly the month passed despite his imprisonment in this room. Before Styx shoved him into it, he had worried the confinement for that long would drive him nuts, what with nothing but investing one million dollars to occupy his time.

But with all of the amenities, not to mention the test preparation, it proved remarkably painless. He easily had one thousand square feet, which included a fully stocked bar, a complete kitchen, including a way to give Styx a grocery list that was filled within a day, an audio-visual system that topped anything Charon had ever experienced, leather furniture, a king-size bed, internet access, and even a phone. He wanted for nothing. He only longed to jog along the beach instead of using the treadmill over and over, though the weight set kicked ass. His room, on the opposite side of the house from the family room and bar, looked onto a channel, so the view was okay, too. Charon spent most of the month completely naked, for no reason other than that he could and nothing really demanded he clothe himself. He jacked off more in that month than he could remember since he hit puberty. Charon even managed to amuse himself with internet porn and never longed for the days of finding a random partner in a bar to fulfill those needs. He tried a private chat with a live dude one time, but the whole concept creeped him out, so he settled for searching for various porn videos or webcam recordings.

Other than bringing things at his request, Styx never spoke to Charon or allowed him to interact with the other two. A few times, Charon contemplated calling an old friend but never knew what to say or how to explain his sudden disappearance. Besides, soon enough he would either be dead or a vampire, and either option meant leaving that old life behind.

But at last, the day finally arrived to end his confinement. Charon clicked into a couple of the accounts he created and double-checked that everything would commence as planned later that night. Yep. All set.

Actually, the organization for this task consumed many of his waking hours. He spent the first week of confinement creating charts and graphs, with all the possibilities about what a vampire might do with one million dollars, and specifically contemplating what he thought Styx meant to test. He knew it contained more than a mere voyeuristic glance into how these three would blow the money. Once he plotted his strategy, it took a lot of cunning and subterfuge to set his plan in motion, to maximize the value during those upcoming three short days, despite not having a penny to his name leading up to it. Thankfully, his previous reputation assisted him a few times to gain access and trust with people who otherwise would delete his messages without a response.

Charon closed the files and stretched. He could hardly wait to get to the next step. He felt confident in passing this test with flying colors and even laughed aloud at the ease with which he thought he could defeat the other two.

He touched his cock, and it hardened quickly, so he decided to sit back and enjoy himself one last time. He beat off to the solo image of some incredibly hot jock using a toy in his ass, then shaved and showered quickly. He pulled out the Armani suit that he ordered from Styx, who had it tailored it to fit him perfectly. His custom-made shirt wrapped around his torso, and the blue tie accented his eyes perfectly, to the point he winked at himself in the mirror and smiled widely.

He checked the time on his Invicta and assumed that Styx would appear any second. As if on cue, his door cautiously opened. When no one peeked in, Charon walked out and started down the hall, almost running into Josh as he emerged from his room.

"Whoa!" Josh laughed. "Look at Pretty Boy all decked out." He brushed the top of Charon's shoulder. "Nice."

Charon eyed Josh from top to bottom. He, too, wore expensive clothing, but just jeans, a sweater, and Nikes. "Nice watch." Charon pointed to Josh's Swatch and moved past him.

"You know you want some of this," Josh whispered in his ear from behind as they walked toward the family room. He brushed up against Charon with his dick.

"Only because I'd love to hear you squeal in pain as I fucked your ass."

Grady already sat in his recliner, wearing sweatpants and a T-shirt. Classy, just as Charon anticipated.

Styx stood in his central spot and motioned for the other two to join them. "A particularly good year for Chardonnay from the Russian River Region in Sonoma County," he said to Charon. "Try it. You two may enjoy your usual."

Charon took a sip of the wine from Lambert Bridge Winery. Divine.

"Well—" Styx grinned widely at the three of them and rubbed his hands together. "Welcome, welcome, welcome. Did any of you read the Hunger Games trilogy? Such a dreadful scenario. Still, the concept startles me with its proximity to the games about to commence right here! One of you will become just like me. The other two will die."

"What the fuck you talking about?" Grady almost shouted the question. "Hunger what?"

Charon rolled his eyes. "He probably can't read."

"Fuck off, faggot."

"See what I mean?" Charon barely glanced out the side of his eye at Grady, instead focusing his attention on how Styx smiled at the repartee.

"But you and Josh certainly understand my analogy."

"Yeah." Josh nodded. "But could we get on with it? Is this cutting into our three days?"

"Indeed, it does. So finally we get your first test underway. Are you all ready?"

Grady smirked. "You're such a tool. Cut with the bullshit. You letting us go now to do this?"

"So impatient. One more thing, and then you may disperse. I'll place one of these bracelets around each of your ankles. It allows me to more easily track you, since I anticipate you all going in different directions. A word of caution. Any attempt to escape or expose me, and I terminate you immediately. This includes if you try to remove the bracelet, understood?"

"Let's roll." Josh stuck out his leg for the first bracelet.

He raced from the room immediately after Styx attached it, prompting Grady to demand his next. Charon sat and admired the dark beauty of the ocean, sipping his wine and again thinking about starting a winery at some point. Styx smiled at him after Grady bounded up the stairs and away.

"You seem relaxed."

Charon shrugged and watched him snap the bracelet around his ankle. "I trust my plan." He took a long sniff at his wine.

"Not even hurrying out?"

"I had to guess a bit at the timing, not knowing when you'd let us go. So my plane doesn't leave for another hour."

"A plane? How resourceful. How did you acquire it without funds?"

"It's the private company I've used for a long time. I explained I had some trouble with my account but would pay them double today if they reserved the time for me. They already received the money in their account because you released our million dollars about two hours ago."

Styx chuckled. "You're definitely the most cunning of the group. Mind if I join you?" Styx pointed to the recliner next to Charon.

"It's your place. And your party."

"It must be expensive to acquire a plane like that. I hope your funds hold out."

Charon smiled. "Not to worry."

Styx and Charon finished the bottle of wine together, never speaking as they watched a couple of boats drift by and a dog run down the beach.

Charon stood up. "Well, I'll see you in three days."

In no time, Charon boarded his plane, and it touched down in Miami right on schedule, where a limousine waited and whisked Charon away, right into the heart of the downtown. He showed his identification and a minute later sat opposite the investment banker.

The man pulled out a bottle of scotch and smiled. "I only use this on special occasions."

"I'm glad this qualifies."

"It's a large sum of money. I've tried to get so many of my clients to collect Bitcoin but they want the security of more traditional investments or government backing, and all those stories about illicit deals and shady practices that involve Bitcoin scare them away, too. That doesn't even get to the volatility. When the Bitcoin value plummeted because of the Chinese, they really freaked. Still, some Vegas casinos started using it. But mostly it's the fear of any impropriety that steers people away. Actually, we had to pull some strings, you know, to get this deal done. Every part of it, I mean."

Charon sipped at the scotch to be polite but wanted complete sobriety for the next two days. "If that's a euphemism for the illegal nature of some of my request, I understand the risk you took. Of course, giving half the profit to you should alleviate most of your concern."

"Still, fake accounts and assumed names. You're playing a risky game. Planning on disappearing or something?"

"I don't imagine that many of your clients answer that question, do they? I'll be around." Charon stood and reached his hand across the desk. "Thank you."

Charon slept well that night in a luxury hotel room overlooking the ocean. He jogged on the beach late the next morning with the sand between his toes, then put a clean shirt and his suit back on. He met three more bankers before finishing for the day. He repeated this routine the second day, bored to tears by the end at having the same conversation over and over, stroking these idiots because he needed something from them. Still it worked, and by evening, he prepared for a night of his more customary partying.

He drove himself in a Mustang convertible out to South Beach and checked into a little boutique motel.

He ate an incredibly high-priced dinner, drank too much Jack Daniel's, then went dancing for a couple of hours before finding a couple to join for a hot threesome. He loved touching and licking another human after a month of only feeling himself up, especially the soft little blond twink with the ruby lips. Their insistence on using condoms annoyed him, only because his unique situation meant either death or eternal life, and he wanted a purer experience if death awaited him at the end of these tests. Still, it felt good to bang a real ass for a change. He even convinced the "strictly a top" jock to bend over the sink for a good fuck. He left them in their hotel and went back to his own for a good night's sleep.

In the morning, he returned to the airport and flew back to Venice, where he let himself into Styx's place and spent the afternoon double-checking everything he accomplished the last few days on his computer. Everything looked in order.

Only now did he wonder how many more tests awaited him. Styx never mentioned it, and Charon doubted he would get a very clear answer, even if he asked. Oh, well, one down, who knew how many to go? At least he felt successful this time.

After a quick nap, Charon woke and showered, choosing a more casual outfit for the next meeting. Soon enough, Styx rapped on his door and called for the three of them to join him.

Chapter Six: Test One Results

14 SEPTEMBER 2011

Venice, Florida

Charon entered the lower level of Styx's house first, noting the three leather recliners that faced the ocean. He could barely see the last vestiges of the sunset. As before, a small end table sat beside each chair with a drink of the person's choice, and Styx stood to the side, watching Charon while occasionally glancing out the window.

"I have just enough power to witness the sun as it descends. Some never get to see it again once they transform. I'm lucky that way."

Before Charon could ask a question or say anything, he heard the other two coming down the hall.

"This is just like a game show," Josh exclaimed as he jumped over the back of his recliner and plunged into it. His tight shorts showed off the large endowment. As if on cue, Josh grabbed it and moved it from one side to the other. "Bracelet acted like a camera, following us around, and now we return to the set. Same positions. Same routine. With our host, Ryan Seacrest, ready to reveal the results."

Charon laughed, though Grady slouched into his chair. Charon thought he never saw a greener-looking person.

"You going to vomit?" Josh asked Grady.

Odd. Charon remembered how Styx carried on about Grady's lack of alcohol consumption. So what made him sick?

Grady rubbed his face with his hands. "Maybe. If I do, I'm leaning your way."

Styx clapped his hands together loudly. "Enough of your intellectual banter. I can't take the highbrow conversation. You'll give me a headache, too. Shall we get to the task at hand? The game has begun, and I'd like to keep us moving toward its finish."

The three men sat silently in their chairs, Grady with his head in his hands, Josh casually adjusting his package, and Charon reaching for his wine for a long drink.

"Good." Styx paced in front of them. "That's better. Now, who should we start with?"

Josh chuckled and pointed to the chair next to him. "Could start with Grady, because it probably won't take long, what with his general health combined with the brain power."

Grady kept his head down but lifted one hand and flipped Josh off.

This time Styx laughed at them. "You opened your mouth. That means you go first." He motioned to Josh.

"What am I supposed to say? What's up now? You didn't give us the game show rules yet."

"Just tell the others what you did with the money and your time, both the month leading up to your release, and the three days you were gone."

Josh shrugged. "That was an easy call. Not much during my month, to be honest with you. I called into my old businesses, like you've been having me do all along, and made sure everything was fine. Kept tabs on the operation, so to speak. Then pretended that we got a windfall investor interested in us. Set that up, got them excited, explained we needed to make some dough on this, you know? That's about all I had to do during the month. Except they freaked when you drained the accounts. I calmed them down, and told them to start rebuilding it. See? To be honest with you, I figured you wanted to test if we could survive as a vampire, you know? Like, invest and shit so we could get a nice place like this." Josh shrugged again but smiled, obviously proud of himself. "They drop chunks of the profit into this and that account, other times I'll show to collect the cash, and I get that new profit plus the old profit still from owning the business. All set up on a nice little nest egg that should keep growing."

Charon raised his hand to ask a question. When Styx nodded toward him, he looked at Josh. "Is your new account in the United States, too? Under your name? A different name?"

"Yeah. Here. Like my old ones, cuz that's what I knew to do. I know how to hide my real name, asshole, though. What are you, Simon Cowell, trying to fuck with me? How else am I supposed to get the money?"

"Just curious." Charon smiled at him. "And your business," Charon made quotation signs in the air as he said the last word, "is still drug dealing?"

Josh squinted his eyes at Charon. "Perfect for a creature wanting to stay under the radar. And, you know, now you know what I did. Enough. Let's get on with it."

"Is that it?" Styx arched an eyebrow. "Why don't you give a bit more detail? Did all the money go into this old business of yours?" Styx changed his voice inflection when he said business, as if also questioning the use of the term. "Where were you during these three days?"

"Yeah, that's about it. I plopped most of it in the old company, because I know it works, you know? I know it makes money. And fast. I trust my bros running the operation. And they haven't so much as peeped about my being gone all this time, you know? So it's all good. To be honest with you, by the end of next month, should be doubled. Otherwise, you know, I just chilled. Went to my old haunts. My favorite barbershop." Josh ran his hand along the side of his head to draw attention to the new cut. "Couple old ladies that liked my attention, if you know what I mean." He laughed, and even Grady smirked. Then Josh glanced at Charon. "Well, you wouldn't understand that last part." This time Grady barked out a laugh.

Styx stepped forward. "Am I correct, then, that you put most of the money in your drug dealing, banked the rest of it, and dicked around the rest of the time?"

Josh grew quiet, some of his cockiness seeming to evaporate. "Sounds crass that way," he whispered.

"Am I correct?"

"Yeah." Josh shrugged again, ever so slightly. He nervously felt to see that his penis still existed.

"Interesting." Styx turned his attention to Josh's right and smiled, but it looked smug to Charon. "And you, Grady?"

"Wait." Josh half shouted and held up his hand. "That's it? You going to tell us if we passed or whatever?"

"Of course." Styx smiled pleasantly. "I'll grade each of you at the conclusion tonight. First, let's get all the stories in the open. Grady, you're next. There are no mulligans for withdrawal, and I don't have the patience to wait until you feel better to get on with it. Speak."

"I'm not a fucking dog," Grady mumbled.

Styx frowned, then spun around and faced the ocean. He spoke in a monotone. "Yet so often you act like a beast of the wilderness. Do you wish to participate, or are you voluntarily exiting the competition?"

"Nah!" Grady practically jumped out of his seat before settling back into it. "No. Stop. Here, I'll talk."

Styx turned around, the grin back on his face. "That's better. Please, enlighten us on your activities, though I think we've all seen *The Hangover*."

"I don't drink." Grady growled the words.

"But you did develop a habit with Ecstasy, didn't you?"

Grady continued to scowl at Styx. "We all got a weakness. You probably do, too, even in your high and mighty state as a bloodsucker. Not much to tell, dudes. Not going to waste your time with a long story like Josh."

Charon hardly believed his ears. "You have the attention span of a dog, too, if that seemed long."

"Fuck off, fag."

"Well, except dogs are smarter."

With Charon's last comment, Grady launched out of his chair but only got a few steps before Styx reached out and with but a grab of his arm tossed the large man like a Nerf ball back into his recliner. It looked as if Grady swallowed vomit as he took a moment to collect himself before continuing.

"It's a vampire test, dudes." Grady regained his cocky attitude rather quickly. "Think about it. Josh fucking around with drug money, who cares? You can murder people all the time and snatch their money. The point, if this is some test to become a vampire, is how we embrace the life, know what I mean? So I just got a limo, headed right up to Tampa, rented the best suite at a hotel, and partied hard for three days. The best meals. The best liquor for the friends I made. Mostly chicks. Scored some Ecstasy because a binge every now and then just feels good, right? Though I think the bitch with me mixed something else into that last batch. Anyway, tossed a lot of bucks at women to get what I wanted. Bought shit I liked. Oh, rented a yacht one night. Cool stuff. Met a couple of dudes who play in the NFL. Showing my prestige to the world."

Grady suddenly got up and raced out of the room. Charon shifted uncomfortably while the seconds ticked away, but Styx simply stood there. Grady returned a few minutes later, smiling and wiping at his mouth.

"Always feels better once you get a good upchuck to clear that shit out. See, alcohol would linger all fucking day."

Styx looked at Charon. "As you may guess, we've been through something like this with him before. But frankly, it's the barbarian in him that I love." He returned his attention to Grady. "Unlike Josh, who I prompted to explain more, I have a sneaking suspicion that you really don't have anything else to tell, unless we wanted the gory details of drunken people around you, sex, how you acquired the drug that put you in this lovely condition, and all other kinds of excess under the sun?"

Grady laughed. Charon marveled that a rosy complexion returned to his cheeks and his demeanor perked up, as if the throwing up really cured him. It almost made Charon want to vomit.

"That's about it, boss."

"Well, we have one more explanation to hear. Charon?"

Charon explained his handling of the million dollars as briefly as possible so as not to give everything away to his opponents but enough to satisfy Styx's request.

"If I may summarize?" Styx asked Charon, who nodded his assent. "You established false accounts and relationships over your month, and then spent most of your time setting up various hidden funds and investments, in various names and all over the place. But you, perhaps like Josh, ended with a bit of pleasure for yourself. Did I get that right?"

"Yes." Unlike the uncertainty of Josh or vapidity of Grady, Charon felt confident in his actions.

Styx paced a bit, then stared out at the ocean. Charon wondered if he possessed better eyesight as a vampire and could actually see the water. Charon envisioned the shoreline at the point where complete blackness consumed his vision because he heard the waves crashing onto the beach, but at this hour, he primarily saw the stars in the sky when he peered out the window.

Styx finally turned around. He went over and poured each of them their drink of choice, refilling Charon's wine and taking some this time for himself. He held up his glass. "A toast. To the end of the first competition." They all held up their glasses, even Grady with his juice, and then took a drink.

"It seems trite to give you grades, but I'm not sure how else to handle this, since it will develop in stages. Nothing here will give you immediate victory or immediate death. Yet you need to know your standing at the end of each trial. It may affect how you handle the next one. So, in the order you presented your achievements, or lack thereof"—he glanced toward Grady—"I'll reveal your current grade. That way you'll have some idea about how it's going at least."

Styx allowed a long silence—what felt like several minutes, though probably nothing more than seconds—before he centered himself before them and tilted his head, like a kind professor about to return exams. Yet the tension Charon could practically feel in the air indicated the life and death nature of the situation.

"Josh. You earned a B."

Josh jumped out of his chair and pumped his fists in the air. "Damn right I did." He settled back into the leather with a wide grin.

Styx motioned for him to calm down. "You established assets and relied on your human expertise and experiences prior to capture. Good. However, your investments and future are quite limited with drug dealing. That will grow your wealth and establish you early in the process of becoming a vampire. Thus the good grade. But long-term, it would expose you and leave you completely vulnerable. It's particularly too tied to your old self, and to the United States. When the government finally catches up with your enterprise, you could lose it all unless you diversify."

Josh nodded. "I get you, bro. To be honest, you're completely right."

"I know I am. Grady." Styx mock-frowned. "Poor Grady. I knew this first challenge would be most difficult for you. Not to fret, because I think you'll recover nicely next time. At least you better, since you're sitting on an F."

"What the fuck?" Grady inched forward in his chair but, perhaps remembering the last time he got thrown back into it, stayed there. Every muscle in his body went rigid.

"I knew that would shock you. But you did everything wrong. You blew the money, exposed yourself, and called attention to yourself. A lot of attention. As a vampire, that could get you killed. There are those who police our behavior. You'd ultimately end up as a homeless vampire or houseboy vampire. If you, indeed, redeem yourself and win this competition, I'll have to train you in the art of finance."

"Whatever." Grady slumped into his chair, his beautiful red lips pouting.

Styx smiled more genuinely when he turned to Charon. "My dear boy, congratulations. You're in the lead with an A."

Charon smiled back but remained casual. He guessed before Styx revealed it that he had won this round.

"A perfect diversity of investments, in different names, different countries, all over the place. I checked before you came out this evening, and you have already at least doubled your money. I especially like the Bitcoin investment. Clever. And all of it long-term. You could lose one asset without feeling it. And your indulgence embraced your wealth but modestly so." Styx held out his arms to all three. "I think you could all use a nice break. To your rooms. I'll see you in one week. Nothing to prepare in advance this time."

PART TWO: GAME END

Chapter Seven: Second Test

21 SEPTEMBER 2011

Venice, Florida

Without Styx assigning any planning to them, Charon took his week before the second test to simply enjoy himself. He had never guessed that captivity could so entertain him, but with all the amenities in the world at his disposal, no chance of escape, and yet the possibility of eternal life, he embraced the moment. He played video games, partook of more internet porn, read two novels, managed the portfolio of finances he put together during the first challenge, and otherwise relished the strange sense of liberation within this jail. Charon never realized how much he liked his solitude and keeping his own company from time to time.

So much so that he almost regretted when the door swung open and he was summoned back to the game show set. Almost, except that he led the competition for a most amazing prize. Unless, of course, he lost.

Which was not an option.

The same chairs, lineup, and drinks greeted him, but no Styx. The last glow of the sunset disappeared on the horizon and the beach descended into blackness. Charon sat down first and inspected the bottle of wine. Tessarae from Garden Creek Vineyards in Sonoma County. He knew nothing about it but took a drink and closed his eyes at the wonderful fruit-forward flavor and smooth finish.

Soon, Grady plodded in and plopped into his chair, followed by Josh, who came around to his recliner, adjusted his package, and fell into it. They all wore casual yet expensive clothes, as if Styx ordered a dress code of jeans and T-shirts or other high-end summer wear.

Charon noticed a distinct edge in the atmosphere, unlike anything to date. Perhaps the grading made it more serious or ramped up the concern. But the playful banter and one-upmanship vanished, and the others took on a cold, determined demeanor.

Except for Charon, who casually drank his wine and quite enjoyed the competition. Even if he died at the end, at least he went out with a flourish and engaged in something completely unimaginable. A game to determine who became a vampire and death for those who lost. It was brilliant.

Styx strode into the room with his usual commanding presence yet easy smile. He nodded to each of them. "Welcome. Welcome. We're almost there, folks. Almost there. I'm so excited to get this next step underway. It's so critical. So critical."

"So what is it?" Josh almost sounded nervous.

"Anxious, are we? But of course. Then let's dispense with the pleasantries this time. You could slice the tension in here with a knife. But I think this challenge is rather easy. I concocted a crime for each of you to commit. That's all you get to know. I'll hand you a sheet of paper with instructions, and send you on your way. We'll gather before dawn this time and discuss your revised grade. Understand?"

Grady snorted. "Not much to understand."

"Good." Styx nodded. "In reverse order of your current status, then, here are your instructions." He waved three note cards in the air. "Return as soon as possible once you've completed it."

Styx leaned down and affixed the monitoring bracelet to Grady's leg and waited until he disappeared up the stairs and everyone heard the front door open and close. He enacted the same routine with Josh before attaching the bracelet to Charon.

"This one will test you most of all."

Charon smiled. "Good to know." He started to leave, but Styx grabbed his arm and gently turned him around.

"You don't understand. There's one defining attribute that distinguishes each of you from the others, and they're all different. You each possess a weakness, despite your confident demeanors. I doubt many guess yours. The other two always had community or people around them, regardless of what they did. They still have family looking for them. You've always felt alone. And while you embraced it and live it well, it sometimes makes you weak. Despite what you would have others believe."

Charon froze and stared at Styx.

He smiled, an icy grin.

"I don't know what you mean."

"I think you do. Go."

Charon hurried up the stairs and out the door, shaking his head to clear it of whatever Styx meant by that exchange. Charon had lived without a family and on his own since he could remember, really his entire life. But he had friends, even long-term ones. He surrounded himself with people whenever he wanted.

He walked briskly down the long driveway about a hundred yards before realizing he never read his instructions.

Take the black Tesla. Follow the driving instructions in it and enter the dwelling. Go into the office and steal the golden eagle on the desk. Return to me. Make sure that no one knows this occurred.

"Whew," Charon said aloud. "This is a strange one. He just wants me to steal shit. At least that explains why he insisted we all wear gloves." He shook his head again, glad that his instructions got him back on track mentally.

Charon jogged back to the garage and found the waiting car. The directions were taped to the dashboard, and the GPS programmed to the destination. Driving carefully so as not to get pulled over, Charon headed through Venice and ended on a small island in Nokomis.

Charon parked the car around the back of a stucco mansion with a columned porch in front and a deck overlooking the ocean in the rear. Just before, as he drove up to it, Charon was awed at the house. Everything about it was huge, including the pillars and staircase leading up to the front door. The cream-colored paint was common in this part of Florida, but there was nothing else ordinary about the luxury of this place, right down to the life-size marble lions that guarded the entrance.

Even the rear amazed him with its ocean view and beachfront, its wooden decks, stone paths, and decked-out pool area. The place smacked of even more wealth than Styx's abode.

Glancing up at the structure, he saw no lights on or anything else. The front was darkened and appeared abandoned as well. No one home. Strange.

Seeing no one around outside, Charon walked to the sliding doors and tried them. They slid right open, unlocked. He walked vigilantly inside and stopped, listening for the sound of any living creature. Nothing.

Wondering about a security system as perhaps part of the test, since Styx specifically wrote that no one should learn about his being there, Charon searched the lower level until he found a small closet with all sorts of electronics. Sure enough, he found the recording system and replayed the shots of him driving into the compound and then walking around outside. It took a few seconds to destroy all of it. He did note that the alarm was off, so no triggers or anything appeared to have gone to the outside world.

Good enough. Now to find this dumbass eagle and get the hell out of here.

Charon walked through the lower level, still watchfully and silently, lest anyone come home or in case he had missed someone being here from the beginning.

The inside of the house sparkled as much as the outside, with expensive furniture, ornate décor, and what looked like original works of art by some of the masters. The basement stairs emptied into a side hall, down which Charon spotted the kitchen and in the opposite direction a large dining room, with a huge glass table and metal chairs around it.

Charon continued the other way until he stood in the living room. He considered an open door on the far end, which appeared to lead to a study of some sort, the one viewable wall housing floor-to-ceiling bookshelves.

Charon crossed the living room and entered the office with its old-world traditional flare, dark wood panels, two walls of books, and an enormous wooden desk in the middle. Though beautiful—and certainly it made a statement—the room appeared out of place with the rest of the house, which distinctly felt contemporary, open, and clean with brighter colors and metal-and-glass accents.

And right in the middle of the desk, illuminated by the lamp, which someone—probably Styx—staged as a spotlight, sat the stupid eagle. Such a weird challenge this time. Was it about the security system? Styx must have intended for more than the simple theft.

Whatever, Charon walked over, grabbed the item, and turned around to leave.

He froze. At last, the challenge revealed. Never having engaged a life of crime or gone through police academy, Charon at once learned the cardinal sin of forgetting to check your back.

There sat an elderly man, tied to a rocking chair with a rag shoved in his mouth. His forehead glistened with sweat, and he trembled.

"Hello," Charon said pleasantly to the old man, knowing he could not respond because of the cloth in his mouth, nor could he move. Strange, as well, that Styx or whoever had covered his eyes with a blindfold.

The gentleman squirmed a bit but, at his age, possessed no power to overcome the situation.

"This is interesting, isn't it? I need some time to think. I'll be right back." Charon smiled at the man, even bowed his head slightly as he left the room.

Clutching the eagle tightly, Charon paced back and forth in the grand foyer, pondering his options and contemplating what this meant. Styx's true test revealed. Yet test of what? Perhaps his willingness to kill the man, but that seemed too obvious. Why go to the trouble of ensuring the man could never identify him because of the blindfold if he merely wanted Charon to murder him?

No, what if this meant that he should allow the person to live, to avoid exposure. Styx reprimanded Grady for the lavish way he flaunted his wealth and status in the first test. A death would bring the police and other scrutiny, much more intense than if the geezer survived but had nothing, what with the destroyed security system, to identify the culprit. Besides, perhaps Charon could scare him into silence.

He set the eagle down in the middle of the floor so as not to forget it, and went back into the office. He removed the rag and slapped the man lightly on the cheek.

"Hello again."

The man trembled but said nothing.

"Can you speak?"

"Yes," he wheezed through a dry mouth.

"Good. I need to ask you a question. Will you answer me?"

He nodded slightly.

"Did the person who did this to you say anything? Give you any hints or such things?"

He shook his head.

"No?"

"No." Then he hesitated and coughed. "Well, one thing. That I was part of a test. And his friend would come to complete it." Drool trickled down the side of his mouth.

That confirmed, of course, that Styx staged the whole thing, not that it surprised Charon in the least.

Charon reconsidered his options again, between murder, assault, or bribing him to keep his mouth shut, sweating now a bit because he wanted to know more specifically what Styx wanted. What the old man said next made his decision.

"I'm alone. No wife or kids. Please, don't harm me. I won't tell a soul. I do have dogs, though. I don't want them hurt. I'll pay you anything."

Frightened. Compliant. No one else, really, to find out. For some damned reason, the plight of the dogs even tugged a bit at Charon's heartstrings.

"One last thing. I'll allow you to live. However, I assume you surmised from my friend's visit and your capture how easy it would be to return and finish the job, so to speak? I think it best if you keep this to yourself. Understood? I'm taking that charming eagle, and nothing else. So no police. Just go about your business. You'll need to fix your security system. But do you understand? You live, so long as you do nothing but repair your lovely home. Got it?"

And so he opted for caution, thinking that Styx would once again reward the more conservative and cautionary action, as opposed to the crass and much simpler murder. Why kill the man unless absolutely necessary?

Charon quickly untied the man from behind. "Don't remove that blindfold until I leave." He shoved the man over harshly in his rocking chair to make it more difficult to get up, especially with his hands still wrapped in the now unknotted rope.

Before the dude even hit the ground, Charon ran from the room, snatched up the ugly eagle, and raced to his car. Within a minute or two at the most, Charon headed down the road and back toward Venice.

Chapter Eight: Revised Grades

22 SEPTEMBER 2011

Venice, Florida

Charon pulled his Tesla into the driveway, ready to get inside and hear his fate after this test. He battled himself the entire way home, one minute confident he outsmarted the system, the next worried he failed by allowing the man to live. Was this the test of whether he could kill or not? He hoped not because Grady and Josh passed that one long ago.

Charon entered the house and raced to the lower level to find Josh and Grady sitting compliantly in their chairs, while Styx paced back and forth in front of the window quietly. The two contestants appeared calm, Grady even with his familiar smirk.

"Yo, Yo, twinkle toes." Josh turned his head and smiled at Charon. "This must have just about done you in." He moved his cock from one side to the other.

Grady laughed. "Bet he didn't even do it right."

Charon walked around and took his place. He stretched out and decided to rest before tasting his wine. He glanced down and noticed that Styx had some mud on his shoes. That struck him as odd, because the vampire always dressed impeccably and had monitored the financial tests from inside. Charon wondered if he spied upon them during the robberies.

When Styx finally spun around to address them, Charon thought he looked disappointed until he smiled widely. "Well, it seems that we'll have a competition after all. I've already determined your grades. But, since you fancy this a television program, we'll need each of you to give the big reveal before I explain how you did."

Charon's heart pounded in his chest. After his doubts on the way back, Styx's words only intensified his concern. A competition meant the grades evened out and Charon lost his lead.

Grady held his hand in the air. "I'll go first. Because I fucking nailed this one, dudes."

Styx nodded and motioned for Grady to continue.

"So, I get this card that tells me to drive over to a little convenience store and rob it."

"I'm surprised you could read it," Josh interrupted.

Grady flipped him off. "It tells me to do it, not by going in the front, mind you, but in the back to the little office with a safe. I'm like, dude, vampire, you got lots of money and shit. Why do you need petty cash from some dumpy little store? I wondered if it had to do with teaching me about money and all, since he thinks I failed the first test."

Styx held up a finger. "You did fail it."

"Anyway, it hits me. This ain't about the money. No fucking way. Got to be about something else. By the time I get there, I got it all figured out, no problem. Right? Obvious."

Grady grinned widely and looked to the other two for confirmation. Josh nodded his head vigorously and returned the smile while Charon sat stoically. Styx stood in front of them, ever the statue.

Charon glanced down at Grady's firm belly peeking out where his shirt lifted slightly at the waistline. Dumb but hot.

"So I park a block away, go around back with my black hat pulled down, my hoodie on, nothing that any camera could use to get me. Like I never committed a crime before, right?" Grady laughed and any sexual allure evaporated with the stupid jock sounds he snorted out. "Quick and easy after that. I walk quietly in the unlocked door, sneak up behind her, and snap her fucking neck before she even knows what hit her."

"Why the fuck was the door unlocked? Dumb bitch." Josh shook his head as if he suddenly became concerned about protecting the innocent.

Grady shrugged, but Styx answered. "I did that as part of the test. Going through the front of the store would call attention to him, and needing to bust or pick the lock would alert people, too. Are you finished?"

Grady's smile reached his eyes. "Nope. I called you on this one." He clapped his hands together and leaned forward in the chair. "Since I know this wasn't no robbery, I left the cash there and headed home."

When Grady finished, Charon grabbed his untouched glass of wine and drained it in one swallow. Fuck.

"Well played, Grady. Thank you. Josh?"

"Me next?" Josh fumbled nervously to check that his package was still there. "You know, same basic shit. To be honest with you, I don't think it'll take long to let you hear it. Must be the night of robberies and murder. Easy enough." Josh grinned, but unlike Grady's pride in himself, he looked at Charon in a kind of triumph.

"First, that motorcycle I got to ride was fucking hot. Fucking hot. I sped away in that baby, got to my destination, and waited, like the note said. That was the worst part, you know? Just sitting there, watching the world go by, and waiting for some dude in a red Volvo to pull up. But he did. So I get off the bike, walk over, and the rest, as they say, is history." Josh danced in his chair with his arms stretched out in front of him. "Unlike mental giant Grady there, I followed orders exactly."

"Fucking tool." Grady laughed at himself.

"Whatever. Jealous or something?"

Styx cleared his throat. "And what did the note ask you to do?"

"Oh, yeah. Pretend I called him for some weed but instead steal it, his money, and make sure no one witnessed the crime. So I spotted the gun in his waistband, you know? Fucking idiot had it right there. It's what I teach my guys all the time. You got to secure the gun. Always be in charge of it. Putting it someplace just so people see it won't scare dudes off. That's for movies and shit. It's your demeanor that matters. He probably thought it showed force and protected him. Instead, it made it easier for me to grab it, you know? To be honest with you, not much else to tell. Snatched it, put a bullet in his forehead, grabbed the cash and weed, and came back." Josh leaned back and crossed his arms in front of him, as satisfied as Grady that he passed with flying colors.

Charon nervously poured more wine and gulped it down.

"And Charon?" Styx frowned. "Your story?"

Charon regained his composure and sat straight up. "Are you seriously going to make me do this? Some form of humiliating people that you enjoy?"

"Did you think I'd treat you differently from the others? I even tried to warn you, or toughen you up before you left."

"It wasn't that."

"Then what was it?" Styx pursed his lips tightly together.

"Yeah, Pretty Boy." Josh punched Charon lightly in the arm. "Spill it."

"I robbed a house of a golden eagle. It's still in my car."

Grady whistled. "A real fucking bird?"

"No. A statue. Anyway, I drove out to some house and took it. It was rather easy. That is, until I turned around and saw the old man tied up and blindfolded. It has nothing to do with toughening me up. I could have killed him. I almost just did it. But I thought that too simplistic. Too much on Grady's level." Charon stared right at Styx as he spoke.

Styx lowered his head, but the daggers from his eyes almost caused Charon to flinch. "Watch it."

"I believe I outsmarted myself." He took a swig from the bottle this time. "After careful contemplation, because the guy could never identify me and I destroyed the security system, I left him there. He'll never tell what happened because I threatened him that the same person who tied him up would return to finish the job if he went to the authorities. That's it. I'm done."

Charon sat rigidly in his chair and would refuse any attempt to yank more information out of him to further his embarrassment.

Grady jumped out of his chair, his arms held over his head to signal a touchdown, and hooted and hollered. "Yes! Yes! He fucked it up! Yes!"

Josh clapped his hands loudly, too, and grinned.

Styx waited patiently for them to calm down and for Grady to return to his seat.

"Well, since we can't go to a commercial for dramatic effect, let's get on with it, shall we?" Styx rubbed his hands together. "This test took careful preparation and monitoring. First, to go in advance and render the lock at the convenience store ineffectual without them knowing so that Grady had easy access, then to call and arrange for the purchase of marijuana for Josh, and finally to stage the home scene for Charon. I intentionally spaced the distances of each crime out, so I could ensure you did it the right way and I had time to get from one place to the next, after you all left. It took mere seconds to see that Grady accomplished the task, and the same to examine Josh's success."

Styx mock-frowned as he walked over to Charon. "Yours, unfortunately, took a little longer. As Josh and Grady figured from the first, the test had nothing to do with the robbery itself, or even some intelligence test. It was all about the kill." Styx gently placed a hand on Charon's shoulder. "Vampires kill, Charon. To feed. To protect themselves. And, I hope you'll see, simply because we can."

Charon's hands shook nervously in his lap.

Styx sighed before he continued. "So I finished the job for you. The man is dead and thrown far into the ocean, thanks to my vampiric strength." That explained the dirt on his shoes.

Styx allowed a long moment of silence to fill the room. Grady and Josh sat smugly in their chairs, while Charon struggled to capture his confidence. He shoved concern for those damn dogs from his mind. He must recover, and quickly, because this test ended but at least one more remained.

Grady finally broke the silence when he shouted with glee. "I never got an A before, dudes! Never!"

Styx smiled at him. "And indeed, that is your grade. You recovered nicely. It put you back in the game. Congratulations."

Again Grady stood and danced around, though his moves looked more like a drunken hyena.

"Enough. Sit." Styx pushed him lightly back into his chair. "Josh, you earned a B."

Josh frowned. "What the fuck? I did the same as him. You a racist teacher or something?"

Styx shook his head. "Hardly. He just set the bar so high when he left the money. I had to differentiate you somehow. But relax, two Bs really puts you in the lead."

Josh clapped his hands together, and the smile returned.

"What, no dance?" Styx stepped back to give Josh some space.

Josh jumped out of his seat. He gyrated around and looked like one of those NFL players doing a touchdown dance. Despite Charon's predicament, he found it incredibly sensual.

Unfortunately, Styx continued the grading. He stepped closer to Charon and again placed a hand on his shoulder. "I'm so disappointed." He sounded genuinely hurt except for the hint of amusement with the slight curl of his lips into a smile. "You earned an F. I think you knew that already. There are others in the world who would do us harm. You can't risk a thing. Death of others in your vampire existence will be inevitable. You'll need to leave your humanity behind if you win this battle—all of it. And forget any loneliness or hesitance inside of you."

Styx turned around and watched the blackness outside for a moment. "Well, at any rate, all of this should make the final test most interesting." He twisted his head back to them, then his whole body. "Don't you agree?"

Charon stared hard at the floor. He learned his lesson the hard way and would never make that mistake again. He hated the way Styx spoke so condescendingly to him, like a lost and alone child found in the woods and incapable of protecting himself.

By his reckoning, that put Grady and him at about a C, with Josh at a B. With one more test to go. He would not fail again.

"Please, return to your rooms." Styx held his hands out to them by way of dismissal.

Grady danced out of his chair and headed down the hall, followed by Josh who moved his cock to one side before gliding after him.

Charon got up leisurely, straightened his posture, and took the bottle of wine to finish. As he got to the hall, without having heard a thing, he felt Styx's presence right behind him. He stopped.

Styx's breath tickled his ear as he whispered into it. "Let it go." He pushed ever so slightly on Charon's back to direct him down the hallway. Charon could swear Styx's lips brushed across his ear as he spoke, especially from the fact that it made his dick grow hard.

Charon slammed the door shut behind him and stalked over to the little bar. He poured the remaining wine into a glass, needing refinement and not some drunk theatrics like he assumed those other two performed after a failure.

He swirled it in his glass and watched the beautiful crimson color. As he took the last sip, he imagined the tint and taste of blood as it flowed down his throat. Lesson learned. As he stared at the channel and turned on some soft music, Charon knew he would recover and win this thing. He had every intention of it. And whatever Styx thought he needed to let go, whatever that meant, it evaporated as Charon became more determined than ever to become a vampire.

Chapter Nine: Final Test

28 SEPTEMBER 2011

Venice, Florida

Charon recovered mentally during the week after his failed test, primarily because of the time alone. Like the second test, Styx gave them nothing to prepare or ponder as they waited for the third and final phase of the competition, which offered Charon all the time he needed to contemplate what went wrong, and why.

Styx had attempted to pin it on being alone and somehow pitying the old fool as he sat tied up and at Charon's mercy. Ridiculous. Charon merely outsmarted himself. He searched for the complications in every situation and assumed that Styx planted intelligence tests and other more important attributes for a vampire than shear brutality. Lesson learned. When next faced with the task of murder, Charon would murder without hesitation. If for nothing else, he would need to in order to save his own life.

He pondered the matter for less than a day, cursed himself quickly for losing the lead and then let it go. Charon spent the rest of the time enjoying his last days as a human. For he no doubt would destroy these other two in the last test. He went as far as to study combat tactics, lest Styx planned a fight to the death.

In fact, despite last time's failing grade, Charon suspected that Styx wanted him to triumph over the other two. Styx's disappointment and softer demeanor toward Charon before sending him down the hall hinted that he had chosen a favorite, even if he held tightly to the original grading scheme.

Charon therefore hurried out of his room and down the hall when the door opened, ready to complete the game show with a victory. He sat down eagerly.

If the room took on an edge before the second competition, you could cut the tension with a knife on this evening. Everyone dressed casually, including Charon, in jeans and a T-shirt. Styx dispensed with the usual lighting and illuminated candles around the room and softly played opera music in the background. Grady sat stiffly in his chair, staring straight into the blackness beyond, while Josh fidgeted nervously, playing with the ribbing of his chair, scratching his balls, and then styling his hair. No one looked at one another; no one said a word.

Styx, too, stood before them with a commanding presence and complete seriousness. Gone was the playful smile or twinkle in his eye at the games. "Let's begin at once. No theatrics. No games this time. Two of you will die tonight. One will become a vampire. Understood?"

All three nodded with varying degrees of enthusiasm, but still no one spoke.

Styx rubbed his hands together. "Good. The first two tests concerned life and survival as a vampire. I gauged your intellect and basic perception of the situation. I attempted to see if you could handle the complicated realities of eternal life and the need to feed off people. Really, you could come upon any vampire wanting to propagate our population and find similar challenges and criteria. Not this time."

Styx turned around and faced the Gulf. He could have silently pondered something or intentionally stoked the tension to a fevered pitch through his silence, to the point that Charon glanced over and saw sweat break out on Grady's forehead.

Then Styx turned around and walked closer to the three men, a mere foot from the chairs, and passed by each of them very slowly. He stared deeply into their eyes until he got to the next chair and thus the next contestant.

Once he finished, he returned his attention to the shoreline and spoke. "The final test is more personal. You see, if a dozen vampires administered this test, each would approach it differently. This scenario has to do with what will happen to me once you become a vampire. This will explain why I selected each of you particularly for the challenge. This takes the mundane, typical vampire life and crafts it into something unique. It's about me." Styx turned around and again stared at them, or really glared at them. "Do you understand?"

Silent nods from the three men.

"I'm about to ask you a question. I'll give each of you a piece of paper upon which to write two one-word answers. Understand? I will ask a two-part question. You will give me two answers. Each one word in length. You'll have up to five minutes to write them. Questions?"

Grady raised his hand, as if back in second grade. "Why not just say 'em, like before?"

Styx smiled indulgently. "So you can't play off each other or give each other ideas. I want only what comes by instinct. What springs naturally from your heart." Styx touched his chest over his heart for emphasis. Charon wondered if a vampire's heart still beat.

Styx went behind them to the bar and grabbed three clipboards and distributed them. Charon looked at one four-by-six note card, with a one and a two already written on it. The pen was attached with a string. Now he really felt that Styx had launched them back to elementary school.

"The clock will begin the second I finish the questions. So please clear your minds." He paused to be sure they were ready before giving them their final test. "What is the greatest aspect of a vampire's life, and what would you add to make it distinct to you? Begin."

Charon turned his head so that he peered beyond the small deck, past the sand, and into the black water that only the vampire could see clearly. He made sure to get all of the other entities in the room, human and vampire, completely out of his vision. Thankfully, the stillness and quiet of the evening persisted.

With his thoughts focused and his mind clear, the answers came all too easily. Charon had won. He knew it. It was palpable in the air as surely as the tension a moment before. Not only had he figured out what might please Styx, he answered truthfully with both words. He scribbled his answers onto the card, set the clipboard quietly in his lap, and waited for the other two to finish.

Josh chewed the end of his pen, still thinking. A minute or two after Charon finished, Grady scribbled something down, then rather violently scratched it out and replaced it with something different.

"Thirty seconds."

By the time Styx gave that warning, it seemed to Charon as if an hour passed. He detected a slight tension building in his shoulders despite his confidence, so he relaxed his muscles and sat back farther in his chair. Grady returned to the imitation of a stone sculpture he had portrayed at the beginning of the night. Just before Styx clapped his hand and reached out to grab the clipboards, Josh wrote his answers.

"Let's see what you wrote, shall we?" Styx smiled for the first time that night, seemingly transformed back to the game show host and levity of earlier competitions. "We'll continue in our now-established order, yes? You should know one thing beforehand. Though obvious, the game has become pass or fail. One of you will pass. The other two fail. Now, your answers."

Styx read each clipboard without giving any hint as to his reaction. He stepped over and stood in front of Grady. "For the first part, you listed 'Eternal Life' as the greatest aspect of a vampire's life. That's two words but acceptable, given the notion you wanted to communicate. We'll simply change it to 'Eternity' for you." Surprisingly, Grady still failed to say a word when the snotty statement by Styx would usually send him into orbit. "And your distinction would be 'Liking to Kill." Again with the wordiness, but 'Kill' shall suffice. Would you like to explain your answers?"

Grady shrugged, a sneer on his face. "Seems pretty obvious." Despite his expression, his voice sounded tentative, unsure.

Styx paused before Grady, then inched over to stand before Josh.

"You wrote 'Lawless' for your first answer. And for the distinction you would offer, you put 'Calculation.' Would you at least like to indulge me with an explanation?"

Josh nodded. He adjusted the position of his dick as he answered. "Sure." He spoke more quietly than usual. "Who wouldn't love that you make your own rules, you know? Not so many to follow. Seems like eternal life is pretty obvious. To be honest with you, I went with the fact you don't have the same rules as humans. And, if it's essentially that a lawless criminal mindset makes being a vampire great, then my calculation and experience will transform me into an even greater vampire."

Styx repeated the routine of standing silently before Josh, letting the tension build again in the room, before he purposefully moved over to stand before Charon. Charon looked up and stared right back at him.

"You wrote 'Power' for the greatest attribute." Did Charon detect a slight grin from Styx? "And in a bit of a contrast to that, 'Refinement' for what you would add."

Charon noticed the other two refused to look back at Styx when he hovered over them after reading their answers. Just like dogs to a master, obediently directing their gaze somewhere else in deference to his rule over them. Charon wanted Styx to know that he gave the best answers. Their gazes met and stayed on one another the entire time.

"Do you wish to explain to the other two?"

Charon pressed his lips together and shook his head slightly. "I never thought that I'd agree with Grady. But I think the words themselves suffice."

Styx gave another second to their staredown before he turned back to the window. He set the clipboards on a small table. Again the seconds ticked by, as if they waited for eternity. What was going through Styx's mind at that moment? Was he really pondering the answers to choose a winner? No, Styx made decisions too definitively, too quickly, to suddenly need time to ponder at the very end of the game. Perhaps he wanted the dramatic effect?

Whatever the reason, what Styx said next surprised even Charon. He turned around calmly, with complete contentment written on his face. "It almost makes me sad to reach this point. So much build-up. So much suspense." This time he smiled at the words. "Alas, the competition can't continue forever. You'll now return to your rooms to await the results. Go."

The three sat rooted to their leather chairs, stunned. Charon was first to get up and begin walking away. He reached the hallway when he heard Grady's voice and turned around. Josh had gotten up, too, but stopped midway across the room.

"No fucking way. What about our grades? You always tell us how we did now." Grady got up and clutched his hands into tight fists at his side. Charon sensed that in any other situation, he would have punched Styx in the face.

"Not this time," Styx answered tersely.

Grady shook his head. "No fucking way. That is fucking bullshit. This is my life. Tell me."

Styx stepped menacingly toward Grady, mere inches from him. Despite Grady's few inches of height advantage, Styx commanded the situation. "I said *go*."

Grady spun around, his face bright red, and stalked by Josh and Charon, who waited until they heard the slamming of the door to follow behind.

Charon gradually closed his door and listened for the lock to engage. It never did. So he went to his bar and selected the bottle of extremely expensive French Bordeaux that Styx sent to him the day before. He opened the cork and smelled it before pouring two glasses. When the door opened behind him, he picked them both up and carried one over to Styx.

Chapter Ten: The Winner

28 SEPTEMBER 2011

Venice, Florida

Charon handed the wineglass to Styx and held his in the air. "To victory." He clinked them together, and each took a sip.

Charon closed his eyes, enjoying perhaps the best taste of anything in his entire life.

"You're rather confident that you won." Styx swirled the wine in his glass and quietly waited for Charon's response.

"Am I wrong?" Charon settled onto a love seat. "I always win."

Styx sat next to him and smiled. He patted Charon's knee. "I loved your answers. Funny, despite coming up with the questions, I never took the time to answer them myself. I just wanted to hear all of you and pick the responses that best matched my outlook without setting up some expectation. The instant I read yours, I thought that I would've written the same thing. Precisely the same. It's the power that's intoxicating. But shear power without some refinement equates to barbarism. What perfect answers. As Josh and you surmised, eternal life comes implied with being a vampire. Not necessarily power. Indeed, I know many who would disdain such an answer, claim that it was too crass or unethical. Refinement is just as important. Good wine." He held up his glass as testament to it. "Art. This house. Yes, I adored your answers."

"Are you admitting that I wasn't too confident? That I passed and they failed, just as I suspected?"

Styx folded one leg over the other. "Yes and no."

Charon arched a brow and couldn't help smiling.

Styx grinned back. "You answered perfectly. Averaging the three competitions, you obviously won. Yet your failure, your complete and utter failure, on the second test must be rectified."

"Ah." Charon nodded and smiled. He anticipated as much, though not necessarily in the form of a continued competition. "You still doubt my ability to kill."

Styx scrunched his brow. "Not necessarily doubt. But I need confirmation. That thread of hurt and loneliness in you, whether you admit it or not, could prove fatal. And, frankly, if you fail, I'm more than content to give the prize to Josh, much as I'd rather bequeath it to you."

Charon leaned back casually. "Who would you like me to kill? Anyone? A random person on the street? One of your enemies? I'll gladly do it, simply to grant myself eternal life. Power. Refinement. All mine for the ages."

Styx stood and drank the last of his wine. "We'll save the rest of the bottle for once you finish. As a celebration. Here's your final test. I'm going to allow you to reveal to the other two who won. And, as promised from the beginning, they will immediately die. At your hand."

Styx allowed his words to hang in the air, dramatically waiting for Charon's response. Again Charon suspected that Styx doubted his ability to do the job. Nonsense. "Any particular method you have in mind?"

Styx smiled. "I'm afraid you won't be able to be as graceful as once you become a vampire. Not because of any failing on your part. It's simply a matter of physics. They're as strong as you, if not stronger. I don't need you to prove yourself unafraid to attack them and risk an injury or some such nonsense for no reason. Or Lord help me if Grady killed you and I was left with him."

"Which gets back to method. Do you want me to figure it out? Because I will."

Styx shook his head, reached behind himself, and pulled out a gun. "I know, I know. Nothing suave about it." He handed the Glock to Charon. "Rather brutal, and terribly messy. Still, this could go on for ages, and really at this point, I'm ready for the next stage. I contemplated gassing them, but that won't give us the test we need, will it? The killing must be direct."

Charon toyed with the gun in his hands, then held it up and aimed out the window at an imaginary target. "I assume Grady's first, so if I fail, Josh is protected for you?"

"That and the fact he failed miserably."

Charon smirked. "Not to offend you, right at my moment of potential triumph, but he does seem a rather bad choice on your part. Comparatively speaking, that is."

Styx rolled his eyes. "I'll explain later, if you complete the job."

"Then let's get on with it."

Styx stood and motioned for Charon to follow him down the hallway. "I left his room unlocked. He's waiting. And actually, if you fail and he attacks, it makes my life easier because he'll dispense with you so I can swoop in and finish him off, leaving only Josh."

"That won't be necessary." Charon walked swiftly away from Styx and down the hall.

Ice ran through his veins as he got to Grady's door. Other than admiring his beauty, Charon despised the complete buffoon on the other side of the door. Good riddance. One bullet in the head, though a swift execution hardly made up for every time he called Charon a fag or made some crack about his being gay. Perhaps Charon could fashion himself into a gay superhero and avenge the victims of gay bashing once he became a vampire. The thought made him laugh out loud as he opened the door and stepped into Grady's room, the gun hidden behind his back.

The stench almost made Charon puke. Grady's clothes lay about the floor, rotting and molding food was scattered about, and Charon would swear that the worst smell came from the bathroom, leaving him to wonder if Grady ever flushed the toilet. All the more reason to make this quick.

Grady launched to his feet and sprinted across the room to stand in some sort of attack pose, Charon guessed. "What the fuck you want?"

"Merely to thank you for participating and making the competition that much easier for me."

"You think you won?" Grady stepped toward Charon.

"Not think. Know." Charon pulled the gun out and shot Grady right between the eyes before he got more than a half step closer.

Charon turned to leave and almost slammed into Styx, standing behind him in the doorway to watch.

"Nicely done." Styx grinned.

"Can we get out of here? How did you allow him to create such a complete stench? Seriously, this could seep into the walls and carry throughout the house eventually."

Styx stepped aside, so he and Charon could stand in the hall. Charon pulled the door closed behind him.

"Your first kill, yet you're worried about the state of the place and not the loss of a human life? Shouldn't you dwell on it a bit? Contemplate it?"

Charon wondered if Styx meant the question as another test, or was it just a total misread of him? Or something else? Whatever, Charon persisted with his honesty. "Nothing of the sort ever crossed my mind, frankly. He was in the way of something I wanted, so I solved the problem. The three of you played up the fact that only I never murdered anyone. And, yes, my failure in the second test exacerbated the perception. But I was being truthful when I explained that the matter simply never came up." Charon shrugged. He held up the gun to Styx. "Is this what you want me to use on him?" He pointed the weapon toward Josh's door.

"It's your choice. Would you like something else?"

Charon thought for a moment. "I may need something to pacify him. A fast-acting drug, perhaps. A tranquilizer. He's not stupid, like the idiot I just shot. He'll know what's coming and fight me immediately."

"I have just the thing. Stay here."

Charon waited patiently for a couple of minutes until Styx returned, holding up a tiny bottle with a little liquid in it. It was the size of an eye-drop container but with a spray mechanism on top. Styx tossed it to him.

"You'll come to find in a bit that I'm somewhat of a magician, as well as vampire. I concocted this but never used it. Never needed it. Spray it in his face and it should do the job. Just don't hit yourself at the same time."

Charon nodded and stepped toward the door. He pushed it open from the hallway but paused before entering. Charon guessed that Josh, a much worthier opponent, would conceal himself and attack once Charon entered, so he prepared for as much.

Charon stepped cautiously into the room, waiting for the assault. The second he passed the threshold, Josh jumped from behind an armoire to the side, grabbed Charon's gun, spun behind him, and pointed it at Charon's head. All too predictable.

Charon smiled widely and even laughed a bit.

"Thought you could saunter in and off me? Like I didn't guess who he favored and what was going to happen. Too bad for you, this bullet's going in your head."

As Josh finished the last sentence, Charon brought one arm quickly up and sprayed Styx's little bottle of magic right in his face. Before he could even pull the trigger, Josh staggered back, slammed into the doorframe, and slumped to the ground. He stared up at Charon, his eyes wide with fright but seemingly unable to move.

Charon knelt in front of him and smiled. "You were an admirable opponent. Thank you. I appreciated earning the privilege of eternal life, instead of vying against two barbarians like our friend Grady."

Charon paused, setting the gun and potion beside him. He ran his hands down Josh's powerful arms, admiring again the size and firmness of his muscle. He felt along his chest and pinched at the nipples. Next he ran one hand from Josh's incredibly hot thigh, all the way up to his crotch, where he grabbed Josh's hardening cock and held it in his hands.

"Well, that's interesting. I didn't expect that." Charon twirled his finger over the tip of Josh's now hard dick, powerful and throbbing beneath his clothing. "All the time you pointed it out and played with yourself, I did want to feel it. Thank you."

Charon stood up, the gun back in hand, and aimed it at Josh. Before he pulled the trigger, Styx stepped into the room and held up his hand to stop him.

"Well played. Well played. I liked that you tortured him a bit before the kill. He'll hate that you touched him that way."

"He seemed to like it."

Styx laughed. "At any rate, if you don't mind, I'd like to kill him a different way. Just to avoid the mess. Try this."

Styx handed Charon a syringe.

"What's in it?"

"Poison."

Without another word, Charon plopped to the floor next to Josh, patted his tummy, and stared into his open eyes, noticing that Josh still moved them to peer around the room, as if cognizant of his plight. Charon leaned over and kissed him on the cheek at the same time he stuck the shot into his arm.

He died in a matter of seconds.

"There. Dead. What's next?" Charon hopped to his feet and brushed off the back of his pants.

"I admit, I thought you'd struggle more. Oh, I knew you'd kill them. I just expected it to cause more angst."

Charon smiled. "Hardly."

Styx nodded. "Well, then, come. I have a couple of things I'd like to explain, and then we're off."

Chapter Eleven: Kaboom

28 SEPTEMBER 2011

Venice, Florida

Charon scrambled to follow as Styx hurried down the hall and into Charon's room. Styx grabbed the wine they'd opened before the kills along with two glasses. "Is there anything you want to keep? You won't be back here again. You won't be able to retrieve anything after this moment."

Charon paused, wondering at the dramatics of the statement, then peered around the room. Nothing but stuff that looked eminently replaceable in his budding vampire life. He doubted he would ever return to his own condo, let alone want an item from a place he stayed for a month. Sentimentality rarely possessed him.

He shook his head. "Nope."

"Follow me." Styx turned around with a flourish and headed back down the hall and up to the living room, where he had first planted Charon after kidnapping him in Ft. Lauderdale. "I prefer it up here. The view's better. The furniture more my style. It's just that I staged the other area specifically for the game."

Charon sat on the couch and waited as Styx poured the remainder of the wine evenly into their two glasses. He sipped it and closed his eyes, loving the smooth taste. The vampire and human sat for a moment in silence, savoring the wine, staring out the window, Charon more than anything waiting for Styx to make the next move.

"I wanted to explain a couple of things to you before we leave," Styx said. "We have one quick thing to do, and then I have a new place to take you. My lair."

"Sounds exotic."

Styx laughed, more naturally this time than Charon ever heard him. "It'll be yours soon enough, if you want it. Though you may want to start anew. Venice doesn't seem your style."

Charon laughed. "Indeed. Venice, Italy, perhaps." Charon stared into his wine and contemplated before asking his next question. "It sounds like you won't remain with me. And here I kept hoping for a seduction."

Styx grinned ever so slightly before he glanced out the window, melancholy spreading across his expression, a sadness seeping into his eyes. After a quiet moment, he seemed to snicker. "You're beautiful enough to turn me for a night, if anyone ever could have. But no. I never desired a seduction with you. I admit, however, to falling in love with you. That's different from sex, though. Shall we get on with it? There's much to tell you."

Just like that, Styx swept away whatever troubled him and focused on Charon.

"Do you need to teach me how to act as a vampire or something?"

Styx nodded, then shook his head and stretched it about on his neck as if attempting to become Linda Blair. They both laughed. "Yes and no. Eventually, yes. Starting tomorrow. That's not what I want to discuss right now, though. I just want to finish the game. Tell you more about it. Well, about the contestants."

"I'd love to know how you chose all of us."

Styx sighed. "I'm an impatient person." Styx leaned forward, toward the window, and rubbed his hands together. "It's always been a fault of mine. Once I figured it out, this magic that I'm going to share with you, I wanted to use it. But I needed the perfect specimen, or it'd all be for naught. That need combined with my haste was not good. So I went too fast. Does this make sense?"

"Not really."

Styx laughed again, then reached over and patted Charon on the knee. "It will. Soon enough. Here's what I mean. I saw you as a kindred spirit. Almost from the first time I watched you. Spied on you, really. Observed you in operation. You lived wholly for yourself and indulged in the moment. But not like some one-dimensional purely evil force. You do it with an allure. Like you almost could have turned me gay just to be near you."

Charon laughed. "Well, you're incredibly handsome. Are you sure seduction is off the table?"

"Not going to happen. I wish that I was like you. But I'm not. I'm a little too sentimental. That's why I invented the game. That's why I sought the contestants. Back to my haste. Grady was a mistake. I was excited. I figured I could find the right contestants in a matter of days and move toward my ultimate fate."

Styx paused, perhaps recalling that part of his past or contemplating this seemingly ominous fate he referenced. Charon began to wonder about where this was leading, because Styx became more cryptic and mysterious as they continued instead of more transparent. Odd. Still, Charon felt at ease and safe, so he waited for Styx to continue.

"Where was I?"

"Getting more wine." Charon smiled.

Styx obeyed, to Charon's surprise, by hurrying down the stairs and returned a moment later with another bottle of the same vintage. He uncorked it, poured them both more, and sat back down.

After taking a drink, Charon prompted Styx to continue. "Actually, you were explaining your mistake with Grady."

"Isn't it obvious? I only watched him for a night. He was a complete asshole. There's really nothing remarkable to share. You could probably guess the scene easily enough, just from your interactions with him. But that disregard for the rules and disdain for others seemed close to what I sought. So I snatched him up and brought him here. Within a couple of days, though, after attempting to talk to him, refine him, and prepare him for the game, I knew it was completely hopeless. Still, I worried that I wouldn't find anything better.

"As with you, I lured him in and offered to let him go until it was too late. I drew the line and allowed him to choose whether or not to cross it. He did. Willingly. I decided it'd be unfair to kill him before I even had the competition. It sounds insane." Styx laughed at himself. "I kidnapped people and forced them into a game, in which the winner gains eternal life and the losers die. Yet some ethical or moral compass insisted that I keep Grady alive and in it, despite sensing from almost the beginning that he'd fail. That's why I'm not like you. See?"

Charon nodded. "I would've killed him. Just because he was so annoying."

"I believe you. And I probably should have. But perhaps it worked out for the best. I developed better criteria, based in part on what attracted me to Grady, and then refined it because of what irked me about him. It took another year of searching to find Josh. I crafted a way to observe people, found likely places to locate them, and waited for them to do something, even one little thing, that hinted at evil or an impurity of some sort. Then I monitored for the sophistication within it. My study of Josh and then you took a few months and additional research. My new criteria and calculation proved much better at finding worthy contestants."

"Which is why you chose Josh."

Styx nodded vigorously. "You know, because of my impatience, I almost went with a two-man game. I liked Josh. Figured he fit the bill quite well. Again with some strange ethic or something guiding me, I decided to find one more person just because I promised myself to hold a contest with three people. Arbitrary." Styx chuckled.

"Did you ever examine women? Why not spice it up a little?"

Styx scrunched his brow. "I'm old. Older than you could possibly imagine."

"What does that have to do with it?"

"I don't see women as equals." Styx shrugged. "I never have."

Charon had never considered such a stance before. He grew up in a vastly different world, and despite all his loathing of people and taking what he desired, he always saw women as equal to himself.

"Well, I guess I'm lucky I have a penis."

The grin spread widely across Styx's face. "Let's finish this story. Josh was perfect. Really, in retrospect, you and he vied for the prize. A third more-worthy opponent may have intensified things more than poor Grady could muster. Anyway, as good as Josh was, he lost all humanity, it seems. He nearly became too much a caricature of what I sought. A cartoon villain of sorts. When I recognized that for sure, which wasn't until I found you, I expected you to win. Wanted you to win. Maybe even needed you to win."

"Because I added refinement."

Styx shook his head. "He could do that, too. Differently, to be sure. But no. Because you have a soul."

Charon frowned. "What does that mean?"

"You won't admit it. Not even now. But in your perfect indulgence, in grasping all the joys of life at the expense of others, and in adding to it that intelligence and sophistication, you long for something."

"Are you going back to that loneliness nonsense?" Charon poured himself more wine.

"Essentially."

Charon sighed. "I disagree." He took a deep drink of the wine.

"I know you do. I know you don't want to see it. That spark of emotion drew me to you. You'll become my perfect vision of a vampire. You'll embrace the power with disregard for the Vampire Rules but add such elegance and chic as to make it seem like a good thing. Some inner light will keep you from slipping into total darkness. That's what I feared most with Josh. Because you don't want a war with the Vampire Council. You just want to fuck with them for eternity."

Charon tilted his head, puzzled. "There are laws? What's a Vampire Council?"

"Later. Not now. In fact, enough of this. Our next activity promises some excitement. But the sun approaches, so we must act quickly. Come."

Styx leaped off the couch and threw his half-full wineglass hard against the sliding glass door. He laughed triumphantly as it exploded, glass and wine cascading everywhere. He hurried over and did the same with Charon's.

"I always wanted to do that. Fun!" Then he picked Charon up and ran him out of the house. Sometimes Charon forgot Styx's vampire strength when they sat around chatting like humans.

Within seconds, they stood on a small hill near the edge of the property but still in sight of the house.

"What's going on?" Charon asked.

"Watch!"

Styx pulled out a cell phone and played around on the screen. Suddenly, Charon fell flat on his ass, partially from the force of the explosion and partially from absolute shock.

Kaboom! The entire compound exploded completely. It looked and sounded like an atomic bomb landed right on top of Styx's house and destroyed the entire thing.

Styx stood next to Charon, laughing hard, until he started jumping up and down and cheering. Before Charon even regained his wits about him, Styx grabbed him by the hand, hauled him to his feet, and sauntered down the short remaining driveway to the street, as if on a Sunday stroll.

"Sweet, yes?"

Charon pointed behind them. "You just blew up your house!"

Styx cackled this time. "Cool, huh? I only have one place left. Only one thing left in all the world. No other hidden dwellings, no bank accounts, nothing but my one secret lair. I can't wait to show you! Only one remnant of my life remaining."

Again Charon developed an odd feeling about these comments and what, exactly, Styx meant. A few times, Charon had wondered about the vampire's sanity, which came more and more into question since the end of the game. Something felt unhinged, unstable.

"Are you going to explain all of this to me?"

Styx waved his hands in the air. "Later."

"Why were you so worried about making a mess with shooting Josh, if you were just blowing the place up?" Charon noted the near hysteria in his voice and realized the confusion welling within him. He took a deep breath to calm down.

Styx simply laughed again. "Good question! Ridiculous, now that I think about it." Then he held one finger in the air. "No. It was good. It forced you to make the kill more personal. A final proof that you were up to the task."

"I could have just told you that."

Styx walked silently a few more paces, still smiling widely, then reached over, picked Charon up into his arms like a bride, and away they went. Charon had little choice but to enjoy the short ride, so he fell into those enormous biceps, closed his eyes, and relished the feel of the rock-hard body holding him.

Styx finally set Charon down outside a small cinder-block dwelling in the middle of a swamp. It stunk. Dampness already seeped into Charon's pores. It was dark and frightening. "This is lovely." Charon started when an alligator swam by.

"I know, I know. Now you understand why I needed the separate house. This lair is where I work. I keep calling it a lair, but it's probably more of a lab. A secret lab. Just like Grandpa Munster."

Charon waited while Styx unlocked a chain and elaborate padlock, then stepped back and chanted something in a foreign language. When he finished, Styx motioned for Charon to open the door. "The locks and such are more visual deterrent than anything, for humans. Not many people, if any, stray into this remote location. What really protects my lab from humans, vampires, witches, whatever, is my magic."

Charon hesitated, baffled for the moment. Styx reached over and rubbed his back, again with the seeming attraction or fondness, which reminded Charon that he won the competition, that this all led to him becoming a vampire. With Styx's hand comfortingly pressed against his back the whole way, Charon walked into the building and waited while Styx closed the door behind him and they descended into total darkness.

With nothing but blackness before Charon's eyes, Styx again chanted something in that exotic tongue, then came up behind Charon and gave him a tight hug.

PART THREE: CONVERSION

Chapter Twelve: Vampire Ability

29 SEPTEMBER 2011

Florida Swampland

The hug in total darkness lasted only moments before Styx released Charon to flip on a light switch and hurry over to a coffin, tucked into the corner. Once again, the teasing nature exhibited by Styx thrilled and frustrated Charon.

Styx opened the lid.

"That's a bit theatrical, isn't it?" Charon stifled a laugh at the scene, especially the pine-box coffin that looked like something right out of a bad western.

"Perhaps. It was the easiest solution at the time I settled into this place." Styx put one foot into the coffin. "I'll be out of it for the day, so to speak. Feel free to do whatever you wish. Tomorrow night is very exciting." With that, he jumped in, lay down, and slammed the lid shut.

First, Charon went to check the door, wondering if Styx locked him in this place. No. It opened, and Charon stepped back outside to stand on the damp ground in front of the little cinder-block building, the swampy water just a few feet away. He admired the raw beauty of the landscape and the complete peace and quiet of the moment, feeling more safe and content than when Styx first plopped him down on this spot.

He had spent most of his life in cities or bustling areas, preferred them, really, but the tranquility of the swamp held an allure Charon had never imagined before in his life. He stood there even as the early dawn approached, watching the sun drift over the trees and reflect across the water, until the nocturnal animals went to bed along with Styx, and birds and other creatures claimed the day.

When his feet became uncomfortable as the wet ground oozed into his socks, he went back inside and closed the door. Styx had said something about Grandpa Munster before he brought them inside here, and Charon thought that an appropriate description of what he viewed. Either Grandpa Munster's dungeon in the basement on Mockingbird Lane, with its test tubes and smoking vials of strange liquid, or Frankenstein's lab, with wires and odd devices all over the place. Styx had referred a few times to knowing some kind of magic, but nothing about being a mad scientist. Again Charon doubted the vampire's sanity.

Charon picked up one jar and held it to the light, the bright-orange liquid slightly glowing back at him. Another jar on a nearby shelf, which Charon refused to even go near, housed some decaying rodent head floating in formaldehyde.

"What the fuck are you up to?" Charon whispered.

Though Styx no longer imprisoned Charon, the location effectively did the same thing. Charon could go outside but not off the tiny island unless he intended to swim back to safety alongside an alligator or large snake. It made for an intensely boring day. No television. No radio. Nothing here for Charon to do while the hours ticked away until the setting sun awoke Styx. Not even a book.

At first he wondered if Styx intended it as another test, some forced solitude to prompt Charon to probe deeper into his own psyche or explore whatever issues Styx invented in his head for Charon. But the competition was over, and Styx had left no instructions before locking himself in the coffin, so it seemed more that Styx paid no mind to the fact Charon still lived through the day.

At about noon, however, when Charon fought to keep his eyes open to no avail, he realized that Styx intended for him to sleep, too. After all, he'd stayed awake all last night and, for the most part, lived nocturnally since the kidnapping. Styx was moving him along the path toward becoming a vampire, so it stood to reason that the next night would also include a full agenda.

Finally exhausted, Charon fell asleep, sitting on the cement floor with his back propped against the wall, and woke only when he felt a hand gently shake his shoulder.

"Charon, wake up."

Charon opened his eyes to see Styx smiling down at him.

"It's time to finally get you in a boat so you can push across me, the river."

Charon rubbed his eyes. "What are you talking about?"

"Our analogy. Charon needs the River Styx to accomplish his task. Remember?"

Charon stretched his arms into the air, working out the kink in his neck from sleeping so awkwardly on the ground. "Got it. But if we're staying here for very long, I'm going to need a bed. And something to do."

Styx grinned. "You'll be busy all night tonight, and we'll figure out something for tomorrow to make you comfortable. Tomorrow night, we convert you. You can suffer through the circumstances just a while longer, until they'll never again matter to you. I didn't think of creature comforts for after the competition. Once you're a vampire, we'll be leaving this place, too. Well, I especially."

"What's that supposed to mean? You keep making strange references about yourself and how it plays into all of this. When are you going to explain it to me?"

Styx lifted Charon to his feet and hugged him. "All in good time!" He clapped his hands and spun around, then laughed. "You're right! This place has nothing we need for comfort. I strictly designed it as my lab. Nothing more. But tonight, we primarily need to talk. Let me think."

Styx paced back and forth, his hand on his chin most of the time. Then he raised his arms to the side and slapped them back down. "Are your clothes okay?"

"They're going to stand in the corner pretty soon, if that's what you mean. Otherwise they're fine."

Again the laughter. "Fine. Fine. Stay put. This will go faster without you. I'll be right back."

Without any more explanation or even a goodbye, Styx shot out of the room. Charon witnessed vampire speed for the first time without being in Styx's arms. Incredible. One moment, Styx stood in front of him, grinning and in contemplation, the next he vanished. Charon noticed a slight swish of movement and then saw absolutely nothing.

Alone in this mad man's workshop, Charon worried he might spend another deathly boring amount of time with nothing to do, but he sauntered around the laboratory and pondered the various items for no more than thirty minutes before Styx suddenly appeared in the doorway.

He entered and tossed a pile of stuff on an empty table. "Here, check this out," he said, then fled away again.

Charon sorted through a pile of clothes, picked a new outfit of jeans and a long-sleeve T-shirt with flip-flops, then took the iPad and phone. Finally, something to do. He had no more settled for playing Angry Birds Seasons when Styx burst into the lab, carrying two camping chairs and a bag of food.

"I could have carried something bigger and more comfortable, I suppose, but this was the quickest solution. And really, it's just for tonight." He lifted another sack in the air, and Charon recognized the outline of wine bottles inside. "I thought this was most important."

Styx quickly set up the chairs and then pulled out one of the bottles to show to Charon. "Arista Winery in Sonoma. They make a delightful Pinot Noir." He took out one of those cheap corkscrews and opened the bottle.

"Damn." He laughed and slapped his thigh. "I forgot glasses. Here." He reached over and grabbed two beakers. "These will have to do."

As he poured the wine, Charon grimaced. "Are those clean? Or did some dead thing float around in them for a while? I'm still human, you know, in terms of disease and shit. Can vampires get sick?"

Styx, still giggling at everything, poured the wine and handed a beaker to Charon. "Not to worry. These are clean. As for your question, you segued nicely into this evening's activity. First, a toast." He held up his beaker. "To vampires."

They clinked their glasses together, and Charon drank the wine. Delicious. He definitely intended to learn more about wine in his vampire life.

"As for your question," Styx continued, "the answer is basically no. Vampires can't become ill. We have complete immunity from human disease." He waved a hand in the air. "Please don't ask me about the technical details of the matter. I have no idea about the science behind it. I only know the simple facts. We can drink tainted blood, be it laced with drugs, infected with AIDS, or expose ourselves to anything of the sort and live through it. Only two things kill a vampire."

Styx leaned over and lit a small burner, which ignited with a beautiful blue flame. "Fire. Not this tiny one, obviously, but incineration. And the sun. Nothing else."

"Holy water? A stake through the heart?"

Styx laughed. Apparently everything in the world became funny once the competition ceased. "All myths. Nonsense. Only fire and the sun.

Now, what else to teach you?" He tapped his fingers on the red canvas of the chair. "I'm not at a loss here, just deciding the order of things."

He poured each of them more wine, then leaned back again. "That sack there has food. Eat what you need. Please." Styx watched as Charon picked out a granola bar and other snacks, then spoke again. "Okay. I know. What else can a vampire do? No shape shifting, either, so no flying around like a bat or running through the woods as a wolf. We're restricted, essentially, to human movement."

This time Charon laughed. "Carrying a full grown man across a state in a matter of minutes with no effort hardly amounts to human limitation."

"No." Styx shook his head. "You're right. But I ran the entire time. So we have supernatural—or superhuman, whatever you want to call it—abilities. Our strength is that of the Greek and Roman gods. Look! Right back to your name. It was fate we came together." He sipped his wine. "I could carry you easily, and run with you, too, but only run. We could get all the way to California in a matter of an hour or so, at most. But no flying unless we're on an airplane, and no crossing an ocean unless we take a boat."

"Couldn't you swim?"

Styx tilted his head in contemplation. "Perhaps. The strength and stamina would be there. It'd be a pain in the ass to do it and avoid the sun and such things. But sure."

"Can vampires read minds? Move things through the air with just a thought?"

Styx shrugged. "I can't. Others may have some magic, not related to being a vampire, that gives them such abilities. But not me. That's really it. We're just super strong and fast. We sleep through the day because of the sun. It forces us to sleep, really. Some withstand the early approach of dawn better than others. And all wake at various times. But that's it."

Charon waited again as Styx slipped back into thought. He suspected something more to all this than the quick lesson Styx just delivered but figured he would learn in time.

"Oh! Another thing before we get to a little history. It's possible for a vampire or even a human to injure a vampire. Say, cut them or break an arm. But vampires heal quickly. Even a severed limb. Let me show you!" Styx practically shouted the last sentence.

Before Charon could protest, unsure that he wanted to witness this demonstration, Styx grabbed a knife and sliced off his left pinky.

Styx just raised his eyebrows and grinned while Charon shouted in agony at the mere sight. But Styx held the detached finger in the air, then pushed it back in place on his hand. Before Charon's eyes, the finger reattached itself. Styx walked over and wiggled all five left fingers in Charon's face to prove the healing.

"Cool." Charon drained his wine, a little unnerved at the display but impressed nonetheless. "Anything else? You mentioned something about history?"

Styx tilted his head. "I think that's it. No! One more thing. After you transform, you'll have a perfectly sculpted body. Like mine." Styx stood and twirled around, then flexed his bicep. "I know you like it."

Charon smirked. "It's quite fine. But I think I've got a good thing going as a human."

"Yeah, so imagine what the vampire blood will do to you. You won't consciously decide this, but your transformation will pick an age to freeze you at. For some, it's younger or older than others. You can't age beyond what you've experienced, so maybe it will freeze you right here. Or it may take you to a younger time. It just depends. Hopefully it won't snap you back to infancy!" Styx laughed heartily.

"Is that possible? It depends on what?"

Styx shrugged. "Calm down. That won't happen. As for the precise age, I have no clue how the process determines it. But I was almost forty when transformed. It took me back into my twenties."

"Righteously awesome. So when do I get this?" All this talk made Charon excited for his own transformation.

"Tomorrow. Patience, young Skywalker." Styx mimicked a pretty good Yoda as he spoke.

"You're not going to try to tell me that vampires use the Force, are you?"

Styx tipped his head back, roaring. "No. Just a little movie reference to break it up. We have a lot to teach you, and a short time to do it. So tonight is all about the lessons. I think that does it for vampire ability and vulnerability. If anything else pops into my head, I'll let you know. Let's do a bit of history, and then we'll get into those rules I told you about."

Chapter Thirteen: The Vampire Council

29 SEPTEMBER 2011

Florida Swampland

The wine continued to flow as Styx allowed Charon a moment to finish eating before he continued with the night's lessons. Charon shifted, a little uncomfortable in the camping chair on the hard cement floor.

Styx glanced to the ceiling before continuing, as if the answers hid above them. "I don't know the origin of vampires or anything as old as that. And this won't be about me, yet, either. Here, let me do this quickly. As far as I know, no one knows the origins of vampires or how far back we go. Perhaps since the dawn of humanity, or a divergence in the evolutionary process along the way. Vampires have existed for eons. But the Vampire Council limits our numbers."

"To how many?" Charon asked.

"Not sure. I've heard to roughly one hundred or so. It's not known. Well, the Council probably knows, but not me."

"Interesting. I would've guessed a lot more, what with the human population explosion. You could help control the overpopulation problem."

Styx opened another bottle of wine. "True. Otherwise the humans will lead to their own extinction, and thus ours as well. Anyway, we can't do anything about our numbers unless the Council permits it. So on with the history. Strange, too, that vampires tend to mate. One on one. Monogamy. I've no explanation for that, either. Because not everyone conforms, and it's not a rule or expectation. There are groups, single vampires, all sorts, but a majority pair up. Perhaps it was the influence of Noah's Ark. Two by two."

"Are you saying that vampires are Christian?" Charon scrunched his face, not wanting to become a part of some religious nonsense.

Styx, predictably, laughed. "No, another silly reference. The coupling has nothing to do with religion or theology—that I'm aware of. It just is."

"But you never coupled?"

Styx slumped his shoulders and fell silent, a sadness creeping across his face. He lifted his beaker and sipped his wine silently. "Later on that. Please. When I'm ready."

Charon nodded his understanding but otherwise remained silent.

"The only piece of hardcore history to teach you has to do with a vampire war of long ago. A brutal war. One faction rose up against the governing Council and almost wiped them out. Those with the Council triumphed, and still rule to this day. But the war made them more cautious and brutal in their enforcement of Vampire Law. That's really the only history I wanted to communicate, because it directly influences us today and relates to one of the reasons I held the competition. More on that later, too. But first, let me teach you about this Vampire Council. How does that sound?'"

Charon leaned forward and smiled. "It's still your show."

"For a time. For a time." Styx copied Charon's position, a couple of inches from Charon's face. "For a dude, you're beautiful." Just as quickly he sat back in the chair.

"I never took you for such a tease."

"Now that you've won, I think a bit of playfulness in our relationship adds the needed tension to our story. We don't want it to become too mundane."

"Can vampires get blue balls?" Charon adjusted his slight erection.

Styx, on the other hand, laughed hard. "I wouldn't know. You're free to pull it out, take care of business, and relieve the pressure if necessary."

"No thanks." Charon smiled. "Maybe later. Now, you keep mentioning this Council. What in the hell are you talking about?"

"Something I despise. Immensely. First, the details. Just the facts. Then the reason for my feelings on the matter. There is a Vampire Council that governs all vampires. The members—unknown to us, though we can summon them if desired and one, or maybe a few, will show up—enforce laws over us. They punish with imprisonment or, for more heinous crimes in their eyes, death. They possess a fierce magic and more power than even most vampires. There is no defying them. Or, at least that hasn't historically been the case."

"That's a drag. I didn't predict all these vampire rules, what with the competition and your requirements."

Again Yoda appeared. "Patience, young Skywalker. No. You're too old. Too old to begin the Jedi training."

"I hope that's another funny movie reference and not the truth."

Styx grinned. "A joke. Well, the Star Wars reference is a joke. Not the Council or their power."

"So what laws? How will I learn them?"

Styx rolled his eyes. "Thankfully, you won't have to. But I'll explain them in general, just so you know. Also, we have access, by merely thinking it, to summon a book of the laws at any time."

Styx closed his eyes, and seconds later, an orange glowing globe appeared, followed by a leather-bound book. It seemed ancient yet in perfect condition, not very big, really.

"See?"

"Cool. What's in it?"

"Stupid rules." Styx snapped his fingers and it disappeared. "Let me give you the CliffsNotes. For the safety and future of vampires, as well as humankind, we must remain hidden. No revealing our vampirism to people. Also, no converting someone without authorization from the Council. That's part of limiting our population."

"So they approved my conversion?"

Styx smiled, drank wine, then spit some of it out as he laughed. "Heavens, no. Not in the least. If they knew about that competition, it'd be off with my head!"

Charon squinted at Styx. "This gets more intriguing by the minute."

"You've no idea. None at all. The most important rule, in addition to hiding from people, is that we only kill those worthy of death. Vampires sit in judgment over all humankind. I've no idea how we decided to take such power, but each vampire has the entitlement of judge and jury. Our feeding can leave a person alive but satisfy us, or we can kill. But the Council only permits us to destroy the guilty. They can detect when we violate these rules, and the justice comes swiftly against us if we disobey. So we must restrict our killing to those deemed worthy of death by that little book I presented. In other words, rapists, murderers, brutes. The vile criminals of the world. I've heard we can euthanize someone who desires it but never tested that one myself."

Charon reflected on Grady, Josh, and himself. "Yet you offered this vampire blood to three people who otherwise seem like folks you ought to have fed off and left for dead. Maybe I was in a gray area at the beginning, but not anymore. And never in my heart."

"Precisely. Even if *I* had killed them, the Council would have allowed it because they were worthy of death. If not, the Council could punish me."

"Wow. Seems even more oppressive than human laws. At least, those here in America."

"It is." Styx's voice filled with loathing, all humor gone.

"So what happens if you accidentally kill someone, thinking they're worthy of death but they're not. How do you know?"

"Typically, it's easy enough to identify just by observing people. But, this actually might be the coolest part of being a vampire, or at least of the killing part. As we drink the blood, even just a small sample from the prick of a finger, that person's life passes through our mind. Almost every bit of it. Their childhood. You feel their emotion. And in those visions, you learn about their deeds. Within seconds, you know if you should continue the kill or stop and allow them to live. Easy as that."

"Well, at least that makes it easy enough, I suppose. Still—" Charon cut himself off, unsure how to proceed. He hardly wanted to imply that he changed his mind about becoming a vampire. Eternal life beat the alternative of instant death at Styx's hand. He originally envisioned power, though, unencumbered by authority over himself and those around him. A life of supremacy and refinement, as he described to Styx in order to win the competition. This Vampire Council sounded like it would put a serious cramp in his style.

As if reading his mind, Styx continued. "You haven't learned everything about my plans yet. I told you, I wanted to explain all of this first, because you'll need that knowledge. Your existence, however, will be different."

"How? Are you setting me up to be some sacrificial lamb? You want to defy the Council but preserve your life, so I get to become a vampire as long as I do your dirty work, at least until they hunt me down and kill me? What happens if I turn on you, instead, just to preserve myself? What if—"

Styx pushed himself out of the chair and stood before him, one hand on Charon's knee, the other covering his mouth to quiet Charon. He shook his head. "No, no. You don't understand yet. Stop. You're getting ahead of us again."

After a moment, Styx calmly took his hand off Charon's mouth and ran a finger down the side of his cheek, then patted it softly.

Charon resisted the urge to grab the finger into his mouth and suck on it. "Well, you better keep with the Yoda analogy and not become the Emperor on my ass."

Styx ruffled Charon's hair. "I get why you don't trust me. Or anyone, for that matter. Since you have no choice, though, you might as well go with the process here. You don't have anything to worry about. This isn't a trick. And while I used Yoda, in fact, don't you want more of a taste of the Dark Side? Aren't you more in league with Darth Vader than the rebellion, anyway?"

"Well, when you put it that way."

Styx walked around behind Charon and grabbed him by the shoulders. His hands kneaded into Charon's muscle, the deep massage feeling ever so good after sitting for much too long in this uncomfortable camping chair. The masculine force of the motion enthralled him, and Charon closed his eyes to enjoy the moment.

After a few minutes, Styx moved his hands down Charon's chest to pinch his nipples.

Charon sighed. "Again with the foreplay."

"I like keeping you on edge."

"Or you'd like a little taste of me?"

Styx came back around and returned to his seat. He sipped his wine, a wry smile on his face the entire time. "I'm straight."

"So you've said. But perhaps not totally straight on the Kinsey spectrum? You seem to have a little wiggle room. You need to catch up with the spirit of the time, vampire. Sexuality is more fluid among the youth. Disdain the labels and just go with it."

Styx slapped his hands on his thighs. "At any rate, no matter my placement in the grand scheme of modern sexuality, we don't have time for such things."

"Aren't we going to have eternity?"

"You will."

"But you?"

"I suppose you're moving us to the next lesson of the night." Styx sighed and stared into his beaker of wine.

Chapter Fourteen: Styx's History

29 SEPTEMBER 2011

Florida Swampland

Styx fell silent for what seemed like hours after saying that he would transition to his story. Charon sensed the moment and remained silent.

"I originally come from an era when we didn't acknowledge emotion. I'm not even sure we understood such a thing as feelings." Styx grew quiet again, just like last time when his personal situation came up amidst the vampire history and rules. He suddenly chuckled to himself, breaking the somber mood. "Though I'm sure you're thinking that I seem rather emotional about it right now. It's complicated, living for centuries."

"I imagine so. It can be complicated just to live for a couple decades."

"Indeed. In fact, I'm going to negate my previous statement entirely. I think it's more accurate to say that we didn't express the emotion. That wasn't considered proper. But we had them. We most certainly had them."

"So you're going to tell me your story? Like, your actual name?"

Styx shook his head. "I'm not going to bore either one of us with the long and gory details of my actual past. It's completely irrelevant, and only interesting to me. I don't want to delay this any more than needed. Let's finish this bottle of wine and get on with it, so we can dispense with the chatter after tonight and convert you tomorrow. That's what this is really about, right?"

Charon held up his beaker for the refill. "Well, it is for me. But you have something to tell me about yourself, yes?"

Styx tossed the empty bottle to the side and watched it clang on the cement and roll away. He held up two fingers. "Two things I'll tell you about myself. First, as I mentioned earlier, most vampires mate for life. As did I, a very long time ago. She was taken from me." He practically growled the last sentence.

"I'm sorry. I was under the impression you were always alone."

"Because that's what I led all of you to believe. And, though we never discussed it, I ensured that the three of you preferred a life of solitude as well. I thought it might be easier on you, rather than risk the loss of a lover and having to live for eternity with the misery."

Charon pondered for a second. "So why did you continue to live?"

Styx glared at Charon, a hatred practically escaping from his pores that Charon had never seen before. "Spite. Hatred." Styx pointed hard at the floor with one hand. "For this moment. This moment right now about to take place. Because I planned for tomorrow for centuries. Centuries!" He screamed the last word at the top of his lungs. Charon noticed tears of blood pool at the corner of his eyes and trickle down one cheek.

Styx slipped into maniacal laughter and wiped at his face.

Charon returned an uncomfortable snort. "You're kinda becoming a comic book villain."

"You've no idea. You'd enjoy that, wouldn't you? As I recall, you've a particular fondness for Loki. Yes?"

Charon nodded. "Yeah. Without the Council, I'd want to be Loki the Vampire."

"Fuck the Council. I'll make you into him. Yes, let's concentrate on that. No more tears."

Charon stood up and grabbed a cloth from a nearby stack. He walked over and gently wiped the blood tears from Styx's face. He stared into the vampire's eyes the whole time, finally seeing the deep sadness they had always reflected back at him. He leaned over and kissed Styx on the cheek.

Styx slowly pulled away. "Thank you. For a pure villain, you have a kindness lurking inside of you. You may want to watch for that, or it might expose your own longings and loneliness."

Charon grinned. "Don't worry. That won't be a problem."

"Good. Because now I want to stir the pot of hatred in you again. As I mentioned, there was a vampire war. A terrible thing. Some demigod of a figure rose to defy the Council. I still don't completely understand it. I was outside the dispute entirely at the time. I didn't back either side. I obeyed the Council because I enjoyed eternal life and wanted to be together with my mate forever. Unfortunately, she picked a side in the war."

"Who did?"

"My lover."

"Does she have a name?"

"As do I. But we're not digging that up. It's become incidental to our story."

A million challenges to that statement ran through Charon's mind, but he would never win that argument. He settled for listening instead. "So what happened?"

Styx clenched his fists at his side to the point that Charon saw blood oozing between his fingers. Charon took Styx's arm and guided him back to the chairs, where he sat Styx down.

"Just tell me." Charon moved his chair closer to Styx so that he could rest a hand on his knee as he sat.

"She was so naïve. So innocent. She befriended one of the vampires who rebelled against the Council. Innocently. She had no idea. And when they struck, she never participated. She had nothing to do with the war, except guilt by association."

Charon understood now. "They killed her anyway, didn't they?"

"They, yes. Particularly one. The self-righteous Anthony. He stormed into our lair one evening, a few nights after the war ended, or so we thought. He accused her of cavorting with the enemy. Oh, true, she knew of the plot. But what could she do? He marauded around our home, breaking things and accusing her of being no worse than the rebels because she failed to tell the Council. To inform them. And then he killed her. Right before my eyes. He reached with some magical power across the room and lit her on fire, burning her from afar until she died. By this time, he stood framed in the doorway, clear across the room, and as she struggled against whatever took hold of her, I raced to her and held her in my arms as she died. I pled with him to take me, too. I insisted that I, too, knew about the plot. But he somehow knew the lie. I had vaguely heard her talk about it but never completely realized the scope of it. I certainly knew nothing of the timing.

"He shook his head at me, the long blond hair swaying back and forth. 'You don't deserve death. The Law allows you to live.'

"I didn't want to live! He left. Without answering me, he just left. I decided to force the issue. I went on a killing rampage in a small village in Germany. As I predicted, he showed up soon after. Again, he refused to execute me." Styx trembled with rage in his chair.

"You violated the Ethic, though? Doesn't that deserve death?"

Styx nodded. "Absolutely. Instead, he comforted me. He said that my rage made sense to him. He stayed for over a month as my warden. By the end, I feigned compliance. I stopped violating the laws and obeyed his representation of the Vampire Council. I pledged to amend my ways. And from that moment on, I did nothing but plot for what will take place tomorrow night. My revenge upon the Council."

Despite the depressing story and weight of the moment, Charon could no longer suppress a wide grin. Styx finally arrived at the point where he picked Charon, and whatever he planned must include defiance of this Council, defiance at the behest of Charon. Defiance orchestrated by the vampire in front of him over centuries of anguish.

Styx returned the smile. "You get it, don't you? I acted the perfect and reformed vampire. In the grandest of styles, I've complied over the years and decades. I performed the role unmatched in all of vampire history. Oh, the willpower it took. Anthony still visits me, at least once a year. Not to investigate, but because he thinks that he supports me. He thinks we're friends, the fool! Because all the while I kept to myself. I never coupled again. And the only thing that kept me alive, all these years? Hatred and anger. A pure loathing. A lust to avenge her. A hatred of Anthony, who I dreamed of choking with my own hands until he lay lifeless on the floor like he left her. Now the moment has arrived. The Council will no longer hold absolute authority over all vampires. And in that act, I will have avenged her."

Styx grew quiet again while a metamorphosis took place over the next several minutes. Frowning and sullen, he withdrew from Charon until his face became placid, like a store mannequin with no emotion whatsoever. Finally, that slight smile spread across his lips, a glow returned to his eyes despite the hollow longing deep in the pupils, and the more passionate, exuberant vampire sprung back to life.

"Depressing, wasn't it? But enough of that. This is about my moment of triumph. No more regret. No more sadness. Are you ready to learn what I've done?"

Charon returned Styx's wide grin. "Ready when you are."

"Good. Let's get on with it."

Chapter Fifteen: The Perfect Foil

29 SEPTEMBER 2011

Florida Swampland

Styx practically launched out of his chair and stood before the tables of experiments, vials, test tubes, liquids, and other scientific tools. He swept an arm in presentation and smiled broadly at Charon.

"I've been working for centuries to perfect this experiment. Centuries. And until recently, until right before I started the competition, I've always failed. I failed because the Vampire Council's magic is so powerful and all encompassing. But nothing is omnipotent, unless God exists out there. There's no sign of such a divine force. And it certainly isn't the Council's magic, because I finally discovered its weakness. You won't believe the key ingredient once I tell you."

Styx glanced over his table of experiments fondly. "Am I boring you? Do you want the details, or shall I cut to the chase about you?"

"I want the full story." At this point, Styx held Charon's complete attention. Charon wanted every detail, the nuances, anything that led to this moment and what it would mean for him.

"I was hoping you'd want to hear it. I've never told anyone, obviously. Another vampire would threaten my exposure, and any human would disbelieve or become my next dinner."

Charon laughed. "What do you mean it took you centuries?"

"After Anthony murdered my lover, I sulked and pouted for a long time, especially after he forced me to continue living. I mean that I moped for perhaps years. I pondered nothing but death, until my sorrow gradually gave way to pure rage. I seethed, day in and day out, letting the anger consume me. Oh, I obeyed the Ethic, if for nothing else than to keep him away from me. But I tortured my victims. I haunted people, scaring the shit out of them without feeding from them, just because of my power and anger.

"One day, while passing through a small village in Poland, I came upon a very old woman. She invited me into her home, where I intended to frighten her and eventually test if she deserved death. She surprised me, instead, when she immediately said she knew about my nature. Intrigued, I settled into a chair and asked how she learned that about me. She was a witch! And a vile one at that, who liked to spy on people, steal from them, inflict illnesses on them. A generally dreadful woman. So we spent the night exchanging stories of torture, hating humanity, and the ills inflicted upon us over the years.

"After a time, she explained that she invited me in because she wanted to become a vampire. She took the risk knowingly, because she was dying, anyway. Unfortunately, I knew that Anthony would never allow it. I explained as much. It disappointed me tremendously, because I came upon a new goal in my short time with her but would need her assistance, at least to get me started. She shocked me by saying that she understood and then asked me for something else, instead. She pled for death. Immediately. At my hands. She wanted me to kill her! She was dying, of cancer it turns out, and feared a long and painful ending, alone and despised. I agreed but insisted that I would need payment for it. And my price for assisting her? She had to spend three days teaching me everything she knew about magic."

Charon reached over and grabbed another bottle of wine, then held it up to Styx to see if he was interested. He nodded. Charon opened it, filled their beakers, and returned them to the camp chairs so he could hear the rest of the story in more comfort.

Charon crossed his legs and leaned back. "And I take it that you learned the magic in order to take on the Vampire Council?"

"Indeed. I suppose it doesn't take Nostradamus to predict that part of the story." Styx chuckled. "I wanted to create a concealing spell. You see, I figured that with some magic, I could figure out how to counter the Council's sorcery and wreak havoc on all of their plans. I desired nothing more than to fuck with them, and especially Anthony."

Styx sighed. "After she taught me as much as possible and I killed her, I assumed that I could learn a spell and figure it out quickly. I burst with confidence. Well, that proved rather optimistic. Fast forward a few hundred years or so, place me right in the middle of the 1800s, and guess what? Same Styx. A vampire who knew magic but not anything to counter the Council. I experimented all the time, and maybe even came close, but every test revealed that they still controlled me. Or at least, I could sense that nothing perfectly hid my actions from them."

"How did you experiment without doing something wrong?"

Styx shrugged. "Oh, a couple of times I revealed my nature to humans, which is strictly forbidden. Once I killed a borderline person, not quite worthy of death. Anthony showed up all three times. Mostly, though, I sensed it. Funny, I finally learned to cast a spell that informed me of whether or not the Council could still detect me. That finally gave me the foolproof test. Unfortunately, it kept telling me that I failed. My big break came when I traveled to Australia at mid-century."

"I thought you just recently perfected this experiment?"

Styx laughed. "I did. Still, it was what I learned in Australia that led to a century of getting close, until I finally succeeded!"

Styx had hid this instability so well throughout the game; Charon thought him an evil genius, perfecting some grand scheme and intending to enlist the winner in some plot to rule the world, to the point Charon thought he might need to fight to the death as a vampire to escape from Styx once he obtained eternal life. Instead, he began to doubt everything. To be sure, he knew Styx was a vampire and felt certain that Styx planned to convert Charon. Otherwise, he sounded a bit off, pining all these years, overwrought with the emotion of losing his lover, and now this centuries-long experiment that apparently contained some fatal flaw. Charon only hoped to receive the gift and get away as quickly as possible.

Charon's doubt intensified when Styx laughed like a crazed person at some unspoken joke.

"Are you going to share the humor?"

Styx nodded and wiped a blood tear from his eye. He began the story again, though, as if the odd interlude never happened. "So I ended up in Australia."

"Why Australia?"

Styx shrugged, a peculiar smile still plastered on his face. "I went because, at the time, it was so remote. So desolate. The British had only begun to settle there and take over the place. It gave me ample solitude to experiment on my potions and magic, with new plants and substances to play with, and interesting native people, along with lots of criminals of all stripes to feed off."

Styx clapped his hands together. "In fact, it was the fur of a kangaroo that proved the missing ingredient."

Charon could no longer conceal his alarm. "I never suspected before that you were completely nuts."

Styx shook his head, but again that grin stayed put. "No, no. Just giddy with excitement right now. I told you that you wouldn't believe it when I told you! It's true! It's true! The kangaroo fur did something to the potion—I've no idea why or how. Oh, it took a few attempts." Styx held his side and began laughing, then fell out of his chair and rolled on the ground. When he composed himself again, he slapped Charon on the knee. "Stop looking so alarmed. It's fine. Here, I'll explain. I've been laughing because with some of the native plants to Australia, I made it possible to create a potion that allowed me to fart butterflies." He laughed hysterically again.

Charon, on the other hand, failed to crack a smile. "You've completely lost it."

Styx waved his hand in the air to dismiss Charon's concern. "It's true. I thought it the final solution, and instead it wiped out all the other magic and concealing that I invented, turning me into a farting butterfly factory."

Charon nearly raced out of the room, if not for the fact that a swamp surrounded it and the vampire could easily track him down. "Can we go back to your being a shrewd and somewhat evil vampire, controlling three rather large men in a game to the death? No one would ever believe that you farted butterflies. That's preposterous."

Styx shrugged but continued to smile. "Suit yourself. Believe what you choose. We can skip that part. Still it was the kangaroo fur that made all the difference. That much you must believe. It's all about potions and mixing ingredients. Don't ask me how it all works. Anyway, I recognized in my experiments the power of the kangaroo fur. Not that I succeeded yet, but it came close. Too close to ignore. Close enough that I sensed imminent success. The power of that element pushed the experiments onto the final trajectory, to today. To this moment!"

Styx jumped up, grabbed Charon on both sides of his head, and planted a kiss on his forehead. When he laughed again, it became so silly that Charon broke his concern and grinned back.

"Is this story almost finished? Or will you continue to freak me out? It seems more and more likely that you're batshit crazy." Charon reached up and held both of Styx's biceps, one in each hand, getting a bit aroused from the feel of the hard body, despite the growing delusions.

Styx continued to tease when he ran a finger down Charon's cheek and along his chest. "I'm not crazy," he whispered. "Essentially, it's over. That was it. A fucking kangaroo. I combined all of the elements, but it took a century to get the right amounts in the right sequence to perfect it. I created this swamp hideaway in the 60s and mostly stayed here except to feed until I finished. And, finally, dear boy, we've come to the point where you'll get involved." Styx brushed his lips lightly along Charon's cheek and then retreated back to his chair.

Styx stared into his wine and grew silent. His expression lost that hint of crazy and snapped back to the calculating and confident vampire. "I didn't mean to alarm you. I'm not insane, despite what you may think. It's just that this took so long, you can't imagine my excitement when I finally arrived at this point. I'm just excited beyond belief. I'll be going to see her soon."

"You've alluded to that a number of times. Something extreme, profound. Leaving me alone. Are you going to explain that?"

"Yes. I promise. So let me tell you the problem. As you know, I recently finished the serum. I know it. We'll test it, to be sure. But I know it's right this time. There's one problem. I always envisioned my swallowing it and seeking revenge, until the entire Council or every vampire combined their power to bring me down." He shook his head, sadly. "But it won't work on an existing vampire. I tried, over and over, but it fails every time. I could spend another three centuries to figure it out, but I never wanted that, anyway."

The picture became a bit clearer, but Charon waited for Styx to continue.

Styx smiled. "You know, don't you? You get it? It can't be me. It has to be someone else, who takes the potion right before the conversion. They'll be hidden from the Council. They'll live beyond its control, to do as they please. To embrace the full power of vampirism, unencumbered by the arbitrary rules. To demand of humanity what it wants, with no vampire enemy able to detect them."

Charon reached down and poured more wine for both of them. Styx restored Charon's faith in the process. To be sure, Charon still thought him completely nuts. But in the calculating mad scientist kind of way, as opposed to the completely bonkers lunatic of a few minutes ago.

"Thus the competition. To find the perfect specimen for this honor. I won't let you down. I think you picked the perfect protégé," Charon assured.

Styx held up his beaker. "A toast. To Charon. My protégé."

"And you're not sticking around, are you?"

Styx held the wine in his mouth a second before swallowing. "No. In fact, the problem with the potion turns out to be perfect for me, really. I don't want to be here anymore. I never wanted to exist without her, anyway. I'm only here because of Anthony's cruel punishment against me. That he forced me to remain, out of some odd sense of an Ethic, that I had to live because she disobeyed the arbitrary law but not me. He will rue the day he failed to let me die peacefully and follow her into the afterlife."

Charon laughed this time. "I'll make sure of it."

"One more thing. I'm not leaving you the potion or teaching you magic. That's my secret. My tribute to her, that I don't want anyone else to know or have it. So that it's special. So that she knows how much she meant—*means* to me."

That irked Charon, but he decided to keep his consternation to himself, though he pondered whether or not he could steal that knowledge from Styx. "So that's it?" he asked to defuse his own anger.

"It may get lonely for you, once I'm gone."

Charon sighed. "You worry too much about that. I've never needed a close companion. Solitude, that's all I ever knew. In fact, after too much time with someone or a group of people, I crave being alone. This will be perfect, actually. I passed all your tests, and would have passed even more if you administered them. I'm ready."

"I do believe you are."

Styx got up, took Charon's beaker, and set it on a lab table. He returned and took Charon by both hands, then pulled him out of the camping chair. He tugged him close, pulling him into a tight hug. Charon grew aroused when Styx pressed their heads together and caressed Charon's back.

"I do believe you are," he whispered into Charon's ear.

Chapter Sixteen: Conversion

30 SEPTEMBER 2011

Key West, Florida

Charon grabbed a bottle of wine and went outside and around to the back of the cinder-block building in order to face west. The sun still reflected off the water, glistening and beautiful on this warm fall evening. He opened the wine and drank right from the bottle. Nothing blocked his vision of a perfect wilderness, with trees, water, and a few animals and birds. Something splashed in the water nearby, sending a rodent of some sort scurrying for cover. Charon smiled and took a couple of minutes to reflect on his last day of humanity as he waited to witness his final sunset.

After Styx pulled him into that erotic hug last night, he had ended up grabbing Charon's ass and letting go, as abruptly and playfully as always.

Then Styx had yawned. "It's time for bed, for me. Not you. Listen, you'll be tired but fight it. I want you to go outside right now and watch your last sunrise. Tomorrow, and for thousands of tomorrows after it, the sun's appearance will call you to sleep. Stay up all day and enjoy the light. Then watch your final sunset."

Charon had adjusted his erection uncomfortably, but Styx paid him no attention, instead getting into his coffin and closing the lid.

Charon followed his orders this day. He watched a beautiful sunrise, though on that side of the small island more trees blocked the view than over here, where water stretched out for several yards before any foliage or land obstructed his field of vision. He stayed outside as much as possible, feeling the heat of the sun's rays upon his skin, warming him to the point of sweating even as he stood still. He sort of expected some philosophical revelations about his life, his humanity, at the prospect of converting to vampirism and never again spending time in the sunlight. He wondered if Styx's warning about his alleged loneliness would suddenly manifest itself and spur him into deep reflection. Instead, he simply embraced his final day while welling with excitement at the prospect of eternal life.

Thankfully, the sun faded gradually across the horizon. It stood huge, like a giant glowing spaceship getting ready to engulf the Earth, until the bright yellow turned orange, until the sparkling water turned black as it disappeared. The final reflection of its rays glinted off the surface and seemed to wink at Charon as they disappeared, as if bidding him farewell. The westward landscape changed to dark blue and then purple, with just a flash of green as the last tip of the sun disappeared.

Charon reached beside him for his bottle, so lost in the moment that he jumped at the discovery of a foot and glanced up to find Styx standing behind him.

"I didn't want to interrupt. Beautiful, wasn't it?"

Charon only nodded, then patted the ground for Styx to sit next to him. "How could you see it, if you're a vampire?"

"Some have more tolerance for the light than others. I can view the very end of the sunset. More than anything, I guessed at what you must have seen. I'm glad it wasn't raining or cloudy today."

Charon handed the bottle to Styx.

He took a big drink. "I don't know how I feel about drinking wine this good like a wino, straight from the bottle."

"As opposed to using your refined beakers?"

Styx cackled. "Touché." He sat silently for a while, lost in thought.

Charon, on the other hand, grew anxious. Before the next morning, he would become a vampire. He wanted nothing more than to hurry toward it, not waste any more time on vampire rules, guidelines, realities, or the awful mindset of Styx over these many long centuries. Tonight belonged to Charon.

At long last, Styx smiled and jumped to his feet. "Ready?"

"Any time. Let's do this."

"Where would you like to convert?"

"What do you mean?"

Styx started back toward the front of the building, so Charon followed. "We don't want to convert you here, do we? It's awful. I built this place merely to be functional. Let's go for something more eloquent, yes?"

"How about Key West? I love it there. On the beach, in the pitch black, with the waves rolling in?"

"I'll get what we need." Styx disappeared inside and returned moments later with a small backpack, which he held in the air. "Two bottles of wine and the potion. Though I think I converted it into an enchantment, let's not risk it."

Without warning, he rushed over, grabbed Charon around the waist, and lifted him into the air. It seemed as though he jumped from one patch of land to another, and when he hit solid ground, they raced south. Or at least Charon assumed they headed south, though the speed made it impossible to see anything or understand direction. Mostly, Charon noticed the rush of wind on his face and felt the force of Styx's hold around him, which ached by the time Styx set him gently on the sand.

Styx unpacked his bag and stretched out on the beach. "Key West will also be good for our first post-conversion activity."

Charon plopped down next to him. "I hope that's the last time you have to carry me somewhere."

"I kind of like carrying you around."

Charon tilted his head. "Are you sure you're not gay? I know your lover was a woman and all, but the connection between us is only getting more intense. Now, you admit you like to carry me around." Charon laughed, but Styx turned stoic.

Finally, he shrugged. "Does it matter? Nothing's going to happen, and soon I'll be gone."

Charon reached for the wine, then laughed again when Styx pulled out the beakers.

"I couldn't resist bringing them, just for you."

They sipped the Bordeaux. Styx started a bit when two souls meandered down the beach, but they passed with a pleasant hello and disappeared around a bend.

"Ready?" Styx asked.

"I thought you'd never ask."

Styx handed Charon a small vial of bright-orange liquid, which practically glowed in the night.

"You sure you remembered the kangaroo fur?"

"Don't jest. You won't think it's funny if I'm mad and made the whole thing up."

Charon glanced at Styx, who thankfully smirked as he finished that sentence. He took the vial, popped off the rubber seal, and downed the concoction. He started to look toward Styx to ask about the next step, but the vampire suddenly hovered over him.

He pushed Charon back onto the sand, pinning his shoulders down with both arms and forcing Charon to spread his legs so Styx's lower body nestled between them. Charon grew rock hard, which only intensified when he felt Styx's erection press into him. Styx leaned down as if to kiss Charon but just before their lips met, Styx turned his head and bit hard into Charon's neck.

Charon's instincts told him to struggle, to fight for his life, and his heart began to race alarmingly. He forced himself to remain motionless until Styx lifted up, licking the last of the blood from his lips. Charon felt dizzy, about to faint. The trees and sky above appeared to waver back and forth, and then a blackness tried to descend over his eyes.

"Stay with me. Just a second longer. This part I designed special for you."

Styx stood up, though he appeared to sway back and forth, until Charon realized his vision blurred, not the man in front of him. Still, he saw Styx drop his shorts to the sand, his solid cock with a curve to the left, his bulging thigh muscles flexing before Charon. Styx leaned over and helped Charon sit up so that he stared right at the hairy balls and glistening penis.

Styx reached down and tore into his own thigh with one hand, right into what appeared to be the main vein. He grabbed Charon by the back of the head and smashed his face into the blood. "Drink."

Charon gulped it down. At first too delusional from his own loss of blood to resist or ask questions, he noticed the tangy iron taste as he came to his senses and then finally lusted for this life force as it coursed through his own veins, bringing him eternal life. He only stopped when the wound on Styx's firm thigh healed itself. The entire time, Charon sensed the transformation taking place. The strength in his muscles. The sharper vision, so that he could merely glance out the corner of his eye and see the pulsating veins in Styx's dick. The heightened sense of smell of the manhood before him.

Transformed. A vampire. At last.

Charon tried to wrap his lips around that wonderful penis, but Styx laughed and jumped away. He grabbed his shorts and put them on, while Charon watched with a smirk.

"My giving you a blow job wouldn't even force you to contemplate your sexuality?"

"Not going to happen. Come." Styx waved at Charon, who jumped to his feet and followed the fellow vampire.

Charon sprinted forward, loving the new speed and power that coursed through every muscle. He grabbed onto a tree, moving too fast for a human eye to see, then spun around and leapt at Styx.

Styx easily sidestepped him and laughed. "Stop it. This is serious."

Charon sauntered back to Styx. "What's serious?"

"Your first kill as a vampire." Styx stared into Charon's eyes, as if gauging his reaction or further testing him.

Charon laughed. "Let me pick some hot little number to off right as he comes."

Styx shook his finger in the air. "Remember the Ethic!"

"It doesn't apply to me! I want my first to be a hot experience. Mix the feeding and the sex. What's one dead dude, amidst the hundreds of thousands out there?"

Styx grabbed Charon's arm and held tight. Charon attempted to shrug away from him, but they equaled each other in strength.

"Wait." Styx said this harshly, speaking as he did to the three of them during the competition, not as the vulnerable vampire of the last few days. "We think the potion worked. Let's play this safe, to be sure. We'll pick someone you like. But we'll also select a gray area, just in case the Council comes snooping. I can defend you that way."

Charon thought Styx a total buzzkill but acknowledged wisdom in the suggestion. "But I can veto whomever you pick?"

"Yes."

"Cool."

"Do you need any instructions before we go do this?"

Charon rolled his eyes. "Dude! I'm a vampire now. You wanted to produce the perfect evil machine, and here he stands before you! I don't want any more fucking lessons. No rules! Isn't that the point of my existence? To fuck with the system? I think I get it, okay? Vampire gets hungry, so vampire feeds off human blood. How difficult can that be? Like a baby's first suck off a tit."

Styx scrunched up his nose. "That's lovely. I thought Charon won the competition, not Grady."

Charon shrugged and laughed. "Just saying."

They turned onto Duval Street and followed the crowds, watching them go in and out of the clubs and stagger down the streets.

"Oh, look at him." Charon pointed to a stereotypical frat boy walking down the opposite side of the street toward them, swaying back and forth with a stare a mile long. He wore his Kent State University hat backward, jeans barely hugging the bottom of his hips, and a tight T-shirt. "Yum."

"You want him?" Styx asked nonchalantly.

"In so many ways."

"Let me test it."

The vampires turned around to follow the guy after he passed them. He spun around completely one time. "Jake! Where the fuck are ya?" He laughed, stumbled off the curb into the street, then righted himself and continued his journey.

"I'll be right back." Styx raced forward, using that vampiric speed that used to make him disappear from Charon's vision. As a vampire, Charon watched him the entire way.

Styx ran by the guy, scratched him on the arm, then hurried around a corner. In mere seconds, he walked beside Charon again, licking blood off two of his fingers. "Tasty." He smiled at Charon. "And a perfect specimen. Not worthy of a kill, according to the esteemed Vampire Council. But no saint, either. We could defend you as a stupid newbie if they catch us. Otherwise, enjoy." Styx motioned for Charon to go after the gent.

"You coming along?"

Styx shook his head. "I'm not into voyeurism."

"Or are you afraid of getting turned on by the gay boys going at it?"

"That one's not gay."

"He will be soon enough."

"Just go." Styx pointed forward, then quickly ran off the other way.

Charon followed Drunk Boy a few more blocks, then hurried up next to him. "Dude, you look pretty fucked up."

Kent State laughed and nodded. "True dat."

"Where you headed?"

"My boy Jake. Promised to hook us up. Need some horny chicks."

"I bet you can't even get it up right now."

The guy grabbed his crotch and moved it around. "We'll find out."

When they came to a corner that led toward a quieter residential street of bed-and-breakfasts and houses, Charon leaned into Kent State and forced him to turn. Drunk, he followed along unknowingly for a minute before spinning around.

"Where we goin'?"

"Back here." Charon grabbed him around both his solid biceps and pushed him into a grove of trees.

Thus concealed, Charon forcibly spun him around and ripped off his pants in one motion. Drunk Boy struggled and yelled something about fags, but Charon held tight, then took a hand and stuck three fingers up the tight ass. It felt so divine.

For the first time, a vampire hunger took hold of him and consumed his every desire, even overpowering the sexual energy and rock-hard dick in his own pants. His fangs descended, he reached up to turn the boy's head and slammed his mouth into the succulent neck.

The blood—delicious, rich, and savory—flowed over his tongue and down his throat, like no feeling of nourishment or satisfaction he had ever experienced. The boy slumped in Charon's arms until he dropped him to the ground, completely full.

But that tight, beautiful ass still peered up at Charon. He unzipped his pants, this time utilizing vampiric speed to rub one out and all over the frat boy, his first kill.

"Don't forget to stage it." Charon jumped at Styx's voice behind him.

"I thought you weren't into watching?" He tucked his softening dick back into his pants.

"I'm not. But then I remembered that you don't like to follow the rules, which, at least for now, we still need to follow."

"We can't just leave him here?"

"No. Wipe up your cum. That's disgusting."

Charon smirked. "You're just jealous that it's on him and not you." Charon obeyed, however, cleaning him up and turning him over. "How does one stage such a thing, anyway?"

"Easy. He was drunk enough for them to consider it alcohol poisoning. We'll just make it look like he stumbled over here to jack off, passed out, and died." Styx rearranged the body as such and walked away.

"How do you know he was drunk enough?" Charon followed quickly.

"Couldn't you taste it in the blood?"

"Oh, that. Yeah. But I was more fascinated by seeing his life. That is a righteous vampire ability. Like getting a movie about his life to run through your head in just seconds."

Styx smiled. "Cool, isn't it? That we see their whole lives pass before our eyes in the blood. Too bad the Council thinks that power exists only to enforce the Ethic."

"With him, I see the gray thing you mentioned. One date rape, but otherwise he felt shitty about it. Still, liked to get in fights. Not totally bad. Not really good. Just a typical straight guy."

"Nice stereotyping."

"Yeah, well, a lot of guys like that were my friends."

"Were?" Styx tilted his head, questioning Charon.

"I left all that behind in my human life, just as instructed."

"Good. So did killing him violate the Ethic?"

Charon nodded. "Probably. Like you said, it's ambiguous, I suppose. Like you wanted. He was no saint. Still, death was a little extreme. But damn." Charon clapped his hands together. "He tasted good." Then he smelled his fingers. "And that tight ass."

Styx winced. "Stop."

"What now, boss? The night's young."

"It's all up to you, newbie. Show the way." Styx gestured with both arms in front of him.

"Dancing!"

Charon grabbed Styx's hand and ran them at human speed back to Duval Street, where he hurried them into the nearest gay bar. The night passed quickly, as they danced and danced until everything cleared out. Too soon, Styx located an empty crypt in which to sleep the day away.

"What, it's my first night so we go all Bela Lugosi stereotypical?"

Styx smiled. "Funny. No, I just forgot to arrange accommodations. I'm used to staying in my territory. This will be fun."

"Right. Fun."

"Go to bed."

Almost as Styx spoke the words, Charon noticed the sun's approach through the slight burn in his blood. Safely locked in the darkened crypt, where no light shown through and they used their extraordinary senses to see, he nonetheless knew when the sun appeared on the horizon. As if drunk on too much wine, he passed out into a blissful oblivion.

Chapter Seventeen: Suicide

12 OCTOBER 2011

Key West, Florida

The next two weeks passed quickly, with Styx teaching Charon the subtle aspects of being a vampire, such as luring victims or making sure to conceal their powers when around humans. Charon loved the authority he commanded as the undead. He feared nothing, could physically do just about anything, and nourished himself on blood, which as a vampire, tasted better than anything he recalled from his human life.

As they strolled down the street on this warm October night, Charon contemplated whether or not to feed again just for fun and wondered how much longer the tests of the Council must continue. He tired of the games and caution, was ready for liberation into the perfect fiend that Styx envisioned when he first started the game.

"Are we done with the gray kills?" he asked.

Styx chuckled. "Gray kills. It's funny that you found a name for them."

"Well, they needed some moniker. It's not like we tried to conform to the Vampire Ethic. But you won't unleash me, either. I'm ready. Wouldn't they have swooped in by now if they knew about the violations?"

"We only tested it two times."

Charon shook his head. "Three. Kent State Boy, the Evangelist, and Crazy Woman."

"I forgot about the Evangelist. But are we sure that Crazy Woman counts as gray? We could make a case for her conforming to Council guidelines."

"She may have been whacked and did shitty things, but it seems grayish. I mean, she had a drug problem, which seems to preclude her from death by the Council's standards. Never killed anyone. Sure, she stole shit. And beat her baby pretty badly. But it feels like that called for saving the baby and throwing her in rehab, again just going by their holier-than-thou standards. I could make the case that the Evangelist was worse, really."

Styx sat down on a bench underneath some blooming tree, which smelled marvelous. Charon leaned over to sniff the flower closely.

"You're right, she's gray. Kent State obviously was. But I'm not sure that the Evangelist qualified as gray."

"There's no way he wasn't gray. No way he deserved death according to their standards!" Charon practically shouted the rebuttal.

"I meant that he may be completely innocent. Maybe he was an even better test of their inability to detect you."

Charon remembered the blood images, of a man who grew up in a pastor's family, never misbehaved, and felt guilty his entire life just because he jacked off as a teenager. Poor dolt. He went to seminary, waited until marriage to have sex, and sincerely believed the religious drivel he delivered on the street corner and at his little church. Pretty innocent, except for the hate that spewed from his mouth.

"Funny, I thought him gray because of the hatemongering. Pisses me off when those religious fucks always go off on gay people. Anyway, that means I totally violated the Ethic that time. No gray there, right?"

"Indeed. And, to your original point, there's no way the Council would allow that to happen without showing up, and fast. I've seen them appear more quickly for much lesser crimes."

"Must mean we're in the clear. Why aren't you celebrating?" Charon jumped to his feet and danced in front of Styx. He tried to pull the other vampire to his feet, but he laughed and refused.

"Why on earth would that make me dance?"

"Dude!" Charon threw his hands in the air. "Don't you get it? You did it! You figured it out! Absolute, positive proof that your potion worked." Charon's fangs descended, and he lurked above Styx with a sinister look. "You've created perfect evil! Let's go do really bad things!"

Styx stood up but stayed in place. "Actually, I assumed as much all along. Sure, I wanted to be extra careful. But the fact I converted you, completely against Council protocol, made me feel pretty secure from the first. They detest illegally making a vampire. You're correct. My potion worked." Styx smiled broadly as a crimson tear trickled down his cheek.

"So no more stupid tests, right? I appreciate you took this cautiously, to defend me if anyone showed up and all. But let's be done with it already."

"No more stupid tests." Styx shook his head.

"So what's next?"

"I've been meaning to tell you something. Follow me."

A couple of blocks down the street, Charon realized they were headed back toward the cemetery. After that first night in a mausoleum there, Styx had rented a house and concealed a couple of pretty nice coffins in the basement for them. Still, he obviously liked wandering around with the dead. It did have a certain vampiric charm to it, these midnight wanderings around the tombstones.

"Want to hurry there? Like vampires?" Charon wiggled his eyes and smiled. "Or I thought you were going to explain something?"

Usually Styx smiled back, but this time he stoically shook his head. "Let's take our time."

"So at least explain what the fuck's going on."

Styx paused in conversation for a few minutes as they continued walking. "As you know, I blew up my house in Venice. Actually, other than the lab where I performed the experiments, I liquidated all my assets. As you surmised during the first test, vampires accumulate wealth all over the place to keep themselves in creature comforts. For your benefit, I consolidated everything into two accounts. You'll want to diversify it, create other false personas and the like. Well, anyway, you understand. I just did two accounts to keep the transfer simple. That way you'll make it more complex but understand it as you go. Oh, and I maintained your Bitcoin investment for you." Styx handed him a portfolio of papers.

"What's this?"

"The paperwork. All my wealth, given to you. It's more than enough to get you started."

"Oh." Charon took the proffered papers as they rounded the corner into the cemetery. They passed the graves of soldiers from the Spanish-American War and eventually ended up outside the crypt that had first housed them when they arrived in Key West. "You still prefer this place, don't you?"

"You've no idea. Actually, I've continued to come here when you went off on your own to feed or explore. I chose it as my special place."

Charon sensed a darkness in the atmosphere, a strange macabre vibe he felt but could never explain to anyone. How did he know of the depressing event about to transpire? Intuition? Or maybe just because Styx had warned him about it all along?

Just as a melancholy began to settle into his being, Charon snapped out of it. He needed all his faculties focused on acquiring one more thing from Styx, which he required to make his vampire life perfect. And it would take all the energy and attention to detail he could muster, because he must do it against his maker's will. There was no time to wallow in sorrow or ponder Styx's mental state.

His plot started a couple of nights ago with a stolen spell, something he had snatched from Styx just as the sun's rays forced them into sleep. He'd spied the book of witchcraft earlier that week, noticed the carefully outlined spells and enchantments, and noted that Styx slammed it shut whenever Charon came nearby. For a couple nights, Charon had monitored that Styx left it in the same place. Styx always stood by it until the approaching dawn made Charon woozy and forced him to hide in the coffin, only returning to his own once Charon slammed his lid shut. Thus, Charon feigned that the sun called him earlier than it did, waited for a couple of seconds until he heard Styx close his coffin, then raced out, carefully cut out the needed page of the spell book, and dashed to his coffin just in time.

Thus he figured out a way to secure the one thing Styx denied him. Magic. He studied the page carefully the last couple days to make sure he memorized the words and could summon the power at the last moment. One time, he worried that Styx noticed the missing page, but something distracted him and he never brought it up.

Now, in the cemetery, walking like a human, with the general blackened aura about the circumstances, the time had come. Charon knew it.

Styx held out his hand. "This is it. Good luck. Give them hell."

Charon tilted his head and grinned. "A handshake? You're leaving on that note?" Charon grabbed Styx's hand and pulled him into a hug. He whispered into his ear. "Thank you for choosing me."

Styx pulled away and went rigid. "Avenge me."

Charon smiled. "Right. I'll give them hell. I'm good at that. And I'll avenge *her*."

Styx paused again after he opened the door, about ready to step in. "You'll want to stand back farther, toward the edge of the cemetery. I don't want all of my hard work with you to get blown to smithereens."

Charon almost laughed, wanted to, really, but decided it inappropriate for the moment. "You're just blowing yourself up?"

Styx smiled, a sad resigned expression, and nodded.

Just before he closed the door, Charon called out. "Styx! One more thing."

Styx peeked his head back out. "What?"

"I'm sorry. There's something you may learn, right as you're about to leave this earth, or go to wherever the soul of a vampire takes you, that you won't necessarily like. I'm doing it, anyway. But still, after what you gave me, an apology seems in order."

Styx frowned. "What are you talking about?"

"It's nothing." Charon turned around and walked to the edge of the cemetery. He heard the crypt door close behind him.

Safely out of range, or at least far enough that he could bolt at the last minute, Charon concentrated all of his vampire senses on the crypt. He closed his eyes and stood completely still, so as to hear every sound in the area and take in nothing else.

There, he heard the shuffle of Styx's feet, his movements as he lifted some metal object and placed it somewhere. He almost missed it, but then realized that the last sound was of Styx picking up some small item, Charon could only assume a detonator. He heard the slight, almost imperceptible sound even to a vampire of Styx feeling the object, brushing across something, maybe to push the button.

Quickly, Charon said the words. Just like the previous night and two experiments before that, he felt the magic reach out of his mind and race through the air toward Styx. Yes, he manipulated that spell easily enough without Styx knowing. This time, however, at the moment he always retracted the spell back to himself to avoid Styx's learning of his plan, he thrust it forward with all his mental energy.

He snatched the thoughts right out of Styx's brain. Every detail, every witch's ability, he stole completely from the vampire's mind.

Charon felt Styx's alarm, then heard the audible scream from the crypt. "No!"

But it was too late. Charon timed it perfectly so that the theft of the sorcery, the magic that Styx so lovingly dedicated to his fallen lover and vowed to take with him to death in her honor, that heist succeeded. It belonged to Charon now.

Reveling in the moment, Charon almost forgot to race away. He hurried backward just as the blast exploded the crypt and half the cemetery nearby. True to his word, Styx went out in a blaze of glory. That ultimate sacrifice, at least, honored his woman. At least Charon allowed her and Styx that special time.

Sitting on his ass from the explosion, Charon began laughing. He hated ruining Styx's grand exit, especially because Styx realized the theft and tried to stop the blast, no doubt to try to pummel Charon for the deceit.

Ah, well, this magic would come in handy. Charon needed it. It was that simple.

Charon stood up, brushed himself off, and walked casually back toward Duval Street as he heard the sirens in the distance. A few people ran by him, no doubt to check out the cemetery.

As for himself, he decided to go experiment with life as a vampire-cum-warlock, one now unencumbered by the brooding vampire who made him.

PART FOUR: BUILDING AN EMPIRE

Chapter Eighteen: One More Test

30 OCTOBER 2011

Fort Lauderdale, Florida

Charon sat at the Naked Grape, the wine bar where Styx first introduced him to the game, waiting for the waiter to bring the most expensive bottle of wine on their list to the outdoor patio. Traffic hummed by on the busy street and passersby waved to one another or stole a glance at Charon, sitting in his tight T-shirt and shorts with the glowing moon above.

He decided to make this one of his official hangouts, for a number of reasons. He started his life toward vampirism here, without even knowing it. The business sat in the heart of the gay ghetto of Wilton Manors, right in the middle of Fort Lauderdale and a quick jaunt to the ocean. He loved the chatty owner, who held court behind the bar and would talk for hours about the wine or whatever other topic came up.

After partying hard for a few nights and feeding off Key West revelers, Charon relocated to Fort Lauderdale in order to clear his head and begin making plans for his future life. With eternity spread out before him, and no damnable Council to control his activities nor a paternal and hot vampire to scold and tease him, he saw infinite possibilities before him, limitless potential for wealth, sex, and power.

To be sure, he intended a good deal of refinement, as evidenced by the wine the waiter showed him and began to uncork.

"Awesome evening," the waiter said. "You from around here?"

Charon shook his head. "Just visiting."

The waiter poured a sample. Charon swished it around, stuck his nose into the glass to take in the rich cherry scent, then tasted the powerful Meritage blend. "Delicious." He smiled at the waiter, who left the bottle on his table and disappeared.

One nagging thought about his freedom and future haunted Charon, however, to the point that he deliberately left his victims alive the previous night and avoided anything that might bring about the Council's attention since Styx's death.

What if the magic depended on Styx? What if the potion that protected Charon from the Council needed Styx alive and concentrating on the magic in order to work? Or what if, enraged at Charon's duplicity in stealing the witchery that Styx so carefully guarded as a tribute to his love, he cast a spell before he died that reversed the protection against the Council?

On the one hand, Charon doubted living under Council strictures would dissuade him too much from the general life he intended to live. But would he choose death over living within their guidelines? Probably not, much like Styx for all those centuries of loneliness.

As he sipped the wine, concentrating on the flavor as it smoothly slid down his throat, he decided that another night of caution was in order. One more test, just to be sure. Actually, he had plotted the test for a couple of weeks now but just decided at this moment to do it.

He laughed aloud. How many times had he scolded Styx about all the testing? Now liberated from the older vampire's control and free to do as he chose, he became conservative and decided to protect himself one more time.

Then again, what was one more night, when an eternity of nights faced him?

Plus, the test he invented would provide an exciting challenge, something more daring than ever before. Something that would simultaneously experiment with just how much power he could unleash.

He took the last drink from his glass, left a too-generous tip on the table and the rest of the wine, and headed down the street and around the corner, until he could switch to moving with vampiric speed. Soon he stood outside the tiny Florida home, with its outside lights off and appearing completely dark inside, too.

The ruse of a typical little winter home might fool most humans and even a majority of vampires, but Charon uncovered a spell during his planning of this test, which could reveal the location of nearby vampires. He located this couple close by and found them the perfect specimen for his last experiment of the Council's reach, or lack thereof when it pertained to him, after studying them for several days. His spells and witchery obviously concealed him from them or the Council during this reconnaissance because no one confronted him or even seemed to notice him, a good sign for future success with the test.

When the first vampire crept out of the house and hurried away, Charon assumed the two vampires would follow the same routine as the last couple of nights and so moved into action. One or the other always left and returned about thirty minutes later, looking well fed, so that the two could then spend the rest of the night together. Sometimes they ventured out, sometimes they remained inside. None of that mattered to Charon or would affect his intentions.

Charon approached the door and knocked, as if he visited on a regular basis. Predictably, no one answered, so he enchanted another spell he had half discovered, half invented just for this test. It concealed everything that he did from the outside world by sealing him inside an invisible bubble, all within about a ten-foot radius of himself. No humans, animals, or even vampires outside the bubble could see, smell, sense, or otherwise detect his presence. Also, nothing could get outside of it or scream for help once in it. A poor cat learned that the hard way.

Safely within his bubble, Charon walked around to the back, quietly opened the unlocked bathroom window, and jumped inside the house. He froze for a second but heard nothing and felt nothing amiss. He crept down the hall and peered around the corner into the small living room, where the vampire sat curled up on the couch, reading a book. He paused, then rushed into action.

In a matter of seconds, Charon pounced on top of the unsuspecting victim, thus trapping him in his bubble as he struggled to get away. Their power matched one another, which the other vampire must have figured out, because after a brief back and forth of fighting, he shoved away from Charon and ran for the front door, except that, after about six feet, he slammed into the bubble and fell to the ground.

He scampered away, scooting on his butt until his back leaned against the invisible wall.

"What do you want?" he snarled, fangs descended.

"I need your assistance." Charon smiled as the vampire glanced around, seeming to search for an escape route. "You can't get out of my little bubble, so don't bother trying."

"We could just fight all night." Yet he remained planted in his spot on the floor.

Charon nodded. "True. We could. To what point? See, if you kill me, you'd just trap yourself inside my bubble." Charon had no idea whether or not he spoke the truth. For all he knew, it might disappear with his death, but it gave him the advantage. Besides, it could be true.

Still tense and ready for a fight, the guy glanced around again but appeared to acquiesce. "So what do you want? Strange to have a vampire burglar or rapist or whatever the fuck you are."

Charon laughed at him. "Neither a burglar nor a rapist, I assure you. I simply require your assistance on a small matter. A test of the Vampire Council."

He barked a derisive laugh. "You're taking on the Council? Good luck. In fact, I'm calm because I know they're going to protect me. Us."

"Us?"

"Marge and me. My wife."

"Ah. Speaking of which, we haven't been properly introduced. I'm Charon." He bowed, mimicking the decorum he found so endearing in films about the 17th century.

"A debonair kidnapper. Sweet." He rolled his eyes. "Jon. The name's Jon."

"Jon. Good."

"So what am I supposed to help you with, regarding the Council?" His nails dug little trenches into the tile floor where he sat.

"We'll chat more about that when Marge returns."

"She's going to kick your ass, too. Two against one. Why don't you just leave while you can?"

Charon opened his eyes wide in mock fright. "I'm sure a vampire couple would scare most people. But as you've seen, you can't get out of my bubble. And she won't be able to get in, or even see that we're here. In fact, let's move into the corner."

Charon walked casually into a far corner of the room, where only a couple of decorative plants sat next to a window. Against his will, the bubble wall shoved Jon along.

Next, as if on cue, the front door burst open and a smiling, whistling Marge entered the room. "I got to kill one tonight," she sang out. "Found a derelict not far from here. Hey, where are you? We still going to the beach?"

Jon spun around and bashed his fists against the bubble wall, screaming for Marge, but she stood with a puzzled look on her face and called out his name again. When she walked out of the room to search the house, Charon walked over and patted Jon on the arm.

"See? No one gets in or out of the bubble without my permission. Will you calm down now? Assist me, in order to protect both of you."

Jon nodded guardedly and slumped to the ground.

"Good. That's good." Charon pulled a cell phone out of his pocket. "It seems archaic, I know, to have to use a phone and such. But I couldn't think of any other way to do it without giving up our presence. Does your wife have a phone number I could use?"

Marge hurried into the room, now distraught as she screamed Jon's name and spun around in circles.

Jon stared at Charon in bewilderment and began shaking.

Charon twirled his finger in the air. "Hurry. Come, come. Answer me. The longer you wait, the longer she stands out there, hysterical, or flees from our grasp."

Jon scanned the room. "Uh, we don't have cell phones. We're vampires, remember? Who needs them?" He continued looking all around. "Wait. The house has a phone. Call it." Jon pointed across the room to a rather old-looking phone sitting on an end table.

"The number?" Charon asked.

Jon pressed two fingers on either side of the bridge of his nose, trying to remember and then shouted the numbers as Marge finally stopped circling and headed for the door.

Charon casually pressed the numbers into the phone. As it began ringing on the end table and in his ear, he talked more to Jon. "Just instruct her to obey me. Nothing else. Trust me, this can only get worse for both of you if you try anything funny."

Marge paused at the door and turned around, staring at the phone in disbelief. She apprehensively crossed the room and picked it up.

"Ah, Marge. How good to talk to you. I'm going to put Jon on the phone. Listen to him carefully, and then I'll return with some instructions for you."

Charon handed the phone to Jon. He grabbed it. "Marge, run! Get out of here. It's a trap. Just—"

Before he could say another word, Charon kicked him hard in the throat and enchanted an incapacitating spell so his vocal cords no longer functioned.

Charon pointed at him and glared. "I'll release you from the spell, but only if you do as I say."

Meanwhile, as Jon contemplated this offer, Marge held the phone away from her face and stared at it in utter disbelief.

Jon wearily nodded and held out the phone, which Charon snatched away from him.

"You'll obey? For her sake?"

Jon again nodded, so Charon returned the phone to him and undid the spell. "Honey, we're in a little trouble."

She gasped and clutched at her throat. "Where are you?"

Jon looked at Charon, who shook his head in answer to the silent question.

"That's not important. I can't tell you. Just listen to me, okay? I'm putting him back on, the warlock or whatever I'm with. He won't hurt you. Just follow his instructions, okay?"

"And tell her no Council," Charon whispered.

Jon trembled as he spoke into the phone. "Right. Honey, don't alert the Council, okay?"

Charon grabbed the phone from him, impatient to get on with it. "There, Marge. Do as Jon says. Which means do as I say. Understand? We have precious little time. Follow my directions and I'll return him safely to you."

"Are you a warlock? A vampire? How did you do this to him?"

"I'm both. And, frankly, the facts of the matter are hardly important right now. I'm in control and you need to listen, or Jon will die. And probably you, too."

Marge remained a statue near the couch, seeming to contemplate whether they really must obey or if some other option might present itself.

Charon pointed his finger at Jon and let out a laser of intense light. While relatively harmless because Charon could do nothing more with this trick, it struck Jon in the cheek. Charon knew from his own experiment that it felt much like a bee sting. In the dark about Charon's power and what he intended, Jon cried out in pain.

"Don't hurt him!" Marge screamed into the phone.

"That's better. No more games. Here's what I need you to do, and you need to do it quickly. Go kidnap the first human you see, but make sure it's an innocent one. Bring the individual to this room. We're watching you. Be fast. And, just to reiterate, no funny business. Especially avoid any involvement of the Vampire Council. Do you understand? I'll kill him. When you get back with the person, I'll call again."

Marge nodded and hung up the phone. She hardly paused before hurrying out the front door.

While they waited, Charon quietly paced, peering down at Jon from time to time, a now shaking mess of a vampire, completely cowed and afraid.

Marge returned just a few minutes later, carrying what appeared to be an elderly woman in her arms. The woman was completely limp as Marge laid her on the couch next to Jon's abandoned book.

Charon redialed. "Is she dead?" he asked, not waiting for Marge to say anything.

Marge shook her head, assuming Charon could see her, even as he and Jon remained safely hidden in the bubble.

"Just passed out."

"Good. Now kill her."

Marge darted her head this way and that, searching the room for a spirit or ghost. "It's not allowed."

Charon rolled his eyes. For his part, Jon began whimpering on the floor. Charon never guessed from his earlier observations that Jon would become so feeble and weak so quickly.

"I'm giving you special permission. Do it, or he dies."

Jon began weeping blood tears. "Please don't do this to her. Please."

"Now!" Charon screamed into the phone and jammed the button to cut it off. He ignored Jon.

After a moment's hesitation, still glancing all around, Marge leaned over and drank from the woman until she died.

Jon pounded on the bubble, screaming for her to stop and begging for Charon to release him. Charon thought to restrain him, then decided to allow the theatrics, since they did no good but kept the whimpering fool from coming after Charon again.

When Marge finished, she threw the body to the ground and paced nervously back and forth.

Charon called her back. "Very good. Now, you're going to sleep for the day. Secure the living room in the dark, and we'll talk again tomorrow night. Sleep right there, on the couch."

She readied the room for a vampire to survive the day, while Charon still tolerated Jon's crying and brokenness on the floor in front of him. Jon fell into a deep slumber long before the sun appeared, but she stayed up, just drifting off the second before Charon joined both of them.

The following evening, Charon woke first and took in his surroundings. He tapped the bubble, which remained securely in place, and frowned at the flies buzzing around the dead woman. Marge began to stir on the couch.

Charon called her. "Someone should come to visit you this evening. I want you to move into the bedroom and wait. Go now. I can see you, wherever you go."

As she started down the hall, Charon grabbed Jon by the collar and pulled him along. He only came to his senses when Charon threw him into the corner of the master bathroom.

Charon stuck a finger in his direction. "Stay there." Jon sat near the shower, out of sight from the other room, and Charon stood just inside the door so that he could see into the bedroom without anyone seeing him, even if they possessed power to see through the bubble.

Marge still held the cordless phone to her ear. "Now what?"

"Just wait until the person shows up. This will be very difficult, but it's what you must do to save Jon. Okay?"

"Don't do it! Honey! Run!" Jon came to life all of a sudden, not moving from his spot but yelling and screaming. Charon cast the spell to shut him up again.

"You're not listening to him, are you?"

Marge shook her head. "Please don't hurt him. He's weak. Sensitive. Afraid. I'll do what you say, just leave him alone."

Charon grinned, having surmised correctly Marge's strength and determination, counting on it to complete this test. "That's good. Now listen. This is very important. I need you to tell the Council member that you killed the woman because you're sick of humans and she got in your way. Express no remorse."

"They might kill me for that," Marge whispered, as if nonetheless resigned to the order.

Charon first thought to tell her the truth, that they might indeed kill her, but then worried that Jon would freak out and upset his test. He admired Marge's calm in the crisis, even thought kindly of her protectiveness of cowering Jon. But his need for a successful test won out over the honor of honesty.

"Listen to me, carefully. Remain calm. There's something I shouldn't tell you, but I can't stand seeing you two this way. The Council is testing a new member, to see if they can obey and enforce the vampire rules without losing it. Then they would become a Vampire Council enforcer. I wasn't supposed to tell you that, because we need this experiment to be as authentic as possible. But it just seems wrong to continue when you're both so worried. Will you play along, without telling them? For me?"

Marge frowned. She was too smart to take the bait that easily. "Do I have any other choice? Can you prove it?"

Charon returned to his bag of tricks. He invented an orange hovering book and sent it over to Marge. Because it appeared the same as the Council's rulebook, she apparently believed the part Charon wrote, that from time to time the Council tested new enforcers and absolved the vampires who participated from any guilt.

"I've never known the Council to sanction innocent kills."

"It's a necessary evil in this case. Just remember, pretend you're guilty, murdered her under duress in order to save Jon, which is actually the truth, and I'll step in before they punish you. It'd take a vampire trial to convict you, anyway."

"Trial?" Marge asked, but at that moment, a beautiful blonde vampire charged into the room, fangs descended, fierce blue eyes glaring at Marge.

Shit. Charon made up the part about a trial and hoped Marge was too shocked and confused now to disbelieve his nonsense.

"You killed an innocent." The blonde vampire suddenly flung out a set of chains that wrapped themselves around Marge.

Marge began to speak, then stopped. She stammered, said nothing, then sobbed. The blood tears streamed down her face and stained the top of her shirt.

"Speak to me." The woman stepped forward, lording over Marge. "This requires instant death, unless you have some sort of explanation."

"But he made me. For the Council's test. To save Jon. You have to believe me."

The Council member frowned. "Jon's your lover. But he's not here. I don't detect him anywhere. Who made you do this? How? I'm taking you with me."

Damn. Charon hoped she would simply kill Marge. Alas, he could only control so much. Thus, he waited as the lovely vampire prepared to transport the now criminal Marge out of the room. It played out perfectly, actually, for him to enact the last bit of his test on the Council's reach.

Just as they exited the room, Charon jumped on top of Jon and jabbed his hand through his chest, clutching the heart and incapacitating him. He squeezed hard until the heart burst into flames, killing Jon instantly.

Charon whipped around to see if the Council member noticed.

Nothing. The bubble still protected him. He killed one of their own, and still he heard her continuing down the hallway.

Marge, however, sensed the death of her lover and screamed out from the other vampire's arms. She said something unintelligible to the Council member, which Charon took as his cue to leave.

He removed the bubble and flung himself out the open bathroom window. He crouched beneath the window and waited a moment, until he heard them return to the bedroom. This last test proved that the Council could not detect him, because the vampire never came for him, even without the protective bubble. He raced away, only stopping once he arrived back in Wilton Manors, and washed the blood off in the river that surrounded it. He observed his surroundings, waiting for the Council or someone to come after him for the crime of killing another vampire.

Still nothing.

Charon sat on a nearby bench and began laughing hysterically. He ignored the odd and sometimes frightened stares from people as the hurried by.

He knew without any qualms that Styx triumphed over the Council. Charon had kidnapped a vampire and killed him, right under the Council's nose, yet they had no clue he was there, no clue that another vampire perpetrated the crime. Brilliant!

And so Charon could, indeed, turn to his bright, limitless future, spread out before him! Time to make a new home, a grand palace for all his desires. And with no more worries about some impotent Vampire Council coming after him.

Chapter Nineteen: A Vampire's Castle

17 MARCH 2012

Nederland, Colorado

Charon sipped from the glass of wine that he'd bought that evening in Boulder, loving that, as a vampire, cost meant absolutely nothing to him. Even in his most hedonistic human moments, he had never dreamt of casually sipping on a two-hundred-dollar bottle of wine, with its floral aroma, its completely smooth finish—the obscene luxury of it.

Speaking of luxury, Charon glanced around his new abode, a hidden castle deep inside James Peak. He smiled widely.

Ah, so many accomplishments completed since he determined once and for all that the Vampire Council knew nothing about him. Indeed, they never came for him in Fort Lauderdale, even after the murder of poor, feeble Jon, even with Marge surviving as a witness to the whole thing. At first, Charon worried that her survival proved a fatal flaw in his plan, but as time went on and nothing happened, he realized that her living only served to prove even more that he was beyond Council reproach. Surely, she confirmed to the Council that someone else, or something else, kidnapped Jon and ordered her to kill the old woman, and presumably her earnest story would convince them of its truth. And Jon's death obviously came from a powerful vampire, or again some potent agent. Nothing tied it back to Charon, even when he spied on the Council members who appeared in Fort Lauderdale, joining the woman who first came for Marge, and inspected the situation, investigated it thoroughly, but never acted against Charon. Brilliant, actually, that he left Marge alive to make it easier to detect him, if they had that power. And comforting to know they failed completely.

Charon remained just a day or two in Fort Lauderdale, securing a computer and network from which to manage all of his various funds and sources of wealth. He converted the couple of large accounts that

Styx had left him into a variety of smaller accounts under various names, then combined it with newer sources of income that he himself plundered or invested in. He marveled at how easily he could hide funds, his identity, and anything else about himself while still working within the established financial system.

However, to insulate himself a bit from the ups and downs of capitalism, and hardly knowing what the future might hold, he also purchased a hoard of jewels and other hard materials that were better protected from booms and busts in the financial world than cash or bank accounts. He also added gold and silver. These items he stored in secret locations all over the place, with his largest stock saved and then hidden here, in his castle near Nederland, Colorado, once he had finished it.

In just a couple days' time, his wealth grew exponentially. He could now look in on it every few months but otherwise live his vampiric life in complete and utter comfort.

By December, financially set, Charon had turned his attention to wanting a permanent home. He'd learned from Styx that vampires own property, and he wanted something for himself. Something grand. Something beyond belief.

True, he planned to travel frequently and see the world, knowing that he could live anywhere as a complete god. Still, something stable had called to him as well. Some place to come to regularly, some place all his own.

First he'd wanted to find the perfect location. With his vampiric speed and power, by running, swimming, or leaping great distances, he traveled the world in search of the spot. He contemplated something completely remote and isolated, especially awed by the Himalaya Mountains. In fact, he decided atop Mount Everest that he would conceal his lair deep inside such a high range.

But the more he traveled, the more he wanted his primary base in the United States. His home. Where he knew the culture, the people. A haven from his other explorations and meanderings around the globe. He found Alaska too remote, Wyoming too devoid of people, California too vulnerable to earthquakes.

Just as he wondered about venturing back east, he stopped for an evening in Colorado and fell in love with it. It offered a vibrant state with lots of people, especially transient tourists and nomads ripe for feeding off, a large gay community in Denver and Boulder, stunningly beautiful scenery, and yet, amidst the bustle of people and opportunities for interaction, a vampire could easily slip into the Rocky Mountains and find places almost completely bereft of a human imprint.

He therefore searched the state for the ideal mountain, dismissing the ski areas on the western slope because of all the people loitering about and because he wanted to be closer to the metropolitan areas. True, as a vampire, he could run to Denver in a matter of minutes, but he hated having to hurry all over the place all the time. He wanted something closer.

At the same time, he required a relatively isolated area, which eliminated Estes Park and all the tourists descending there in the summer because of Rocky Mountain National Park.

Another crazed laughing spell consumed him when he ventured upon Nederland. The perfect solution. A small town, less populated and not as bustling as some of the other areas, but only a short jog down to Boulder or even Denver.

More splendidly, it butted up against a national forest and other federally designated regions; land protected, ostensibly for eternity, from development by the government. He could pick his mountain there, never worry about some awful settlement landing on top of him, enjoy the great scenery, yet still be close to gay culture. And victims. Lots of victims.

Without much more effort, he chose his mountain and began the process of converting it from a big stone lump into a castle that would rival the grandest of them anywhere else in the world.

Even with his vampiric speed and strength, this construction took him nearly two months.

He went high onto James Peak but stopped several yards from the edge of the tree line. There he started to dig his tunnel in a place where few humans, even the people who hiked onto this mountain, would end up. Thankful for his vampiric strength, he concealed the slight hole he made into the mountain with a gigantic boulder, which in the winter would often be covered completely in snow.

It took forever to first dig his tunnel and then to pull out the rocks and smash them into tiny bits. He then transported the debris all over the state, so no one would see a pile of rubble or all the rock in one spot and suspect anything. Thankfully, he utilized certain bits of magic to assist him, though his attempts to make things vanish or to do the work with but a twitch of his nose always failed. So much for mimicking *Bewitched*. He also dodged any people wandering about, thankful that the dead of winter kept most humans far away. Dynamite or explosives would have sped it up, too, but he hardly wanted to call such attention to himself or risk such exposure.

By January, he mined a tunnel that went a couple of miles into the mountain and then excavated a wide open space deep within James Peak, big enough he assumed to put a gigantic mansion inside. He lined the area with torches simply by wishing them into existence, then adjusted them with more magic so their smoke disappeared after a couple seconds of it drifting into the air.

The mined area mirrored a large cave, however, hardly the image of Charon's dream castle. Thankfully, concealed completely inside the mountain and without threat of exposure to anyone, Charon worked at vampiric speed on his next task; he smoothed the rocks surrounding the entire area until he stood within a perfect rectangle, an enormous one, with every surface polished perfectly. He replaced the archaic torches with an electrical lighting system that he powered with a magical, gigantic quartz rock that he animated with energy, even though even he could never explain exactly how it worked so perfectly and safely.

His next task slowed him down again, as he had to build out the interior of this place, starting with walls, floors, and following that with drywall and the various other infrastructures needed to construct a building. Unfortunately, nothing in his repertoire of sorcery helped him here, frustrating him that, even after stealing everything from Styx, he still knew so little, still confronted dilemmas that provided no easy solutions despite his witchery. While he could work extra fast when alone inside the mountain, acquiring the goods took longer because he sometimes shopped for them, sometimes stole them, and had to carry it all up the hillside and down his tunnel, again doing so secretly lest anyone discover his hidden lair before he even finished it.

The biggest thing that sucked, he pondered as he finished the third and final floor to his buried palace, was doing all this work himself. After the wine and wealth and thinking that vampirism put him on easy street, here he forced himself to learn the art of construction, and then performed all the work alone. Why? Because his new solitary life required it. And his attempts to use magic often frustrated him because it took too long to learn and sometimes never worked. No wonder it took

Styx so fucking long to invent the potion that concealed Charon from the Vampire Council.

The thought suddenly hit him and brought a smirk at the idea that he drew the line at slavery but not necessarily killing the innocent or torturing people. He sighed. Ah, the complications of living without the constraints of society's ethics.

When finished, his palace included dozens of rooms, many of them without an official use at this time, but he planned for the future and might one day need to expand. He set up one as an office, another—the most elaborate and largest room—as a bedroom, including a completely sealed chamber for sleeping through the day on a king-size bed and a hidden lab for experiments. He built out a perfect wine chamber, a television/movie-viewing room, as well as a nice kitchen, in case, for as of yet undetermined reasons, he ever wanted to host a human. He also established a more formal living room area, perhaps for reading or hanging out. It included a gigantic brass chandelier, ornate furniture styled after Louis XIV—nothing contemporary in this room. He provided for himself the ultimate in refinement, something the former kings and queens of Europe might envy, something even Styx never dreamt of acquiring.

At this point, a couple weeks ago in early March, he had bored of spending night after night with himself and decided to take a break before turning his attention to furnishing the rest of his rooms and such with furniture and decorations.

He made his way to Tracks Denver, a lovely club for a night of drinking, dancing, letting loose, and watching the hot boys dance around.

He grabbed his Jack and Coke, stood beside the dance floor, and scanned the room for a delicious specimen, maybe for sex, maybe for dinner, maybe for both. One gorgeous twink attracted his attention right away.

His straight black hair hung down to his shoulders, his eyebrow piercing added a certain allure, and the tattoos of fire crawling up both his arms enticed Charon with their vibrant red and defiant attitude. He glanced at Charon with hazel eyes, smiled, then whirled around and continued dancing. When he turned back toward Charon, he smiled with thin but bright red lips.

He walked right up to Charon, his eyes twinkling, and jerked his head in greeting. "Jordan."

Charon smiled and held out his hand, to formalize their meeting. "Charon."

"Strange name. May I?" Jordan pointed to Charon's drink on the table.

"By all means. Here, let me buy another round." Charon moved them to the bar as he answered the comment about his name. "It's C-h-a-r-o-n. Greek mythology. A long story. A little boring for tonight."

"That's cray-cray." Jordan grinned and walked away while Charon ordered two more drinks.

He found the young man, probably just turned twenty-one or even here with a fake ID, alone in a more isolated part of the bar and handed his drink to him.

He held his glass up and tipped them together. "Cheers."

"To what?" Jordan asked as he took a drink.

"Nothing in particular."

Jordan nodded. "You're totally slammin."

Charon laughed. "I appreciate the compliment, though it's a bit forward."

"Well, actually, I should tell you something. See, I come here to work. Well, and play. Play a lot. Play is work, though. They're the same. You catch my meaning?"

Charon grinned. "You're a prostitute."

Jordan shook his head. "Makes it sound nasty. Just another hoe. Or girly. But I give blow jobs and shit for money. Nothing dangerous." Jordan reached into his pocket and held up a condom.

Charon reached over and patted the young man on the shoulder, swallowing his snide comment about how he could call himself whatever he wanted or dismiss the label of a prostitute, but a whore was a whore in Charon's book.

"Very intelligent of you." He tapped the condom. "I hate to end our association so quickly, but as you can see and pointed out—" He motioned up and down his body. "—I don't exactly need to pay for it."

Jordan held his hands up to Charon. "Wait. Wait. Don't go. I'd do you for free."

Charon squinted at him. "What's your story?"

Jordan shrugged. "I said I'd do you, not go into therapy or share my life. That's private."

"So you're homeless."

Jordan took a big drink. "Maybe." He emptied his glass. "We doing this or not? Cuz otherwise I got work to do."

Charon downed his drink, too. "Where to?"

Jordan smiled, the wide grin reaching all the way to his eyes. "Follow me."

Jordan led Charon outside and around the back of the bar, down an alley and then stopped in a darkened, isolated spot. Charon almost commented on the danger of it, but why did he feel protective of this one, and what good would his words do, anyway? Instead, he reached over, lifted Jordan's chin, and kissed him hard on the lips.

They fell into a deep kiss, a long and affectionate one, surprising Charon who usually kissed merely as a means to getting on to bigger and better things. He soon unbuttoned Jordan's shirt and bit a nipple. Oh, how he wanted to reveal his fangs and bite harder, to taste the delectable blood, but not yet. No.

Casually Charon turned Jordan so he faced the wall, with both hands on it to hold himself up. Charon reached around and undid Jordan's belt, then slid his pants and underwear down. Jordan pushed his tight shaven ass out toward Charon, who jabbed his tongue into it and swished it all over.

Unable to control himself any longer, he stood up and pulled out his own cock, then paused and actually put the condom on when Jordan whispered the request. No disease could infect a vampire, nor could he transmit something to a human, but why argue and ruin the moment? Leisurely inserting himself into the pink hole, Charon closed his eyes and lost himself in the sheer pleasure of the moment. God, that felt good.

Maybe the time off from sex or interaction heightened Charon's sensitivity, or maybe the sexiness of this homeless youth captivated him, but it took about ten or eleven thrusts, even with the condom, and Charon shot his wad long and hard.

He pushed farther into Jordan, then grabbed the guy's hard penis and stroked him to completion while licking his ear and neck. Again for unknown reasons, Charon decided to resist the urge to bite into him and taste the luscious blood.

"That was righteous." Charon finally pushed away and started to dress himself.

"Totally. Swag." Jordan dressed quickly. "Well, no time for long goodbyes or anything. Thanks for the ass grind."

Jordan pretended to tip a hat from his head as he sauntered down the alley and back toward the bar.

Sated for the time being, Charon turned toward his castle, walking through Denver because he wanted to take a night off before delving into the matter of furniture. Except that he passed a house with a kick-ass lamp in the window. Tiffany, or at least a replica, with blue and purple stained glass, dragonflies separating the various panels, and a brass butterfly on the base. He peered around, spotted no one, thought of his lesson with Styx but found no security system, so he walked right up to the window, smashed it, grabbed the lamp, and ran away with vampiric speed before anyone could see him.

Charon spent the next couple weeks, up until St. Patrick's Day, stealing, buying, and otherwise acquiring all the furniture he wanted for his mountain palace. He walked through the entire place, from room to room, even the ones he kept empty, then grabbed yet another bottle of wine, this time a splendid Chardonnay from Arista Winery, and poured himself a glass while sitting in his formal living room. He stayed in his cave-turned-castle on this night, contemplating his next move, when the thought of Jordan pounded into his head. He got hard, remembering the bubble butt, then came upon an idea to solve the one thing missing from his domain. He needed servants.

Chapter Twenty: Jordan

19 MARCH 2012

Nederland, Colorado

Charon woke the night after St. Patrick's Day, thinking perhaps he'd drunk too much green beer until he remembered that he hated most beer and only drank expensive wine these days. Nor had he ventured out of his domain. But how else to rationalize the insanity in his head? What, then, explained this sudden need to inhabit his perfect dungeon of a lair with humans, who might just get in the way? Why hit upon that as a desire, one that somehow stayed with him into the next evening?

Servants. As simple as that, Charon understood his craving. He required servants in order to make the most of this palace and his life. Why do all the work himself? If his magic included limitations, why subject himself to doing all the menial tasks if he intended to live the perfect vampiric life?

The answer against this notion at first went back to his disdain for slavery, because how else could he get people here without them knowing the palace's location or about him being a vampire? They would never be able to return to civilization. His power to kill them would frighten them away, so it seemed to leave him with little choice.

Too, he remembered Styx constantly dwelling on Charon being alone in life. No way he wanted to think that this yearning for a staff was related to a latent need for companionship. Bullshit. That thought alone smashed the idea into the back of his brain for the rest of the night, during which he went out to feed instead.

He returned to Denver rather than thinking about this odd idea about a staff, lurking around the bar once again until a pleasant-looking specimen crossed his path. Small. Cute, though upon closer inspection a little older than Charon went for, what with the slight wrinkles around his eyes and graying at the temples. He thought to approach him, perhaps have a quick fling, but as he got near, a rumble in his stomach took control of the situation.

He moved into a vampiric run, grabbed the man by the waist, and raced to a secluded and deserted park nearby, where he threw the screaming man to the ground and shouted, "Shut the fuck up!"

The man backpedaled, tried to get to his feet, and fell over but at least stopped screaming. Charon contemplated what to do next when the guy made the decision for him. He jumped to his feet and sprinted away, so Charon caught him, and when the shrieking recommenced, Charon drank him for dinner, then unceremoniously dropped the body right there.

He chuckled at the thought of leaving the bite marks of a vampire on the poor victim, wondering if the Vampire Council would ever catch wind of it and attempt to figure out who the hell did it without their knowledge. Then again, the stupid humans would focus on the broken neck and think some kinky romp went awry. Whatever.

Besides, maybe Charon did the guy a favor. Lonely middle-aged dude desperate for a relationship but, from appearances in the blood visions that flooded Charon's mind as he fed, a little too clingy and needy. No doubt a violation of the Council's precious ethic, but fuck them. Why did Charon even think about them anymore?

He went to bed the next morning, hoping the weird idea about a staff would dissipate, but instead he woke with the same contemplation. He reached down and felt his rock-hard dick, wanting in the worst way to get release through something other than his own machinations. What if his staff included those to pleasure him, at his will?

As he rubbed his cock, falling into the pure carnality of it, loving the sensation at the tip of his penis as it percolated toward orgasm, the vision of Jordan's beautiful ass popped into his head. As he shot a load all over himself, the intense release combined with the realization of the perfect solution to his staffing needs.

He dressed hurriedly and raced to Denver, first to Tracks Denver, then combed the various neighborhoods and other bars in search of Jordan.

Charon discovered Jordan behind a dumpster, giving some Republican-looking dude in a suit and wearing a wedding ring a blow job. "Unless you want to explain this to your wife, I'd suggest you zip it up and leave."

Mr. Republican jerked with fear and pulled back, his bright pink pecker glistening with Jordan's saliva and bobbing up and down. Charon tilted his head and smiled, then noticed Jordan underneath, grinning and wiping his chin. When the guy turned to leave before even buttoning his trousers, Jordan shot to his feet.

"What about my money?"

He stumbled to a stop and turned around, finally securing his pants. "You didn't finish."

"Not my fault." Jordan shrugged.

"Better pay him." Charon smiled, but the man heard the threat of the words. He dug into his pocket and handed Jordan some cash before scurrying away.

Once he rounded a corner, Jordan fell to the ground and held his side from laughter. When he recovered, he jumped up and grinned broadly. "Wicked. Totally wicked. You come back for more of this?" Jordan spun around and grabbed his ass for Charon.

"Maybe later. First, we need to talk."

Jordan turned back around and rolled his eyes. "I thought we established I'm not really into that, bro. Again, if I decide it's time to settle down and play *Little House on the Prairie*, I'll definitely give you a shout-out. It's just not where I'm at."

That made Charon laugh. He glanced around, looked at Jordan, and burst out again. "I see. Well, I certainly understand how blowing old dudes in red ties beats anything I have to offer. Still, maybe I can make it worth your while." Charon pulled out a hundred dollar bill and waved it in the air. "I'm not looking for some fucking relationship, either. But I do have a business proposition. A lucrative one. At least hear me out. If you come along and listen, this money is all yours, regardless of your decision."

Jordan squinted and looked at Charon suspiciously. "You a serial killer or something?"

Interesting question, and if Charon worried about telling the truth, he'd have to think long and hard about the honest answer. "No. I just want to make the business proposal to you."

"That's a ginormous wad, just for a chat."

Charon sighed. "I'm filthy rich. It allows me to toss this shit around at will." He took the bill, wadded it up, and threw it across the alley before pulling out another one. "Do you want to earn this or not?"

"Nothing off here? Seriously no killing me?"

"Let's be honest. You're taking a chance, right? We fucked in an alley once, you know nothing about me, and I'm flashing cash in the air to get alone with you. It's a risk. On the other hand, a homeless gay kid, who picks up tricks left and right, already lives with a steady dose of risk-taking, doesn't he? So weigh the odds and tell me what you think."

Jordan frowned and lost himself in some contemplation while Charon attempted to wait patiently. "Okay." Jordan started walking toward the street.

"What, you suddenly know where we're going?"

Jordan spun around and held his hands in the air. "Well, filthy rich guy, I doubt you transact much shit in a smelly-ass alley. I figured you wanted something more posh."

Charon chuckled. "Posh wasn't something I anticipated in your vocabulary."

Jordan flipped him off.

"Okay, okay. You're right, let's go somewhere else."

They started down the alley when Jordan turned around and ran back to the dumpster. He knelt over and picked up the hundred Charon had tossed away. "Finders keepers."

Charon merely turned back and continued down the street. They walked silently a few blocks, until Charon signaled for a cab and requested that it take them to the downtown Marriott. Jordan hung in the background of the lobby once there, fidgeting awkwardly at the surroundings until Charon secured a suite and motioned for him to follow.

Once in the room, Charon locked the door as Jordan took in the luxury. Where Charon saw just another hotel room, he reminded himself that the kid slept outside somewhere most nights. "Why don't you go shower? There'll be a robe in there."

"Thought this wasn't about sex."

Charon shook his head. "It's not. It's about not wanting to smell old man cum on you all night. Go shower."

Twenty minutes later, while Charon sat watching an entertaining rerun of *Arrow* on the CW, Jordan bounced into the room, wearing the robe but without tying it in front, so his cock swayed back and forth.

He felt the material and smiled. "Swag."

"One usually ties it up."

Jordan looked at the ceiling with exasperation. "You've had your cock jammed up my ass, my spunk all over your hand. Now you want to be all prude on me?"

"No. It's just not as conducive to business if I sit here wanting to throw you over the arm of the couch and fuck your brains out. Capisce?"

"What's kap-ish mean?"

"Capisce. Italian. It basically means: do you understand what I just said? I figured you'd know it, since you threw *posh* my way before."

Jordan giggled as he tied his robe and then flopped onto the couch with his legs spread wide open, thus the re-emergence of his penis. "I learn antique words and shit from tricks. So some I know, some I don't. Dude takes me to his house, old one—both the dude and the house, decorated all nice but kinda like a movie from the Civil War. I said something about it, and he says he likes his surroundings posh, or something like that. Then defined it for me. Thus, posh is added to my dictionary. Whenever we hook up, he likes to teach me something. Maybe it's part of his charitable work. I don't know if I can wrap my head around kaa-peeesh." He said the last word deliberately. Smartass. "So, you've a proposition, huh? Though the offer to throw me over the arm here does sound enticing. Especially for two hundred."

"I said one hundred."

"I was just counting the one you chucked away, too."

"Perhaps later. First, the business. What I'm about to explain will shock you. Even you, who thinks you've done and experienced it all. Don't be alarmed. Again, in some ways you've passed a point of no return. And I have no intention of harming you."

Jordan scrunched his brow, confused or annoyed or something.

"Let me try this another way. My name. Charon. In Greek Mythology, he rowed people across the River Styx toward their death or to purgatory."

"Cool. Your 'rents gave you that name?"

Charon shook his head. "No. My college friends. Anyway, you're in that boat now. So it's all a matter of where I row you at this point."

Jordan pulled his knees to his chest and hugged them tightly. "So you *are* a serial killer."

Charon laughed. "Not really. And I'm not going to harm you, no matter what you decide. I admire your spirit. The world is more interesting with you in it, whether or not you go into business with me. Though I certainly hope that you will."

The legs flew out again. "It's hot." The robe came undone. Apparently Charon chilled out Jordan's anxiety again, which heated up his tight little body. "So what's this proposition? Lay it on me. I'm pretty open to all sorts of shit, as long as it's safe, like I said before."

"This isn't just about sex."

Jordan's eyes opened wider with surprise. "But there's some of that involved, right?"

"Probably. Actually, most definitely."

"Cool. Cuz I gotta have it."

Charon sat on the opposite side of the couch, where he reached over and patted Jordan on the foot. "This is going to take all night if you don't stop yammering. Listen, then you'll have all sorts of shit to react to."

"Pushy. But you're sexy, so it's cool."

Charon rubbed Jordan's thigh, watching his dick begin to stiffen slightly before he stopped and folded his hands in his lap. "I'm in need of a staff. But I lead an extremely unconventional life, which brings with it unconventional requirements for this new group of employees. They'll all be hot young men. I'll transport them to a hidden location, my home, where they'll work for me. They'll live there, only leaving if I permit it. They'll do the work I require but have ample free time to do as they please, within the confines of my home. They can't know where they are. They won't be able to leave or sneak away. But the castle is enormous, and everyone will have their own room. Everyone will arrive of their own free will. I'll also buy almost anything and everything they want. In return, the staff will clean, do other chores as necessary, meet my sexual desires when needed, and other sundry tasks in the palace." Jordan's face gave away with every sentence that he thought Charon was nuts. "Before you get any more alarmed, I'd like to put you in charge. You'll have a position of privilege. The position of privilege. No one above you except me."

Jordan stared at Charon in complete disbelief. "So you are totally cray-cray?"

"I can see why you think that, but no."

"You don't think anything you said was off? Even a little?"

Charon laughed. "It sounds completely insane. The ravings of a madman. I understand. However, it's a serious offer. And in a minute, depending on whether or not you decide to progress with the agreement, I'll demonstrate what makes it, if not less crazy, more explainable."

"Why me?"

"Because you aren't attached to anyone. You can disappear without a trace. You're obviously intelligent, if uneducated. Which we could also rectify. You're not afraid. And you're hot. So you fit the criteria. If my instincts are right, this is something you'll jump at."

Jordan sat silently with his attention glued to Charon. "At least you're a gorgeous nut job. What could possibly explain this? Do I get to know, or is that the point of no return, to quote *Phantom of the Opera*? Is that why you keep saying that? A big Phantom fan?"

"Did you learn about these musicals from the same guy who taught you posh?"

Jordan giggled, with his adorable little smile. "No. Another guy takes me to shows. Pays me to accompany him but doesn't even hold my hand. After, just lets me go. Well, first we go to dinner, then the show, but it's all formal and fully clothed. Not so much as copping a feel. So, where we at here?"

"You were correct. We arrived at the point of no return. I'll explain the reason to you, show you, actually, and you'll either accept the position, or I'll do something to remove you from my presence immediately and for good. You'll wake up somewhere else, not even in Denver or Colorado, and if you try to tell anyone about this, they'll think you're the batshit crazy one. Cray-cray, to use your lingo."

"You act like you're so much older than me. Please."

"Right, around a decade. But more worldly. And it gets back to that issue of education."

Jordan fiddled with his limp penis. "At least this is sick somehow. Like, chill-tastic. In a badass way. At least it's entertaining."

"You're not scared, are you?"

Jordan shrugged. "Not really my style. Hasn't been an option, really, since they kicked me out when I was fourteen after they found me munching on that other boy's pecker."

"You have a lovely way with words."

Jordan smiled. "Tell me, what will convince me you aren't bonkers?"

Charon began to speak, but Jordan held up his hands and yelled. "Wait! Wait! One more thing, since this may be it for us, after." He launched himself across the couch and onto Charon's lap, then kissed Charon hard on the lips, jabbing his tongue in and out and grinding his ass cheeks into Charon's growing erection. After a moment, he pulled away, his hard cock smashed between them. "I just wanted another taste, to go. Unless I stay. I'm already contemplating it, just so you know."

Charon smiled. "Then watch this."

He opened his mouth wide, his fangs descending while he stared at Jordan, who watched with amazement but did nothing to pull away from Charon. Once he looked the part of a vampire, he stood up with Jordan in his arms and effortlessly carried him around the suite. Charon opened the balcony doors, winked at Jordan, leapt over the side of the building, and plummeted dozens of stories down to the pavement, where he sprinted away at vampiric speed. He set Jordan against a tree along some quiet residential street, then waited for the next passerby. He laughed to himself at the fact that Jordan did nothing to cover himself despite being in public and the chilly temperature. When an older woman ambled by with her dog, Charon grabbed her, bit her neck, and drank her blood. He called Jordan over and showed that they would leave her, breathing but passed out, simply because he feared scaring the shit out of Jordan, who to this point seemed to take the whole thing in stride. Even now, after he attacked the woman, Jordan appeared to watch with interest, the same way someone might watch the Discovery Channel. Minutes later, they sat comfortably next to each other on the couch inside Charon's suite.

"I didn't expect you to be this calm about it." Charon opened the bottle of wine that he'd snatched from a store before bringing them back. He took a swig and handed it to Jordan.

Jordan drank a big gulp, and Charon reached over and wiped the wine off his chin before it trickled down to the robe. "Well, not much choice, really. I thought you were just cray-cray. Maybe thought I met my end with someone who would cut me to pieces and eat me for dinner. Crazy as it seems, you're right. A vampire. That explains a lot. Like, who knew they were real? But it's not like I had time to worry about it or get away or anything. So I just went with it. WTF, right?"

"So you're not freaked out?"

Jordan shrugged. "You should see some of the penises I've seen and had to put in my mouth, even with a rubber." He grinned.

Charon threw his head back and laughed. "Seriously, you just experienced a vampire. Not a legend. Not an acid trip. A real vampire. I could kill you. Easily."

"Yeah, but you said you wouldn't. Besides, at some point, like I said, or maybe you said it, can't remember, I risk that every night. Except I can take care of myself. I do. It's not like this is the first dicey situation in my life. Though, yeah, a bit intense and all. And, if it's lights out, at least I had a good run. Pretty happy, for a homeless fag who produces spunk for a living."

"What about the job? You want it?"

Jordan frowned, tilted his head, and stared at Charon. "Like, I do. Sounds delish. Except the trapped part. You know? I'm kinda used to freedom. But I'd be in charge, right? That's cool. Can I see the place before I decide? Or something?"

"Here's the deal. Yes, you'd be in charge. And since you're in charge, it gives you a very special status at the palace. You can come to me any time you want to tell me it's time to go. I promise not to kill you, ever. You say the word, and I'll take you to freedom. Now, that won't be true for the other boys. You'll have to keep this a secret between us."

"Can I become a vampire?"

Charon shook his head. "No." He did not want to risk the Vampire Council learning about it. As far as he knew, only he received immunity from Styx's spell, not his progeny as well.

"I probably shouldn't trust a vampire. But I believe you. So, yeah. Okay. Let's give it a whirl. It'll be a nice change of pace for me, as long as there's sex involved. With you. The other staff. Whatever. I'm pretty addicted to cock and coming."

"We'll have plenty of that. You can even pick a special fuck toy to bring along."

"Righteous! So, what's first, boss man?"

Charon grinned, leaned over, and kissed Jordan. "Bend over that chair."

Jordan leapt to his feet and dropped the robe to the ground before doing as ordered, his tight little ass swaying back and forth in front of Charon. Charon hurried to remove his clothes, then dropped to his knees and planted his face right in that delicious butt, his tongue diving in as far as it would go.

They fucked. Cleaned up. And right before the sun rose, Charon raced them to James Peak with Jordan tightly blindfolded and Charon moving too fast, at any rate, for Jordan to figure out the location. He lay Jordan on a couch and bid him good night before disappearing into his bedchamber and the confines of his enormous coffin.

Charon cast a spell to keep anyone from getting into his room, as well as another new spell to conceal the tunnel exit and prohibit anyone from leaving once Charon brought them here.

Chapter Twenty-One: Jordan's Boys

20 MARCH 2012

James Peak, Colorado

Charon woke the next evening to find Jordan flitting about the first floor of the palace, completely naked but dancing wildly to Scissor Sisters.

"Where are your clothes?"

Jordan twirled around. "Dude. You brought me buck-ass naked. Couldn't find a damn thing here. Even the fucking Marriott had a robe for me. Figured you wanted it this way. Also, where's the gym?"

"We'll have to add one. And no, you won't be expected to be naked all the time, unless you so choose. It might be a bit uncouth."

"Un-what? Never mind." Jordan rolled his eyes. "No more words. It's too much. So, as head of staff, I've a couple of comments. First, there's no fucking staff. Just me."

"We'll attend to that soon."

"Good. Then the gym. If we're trapping hot boys here, we need one of those big-ass empty spaces upstairs to become a kick-ass gym, or we'll be pudgy hot guys."

"I'll get that done. It was an oversight, given that I never workout anymore."

Jordan stuck his tongue out. "That's bullshit. But the rest of the joint is swag. Modern, old, all mixed together. I like it. Yeah, I'm good here. You know, when you said palace, I didn't really absorb the meaning. I mean, we don't need to define palace or castle. I know them. But, in some weird way, it was a gross understatement. However, I noticed there's no exit. Or windows."

Charon nodded. "And there won't be. You're deep under the earth. The others will not be permitted to leave. You'll have the opportunity to come and go with me, but never to learn of this location or to leave of your own will."

Jordan twirled his finger in the air. "We went over that. Got it."

"Good. Then let's get started."

"What's first, boss man?"

"I should think some clothes. This way." Charon pointed toward the hallway and motioned for Jordan to move in that direction.

Jordan's cute little ass moved in front of him. Charon escorted Jordan to a smaller room near the back of the castle, far away from the actual tunnel, and decided to make this the official exit and entry point to his kingdom. He once again blindfolded the naked youth, picked him up, and used his vampire nature to dash to Denver.

"Usually I arrange for a clothier to meet me somewhere after hours," Charon explained as they sat in the park opposite a number of very wealthy mansions. "We didn't have time for that. So we'll have to steal something. Do you know anything about the people who live here?" Charon motioned toward the homes.

"Fucking rich dildos. That about sums it up."

"Yes, that was tremendously helpful. Let's start over, without the coy bullshit. You grew up one street away. I need to know if any of these houses contain a late teen, early twenty-something male of about your build. We need to steal his clothes."

Jordan pouted next to Charon. Funny, he sat on a metal park bench completely naked and fine with it, but pointing out that Charon knew about his old home pissed him off.

"How'd you know that?"

"Records. People I know. I'm a vampire, remember? I can get all sorts of information. Remember those hundreds you snatched up last night? They buy all sorts of stuff. Like information from your friends, like your full name."

Jordan nodded, took a moment, and appeared back to his old self. "Well, they threw my shit out, and it wouldn't fit anymore, anyway, so no need to go to that shit hole. I did steal from them sometimes. Fuckers. Pissed in the middle of the living room, too. That was when I was sixteen. I figured if they called the cops about it, they'd get just as much shit for my delinquency as me. I almost shit on their bed, but that seemed deranged."

"Not that I didn't enjoy the meandering down memory lane, but you're completely bare in the middle of a park. I'd rather not call attention to us. Can you answer the question I actually asked? Though I agree, that would have been deranged, to defecate there."

Jordan flicked his penis and pointed it at Charon. "Like you can't hightail it out of here all of a sudden if peeps show up. But okay." He nodded and motioned his head toward the subdivision. "Chad. He lived a couple streets away. He's like a few years older than me, just graduated from college, but lives at home. He might be there, though."

"Take me to his home and leave the rest to me."

Jordan walked casually down the street, turned the corner, and stood before a large yellow brick home with white pillars holding up the porch roof. "There. Where should I wait?"

"Over there." Charon pointed to a grove of trees.

It took mere minutes for Charon to sneak into the house, grateful to find the young man's room empty, and steal about five shirts and pants for Jordan. He also grabbed a pair of sneakers. Outside, he got Jordan to put something on but threw the shoes away when the boy repeatedly complained they were too big.

The ordeal exhausted Charon mentally, so they returned home and spent the rest of the evening ordering Jordan anything and everything his heart desired, shipping it to one of Charon's financial advisors in Denver. He sent his accountant a message to leave the items in boxes outside his office upon arrival, and Charon would pick it up at his convenience. They shipped everything overnight, so in less than a week, the vampire furnished his boy toy with all the clothes he wanted, as well as other things for his bedroom, including some new furniture.

Next they turned their attention to the gym. That, too, went quickly and easily. The only annoying part was carrying all the shit himself to the palace, much like all the building supplies when he constructed the inside. Still, because of the need for secrecy, no other choice presented itself.

Charon leaned against a treadmill after they completed the gym, watching Jordan polish the second wall of mirrors. "Are we done? This was boring. I hired you so I didn't have to do this shit."

Jordan finished a spot and picked up the cleaner. "Yeah, well, you chose a twink." Wearing tight shorts and no shirt, he flexed his bicep at Charon in a muscleman pose. "Bodybuilder would have been better to move this stuff around. I can't do it. Look at this little muscle." He pointed to the still-flexed bicep.

Charon nodded. "So we'll need some buff guys, too."

"Yeah. For more than just moving shit, too." Jordan grabbed his ass and started a mock rendition of getting fucked.

"Are you ready to start that process? We need to pick our guys to join you."

"Sure. How many?"

"We can decide as we go. Maybe ten or so?"

Jordan nodded. "Look at me, the big vampire CEO! I'll whip 'em into shape."

"First we need to acquire them."

"Yeah." Jordan scrunched his brow. "How we doin' that?"

It amazed Charon how quickly they assembled the staff of nine other boys to add to Jordan's services. They accomplished it over a three-month period, each time going to a different city and hunting down the perfect specimen.

Jordan had a knack for scouting out the situation and ingratiating himself with the homeless youth of a city in a matter of a couple days, if not hours. He befriended the gay boys, plied his trade from time to time because he missed it, or so he told Charon, and then picked the future employee. After hiring him, Charon had sex with the newbie, sometimes with Jordan, sometimes without. They offered the opportunity without revealing the vampirism and only let that out once the prospect accepted. Charon escorted each, one by one to the palace, gave them a room, furnished it to their specifications, and then joined Jordan in the next town, where he traveled ahead and already determined the next person to approach. A few declined, but a majority that they selected decided to give it a try. Charon marveled at how many homeless gay guys haunted the streets of America, unknown to almost everyone except themselves, those who preyed on them, and a very few who tried to help.

They initially picked nine.

From San Diego: Joe, with his long braided hair down to the middle of his spine, of slight build and African-American. His flesh glistened, his gaze held longing for Charon to take control of him. He smiled a lot.

Cleveland: Kiki came most easily, ready to escape the prejudice of his mother's church where they constantly tried to "turn him back to straight" after she found the pictures of naked guys tucked under his mattress. He was a big, muscular football player at a local college, so not exactly Charon's type, though he admitted that watching the guy fuck Jordan and then Joe got him plenty aroused.

Washington, DC: The powerfully built wrestler from Georgetown had almost jumped off a bridge when Jordan spotted him. Too macho to come out, he explained when Jordan bustled over and talked him off the ledge. Too afraid to lose everything. Charon smiled at how Jordan recounted the scene to the vampire when he introduced Jason. "So I'm like, well, I have an offer for you. Allows you to live and jump off the bridge at the same time. As a bonus, I'll suck your cock dry." And so Jason came to join their ensemble.

Fort Lauderdale, Charon's previous base: he actually remembered Phil from a night out with the boys during his human years. Built almost just like Jordan, Phil smiled widely when Charon approached, jumping into Charon's arms right in the middle of the sidewalk. "You're back! I thought we were a one-night thing. I cried myself to sleep after, stupidly hoping you'd take me in after I told you my story." Charon kissed him on the cheek. "Well, of a sort, that's why I'm here. I want you to meet someone." Jordan took over with his well-rehearsed spiel. Charon loved having Phil in his bed almost more than Jordan, his vulnerability heightening the sexual pleasure.

New Orleans: It took longer to convince Travis of the truth of the vampire because so many wander around the old city, pretending to be vampires because every author seemed to set their undead here, from Anne Rice to Poppy Z. Brite to almost every movie or television show ever created about Nosferatu. Even the fangs descending failed to appease him. Only witnessing the sucking of a victim's blood convinced him, and he then joined the team readily, more excited than before. He was the only Latino, somewhere between a muscular hotty and a twink. Jordan laughed as he discussed it one night. "I guess he goes both ways."

Detroit: Alex. Bodybuilder. Very large. Almost played the part of an idiot jock, which reminded Charon of Grady, and not in a good way. But Jordan pouted and insisted. Reminded the vampire they needed big guys to carry shit around the palace. "Or is this more of a sexual decision on your part?" Charon asked. Jordan smiled coyly. "Both?"

Sonoma, CA: Unusual to find a wandering young twenty-something and his dog hitchhiking along the road in the middle of the night. Brian, an all-American boyish dude underneath the long unkempt hair and goatee, ready for a three-way right there amidst the grapes, chatting afterward about how he was searching for his purpose in life, and so why not try this hidden realm. Maybe the pot coursing through his veins made the decision easier, and he immediately set up a corner of his room to grow weed in the palace after he settled in.

Chicago: Benjamin liked Jordan, a lot. Charon worried that Benjamin fell completely head over heels in love with Jordan, but Jordan explained emphatically to him that he'd just be one of the others, nothing more, and that slight Asian dudes weren't his style. Charon, on the other hand and for his part in the selection, thought his soulful eyes and pouty lips simply divine. He, of all the boys, liked how the vampire appeared without warning and commanded sex. Surprisingly, despite his apparent uptight nature, he loosened up in bed and would go anywhere, do anything. He even managed to convince Jordan on several occasions to fuck him. "You only encourage his romance with you," Charon explained, "when you give it to him." Jordan merely smiled and wiggled his eyebrows.

The choice from Pittsburgh, however, went up in flames and brought the number that Jordan oversaw from nine down to eight all too quickly. It also prompted Charon to think he needed more oversight of future selections, lest Jordan lose himself again in allowing his penis to make decisions instead of his brain. Jerome was simply gorgeous. At least six five, with a swimmer's build and the confidence of an Olympic champion. He wore it all well, and knew how he appeared.

Still, he was lost, he claimed, despite living in a dorm, with a loving family somewhere in rural Pennsylvania.

"He doesn't really fit the part," Charon told Jordan one day.

"He's lost, just like the rest of us. All alone, like he said. He wants this."

"Or do you want him?"

Jordan grinned. "Haven't we done this before? Can't it be both?" He mock pouted, gave Charon a delicious blow job, and thereby brought Jerome back to the castle.

Jordan knocked lightly on Charon's door two nights after they determined not to add anyone else to the staff, and sheepishly entered the room. "We've got a situation that may be above my head."

Charon arched a brow. He intended to spend a quiet night on financial matters, commanded that no one interrupt him, and assumed Jordan understood to come only in an emergency. "This can't possibly wait?"

"He's kinda getting the others riled up. Listen, you were right. Not a good choice, I admit. My bad. Ginormous mistake. Got it. But I need your help correcting it."

"Correcting what?"

"Jerome wants to go home."

Charon drew in a deep breath. "I thought we explained to them that was impossible? Didn't we emphasize all of this?"

Jordan nodded. "Yeah. A million times. But they came of their own will, so I guess he changed his mind of his own will."

"Bring him to the exit room." Charon got up and rushed by Jordan without another word.

"You won't kill him, will you?"

Charon waved his hand in the air and left Jordan behind him. A few minutes later, Jordan escorted Jerome into the room.

"Is everyone else okay?" Charon asked him.

"Yeah. All good. We ordered some video games, which distracted them. Old-school arcade games. Oh, can you get them for us tomorrow? They're huge."

Charon rolled his eyes. "Yes. If it'll appease everyone. Now, you." He turned to Jerome, then looked back at Jordan. "You're dismissed."

Jordan hesitated, then nodded and backed out when Charon glared at him.

"You're sure you want to return? You can't possibly get over this and stay?"

Jerome shook his head violently back and forth. "Way too weirded out, you know? I think I lost myself with Jordan, didn't really think it through. I just want to go back. No harm, no foul, right? I won't tell anyone. Promise."

Charon threw the hood at him. "Tie this over your head."

Charon raced out of the building, up the tunnel, and moved the rock out of his way in seconds, even with the large young man in his arms. He bounded over James Peak to the western slope and stopped on a snowy, remote mountainside. He dropped Jerome unceremoniously into a mound of snow.

Reaching down, he ripped off the hood, then decided to rip off all his clothes.

"Where are we? This isn't home." Jerome's words started loud and angry but gradually softened to a frightened whisper as he shivered on the mountainside.

"I just wanted you to experience my annoyance with you before you died. I didn't think you deserved swift justice."

Jerome flung his arms and legs around as he tried to stand, to get away. Charon watched him for a minute, like monitoring the plight of a little bug stuck on its back, then in one motion hovered over the young man. He lifted him with one arm, took a second to admire the trimmed, hairy chest and muscular legs, then bent over and stabbed his fangs right into Jerome's pulsating bicep vein. It took longer to drain a person if a vampire stayed away from a main artery, and Charon noticed they felt more of the pain that way.

Typical, spoiled brat's existence revealed itself in Charon's mind as Jerome's life passed through the blood that flowed down his throat. Ugh. Depressingly mundane. Too obvious that he would fail at living in Charon's underworld as a minion. He should have tested their blood before selecting them, he thought, to see their life. Oh, well. Too late.

Charon licked the wounds to heal them, then carried Jerome over to the mountain lion who watched the whole scenario with an animal's fascination. He tossed the carcass to it. "Bon Appetite!"

Back at the palace, he called Jordan into his office. His boy toy leader already snapped back to his usual self. "All taken care of?"

"Done. And I assume we learned our lesson?"

Jordan shook his head and twisted his lips in a strange shape. "Like you said the other night again, my cock makes a great toy but not so great a thinker." Jordan grabbed it through his pink underwear, the only thing he wore tonight.

"Good. You're dismissed."

"Okay. We cool? No worries, right?"

Charon nodded. "No worries. Let me finish. But be ready tomorrow night. You need to be punished. Appear at my door, promptly at midnight, and naked."

Jordan grinned widely. "I'm not supposed to enjoy punishment."

"Sometimes it's okay to like it. But to make it hurt a little more, bring Kiki with you. You need a big cock in one end, mine in another."

Jordan spun around and flashed his ass at Charon before he departed. He also, instinctively perhaps, learned another lesson about the situation and avoided asking what happened to Jerome after he left. What he never learned could never hurt him.

Charon finished his finances, played a computer game, then pulled up the video monitor in each room to admire his staff. Jordan and buff Jason were cooking dinner, while twinky little Phil chatted away on a stool next to them. Joe, his long braided hair swaying back and forth with a huge grin on his face, danced with Brian, who had shaved the goatee and cleaned up from his Sonoma wanderings but demanded that they keep the dog, which lay on a couch nearby. Jordan pled his case, saying a pet around would make things happier, and thus the mutt resided with them and one room became a mock backyard. Benjamin locked himself in his bedroom—Charon grinned that none of them knew about the surveillance system—with an enormous dildo shoved up his ass as he jacked off at feverish pitch to a porn video. Meanwhile, two of the football players, Kiki and Alex, were in a large room they re-carpeted with artificial turf, teaching tiny little Travis to catch passes, or at least attempt to catch them. He dropped more than he caught.

Charon smiled, satisfied. Yes, his palace needed this staff. A perfect complement to his divine castle. He climbed into his extremely large coffin—the width of a king-size bed with a mattress and silk sheets—content and happy with how things turned out to this point as a vampire. He only wondered how to make it even more exciting and better in the future.

Part Five: A Vampire's Pastimes

Chapter Twenty-Two: Visit from a Ghost

2 SEPTEMBER 2012

Essexville, Michigan

Charon stared out at Saginaw Bay as he reflected on his vampire life to this point. In less than a year since Styx transformed him, he had created his empire and set out to become the perfect fiend of a vampire that Styx had imagined would torment the Council, or at least defy their laws at every turn.

Charon lived that life to perfection. He acquired what he wanted, when he wanted, and kept most of it in the most amazing underground palace ever constructed. Louis XIV and his Versailles Palace paled in comparison. Charon staffed it with a throng of gorgeous young men, all content and happy with their lives despite the permanent imprisonment. He tormented people when the spirit moved him, kicked back and enjoyed the company of whomever he chose for a night, and otherwise answered to no one. He could travel to wherever he chose. And would never have to obey a soul.

Charon thanked the vampire gods that he could wake early enough to go out with dusk still lingering, to allow him a brief glimpse at the sun's last beams before it went down for the night.

So why this nagging concern in this head for an old friend? He had left behind all the other humans from his previous life without regret. He thought of them rarely and seldom even wondered what became of them. Of course, because of the way he insulated himself and lived a solitary life, even as a human, not many people knew he'd vanished. Still, his small group of friends from college and a random person here and there must have pondered and even worried about what became of Charon, who simply disappeared into thin air one day.

He googled his real name one day, but Blade Haden came up with few results, all of them old entries, stories, or addresses from his time in college. So no one had informed the police, most probably believing he went off to do his own thing as he had a thousand times before. Nothing unusual there.

He converted to vampirism without a hitch. Perfect.

So why did the murky water reflect his image back to him and send him into this moment of reflection? Was he going soft, already? Why the last two weeks of preparation, for tonight?

That forced him to chuckle aloud. No. Nothing else hinted of such a calamity. Just this concern for Bill. He'd woke a couple of weeks ago and remembered his friend the night of his capture, as they hopped from club to club and Bill had attempted a heart-to-heart conversation with Charon. Charon had rebuffed it. Thought it the ravings of a man regretting his past because of his Christian upbringing and thinking too hard about his future. Still, few people in Charon's past, going all the way back to his childhood and continuing from one foster family to the next ever showed any lasting concern for him. Almost no one had ever expressed their feelings for him with the kind of attention Bill had given him, more than once.

It'd usually annoyed Charon. Now, thinking he would never again see Bill, he found it somewhat endearing, even if he continued to disagree with the sentiment behind it.

The lone boat came into dock as the last glimmer of light disappeared on the horizon and plunged them into darkness.

Charon sauntered away from the water's edge and pulled out his iPhone. He typed in the password at the bank website and confirmed that the funds had all transferred into the other account.

He gradually sped up and hurried through Bay City and into Essexville, down the main drag and by the fancy Victorian houses that dominated much of the street until he got to Maple Street and walked swiftly by the modest middle-class homes. A tricycle blocked the sidewalk outside one, a fallen branch from the recent storm another, a swing hung from a branch next door to a meticulously kept front yard. Most windows were completely darkened for the night, kids safely tucked in bed, only the occasional glow from a television in a living or family room to indicate human life.

One man stood on his incredibly green lawn with a hose, spraying a flower bed that contained a kaleidoscope of colors with the flowers in full bloom, as if he could see them in the dark. He nodded and smiled.

Charon returned the gesture and continued the last couple of houses until directly across the street from his destination. It was a cute single-story home with gray siding and darker blue trim. Plants filled the bay window in the front; an American flag flew from a pole attached to the porch. Despite the two-car garage around the rear of the house, Charon recognized Bill's Saab in the driveway. He smiled as he walked up it, seeing how carefully Bill wound the hose up on the side of the house and edged lawn, not a blade of grass out of place. Ever the anal retentive one.

He opened the back gate and walked into the yard, which appeared even more fastidiously maintained than the front. The swimming pool contained crystal clear water, the fountain bubbled down the rocks next to it, the deck looked newly stained. Beautiful. A perfect slice of Americana.

"Hey," an alarmed voice shouted as a sliding door open. "Who are y—" Bill stopped himself, a wide smile spreading across his face. "Charon?"

"Bill." Charon stretched out his hand and shook Bill's.

Bill glanced inside, then held up a finger. "Wait here. I'll be right back." He returned momentarily, holding two beers from the Great Lakes Brewing Co. and still grinning. He stepped outside and motioned them over to chairs beside the pool. "Shelly's asleep, or I'd invite you in."

"Already in bed?"

Bill smiled even wider than before. "She's pregnant. It's got her all out of whack."

Charon returned the smile. "You two didn't waste any time. Congratulations."

"Yeah. We're excited. We think we want a big family, so might as well get going while we're young. Missed you at the wedding. After you disappeared there last year, well, I thought at least you'd show up for that."

Charon pondered his answer, the various lies sounding hollow, knowing Bill would see through any of them, anyway. The truth, well, that must stay with him, too. The silence extended for several minutes as they quietly sipped their beers.

"I didn't mean it that way." Bill spoke quietly. "It's just, well, I thought you were gone for good this time."

Charon nodded and smiled. "Actually, this will be the last time I can see you. I'm not going to explain. No lies. Still, I wanted to say goodbye and give you a parting gift."

Bill nodded and sipped his beer, not prying or pushing. Charon remembered the easy comfort of sitting with him, even in complete silence, and simply enjoying each other's presence.

"What are you up to these days?" Charon set his empty beer on the table. "How did you end up here? Essexville didn't strike me as a destination for any of us."

Bill threw his head back and laughed, then lurched forward and slapped his hand over his mouth at the loud noise. He shook his head, turning bright red. "No. No, it didn't seem likely at one time. Still, we're really happy here. Seems like it'll be a good place to raise a family. I got a good job. I'm really excited about it."

"Doing what?"

"Children's minister."

Charon's eyes grew wide with shock. "Following in your father's footsteps?"

Bill tilted his head back and forth as he pondered an answer. "Kind of. But not really. Going into the ministry, yeah. Because I believe. Because I want to help people. I sewed my wild oats, so to speak, and found that life wanting. This is what I want. It's perfect for me, really. But I'm not like him. I never will be. Not judgmental. My church is open to everyone, the head pastor insists upon it. It's great. That's not like my parents' church. My dad doesn't like my church, if that tells you anything. Still, they're excited to become grandparents."

Charon laughed. "You as a father would take some getting used to. I think I'm glad I won't be here to see it." He paused and turned serious. "But you'll make a good father and husband. You're the only redeemed one of us. I'm happy for you."

Bill got up without a word and returned a minute later with two more opened beers. He handed one to Charon and sat down, took a long swig from his bottle, and then looked deeply into Charon's eyes.

"What's up? Why the dramatic night entrance? Why is this the last time? I thought you disappeared for good, but here you've returned, only to tell me you really will disappear. What gives?"

"I'm not going to tell you. You don't want to know. I'm happy, though. You don't need to worry about that." Charon paused a moment to consider how to continue. He had rehearsed his speech before he got here, but Bill's steady gaze unnerved him, took him away from telling any lies. "Still, you know more about my past than anyone. I don't recall anyone else really caring about it the way you did. I mean, you actually listened. I appreciate it; I always did, even if I rebuffed you and never followed the path you wanted for me. I don't really give a shit about adding goodness to the world."

Bill actually laughed, Charon assuming more at the truth of it than anything. "You always did say there was no redeeming people, especially yourself. The world was doomed."

Charon grinned. "Is doomed. I haven't changed my opinion."

"I won't give up hope on you."

"You should." Charon finished his second beer. "I'm happy that you at least alleviate some of that suffering. A ray of hope in a dark world. Who knows, maybe there's some poor gay kid here in the middle of Michigan, despondent and afraid. He'll be safe with you. I like to think things might've been different for me if you'd been out there."

Charon sighed, tired of the sentimentality. Or perhaps afraid of it. He admitted that possibility to himself, too.

"It's never too late for you to change. You don't have to be alone. I'm here. I'll always be here for you. Others would be, too, if you let them in. I'd help in any way you let me."

Charon smiled, the villain creeping back into his bones and pushing out whatever drew him to Bill on this night and allowed these feelings to seep to the surface. "It's too late for me. Because I'm happy without reforming. I disdain the thought. That's just the reality. I've found satisfaction in a completely different way. However, I want to give you a parting gift."

"I don't need anything from you. Especially if it's ill-gotten."

Charon shook his head back and forth. Then he laughed and shook his head. "It's completely legitimate. I know it may be hard to trust me, but I'd never do that to you. It's a thank-you."

Bill shook his head. "Okay. I do trust you. You're too brutally honest. At least when we talk, that is. Or maybe I should just say I know when you're full of shit and I don't sense that going on tonight."

That made Charon laugh, and Bill joined him.

Bill shrugged. "I didn't say I should or that it was a good idea to trust you. I just do."

"Well, I'm glad you do. The gift, it's a small token of my appreciation. It should make you, Shelly, and however many kids, quite comfortable. That way, you don't have to worry about money. You can just do your work and help people. No worries."

Bill finished his beer and tilted back on two legs of his chair. "Even if I trust you, I can't accept that. I assume you're talking about money. I can't take it from you, just for doing what a friend should. Besides, you need it." Bill pointed toward his house. "We're fine."

Charon leaned over, close to Bill, and clutched his knee as he stared into his eyes. "If you really trust me, then you'll know this is true. It's but a tiny part of what I own. What may make a world of difference to you means nothing to me. Let me do this kindness. It may be the only one I ever feel like doing again. Besides, it's already done and can't be undone. It's untraceable. Unreturnable."

"How will I know what it is?"

Charon leaned back in his chair and smiled. "I'll be leaving soon. Again, thank you. Just log in to your bank account."

"Now?"

Charon nodded. "Sure."

Bill reached into his pocket and pulled out his phone. When he concentrated on it and began to type on the screen, Charon went into vampiric speed. He pushed out of the chair and climbed high into the nearby tree in seconds, where he could peer down at Bill and still see him clearly with his vampiric eyes. Bill appeared to enter a password and tapped in a couple more clicks. He jerked his head up to look at where Charon had sat, his eyes wide with complete shock. He scanned everywhere, then rubbed his face.

Leaning forward, Bill set his phone down on the table, his hand trembling noticeably. He breathed deeply, then gradually sat back into his chair. After a few minutes, he shook his head and a smile crept across his face.

"Ah, Charon. Thank you." He lifted his beer in a toast and drank the last of it.

Bill said it as if he knew Charon sat watching, as if he knew Charon could still hear him. He eventually went back inside, closed the door, and locked it.

When the family room light went out, Charon pushed himself off the high branch and jumped all the way over the house roof to the front street below. He whistled a dance tune he'd heard the other night in a bar as he sauntered down the middle of the street.

Chapter Twenty-Three: A Parade on Halsted

31 OCTOBER 2012

Chicago, Illinois

Charon snapped out of whatever funk sent him to Bill rather quickly by the end of that night and returned to his devilish ways easily enough. He decided that the Michigan episode amounted to purging whatever tiny bit of human remained inside of him, lurking to undo his perfect villainy.

After all, he had a life to live. Fun to have. An empire under his control, and nothing but pure pleasure to satisfy himself. Not to mention an eternity to do it. Every night provided a new source of excitement and entertainment, from staying in his room alone to watch movies or deal with finances, to sex with one of the house boys, to venturing out to feed or find fresh meat for something else entirely. He traveled a little, but so far he enjoyed staying close to his palace. In time, he thought it might get tiring and compel him to travel the world more, but for now, plenty kept him occupied right there.

However, just the day prior, he'd read in the *Windy City Times* about the huge Halloween parade taking place the following night on Halsted Street, right in the heart of Boystown. The idea struck him that he simply must attend the festivities, and more than that, he must contribute to people's fears. They wanted to celebrate Halloween as a perfectly spooky holiday, when ghosts interacted with the humans, when fall pushed the world toward winter, when everyone dressed up to be someone else for a night or two. So be it. As with his gift to Bill, he felt like giving back what he could, and he could definitely scare the shit out of people to help their revelry.

However, he woke on Halloween with an added thought, and thus called Jordan to his rooms. "We don't have much time to chat about this if we're going to do it, so listen closely."

Jordan smiled and sat across from Charon, in nothing but red bikini briefs. "What? Don't tell me. You're a vampire?"

Charon grinned. "Smart-ass. And here I was just about to reward you."

"Oops." Jordan continued to smile as he lifted one leg over the arm of the chair, pressing the tight underwear up and around his balls and cock. "I'm all ears."

"Good. It's Halloween! We need to do something. Something radical. Something profound, so we can celebrate the holiday. What good is being a vampire if you ignore the scariest night of the year? There's a huge costume parade in Chicago every year. Let's go. It's tonight. If you're up to it, you can assist me. Then I'll hide out in Chicago for the day and you can shop or whatever you want to do."

"Cray-cray. And I mean that in a good way. Let's do it." Jordan jumped to his feet.

"We need costumes. It's unseasonably warm, which is good. Any suggestions?" Charon seldom dressed up for Halloween, but the mood hit him tonight. He needed assistance.

"Let's wear as little as possible. White tight underwear for me, red for you. We'll deck you up with glitter and stuff to be the devil, and I'll be a little white angel. Sex sells, you know. It's gay Halloween, not just Halloween. No plastic costumes from Walmart."

"Do we have time to get that together? We need to leave soon."

"No prob. I'm on it."

In just a few hours, Jordan transformed them into the sluttiest demon and angel imaginable, and Charon transported them across the plains and all the way to Chicago. He stopped carrying Jordan at vampiric speed in a back alley, where he set the guy down and adjusted his boner. To pass the time, or at least he claimed, Jordan had fiddled with Charon's cock the whole way.

Jordan giggled. "I wonder why you let me fuck with you, when you'd probably kill anyone else."

"I wonder the same thing."

Jordan walked toward the main street, his ass swaying back and forth delightfully with every step. "In fairness to myself, you're so fucking hot in that getup, well, my hormones were in overdrive."

Charon grabbed Jordan from behind and licked his ear. Then he whispered to him as he felt around front for his hardening dick. "Listen, little angel, don't forget that you're fucking around with a demon tonight." Charon stopped and stared hard into Jordan's eyes. "Literally."

Jordan nodded, then grinned. "I'm good. I get it. Besides, it's different when you're on the demon's side. You could snap at any minute. You cautioned me about the risks when you brought me on board. Besides, I think you need me around. And, well, I fuck with a demon every night I'm with you, don't I?"

Jordan swirled around and headed back toward the festivities. Feisty. Charon liked that about him.

The street, lined by clubs, restaurants, and other businesses, teemed with people milling about, some in costume, some there just to watch. A few catcalled at Jordan and Charon, making both men smile, while others stared with lust. Charon winked at the big burly ostensibly straight guy, tightly holding the hand of a brunette bombshell with enormous breasts, as he stared at Charon the entire time they walked past one another.

"What's first, boss man?"

"I was just pondering the same thing." Charon walked on. "The actual parade doesn't start for a bit. How about scaring someone on the way?"

"Name it." Jordan grinned widely.

They turned down Roscoe Street, heading west and away from the crowds, until they got to a more secluded, quiet residential street a few blocks away. Still, with the expected crowds on this night, a few passersby meandered their way toward Halsted every minute or so. They both leaned against a tree.

"Um, this was the big plan?" Jordan yawned as he asked his question.

"Glad to see you knocked the smart-ass out of you. Here's plan number one. I'm going up in this tree, way up into it. You're sticking around down here, picking a guy to make out with against this same tree. Watch the festivities commence."

Without waiting for a response, Charon leapt high into the tree in one motion, then stared down at Jordan, who squinted up to see him with his head tilted.

"It's not going to work if you're staring at me the whole time," he shouted down.

Jordan laughed and gave him a thumbs-up before looking away.

A couple dudes and one couple sauntered by, followed by a woman pushing a baby stroller, but Jordan merely smiled politely or exchanged pleasantries about costumes. Finally, after Charon took his turn getting bored, a medium-height average-looking guy walked swiftly past in his Blackhawks hockey costume.

"Man!" Jordan called to him. "That's delish. I love basketball."

The man glanced at Jordan and slowed but kept walking. He smirked. "Sweet of you to notice," he said in a more twinky voice than Charon expected from someone in a professional sports get-up, "but you don't even have the right sport."

Jordan jumped in front of him to stop his progress. He shrugged and hooted. "So teach me."

"Something tells me you don't really want to learn about it."

Jordan laughed and touched the guy's arm, who relaxed a little more but now looked all over the place. He chilled a bit when a straight couple dressed as Raggedy Ann and Andy walked by on the other side of the street, chatting loudly.

"Okay, you got me. Here's the thing, though. My friends and I have a bet. We're all dressed as angels, and there's a competition for the one who kisses the most guys with our angel charm tonight. But we can only kiss cute guys. You interested in becoming my first?"

The Blackhawks fan paused, seeming to contemplate the offer, but was speechless. Jordan stepped closer, pushing his stomach against the guy, and stroked his leg with one hand. Charon forgot from time to time that Jordan was a professional.

When Jordan seductively pressed into him and guided him toward the tree, the dude complied with the movement but still seemed dazed and afraid.

He pulled back a little when Jordan leaned in the rest of the way and planted his lips on the guy, at the same time grinding his crotch into the man's leg. Yet he opened his mouth readily to accept Jordan's tongue.

"You taste so good." Jordan licked across the guy's cheek and nibbled at his ear.

Charon took that as his cue. He pushed himself off the high branch and landed right next to the two. Jordan at first continued to kiss the guy but remembered the game and jumped back a little, though then he stood there frozen, almost grinning. Well, Charon never tested his acting ability.

The Blackhawks guy, however, slumped down, scrambled to get back up, tripped, and did all this in the two seconds that Charon observed the scene.

Charon scowled and reached out to grab him by the jersey, pulling him close. "This is a night for demons, not angels. You dare interact with a righteous one and defy my intentions?"

Jordan giggled behind him.

Thankfully, the man was so scared by Charon lifting him a few inches off the ground by his shirt with only one hand that he began crying and shaking uncontrollably, seemingly unaware of the twit behind them.

"What are you?" he asked.

Now Charon stifled a laugh, thinking of the time a villain asked Batman that very question in a movie. Great, his grand night of scaring people devolved into a superhero flick, with the goofy sidekick and overwrought victim.

Charon let go of the guy and shoved him into the street. "Go home."

He sat trembling in the middle of the street, not moving.

Charon stormed toward him and pointed down the street. "I said go!" His voice echoed back and forth off the nearby homes.

This time Blackhawks fan took but a second to jump to his feet and sprint the other way. Charon turned around to see Jordan bent over, laughing his ass off.

Charon reached out and made him stand up, embarrassed at the people passing by and laughing at the sight of them.

Jordan smiled widely. "Well, that was fun."

"Not really what I had in mind," Charon muttered.

"He was scared. Shitless."

"Right. But in a comical isn't-it-hilarious-to-meet-a-vampire kind of way. Again, not what I had in mind."

"You didn't specify the plans. Besides, we have all night to get it right."

Charon eyed Jordan up and down, almost forgetting his Halloween intentions when a sexual energy seized control of him. "What if I change my plans to ravaging your body instead?"

Jordan rolled his eyes. "That will be delightful. But we can do that any time. Come on, one more fright at least. Then I'm all yours."

Chapter Twenty-Four: Deadly Halloween

31 OCTOBER 2012

Chicago, Illinois

Jordan and Charon walked arm in arm back toward the parade.

"Uh, since we failed your expectations last time, what did you really have in mind?" Jordan asked.

Charon paused. He intended to kill someone, for dinner and for fun, but in a Halloween-style kind of way. He hesitated to tell Jordan, however, wondering how he might react to witnessing an actual death. Then again, he worked for a vampire and came along tonight, so what did he expect?

Jordan apparently read his mind. "It's not like I don't have a clue about what you do, you know. I get it. Signed up for that part, too. You're a vampire, and a fiend of one, who kills to eat, probably enjoys it. I figured it out. Remember that night when Jerome freaked, wanted to return home? I know that you killed him. That you left to pretend to take him back but really offed him. So let's get this straight."

Jordan came to a stop and yanked Charon's arm so he stood in front of him. "I work for you, knowing all this. I don't give a shit about humanity any more than you. Okay? It left me to fuck old buggers in alleys. I don't really owe the world anything. I like the arrangement here. You let me live in a palace and order hot guys around. We get to fuck once in a while, too. It's all good. Murder away! I'd prefer you didn't kill me. I enjoy living and all. But I took my chances with this job, I get it." Jordan sighed and looked at the ground. "Just do it, okay? I'm not asking to become Robin to your Batman, since we're on a comic book kick here, but it's out there now so let's live it. Okay?"

Charon smiled. "Where'd that come from?"

Jordan shrugged. "It's been on my mind."

"Good. Then you don't mind helping me pick dinner?"

Jordan grinned, then frowned. "As long as you're not inviting me to join you."

Charon put his arm around Jordan and started them back down the road. "Absolutely not. We'll get you a nice raw burger afterward, to go along with it."

"That will go right to my ass." Jordan reached around and grabbed each butt cheek.

"We'll work it off later."

The parade had already begun back on Halsted, with a steady stream of people walking down the middle of the street, modeling their costumes and enjoying the audience. Charon marveled at the intricacy of some costumes, seemingly right out of a movie set, while others wore almost nothing, like Jordan and him, and still others entered the parade with the shittiest costumes he'd ever seen.

Charon pointed to one, wearing some rather pedestrian-looking Storm Trooper outfit, screen printed onto just the front of a T-shirt and a cheap-ass mask. "You know the reference you made to the plastic costumes from Walmart?"

"Yeah." Jordan snickered.

"Isn't that one, right there in the parade?"

Jordan laughed loudly. "Sure is. Why the fuck would he enter himself in the parade? Oh, I see why."

Charon scrunched his brow but then noticed after the Star Wars character passed by. He wore ass-less chaps and walked by with one of the tightest, most amazing asses Charon had ever seen, and that was saying something.

The three people doing ballet down the middle of the street enticed Charon, too. They all wore nothing but bikini briefs, much like the two of them, flamboyant scarves, and ballet slippers. With buff bodies and the moves they made, they had to be professionals. They all wore clown makeup, too, with bright red noses, white skin, and other accent marks.

"Delicious." Jordan said it loud enough for them to hear, so they bowed to him.

"Likewise, cutey."

Charon rolled his eyes at the next family going by, dressed as characters from *Finding Nemo*.

"What's that look for?" Jordan asked.

"Families annoy me."

Jordan laughed hard. "Ah, it's cute. Sweet."

"Yeah, until the nose pickers grow up and become assholes like their parents."

"I didn't turn out like my 'rents."

"You didn't exactly become someone out to save the world."

"Touché!" Jordan motioned a sword thrust toward Charon.

"There you go with another old reference. What? You used to sword fight on the streets? Or was this another old-guy lesson?"

"Funny, that. Wicked assessment. Yeah, same guy as before, said that all the time before I stopped and asked what the fuck he meant. He explained, then hired me one night just to teach me fencing. I sucked at it, then sucked him off and called it a night."

Charon and Jordan continued to watch the parade and make their snarky comments until Charon spotted an interesting group heading down the street. They caught his eye, to the point that he moved Jordan along so they could follow them.

One dressed as an enormous brown bat, with a fanged mask and working wings that flapped behind him. He seemed almost blind, too, not knowing exactly where to walk. The woman on each side appeared as gothic vampires, with prosthetic fangs, not the fake shit, delightfully intricate white and black makeup, and moved the bat along with chains and a padlock around his neck. Two guys, a tall and a short one, similarly dressed but in black suits, followed them. Every one of them except the bat wore some kind of contact lenses that gave them disturbingly blue, piercing eyes, rimmed with a ring of red. They played their parts perfectly, never smiling or reacting to the crowd, which seemed as enamored with them as Charon was.

"They fit the bill, huh?" Jordan smiled as he asked the question.

"Indeed."

"So how does this play out?"

"Let's just follow them to the end. We want them alone, so I can handle all of them."

"Fuck. You're thirsty. I didn't know it took that much."

"It doesn't. Just one from time to time. But they look so delicious."

The vampire group continued down the parade route, never noticing that Charon and Jordan followed along, and never once breaking character. They absorbed themselves completely in the charade and embraced All Hallows' Eve as a celebration of their fantasies. Even at the end of the parade, when others dispersed, turned to watch their fellow revelers, or headed toward the nearest bar, this group seamlessly went around the corner and continued down a sidewalk, still acting the part of perfect Nosferatu.

Charon allowed them to get about a half block ahead before he determined his strategy. "Are you sure you want to join this? You can go the other way and I'll find you later."

Jordan contemplated a moment as they walked down the street. "Nope." After all that thinking, he sounded as nonchalant as ever. "This should be wicked. It's something I need to see, what with you being my boss and all."

Charon nodded and quickened his step. Before the vampires and their bat reached the next busy street, Broadway, Charon trotted to catch up with them and motioned for Jordan to follow. He called to them just before they reached an alley, full of fire escapes, wooden decks, a few dumpsters, but no sign of humans, even on this busy night in Chicago.

"Hey!" he called out. They kept moving. "Dudes! Stop, please."

One of the young male vampires turned slightly to see who called and if it was intended for them. Charon smiled widely and waved.

"Can you stop a minute?" Charon asked.

The man poked the other man's arm, who glanced back, then said something to the rest that brought them to a halt. Charon pretended to lose his breath as he approached, grinning and with Jordan in tow.

"I've never seen more righteously awesome costumes. I mean, these are totally great. Do you do the whole vampire thing year round, or is it just for Halloween? It's so awesome."

One of the women finally broke character and smiled broadly. "Thanks! It's just what we do."

Charon continued to smile and nod, as if her ambiguous comment answered his question. "Could we get our picture with you?" He pointed to Jordan. "He's got all sorts of vampire fantasies. Pretends he works for one sometimes. He loves the get-ups, and that bat is wicked."

"Yeah," Jordan jumped in. "Swag."

"We'd love to." The woman began organizing them for a picture, never noticing that neither Jordan nor Charon carried a camera.

"Wait!" Charon called out excitedly. "Let's do it someplace dark and creepy. How about farther back here in the alley? That's a better setting."

The vampires chuckled and looked at each other, but one shrugged and led the way.

"Where the fuck we going?" the bat asked, speaking for the first time. "I can't see shit in this thing."

"Just follow us, bat. You're not supposed to talk."

"Fuck you," the bat answered but laughed.

Tucked away from prying eyes, with a delightfully spooky Halloween setting and revelers all decked out for the occasion, Charon took his turn to play the part of vampire.

"Before we do this, do you want to see a real vampire?"

The two women laughed, the bat stood stoically, and the two guys glanced around, seeming to grow nervous.

"Sure." The lead woman laughed.

"Let me have the cute one." Charon pointed to the shorter male, slight but well built, pale in his makeup but with delightfully long hair that curled down to his shoulder.

When he failed to react, their apparent leader pushed him forward, still laughing. "Don't be a party pooper," she insisted.

He stumbled toward Charon, who caught him in his arms. Charon whispered into his ear. "Relax, beautiful. I just want a taste of you. You're scrumptious."

Charon wrapped his arms around the man, who trembled slightly, but the bulge in his pants gave away his excitement. He licked along his neck, then spun him around so Charon's back faced the group and hid their friend. In what looked like the embrace of a deep kiss to them, Charon's fangs descended and he sunk them deeply into the guy's neck. The blood flowed through his system, tasting delicious. He blocked out the bloke's innocent life, not wanting to stop until the heart faltered first because it tasted that good.

One of the women, the quiet one so far, hooted and hollered just as the man died. Charon dropped him to the ground and spun around quickly.

He guessed at the grotesque sight that greeted them, the blood dripping down his chin, the fangs fully descended and also covered in crimson, the feral look in his eyes as he chose his next victim.

Quickly, he jumped over as the women began to scream, and snapped their necks, one in each hand, with the ease of someone swatting mosquitoes. The remaining man attempted to hit him but missed as Charon punched the bat in the stomach. As the other one jumped on his back, Charon choked the bat's life out of him.

He easily flipped the remaining victim onto the ground and jumped on top of him. "You're cute, too." Charon leaned over and again sucked the life out of this victim, the blood stronger and more defiant than the first but equally as delicious.

Finished, he stood up and stretched as he scanned the scene around him. "This is a fucking mess."

He'd almost forgotten Jordan's presence until he heard the young man snicker at his comment. "True dat. Good thing I don't have a weak stomach. You have to hide this or anything?"

"If I lived according to vampire law, yes. But I don't. This will make a delightful crime scene. Maybe they'll have to cancel the whole parade next year because of the threat of violence. I don't have time to hide it, anyway, because my next victim calls to me."

"Who's that?" Jordan stepped right next to him, seemingly unfazed by the carnage around him.

Charon pulled him into a kiss and clutched at his ass. When he finished, he stared into Jordan's eyes. "Eating those sexy boys made me horny. I need a victim with a willing tight ass."

"Then let's get at it."

Charon intended to go somewhere else, but Jordan ripped his small undies off right there and grabbed hold of the fence, pushing his tight little ass out toward Charon. With the bodies cooling around them, Charon pulled out his penis and fucked Jordan until an explosion of cum shot out of him and deep into the boy's ass.

Lost in his own sexual sensations, Charon had no idea when Jordan came, but noticed the cum dripping down the boy's hand when he turned around.

Charon grinned. "We better get going. Two naked dudes with cum all over and surrounded by dead bodies might look suspicious."

Charon grabbed Jordan into his arms, ran them through the streets of Chicago, and then broke into a home that looked deserted for the night. He took them into the basement, initiated another round of sex, and then hid them beneath a staircase for the day lest anyone show up unexpectedly. Jordan refused the idea of hanging in Chicago because he was exhausted and instead wanted to stay in Charon's arms.

Chapter Twenty-Five: Playing God

24 DECEMBER 2012

Oostburg, Wisconsin

Charon enjoyed the month-long buildup to this particular kill, even heightening the anticipated pleasure by refusing to eat since the charade began. Alas, he set Christmas Eve as the fateful day and almost regretted that his act as an angel would soon end. Next time he might give himself more than a month to torture a self-righteous asshole.

He got the idea from Jordan's Halloween costume, actually. After playing the devil for that holiday, Charon determined to play an angelic role this time. But he fancied himself more like the Archangel St. Michael, who terrorized people and forced them to do his bidding upon the threat of death. No angel of mercy, Charon terrorized his chosen target, building toward this ultimate judgment day, with the poor fool unknowingly condemned to death despite any reform he achieved or any repentance he expressed before or after. And certainly despite the fact that he failed to meet any criteria established by the Vampire Council for putting a human to death. Unfortunately for the world, being a conservative asshole failed to qualify according to that body's pretentious wholesomeness. Unfortunately for Pastor Jeff, Charon could give two shits about the Council's sentencing guidelines.

Charon strode through the streets of Oostburg, a typical small Wisconsin town, and smiled at the stares from a couple cars that passed by. They seldom saw outsiders here, let alone hot ones in tight leather pants and a bright red shirt, wearing no coat despite the frigid temperature outside and snow drifting down from the sky.

Charon opened the door of the small brick church, so much a slice of Americana in its appearance, with the lit manger scene outside, the garland decorating the banister up to the door, and the sign that falsely claimed to welcome all to its midst.

The pastor, during Charon's previous visits, assured Charon the church would be vacant when he arrived because they only had one service this year, the candlelight service at 8:00. Charon figured that gave him an hour or so to complete the deed.

He paused outside the pastor's door until he heard Jeff shuffling papers around nervously.

Charon ran into the room, too fast for a human to see, and planted himself right behind Jeff's chair.

"I see that you're alone, as instructed."

Jeff almost jumped out of his chair when Charon spoke. He spun it around and nodded, sweat already breaking out above his upper lip.

"What have you to report?" Charon asked.

"I did what you asked. I promise."

"Like the first time?" Charon growled.

Pastor Jeff shook his head back and forth, vehemently denying the accusation. "I never disobeyed after your second visit. You have to believe me. I didn't believe the first time. I was weak. I thought a demon tested me. I thought maybe I hallucinated the whole thing. So I just went about my business, as usual, until you returned. Then I delivered the sermon, just as you instructed the second time, to tell them to love everyone. Even the homosexuals. You said you watched me deliver it, that you knew I did."

Charon sneered. "You still say homosexual like it's a disease. Like it pains you to utter the words. That displeases your Lord."

Jeff grew pale but spoke firmly. "Still, you've visited once a week this month, always with the same threats and messages. I've been thinking." Jeff hesitated, now his armpits sweating profusely. "I need a sign. A sign that you're really an angel and not a demon sent to distract me. How do I really know? Everything you command contradicts all my training. Everything I've ever taught my flock. I don't mean disrespect." Jeff held his trembling hands up as Charon stepped forward. "But I'd rather die at the hands of the devil than to get fooled by him."

Charon laughed at that. "So you would doubt me again, like the first time, despite what you've witnessed? What else would you have me do to prove it? On my first visit, I descended from the sky, the second time I stole you out of bed and carried you to the abandoned barn without your knowing, and last time I exposed your secret stash of pornography, that you even hid from your wife."

"I got rid of it!" Jeff shouted. "All of it."

Charon stifled a laugh at the thought that the innocent-looking man before him, skinny with medium-length wavy hair and a pastor's easygoing nature, enjoyed masturbating to images of obese women in the privacy of his office.

"What else do you need? Your doubt tires me." Charon yawned for effect.

Jeff shook his head, searching for an answer. "Something good. As in, delightful in the eyes of the Lord."

Good Lord, still with the nonsense. What the hell did "something good" even mean? "What about my previous visits disappointed you? I thought I commanded goodness of you? Isn't that enough?"

Jeff nodded vigorously. "You did. You did. And yes, for the most part. But the first time you just told me that I was wrong about homo-hom-homosexuals. Warned that you'd come again under harsher circumstances if I failed to change my message. I didn't. I admit it, because that was so little to go on, that a thing fell from the sky and told me to accept that sin."

"I'm not a thing. It's not a sin." Charon spat at Jeff. "And, in response, I miraculously moved you as you slept, then told you about your childhood, your entire history, by way of showing that as an angel of the Lord I knew all about you." Charon's mouth watered at the memory of pricking Jeff's arm ever so slightly before he woke him that night in order to see his life pass before Charon's eyes in the blood. So sweet. So delicious. Waiting for Charon tonight to take the more complete, lasting drink of it.

Jeff sighed. He was scared, shaking, but somehow still sure in his hateful convictions. It angered Charon.

"And it convinced me that night." Jeff added labored breathing to the disgusting sweat. "To the point I delivered the sermon, as you commanded. But a few of them, they've come to me in the last weeks, saying it's not right." He pointed out the window, presumably to his parishioners. "They could tell I didn't believe it from the way I proclaimed the Word to them. From the change in my voice as I spoke. Then, then, the last thing. It has my church in an uproar. No one agrees. I don't think I do, either. I only did it because I'm afraid of you. That's not good enough."

Charon paused for a long moment, fighting to maintain his composure. He wanted to play this out to the fullest, not simply snap the man's neck or drink from him too quickly because of his out-of-control rage.

"So after my third visit, and after I listened to your sermon on high and knew you obeyed"—Charon almost laughed again, with Jeff believing he listened to the sermon live and forgetting that he posted every sermon online—"you actually attempted to open a center for LGBT youth, or those who support them?"

Jeff sighed. "Yes. And as I told you, no one came. No one but three irate families that threatened my job. I was so worked up by them, I told them the truth. That you'd visited me. That I wasn't sure of the truth anymore, either. They think I've lost my mind. Maybe I have. There aren't any gay youth in Oostburg! What is this all about?"

"There aren't any *out* youth in Oostburg," Charon corrected him. "Partially because of your hate. So what kind of a sign do you need this time? I'm growing tired of your refusal to obey God's Word."

"I told you." Jeff pushed back in his chair until it slammed against his desk, trying to put some distance between himself and Charon. "Something good. Not just orders. Or something about myself. Something that proves you come from God."

Ugh. Pastors annoyed him. All he wanted to do was torture some conservative asshole for a month, and do it with a fun game of being an Angel of the Lord. Instead, he got this complicated mess in front of him and kept having to come up with other ways to convince him. He should just kill him and be done with it.

He searched his brain for a suitable way to appease the idiot. Why, he had no idea, since one way or another, the end would come tonight.

"Alright. Though I warn you." Charon pointed a finger at the pastor. "I don't recommend testing the Lord, even one of His angels, in such a manner ever again."

Charon thought for a few silent minutes, completely at a loss as to what might appease this pastor in the heart of Wisconsin. Shit. If he asked for a sex tip, better way to torture people, or simply a way to indulge himself, Charon could answer quickly. Spontaneous goodness, on the other hand, hardly fit his field of expertise.

Then he hit upon the one thing that he could control, quickly and efficiently. "Tell me your favorite three charities."

Jeff, fidgeting all over the place, scanned the ceiling for the answer. "Um, this church, of course."

Charon twirled his finger, hating that answer. "More."

As the pastor contemplated, Charon utilized a vampire's speed to grab the nearby iPad without Jeff noticing. "Spin around and look in your records to give me a better answer."

Jeff obeyed, nervously as expected, typing into his computer and pulling up a spreadsheet. Before he even voiced the other charities that came up under tithing, Charon picked one and sent a sizable donation in Jeff's name.

Only the internet's speed slowed Charon as he erased the history of what he did from the iPad and sat it back on the desk.

Jeff's voice wavered as he spoke. "Okay, we give to the local orphanage. My daughter started us with the local animal shelter, where we got our dog. She even gives part of her allowance."

Before he continued, Charon broke in. Jeff turned his head to listen to Charon as he spoke. "Don't even bother mentioning that other one listed there, that pickets at funerals and other detestable behavior with its antigay agenda. It will only anger me further. Besides, while you took eons to remember the four whole charities to which you give, I made a sizable donation to the animal shelter in your name. You can check your inbox to verify it. If that doesn't suffice as enough of a miracle, then I'm afraid that you and I have a serious disagreement."

The pastor returned his attention to the computer, where he accessed his email account and clicked into the message from the shelter, which thanked him for the ten thousand dollar donation and instructed him to save that message for his records.

"You did this? With what money?"

Still with the doubt. "God's." Charon spun the man around so they again faced each other. "Don't worry. It wasn't yours. I'm serious. It was money from above."

Jeff trembled in his seat. "I'm sorry. I always thought a divine experience would be different."

"What? You expected praise for your faithful life? Some kind of divine adoration? Because you never sin, is that it? The second coming, apparently, right before me and I missed it, despite being an Angel of the Lord."

Jeff began to weep. He shook his head. "I just expected something else. Not the sarcasm. Not the anger."

"Maybe you should have spent more time reflecting on what God's Old Testament wrath might mean to you, instead of accusing everyone else of Godlessness. I'm done playing. You've learned nothing from my visits."

Charon moved toward Pastor Jeff and swiftly clutched him by the neck, lifting him out of the chair and high above. Jeff's face turned beet red, and he grabbed at Charon's hands in a futile attempt to free himself.

Charon casually carried him out of the office, through the hallway, and right into the sanctuary, carefully decorated for the special service that night. He threw the pastor into the advent candles, which fell over and crashed the iron candelabra to the ground. Jeff slammed his head into the nearby pulpit.

Jeff stumbled backward, praying, then pleading with the vampire for mercy. "Please. I'll repent. I'll do it this time. Whatever you want."

Charon shoved him into the altar. "Too late."

"I have children. A wife."

"So do the loved ones you cast out. Tell that to the youth who committed suicide because of your vile message."

Charon worked himself into a complete state of disdain. The game he began, where he toyed with a pastor and played with him as a cat with a mouse, faded into a righteous indignation at the hateful person before him. Oh, that the Council would target this blasphemy and hatemongering instead of being so blameless about whom they would sentence to death. A campaign against this hate meant just as much as going after murderers and rapists. How many people did these hateful idiots assassinate every year with their message?

He grabbed Jeff around the waist, lifted him high in the air, and dropped him on top of the altar, splashing the waiting wine for communion all over the place, sending the wafers scattering across the floor.

As Jeff wept, screamed, and prayed, Charon stood over him and his fangs descended.

Ah, the bitter taste of the self-righteous blood as it cascaded down his throat. Ah, the luscious gift of food that the pastor gave as his final sacrifice. Sated, Charon wiped his mouth and turned to leave. He ambled between the rows of pews, turning halfway down to admire the artistic display he left for the expectant churchgoers that night.

He only hoped it gave each and every one of the conservative assholes a nightmare that would return night after night for the rest of their lives.

Outside, he stretched, cracked his neck, and chuckled before heading toward Colorado for a Christmas festival the next day with the boys.

Chapter Twenty-Six: Christmas in the Palace

25 DECEMBER 2012

James Peak, Colorado

Charon marveled again at the power of the sun over him. With the help of Styx, he had overcome the authority of the Vampire Council. With his vampiric senses, supremacy, and blood, he held dominion over humanity. His nocturnal habits gave him complete control over the night. Yet no matter his strength or how deeply he went into the ground, far away from the sun's rays or illumination, once it peeked over the horizon and lifted into the air, its grip drove him into a deep sleep.

He woke Christmas evening and stretched, knowing that his enemy in the heavens drifted over the edge of the Earth and allowed him to prey upon the darkness. Tonight, however, he intended to hang with the boys here in the palace, celebrating the holiday in their own way. No desire to feed called to him. He only wanted to spend time with the lovely gaggle of hot men he had assembled to work for him.

Still trapped mentally by the machinations of the world outside, he grabbed a pair of gym shorts and put them on, though nothing else, preferring that slight modesty to walking around naked, even though at least half of the staff meandered about naked on most days. He wondered if a couple of them ever put an article of clothing onto their body anymore, since Jordan maintained a perfectly comfortable temperature throughout the castle at all times. Except during their beach parties, when he cranked the heat in the party room in order to create a tropical paradise for the afternoon.

Stepping outside his dominion on the very top floor, where he allowed no one to enter without his presence and permission, he stood at the edge of the stairs and heard the pounding music down on the first floor, where the Christmas festivities probably began hours ago. He doubted that he would discover any sober people.

He drifted down the stairs, smiling with anticipation. On the second level, moving toward the grand central staircase and thus past a number of the boy's rooms, he almost bumped into Joe when he bounced out of his room.

Joe chuckled. "My liege." He bowed before Charon, his long braided hair flopping over his shoulder.

Charon patted him on the head. "Cute. Having fun today?"

Joe lurched up and swayed before Charon. "Jordan gave us no tasks for the holiday! All play today!"

Charon leaned over and kissed the lovely boy on the cheek. "Adorable. Now go."

As Joe whipped around and skipped down the hall, Charon swatted his fit bubble ass and hurried behind him. Down the stairs and into the living room, Charon lurched to a stop with awe. He marveled at the scene before him. Despite everything he'd accomplished in creating this underground castle, and although he himself carried all of the shit Jordan requested from Denver a couple weeks ago, the boys had completely outdone themselves this time.

A gigantic, at least fourteen foot, Christmas tree stood in the middle of the living room, completely decorated with a mixture of the new multicolored LED lights and old-school bubble lights, tinsel, and a ton of different ornaments and candy canes. Every picture was replaced by a painting or print of a Christmas scene: little snowmen, Santas, and elves sat, stood, and adorned the tables and other spaces, garland lit with clear lights brightened the mantel, and a bar at one end of the room was stocked with every Christmas drink imaginable—eggnog, peppermint schnapps for hot chocolate, red wine, and other holiday delights.

Charon counted to confirm that all nine of his staff partied and carried on before him.

After a minute of jumping up and down and screaming his head off, the others at last noticed Joe in the middle of the room, who almost fell into the Christmas tree, trying desperately to get them to shut up and listen to him. He motioned toward Brian, sitting with a glass of wine and next to his dog, to turn the music down. Brian reached over and obeyed.

Joe took a deep breath and paused a moment, apparently exhausted from his efforts. "Dudes. He's up, finally." Joe pointed toward Charon.

"Boss man!" Jordan screamed and ran over to Charon, embracing him in a hug. "We've been waitin'."

The others clapped and cheered as well. Charon smiled but also lowered his brow, suspicious of this display. "Gentlemen."

"We've been waiting for you!" Kiki repeated the theme and joined Charon and Jordan, wrapping his huge football bicep around Charon's waist and hugging him.

Charon laughed now. "It doesn't look like you waited for anything."

This caused the throng to laugh.

"So we started the party. Still, we got something for you. A gift, but not wrapped or anything we bought." Travis, his twinkling brown eyes glistening with excitement, shrugged his buff shoulders and grinned. "Cuz you get whatever you want. It's not like we could get you anything."

Burly Alex snorted. "And we ain't doing arts and crafts for you."

"What, then, do you have for me?"

Jordan pulled Charon toward the couch, which now sat off by itself, almost against the wall, now with a large space in front of it. "Sit." He motioned toward the center of the sofa, so Charon obeyed, more curious than ever as to their aims.

They milled about a little, took certain spots, Jordan tweaked the formation here and there, then all of them stripped down to bikini briefs, either red, green, or with a special Christmas print. Charon's favorite was slight little Benjamin with his Grinch undies, the grumpy Christmas icon seeming to stare at the tip of his penis beneath the cloth.

Jordan hummed a note, and suddenly they broke into song. They sang two Christmas carols in a row, including choreographed dance moves and taking turns with flirting with Charon on the couch. Not everyone sang, some just danced, but Charon found it endearing.

Indeed, he risked being overcome with emotion at the display, which threatened to bring out a sentimentality or love for these men, which might expose some lurking human emotion or longing. Still, why not lose himself in the moment? In their kindness. In fact, what he planned to deliver later to them, and planned several weeks before, would reveal these realities, anyway. And all because he orchestrated it himself.

The final number, a seductive version of "Baby, It's Cold Outside," flipped Charon's overwrought emotion and melancholy into a full blown hard-on and lustful bacchanal as all of the boys launched onto the couch and kissed and fondled every surface of his skin.

One by one, they came to him. Twinky little Joe, his hair tickling Charon's cheek. Kiki's skin glistening and sliding against Charon as the football player licked his ear. Stud Jason, unceremoniously jamming his tongue down Charon's throat and grabbing his balls. Blond Phil, smiling and gently placing his lips on the tip of Charon's nose. Travis, eschewing the kiss and instead landing on his knees, stripping off Charon's shorts, and licking the length of his cock. Alex, at the same time, wrapped his lips around one of Charon's nipples and bit, hard and passionately, joined on the other one by Brian, who eventually moved up to nibble on Charon's ear. Benjamin stood off to the side, masturbating himself, until Jordan pushed him forward and he hopped onto Charon's lap and grinded away. Last, Jordan lifted Benjamin into Kiki's arms and straddled Charon himself, planting a deep, longing kiss on Charon's mouth.

As Jordan and Charon continued their impassioned embrace, the others fell around and on the couch, touching Charon, sucking on each other, engaging in a full-on orgy, the first Charon thought he had ever experienced. Certainly one of the hottest sex scenes ever.

Charon and every one of the fine specimens around him took little time before they exploded all over the place, sending them back into laughter, revelry, and to their drinks. Charon even left his discarded shorts in the pile of everyone else's garments. The holiday celebration now became a completely naked one. Charon liked it, to the point he could hardly imagine what New Year's Eve would hold in store a week from then.

After a while and one glass of wine, a very old French Bordeaux, Charon slipped out of the room and went back upstairs to his quarters, where he grabbed the nine jewelry boxes, all wrapped nicely with blue paper with little white snowflakes. It took some doing over the last month to figure out their finger sizes, but again his vampiric speed assisted, along with the fact that at one time or another they either lay asleep in his bed or passed out somewhere else in the castle, making it possible to get the measurement.

Charon returned to the living room and again turned off the music, which they had switched to a loop of traditional Christmas tunes. He smiled, thinking it out of place with this crowd, but perhaps the season, even with them captured and trapped deep in the bowels of the earth, brought out a longing for tradition, for Christmas or holiday celebrations they experienced as kids.

When the music stopped, they all lurched their attention to Charon.

"My staff." He smiled, not really knowing what else to call them. "Actually," he thought about it, "in my mind I usually think of you as my boys."

A few of them cheered; they all smiled.

"I have gifts for you, too. Wait until I distribute them, please, so you can all open them at the same time. You'll notice there wasn't a great deal of creativity here. You each got the same thing."

Charon passed them out, then signaled when they could unwrap their gift.

He knew, of course, what lay inside. Each now possessed a wedding ring, made of twenty-four karat gold, with a genuine ruby in the middle. On one side of the ruby, he instructed the jeweler to imprint a C and, on the other side, a half moon to signify the night and therefore his command of it and, in turn, of them. On the ring's interior, Charon inscribed their first names, more than anything because he knew they would lose them, mix them up, and leave them around the castle, and ultimately need help identifying them from time to time.

He listened as Brian whistled, others cheered, and everyone seemed to enjoy them. One by one, he circled the room and kissed them again, admiring the ring on each of their fingers.

For the rest of the night, he sat around, listening to the music and watching them party, occasionally conversing when someone approached him but more than anything just observing, as if he enjoyed a reality television show. The electric train sped around the Christmas tree, controlled by Phil, his adorable and tight little ass often sticking in the air when he leaned over to fix a derailment or add more steam so the engine would churn out its candy-cane-scented smoke. The peach fuzz enticed Charon, as did the tight pink hole as it winked at him.

Wanting some time to himself before going to sleep, Charon kissed each one of them one more time and started up the stairs. He heard someone pattering behind him but waited until the base of the stairs to his realm, where they could not follow, to turn around.

He knew before he saw his smiling face and the flip of his head as he moved a strand of hair away from his eye that Jordan wanted a moment alone. He knew the boy's cadence as he walked. He recognized his scent, a combination of French cologne and his own sweat.

"Jordan." Charon grinned.

"I just wanted to say thanks. I noticed, despite what you said about everyone getting the same thing." Jordan held up his hand and showed Charon the wedding ring to explain his statement.

Charon looked down at the jewelry, designed the same as the others but with a diamond at its center, twice as big as the rubies the other boys possessed. On either side of the diamond, between it and the C and moon, rested two rubies.

"You needed a more powerful signet ring. What with being Pharaoh's number two, and all."

Jordan blushed, then rushed forward and hugged Charon. "I know you're not into all this attachment bullshit. Me neither, usually." Jordan pushed away, and it was obvious the embrace excited the young man. "Still." He shrugged. "It being Christmas and all. Chill-tastic gifts, these. Delish. Thanks, boss man."

Jordan spun to leave.

"Jordan. Wait."

He stopped and turned around. Charon closed the distance and reached up to hold Jordan's chin in his hand. He lifted his face, bent himself over, and gently kissed the adorable little guy. He cupped his head in his hand and pressed their foreheads together.

After a moment, he kissed Jordan's forehead and squeezed his butt. "Go have fun."

Charon turned toward the stairs, knowing that Jordan watched him go but never turning back. He smiled once inside his bedroom. He felt a sense of peace wash over him, that he had constructed for himself the perfect kingdom, perhaps better than what he'd envisioned even after Styx and he confirmed his complete autonomy from the Vampire Council or other forms of control.

He commanded an empire. Including a palace; a lovely staff; dominion over humans; a lust for life, power, and sex even more potent than he experienced in human life. He jumped onto his coffin-cum-bed and jacked off to images of Phil's butt, Jordan's bobbing cock, and Ben's ass pushing down on him.

He finished the evening by watching Johnny Depp in *Sweeney Todd*, remembering the Christmas he took a group of friends to see it, mostly because he found it funny to take them to something that dark and macabre on the sacred holiday.

He cast his magic spell over his floor, then a more powerful one in his room, and fell asleep as the sun rose miles and miles above him, again claiming control over his being.

PART SIX: COMING TO LIFE

Chapter Twenty-Seven: Bucharest Ghosts

12 MAY 2014

Bucharest, Romania

Perhaps Charon had grown lazy over the last year and a half since that peaceful feeling of contentment that had overcome him as he went to bed following the 2012 Christmas celebration at his palace. He had accomplished the perfect life as a vampire: hunting, playing with humanity, enjoying his staff of boys and the luxury that surrounded him. The Vampire Council never threatened, as Styx's spell continued to protect his activities, even when he left bodies carelessly strewn about for others to find; even when he killed the innocent from time to time just for fun, as on Halloween with those wannabe vampires, or for vengeance, as with his new tradition of targeting a conservative pastor every Christmas for assassination. He loved that the FBI opened a case file on the "Christmas Eve Vampire" after the same scenario developed two years in a row in completely different parts of the country. Life moved along swimmingly. Just as expected, he reigned as king over the wicked.

He positively loved his existence, with no complaints, plenty of excitement whenever he wanted to create it, and refinements beyond belief, but in the midst of this revelry, he forgot that threats must still exist against him. Maybe from other vampires, or heaven forbid the damnable Vampire Council. What if they finally figured out a way to track him? Could he feign ignorance of their laws and save his life against their wrath? Or, better yet, fight them off? Other dangers must lurk, too. Maybe from vigilant humans, vestiges of the past who might stalk the Earth, still believing in vampires while everyone else gave them up as legend, and thus hunting for his kind; perhaps they watched for signs that the undead were near and attacked them when most vulnerable in the daylight.

Part of Charon hated these thoughts. This caution. He was not supposed to have such worries, no matter how common to everyone else in the world. Styx guaranteed it, after all. And nothing challenged that autonomy to this point.

Still, sipping his drink here in the heart of Bucharest's city center, the nagging feeling of being monitored came across him for the second time that week, ever since he arrived in this ancient metropolis. He pinched the bridge of his nose in order to block out this negative sense and to focus on his reason for coming to Romania.

He had ventured across the ocean for the first time since becoming a vampire specifically to visit this place, the country of legends, the home of Vlad the Impaler, who founded Bucharest because of the vantage point on a river and within fifty miles of the Danube. Central to his area of control, Vlad wanted it for the defense of his lands.

Interesting that the man whom Bram Stoker did so much to make a feared villain to the rest of the world served more as a hero in this nation, for defending Christendom from the invading Islamic Turks, for protecting the homeland from outsiders. Charon wondered if, without the influence of a piece of English fiction, Vlad might have enjoyed a different legacy because of this heroic image. True, historians pointed out his less than wholesome appetites for violence and punishment, the verifiable sadism that he inflicted upon enemies. But it was a different time and other famous individuals overcame similar blights on their record because of their overall deeds and the love their country had for them. Thomas Jefferson owned slaves yet Americans revered him. Centuries after Vlad, even, Harry Truman blasted the most lethal weapon known to humankind atop two cities full of innocent civilians, yet most Americans never condemned him to the fate that Vlad suffered.

Nonetheless, regardless of ruminations on history, Charon had come because life in America grew a bit complacent and he sought his next adventure. He left the boys well stocked in the castle and promised to return no longer than one month from leaving them; in turn, they promised not to destroy the place with their partying in his absence.

Scanning the internet for places to visit, almost like a typical tourist, Charon chuckled to himself when he came upon a brochure for Dracula Tours of Romania. While hardly wanting to join some awful tour group, not to mention the fact they probably ventured about in the daylight, the idea of visiting famous Vlad sites and exploring this ancient land, one he had never visited during his human life, intrigued him.

In his first week, he had visited Snagov Monastery, the original burial place of Vlad, as well as the beautiful towns of Brasov and Sibiu. He enjoyed the old history of Romania, the stories, the culture, and especially their national icon, Vlad Dracul. A refreshing break from the United States, and he loved the dark-haired olive-skinned men of this nation. So much so that he'd reveled in sex even more than usual and only fed on a couple of them, not wanting to strip the world of their beauty. Perhaps sating himself on those Orthodox priests after he first arrived kept his appetites at bay for the time being.

He had meandered his way over the Borgo Pass and through the Carpathian Mountains until coming upon this, the largest city in Romania. The architectural changes as one traversed from outer Bucharest to the interior fascinated him. It began on its fringes as any large contemporary city, with an international airport, malls, shopping centers, and suburban homes. Next came modern office buildings and signs of economic growth, like a skyscraper here and there, huge industrial complexes, and other attributes of a thriving place. Yet a few miles later, between this newness and the oldest part of the city, Charon found himself shot back to the Communist era, as if the Cold War lingered here. Concrete building after concrete building showed no sign of originality because they'd built them strictly to pack people in on top of each other. Functionality ruled the day, as well as cheapness. Nothing distinguished one of these residences from another, though some appeared to get a fresh paint job or attempted modernization with air-conditioning dangling from the sides of the building or a new entryway smashed onto the front, to help it appear more luxurious. Everything looked and smelled the same, as if the Cold War clung to the land like a mold.

Then Charon stepped into the oldest part of Bucharest. Once run-down and controlled by the homeless and nomadic Roma gentrification saw it revitalized with nightlife, restaurants, and the excavation of old ruins, including more artifacts and signs from the life of Vlad the Impaler.

Charon loved it here. Vibrant. Alive. Yet balanced with an aura of unrest, of the undead still haunting this earth.

He took another sip of his drink, a Romanian red wine. Not as good as what he usually imbibed, but he enjoyed the local flavor of it. When in Rome, as they say.

When Charon's neck tingled slightly, not from the alcohol but from that feeling of being watched, he remembered again that he needed to consider his safety, or at least become more aware of his surroundings. His attempt to get lost in Bucharest and its culture failed him again.

In fact, this intuition had first hit him in Brasov, the Hollywood of Europe, or so they claimed because a lovely mountain that overlooked the city housed a gauche white-lettered sign that mimicked the Hollywood sign in California. It was a gift from the movie industry, a sign to the area of how many movies they now filmed in Romania because of its breathtaking landscapes and, relatively speaking, cheaper production costs. Charon thought the sign hideous, especially overlooking the charm of the ancient part of the city there, with its grand architecture and history that took a person clear back to the 1400s and beyond.

He sat at a table on the pedestrian walkway of the historic part of town, the bottle of wine almost finished, when his nerves tingled in alarm. He glanced around to see if something threatened but only saw people chatting at other tables, ambling by arm in arm, or otherwise enjoying the lovely spring evening. The only danger he sensed came from a dog of medium build that sauntered by, seemingly on its own. The dog perked its ears toward Charon and stared at him as it passed, but otherwise went along its merry way. Charon laughed at the time because, from whatever freaked him out, he thought the dog a vampire despite the impossibility of such a thing.

Charon dismissed that episode, perhaps thinking that vampires suffered from a form of jetlag or that the Romanian wine upset his refined tastes, until it occurred again in the forests of the Carpathian Mountains. Tired of people and wanting a night alone, Charon made his way through the beautiful landscape and even decided to conceal himself through the day in an abandoned cabin. Hardly the luxury he typically sought but fun to think of himself as an old-school evil vampire seeking out the most depraved of places to hide from the peasant hordes who hunted him. Or from Jonathan Harker and the band of fools who followed him.

When he woke the next evening, regretting his venture into this version of vampire camping because of the dirt and grime that covered him, he lurched to a stop, listened carefully, and swore that something watched him from above. He scanned the trees but saw nothing but an owl, leaves, and the stars peering down at him.

Still, he remained frozen for several minutes, waiting for the attack, waiting for his nemesis to reveal itself. It hit him, just before he again dismissed it as an overactive imagination because of the setting, that a vampire stalked him. But how? And why? Still, with no sign of an attack and nothing else to concern himself, he pushed forward and arrived in Bucharest to continue his exploration of Romania.

It became much harder to let go of the fear because it consumed him for a third time. Charon drained the remainder of the wine in his glass and, yet again, scanned the crowd and all around him for any sign of danger. Nothing looked amiss. No one threatened him. It was exactly as one might expect in a typical European city at this hour; mostly people in their twenties, out for a night on the town, drinking, flirting, and otherwise enjoying themselves. The only unrest came from the pickpocket scanning the crowd, but he hardly concerned Charon.

Charon paused his surveillance on the hot little number sitting a few tables away by himself. Long curly hair, slight build, with a stunning presence. He was reading a book with a drink in his other hand, seemingly content by himself even while everyone else around him enjoyed each other's company. Charon's loins stirred at his simple beauty.

But something bothered Charon. Did the threat emanate from that seemingly innocuous man in his twenties? Was he a vampire?

Nonsense. Charon would sense it and know the danger. Charon closed his eyes and pressed his fingers tightly against the bridge of his nose, to see if he could squeeze the concern out of himself. Impossible. He well knew the sensation that overtook him when a vampire came into his midst, and he recognized by now how his body alerted him to a serious peril. Nothing of the sort overcame him. Just a slight nagging that a being—or vampire?—monitored him.

By the time he opened his eyes to inspect the little hotty, the young man had disappeared. Charon surveyed the crowd, thinking that the guy could not have gotten far in the brief time Charon closed his eyes. Of course, if he completely vanished, that would certainly prove the danger. Then Charon saw him. Just a few yards away, sauntering down the sidewalk with his book in hand and his back to Charon.

Charon laughed at his own theatrics. Perhaps, despite everything Styx had said about their immunity to viruses and illness, Charon had contracted some cold or fever that caused him to hallucinate. He'd contracted a vampire cold, that's it. No one else paid much attention to the guy, except women and a few men who, like Charon, paused on their journeys to admire his beauty.

The tight ass walked away from him, turning Charon's fear into a fantasy of driving his tongue deep into that one's anus, when again he started. Did that dog, the one from the night before, the one he almost thought was a canine vampire, just join the young man on his walk?

The cute twink and the dog turned a corner before Charon figured it out.

Charon jumped up to follow but stopped himself, again remembering his complete dominion over humanity and total protection from the Vampire Council and any other supernatural threat. The feeling of concern evaporated, and for yet another time, Charon calmed himself down.

What he needed, what could really alleviate all concern, was to hunt. Charon stood and began to meander around the old city until he spied someone alone. Hunger so overtook him that he attacked the woman who wandered down a deserted street, feeding off her in mere seconds and leaving the body on the sidewalk for someone to find.

As he continued to explore, perhaps needing yet another victim, it hit him that he knew so little about the country that he had not even visited a gay bar yet. Surely Bucharest, despite the Romanian Orthodox Church and the country's slow plodding into modernity, supported such an establishment?

Several groups of people milled about until an obviously gay group of guys walked by, laughing and singing and hailing a cab. Charon concealed himself in a darkened corner for a couple of seconds and then moved fast enough to hide himself from the human eye and followed the cab until it stopped outside Queens, a dance club, Charon assumed, from the pounding music and hordes of attractive men venturing into it.

Other than the different languages, Charon found himself inside a typical gay bar, full of dancing, cruising, and laughing men. He ordered a Jack and Coke and began to observe his surroundings. There, in the corner all by himself, stood a cute guy, British or American by his light complexion and long blond hair—not to mention the NFL T-shirt—sipping a drink and looking around nervously. He brushed a strand of his hair off his forehead and leaned against the wall. His green gaze paused on Charon, but he looked to the ground quickly when Charon returned the stare.

Charon pushed away from the bar and crossed the room. "Hey," he said when he stood next to the guy. "You don't look very Romanian."

He blushed. "No. American."

"Charon. An American myself." Charon held out his hand, which the young man took with his own trembling one and shook briefly before yanking it back to himself.

"Todd."

"What brings you here?"

Todd sighed and wiped his free hand against his pants as he held tightly to his drink with the other one. "Uh, I can't really tell."

Charon squinted, then smiled. "You're in the closet. Ever been to a gay bar before? Relax." He placed a comforting hand on Todd's shoulder. "Let me show you around."

"No. I've been before. Well, in America." He paused, shifting his weight from one foot to the next. "Just a couple times."

"You ever even been with a guy?"

After what felt like several minutes, he hesitantly shook his head.

Again Charon patted him on the shoulder. "Seriously, closeted young man from America, all the way in Romania, and somehow in a gay bar by himself. You have to admit it sounds a little odd."

At least Charon got a slight grin this time before Todd spoke. "Mission trip."

"Mormon?"

Todd laughed. "No. Presbyterian. Just my college doing a thing in Romania. We have to do a service-learning project before we graduate, so I picked this. They bring us over to help for a while. I snuck away tonight. It took me forever to figure out how to get here." Todd pointed to the floor to indicate the bar. "I mean, I learned about it from the internet and all. But I had to get a cab and I don't speak Romanian or anything."

Charon leaned over and whispered into his ear, making sure to brush his lips along it before he pulled away. "Want a ride back?"

Todd's eyes grew wide and his hands shook, but his body leaned toward Charon and spoke volumes before he uttered a word. He desperately wanted to fall into Charon's arms but was terrified of the reality, of the contact, of his first time with another man, of the presumed danger. And he had no idea about the truth of what threatened him here. Charon could read all that and more in Todd's subtle body language.

"Maybe," he whispered.

Charon leaned toward Todd again and kissed him on the cheek. "I'll take care of you."

So as not to frighten him to death, after Todd followed Charon outside with hesitant steps, Charon hailed a cab and they arrived at one of the nicest hotels in Bucharest moments later. He assumed correctly that the wealth and formality would give Todd a sense of security. Safely in the room, Todd paced back and forth and fumbled with the remote control, a glass, the button on his shirt, and finally sat on the edge of the bed and kicked his legs back and forth.

Charon plopped down next to him. He hugged him with one arm. "Listen, you don't have to do anything you don't want to. Okay? Here, let's play a game. I'll do something to you. If you like it and are comfortable, return the favor. If not, we're done. Okay?"

Todd thoughtfully nodded. God, Charon almost burst out of his pants before he even started, this game so enticed him.

First he reached over and held Todd's hand. He grabbed back tightly. Charon kissed him on the cheek. Todd kissed him back. So Charon leaned over and gently, ever so slowly, pressed his lips against Todd's and held them there for several seconds, until he felt Todd's tongue urgently push inside of Charon's mouth. They kissed for a long time before Charon pulled Todd into a tight hug. Todd returned the embrace.

Gradually, Charon let go and began pulling off Todd's shirt while continuing their passionate kiss. Todd became a little more aggressive and reached down to untuck Charon's shirt. Together they yanked it off and over Charon's head. Soon Todd had also lost his shirt and they pinched each other's nipples.

Charon's hand landed on Todd's knee, then deliberately moved up until he felt the solid cock underneath the pants, aching for release. He rubbed it, felt it, and Todd shoved his hips against Charon's hand.

The tentative feel of Todd's hand against his own penis again sent a wave of passion through Charon. Whoa, the newness of this, the thought of this innocent virgin in his bed, nearly sent Charon over the top.

Charon stopped and ran his fingers through Todd's hair. "You okay?" He wondered at himself, at this moment, at the gentle way he treated

Todd. He loved that his perfect evil could also lose itself for an evening and appreciate the tenderness that life offered, that he could fall into the role of protective lover and safeguard an innocent little bottom for the night.

In answer to Charon's prompt for them to unzip each other's pants and rub their cocks through the underwear, and far from what Charon anticipated, Todd lunged at him, pushing Charon onto the bed with Todd on top. Todd's hands explored every inch of Charon's torso, his lips and tongue moved down Charon's neck, along his arm, and finally played with the nipple as Todd fumbled with Charon's belt buckle and undid his pants, moving down and sliding them off Charon by first removing his socks and shoes.

Charon quickly stripped Todd until he stood naked at the foot of the bed, his cock dripping precum and angling slightly to the right. The timid, frightened boy from the bar surprised the hell out of Charon at this moment, the nakedness, his first touch with another man, seeming to bring out the animal in him.

Todd jumped onto the bed and sucked Charon's dick, slurping at it desperately. "Ow." Charon held Todd's head still with his lips still wrapped around the cock. "Cover your teeth with your lips." Todd more carefully continued.

"Here. Let me show you." Charon used his strength, but again not too much of it, to flip their roles. He swallowed Todd's crooked cock until the wild pubic hair hit him in the nose. Quickly, oh so fast because Charon hardly moved up and down a couple of times, the hot semen shot out of Todd and down Charon's throat.

When the penis began to go limp in his mouth, Charon released it and looked up at the young man, breathing heavily and glistening with sweat. "I wanna help you, too," Todd gasped between breaths.

"Glad to hear it." Charon smiled. "What are you up for?"

"I don't know."

"Here. Just try this for the first time." Charon lay on the bed, his own dick ready to explode as it bobbed up and down against his belly button. "Just lick and suck my balls while I jack off. You cool with that?"

Todd answered without a word as he dived facefirst into Charon's crotch and began licking up and down his testicles. He stopped only one time. "It's really hot that you're shaved. Can we shave me?"

"Oh, yeah." Charon pushed Todd's face back into his balls and stroked fast and furiously with his other hand until cum shot out of him, hitting the headboard above him, splashing along his cheek and down his chest, and continuing to ooze out of his penis for several seconds afterward.

He reached down and grabbed Todd's head, moving him from cum splotch to cum splotch, nearly ready to come again as the young man ate his essence hungrily.

Without a care for the mess, Todd scrambled up and lay completely on top of Charon, the remaining cum mushing together between them in a carnal bond.

Chapter Twenty-Eight: Newbie

13 MAY 2014

Bucharest, Romania

Todd fell asleep on Charon, who again surprised himself by sitting wide awake for several hours, enjoying the feel of this young man as he clung to him in his sleep. Charon regretted that dawn approached too soon. He shook Todd awake and gently pushed him to the side.

Brushing the blond hair out of his eyes, Charon kissed Todd's forehead. "I have to go. Do you want to stay here? You can."

Todd scanned the room, rubbed his eyes, then a panicked look spread across his face. "Uh," he stammered but nothing else came out.

"What? Do you need to get back? Talk to me."

Todd's eyes welled with tears, but he remained completely silent.

Charon grabbed him into a tight hug. "I have a plan. You do what you want today, but I'll come back this evening. We can hang together again."

Todd nodded, his head resting softly against Charon's chest.

"Do you want to stay here today?"

Todd indicated agreement again without a word when his head nodded just slightly against Charon.

"Okay. Stay here. I'll be back tonight."

Charon dressed quickly and hurried away, while Todd never left the bed or moved as he watched Charon the entire time.

"Order room service. Watch movies. Do whatever you want, okay? I'm rich. No worries."

Charon arranged to stay in the room for at least another night at the front desk before dashing out and finding a darkened quiet basement to conceal himself in for the day. Thankfully, dusk came quickly so that Charon could race back to the hotel, where he knocked softly on the door and entered the room when Todd opened it.

Todd, completely naked, stepped back to allow Charon to enter. He walked over to the bed and sat casually on the end of it. He smiled. "Sorry about this morning."

"No problem. You okay? Did you just stay here?" Two trays of dirty dishes sat nearby, and towels were piled on the floor by the open bathroom door.

"Yeah." Todd shrugged, smiled, then seemed to hold back more tears. He pointed to his cell phone on an end table. "They've been calling me all day, but I never answered."

"We better make some decisions, then. They probably have connections to the embassy and will trace the phone. I assume you don't want them showing up at our door?"

"What are my options?" Todd sighed and ran his hands through his hair. "I mean, what's going on?"

Charon paused, unsure how to proceed. What did Todd want to hear? "I don't know. I'm not in love, if that's what you mean. We can't run away happily ever after. It was just one night."

Todd nodded. "I figured." A tear dripped down his cheek. "I wasn't necessarily anticipating a fairy tale here, even if that'd be nice. I can't just go back, though, without a story. I'm not even sure I want to return. It's not a good idea. I don't know." His shoulders slumped.

Something stirred in Charon. "Let me do this. Do you mind if I go hide your phone away from here? Safe, in case you want to go back and need it, but also to protect us for tonight?"

Todd shrugged. "Sure."

Charon took the phone and walked out of the room until safely away. Then he ran several blocks and hid the phone on the roof of a restaurant. Afterward, he hurried back to Todd.

Todd seemed okay, still naked, but something lurked in the atmosphere. Charon moved into action before his evil nature took hold. After all, part of him screamed to off the kid, end his miserable life, and save Charon a lot of trouble.

"I'm going to give you a new option. You won't have much time to consider it, but first you have to tell me your story. Agreed?"

"What do you mean an option? And what story?"

"You can either go back to your old life, and I'll take care of everything for you so that they won't freak about you having been gone. We'll come up with a plausible story. Or, I'll give you a way out. But I can't do that until you tell me about yourself. Your story."

Todd began to tremble again, much like he had the night before in the bar when Charon first approached him. Charon crossed to the bed, picked Todd up, and held him tightly in his lap as he sat on the edge. Todd, lost in whatever frightened himself, either failed to notice or ignored the strength it took Charon to accomplish this position.

Petting Todd and gently kissing his forehead, Charon spoke softly. "Let it out. Cry if you need to."

"I probably won't do that anymore. I kinda cried myself out this afternoon. My story." Todd paused, again resting his head on Charon's chest. "I don't like to talk about myself. I'll do it, but just a summary. Is that cool?"

"Yeah. That's cool. I just need to get a sense for it."

Todd wrapped his arms around Charon's chest and spoke into his stomach, never looking up and hardly moving a muscle.

"First, you gotta know my parents love me. And both my brothers. But they're way religious. Our church became its own thing when the other Presbyterians started accepting gays. They left the denomination. Our house is super strict. Religious stuff and all. That's why I go to school at a small Christian college. They all hate gays, too. See, Dad warned my brothers and me, if we're gay, he's kicking us out. Won't allow Satan under his roof. Thing is, he had all three of us at the table for the lecture but stared at me the whole time." Todd waited a moment before he continued. "I don't know why he suspected. I never did anything on the internet or brought home pictures or risked it or anything. He just knew. Mom, too. But she pretended she had to cook dinner while this went on. So, that's my story, okay? Pretty typical growing up in a loving family but way intense with the God thing. I always obeyed. Did well in school. Just, you know? The gay thing kept coming back to me. So I snuck to bars a couple times last summer but chickened out. Didn't know how to hit on anyone or things like that. Until you found me last night."

Todd signaled the end of his tale by beginning to unbutton Charon's shirt. He ran his hands along Charon's chest, felt along his bicep, then pushed away to remove the shirt completely. Charon cupped his balls and felt along Todd's rock-hard dick, then kissed him gently.

That pent-up sexual energy escaped from Todd again, who rushed to get Charon's pants off and this time covered his teeth with his lips and gave the most delightful blow job Charon had ever experienced, only removing his mouth when he gagged as Charon thrust into him and shot his load. Charon jacked Todd off, then held his gooey hand up for Todd to lick his own cum after he finished.

Charon sat up in bed, and Todd again wrapped himself around Charon. "So, what's my option? I mean, other than getting kicked out by my dad."

"I'm taking a radical step here. And, the person in charge of my boys usually vets candidates, too. But I'm willing to take this drastic step, if you want to believe, and if you want to leave everything in your life behind."

Todd looked at Charon with a scrunched brow. "What are you talking about?"

"I live in a hidden palace. It's gigantic. My only employees are beautiful young men such as yourself. All gay. All who left their families behind. A requirement of employment is that you cannot leave the castle. Ever. I provide everything you need. Clothes. Food. Entertainment. Really, anything your heart desires. Except for freedom to leave. Jordan is in charge. But the only work is to keep the palace clean and other similar chores. As far as I can tell from when I'm there, they mostly party and have fun. Your option is simply to join me there. Or, as you said, return to your previous life."

"Wouldn't they search for me?"

Charon shook his head. "They'd never find you. We'll make it seem like you disappeared in Romania."

"What about my passport? They'll track me that way. Is your castle here?"

"No. In America. And you won't be leaving the same way you came. You won't need a passport."

"When do I have to decide?"

"Tonight. But there's one more thing you need to know."

"What?"

"I'm a vampire."

Todd sniggered. He licked along Charon's chest, then playfully bit at his neck. "Edward Cullen, huh? Is that some role-play you make us do?"

"Stop." Charon moved Todd to his side and lay next to him, so that they stared into each other's eyes. "I need this to be serious. Do you understand what I expect of you, if you come along? You're leaving your family and friends and everything behind. Forever. No returning."

Todd nodded. "That's hard. You know? But I get it. That'll probably happen, anyway, right? I mean, after tonight, I'm coming out. I'm not going back to the closet. Am I deciding now?"

Charon shook his head. "You don't have to yet. I just wanted to make sure that you comprehended that completely."

"I do." At least Todd had stopped shaking, but Charon could practically see the wheels churning away in his head.

"Now, about the vampire thing. It's true. I'm going to show you. Promise you won't freak?"

"Promise." Todd grinned slightly.

Charon stared hard at Todd and then opened his mouth, transforming into a vampire by letting his fangs descend and then smiling, a diabolical grin of complete control and power.

Todd lurched back and almost fell off the bed. "Whoa."

Charon tilted his head back and roared with laughter as he returned to his more human self. "Whoa? That's what you've got for me?"

"Well, I thought 'fuck' first, but I'm not supposed to say that."

"Depending on your decision, you'll need to get used to cussing. I don't think a lot of proper English or religious discussions take place at the palace."

After a quiet few minutes, Todd scooted back toward Charon. "So do you feed off us or something?"

"No. I don't allow you to witness my hunting or feeding. I have sex with you, when the mood strikes me. And you do my chores, as I said. That's it."

A light bulb went on in Todd's head. "That's why you vacated this morning, yeah? The sun and stuff?"

"Yes."

"Wow. Okay. So, when do I have to decide?"

"Before I leave again for the day."

"What we doing until then?"

Charon shrugged. "It's up to you."

"Good. Let's do that shaving thing." Todd spread his legs to reveal the pubic hair, his dick growing hard in anticipation.

For the next hour, Charon carefully shaved Todd's ass, then his balls, then other areas of his body. He tasted every inch of the boy, especially relishing the taste as his tongue drove deep into the tight anus and Todd moaned with pleasure. Charon decided to wait before introducing anal sex, sensing Todd needed more time before taking that step.

When they finished having sex for the second time, Todd cuddled into Charon. "Okay. I'll go. It's what I want, I mean. I think my family will freak when I disappear, but I think that's better than putting us all through the awfulness of my coming out. Like I said earlier, that would separate us, anyway. Right? This way, no drama. For Mom, I probably remain pure in her head. For Dad, he gets rid of me. My brothers? Well, whatever. I want to go."

Charon pushed Todd's head away gently and looked for any sign of questioning. Todd's green eyes stared hard back at him with no hesitation.

"Good. We leave tomorrow night. Sleep as much as you can through the day."

Across an ocean, and with Todd experiencing Charon's vampiric speed as he swam the ocean and then ran across America with the young man in his arms, Charon escorted Todd into the entryway to his palace with the poor guy bewildered and completely unaware of where they were, despite Charon never blindfolding him. He summoned Jordan immediately.

"Boss man! Back from your European adventure!" Jordan spun around the corner, wearing nothing but a silver sequined G-string. "I've been studying go-go dancing. Benjamin, Joe, and me. Cray-cray, right?" Jordan lurched to a stop and his jaw hit the ground when he finally noticed Todd. "Did you steal someone? Usually you just bring supplies. This one's delish."

Charon smiled. "Todd, meet Jordan. For some unknown and completely insane reason, I put him in charge here. Jordan, this is Todd. Our newest boy."

Jordan curtsied. "Pleased to meet you."

Todd smiled sheepishly and half hid behind Charon. "Hi."

"Oh, he's shy. Hot."

"Listen up." Charon put one arm around each of the guys. "Show him around. Teach him. But listen closely to this. He's a newbie. He's only had sex twice. Both times with me, over the last two nights. He's an anal virgin, and no one better lay a hand on him against his will, or I'll take care of them myself, and it won't be pretty. His virginity remains intact until I take it, and only when he's ready and wants it. I'm holding you personally responsible for acclimating him to the insanity around here. Got it?"

Jordan pulled away and stood at rigid attention in front of Charon, then saluted. "Aye, aye, Captain."

Charon pushed Todd gently toward Jordan. "He'll take care of you."

Jordan wrapped an arm around Todd's waist and began walking him away. Charon reached out and snapped the back of his G-string, which brought a nice ass wiggle in response. Charon followed them down the hall for a while until he turned toward his own quarters.

If, despite his belief to the contrary, some judgmental God would place him on trial were he ever to die, Charon hoped this act of compassion toward Todd might earn him a slightly reduced sentence.

He laughed aloud. "Or maybe just some good karma in the future."

Inside his bedroom and contemplating the journey to Europe that brought him Todd, Charon suddenly remembered that feeling of being followed in Romania when the hair on his neck tingled. The vampire dog. That hot little number who Charon almost thought was a vampire. That feeling that something was amiss.

Maybe he would need that karma.

Chapter Twenty-Nine: The Oriental Theatre Lives

8 JUNE 2014

Chicago, Illinois

Needing an escape, a vacation of sorts, Charon read about Michael Bourne's retelling of the *Sleeping Beauty* ballet as a vampire story while searching the internet for some cultural entertainment. Sometimes he needed a diversion from the castle and his gaggle of boys. The idea of this ballet called to him, especially the reviews, which described it as enchanting in its beautiful wickedness. He purchased front row tickets, traveled to Chicago, rented an apartment for the week, and enjoyed the city by himself for a couple of days with feedings, hooking up a couple of times, and generally admiring the architecture until he now sat in the Oriental Theatre.

Charon adored the grandeur of the theater, from the marble lobby and ornate architecture, to the crimson seats and curtain that concealed the stage at the moment. The carvings on the walls and framing the stage spoke of a different era, when luxury and elaborate décor adorned every public venue, where only the rich and famous gathered to celebrate their wealth.

No doubt a big dose of racism went into the oriental flavor of this space, but it spoke of a long gone and elegant past.

A seahorse looked down upon him, as well as dragons, an enchantress, winged demons, and other designs that the American designer fancied as bringing forth a flavor from India when he created it all in the 1920s.

Too soon, for Charon wanted more time to revel in the theater itself, the lights dimmed and the curtain rose, with the sounds of Tchaikovsky filling the air as the live orchestra in the pit went into action. Charon lost himself in the elegant dance, the ballet more beautiful than he'd imagined when he purchased the tickets. Of course, the muscular men pulled Charon into the show, too, especially the asses moving and straining before him in those tights.

The modern twist, to place a vampire story amidst the fairy-tale ballet from the turn of the previous century, amused Charon. It painted darker colors onto the canvas, adding a horrific element, but without seeming cheesy or out of place. *Perfection itself, this blend of the classical music, old-world dancing, and modern fascination with the undead.*

The lead vampire acted as if truly a vampire, with his smooth ways, pulsating power, and a menace oozing out of his pores.

Just as quickly as the ballet began and yanked Charon away from his revelry about the Oriental Theatre itself, intermission arrived and the curtain descended. Again Charon struggled with a disappointment in the transition, wishing the ballet could last all night until the sun called him to sleep.

Charon stood and stretched, more to give himself an excuse to scan the crowd than from any physical need. He loved admiring the gay couples, or even the hot straight men, and again his gaze drifted to the ceiling and the grandeur of this space. It propelled him back to the art deco of the 1920s; he imagined the tuxedoed men and women in their flapper outfits or, for the more traditional, a long gown, as they meandered about the place and chatted, wanting to be heard and seen more than any desire for entertainment.

Charon jerked to a halt as he started up the aisle when that sensation again crept along his spine, up his neck, and finally stood his arm hair straight up. As if snapped back to Romania, those warning signals shot through his body. Something, or someone, observed him. It almost felt like a vampire, but not quite. It almost seemed threatening, but again not to the point that Charon had to act.

He turned around and walked cautiously back to his seat, scanning the crowd for any sign of danger or observation but seeing nothing but ordinary humans. Anyone who spied on him did so out of lust, nothing else. In front of his seat, he spun around guardedly, making sure to pause with his glance on each and every individual.

Just as the orchestra struck a chord and the lights began to dim, Charon saw him. Front row, center balcony. Staring straight down at Charon. The long curly hair falling gently over his shoulder, the hazel eyes piercing Charon, the slight build casually leaning against the railing. Did he wink?

Charon quickly turned around and sat down, feeling as if some human instinct of fight or flight might take hold of him at any moment. His heart pounded at seeing that hot twink from Bucharest, only missing the dog this time.

Observing him that closely, if for but a moment, confirmed Charon's worst fear. A vampire. No doubt. But one who could conceal himself from Charon that well? Was he from the Council? Why stalk him thus, from Romania all the way to Chicago, but never confront him? Was it a trap?

Charon hardly noticed the beautiful dancing as complete panic took hold. Desperation.

A voice drifted into his head. *Relax. We need to talk.*

Instead of relaxing Charon went into full-blown alarm. How did this vampire talk into Charon's head like that? It hit Charon. In addition to being a vampire, he was a witch.

With no time to contemplate or wait to see what occurred, Charon mustered his own magical powers and determined to send the entire theater into a complete panic, hiding vampire and witches from the humans or exposing the supernatural to them be damned.

First, Charon enchanted the seahorses to squirm to life and fly through the air, as if floating in the ocean. People gasped and pointed, but lost in the production assumed that some magical trick of the theater orchestrated the illusion. Just as a couple of the ballerinas noticed and hesitated in their dancing, Charon pointed directly over his head at the Hindu woman sitting in a Buddha-like pose and brought her to life. She launched out of her spot high above and began moving through the air, scowling at the crowd and gesturing her arms back and forth in some ancient dance. The men kneeling on either side of her also got up and stretched, walking on the air at her sides, as if protecting her dancing journey into the unknown, their gold muscles rippling with every move.

The winged dragons below where she had sat flapped their wings and pulled away from the wall, transforming from creatures with half their body in relief to the audience into three-dimensional beasts flying above. Unlike their dancing and floating counterparts in the rest of the auditorium, they flew in order to hunt and torment. One swooped down upon the crowd, snatching a little old man into its claws and soaring back toward the rafters, its prey firmly clutched in sharp talons and bleeding onto the crowd.

A performer yelped and pointed. The audience came alive, suspecting that more than a theatrical stunt threatened them. Pandemonium ensued. Charon tightened every muscle in his face to concentrate all his magical energy on this building before he opened his eyes, readying for one more act before getting out.

To ensure total panic, the skeletal-looking dragons on either side of the stage and high above the audience roared to life. Their tiger-like heads spit fire at the balcony as they leapt with their bony legs from their perches high above and landed in the aisles, on top of a row of people, on the stage, and one clung to the curtain.

Total bedlam consumed the humanity here. People screamed. They trampled one another. The fire lit a side curtain ablaze near a private seating area. Alarms bellowed throughout the auditorium.

Plaster birds and ancient beasts soared through the air. The light purple walls began to glow just as the electricity went completely out and the fire's glow eerily flickered along the walls. Now the humans harmed each other even more than Charon's creatures in their haste to escape. The elderly or infirm stood no chance as middle-aged and otherwise quite proper people ran them over like ants on the sidewalk.

To add one more touch to his creation, Charon pointed a finger at the women holding the tambourine and brought the giant statute to life. She danced and clanged her tambourine in celebration but, in the process, stepped on a woman and clomped through the audience, the entire balcony shaking with each thudding step.

Charon darted toward the open side door. He glanced behind quickly to see the vampire standing with wide eyes at the scene before him, never looking at Charon, instead seeming to call forth his own magic, countering what Charon had wrought.

Charon was at the door when he saw one of the seahorses lurch back to its appropriate spot on the wall.

Not stopping to see what else the vampire could accomplish, Charon ran away. As fast as his vampiric legs would take him, he sprinted through the streets of Chicago and into the suburbs, along the Eisenhower Expressway shoulder and out past DeKalb in the countryside, through rural Illinois, into Iowa, and all the way to Omaha, where he finally paused.

He considered racing directly to the safety of Colorado and his palace, but what if the vampire witch followed him? He must protect his lair and not act in too much haste.

He paced back and forth in front of the darkened arena on one side and the black river on the other. He scanned his environment for any sign of danger, but nothing alerted him to any threat. Not the presence of a vampire. No witches spied upon him from a corner. He especially felt to see if the hair on his neck stood on end. Nothing.

Perhaps the vampire stayed behind to deal with the Oriental Theatre event.

To be safe, Charon decided to remain in Nebraska for the night. He had never visited Omaha before, really never had a desire, but its small urban environment enticed Charon enough, as well as the fact it would keep his palace concealed, lest the witch show up and pursue him.

He hurried toward the downtown area, swiped a cell phone from an unsuspecting teenager, and used it to find a nearby gay bar. He entered the establishment and downed two shots of Jack Daniel's before his nerves calmed and he leaned against the back of his stool.

The pounding dance music soothed him. The young men dancing and laughing helped him ignore what concerned him. He'd never guessed that the allure of hot farm boys gyrating away could entice him so much. Charon turned back toward the bar and signaled the bartender.

"Another shot?" The tall bartender with the buzzed head, not to mention the full, thick, and beautiful lips, smiled. As the bartender wiped his hands on a towel, Charon admired the biceps. Yum.

"No. Make it a Jack and Coke this time. I'm much better than when I arrived."

Still smiling, the bartender nodded. "Yeah. Nothing to do here but chill and enjoy. Hotty like you should be used to that, right?"

He scooted away to grab the alcohol and make Charon's drink before getting an answer.

Charon watched him the whole time, losing himself in the young man's beauty.

He grinned widely when he returned with Charon's drink. "Here you go, cutey. Five fifty."

"That's it?"

He shrugged. "You can always tip a lot if you think it's not enough. Where you from?"

"I just got in from Chicago."

"Ah." The bartender nodded. "That explains it. Everything costs a shitload there. But it's a great city."

Charon handed him a fifty. "Keep it."

His eyes grew wide. "I knew Chicago was expensive, but damn. I can't keep this."

Charon leaned across the bar. "It's yours. If you want, you can thank me again when you get off work."

"I might just do that." He tapped Charon on the nose and held out his hand. "Nate."

"Charon."

"Nice to meet you. I gotta get back to work. Stick around."

He walked away, and Charon again admired the back view.

Then Nate spun around, a look of revelation on his face. "With a C, right? Not K-a-r-e-n. Something different?"

"Yeah. How'd you know?" Charon usually had to explain the Greek mythology before people understood, if ever. At least Nate forwent the irritating references to a woman's name.

"You got a note here. Guy called about five minutes before you arrived. I told the dude we didn't have some PA system or way to find anyone. Like some local dive bar. Or Cheers. But he insisted. Damn if he wasn't right. He said that you'd be chatting with me, and he really needed to get this message to you. Let me get it."

Chapter Thirty: A Note

8 JUNE 2014

Omaha, Nebraska

A whirl of emotions twisted through Charon's mind as he waited for Nate to retrieve the message by the cash register, which apparently got lost in a pile of receipts and God knows what other notes and scraps of paper people smashed into the small drawer underneath it. Anger that something—or more accurately a certain vampire someone—hunted him. Fear at what it could mean. Really, that fear bothered him the most. Charon feared nothing. No being or circumstance scared him, even when he was a mere human but definitely not since becoming a vampire. Yet there it lurked, a certain unease about the lovely vampire who stared at him from the theater's balcony. Still, despite this negative feeling, a slight hint of intrigue crept to the surface. After all, his pursuer passed on opportunity after opportunity to confront Charon or surprise-attack him. Even in the Oriental Theatre, he seemed more content to counteract Charon's magic and protect the ridiculous humans than to combat Charon.

"Here you go." Nate's voice startled him for a second, having lost himself in this self-reflection. He handed Charon a napkin, with a message crassly scratched on it. "Almost lost it. Seriously, I never thought you'd actually show up, and even if you did, that this would get to you." Nate smiled and spun around when someone called his name from the other side of the bar.

Charon glanced at the note, which puzzled him all the more about whatever game he played.

Relax. No harm intended. Quit freaking. I'll leave you alone, for a while.

Charon read it three times, then crumpled it up and tossed it smoothly into the wastebasket behind the counter. He shook his head, frowned, and laughed to himself. Rather than clarify anything, this note compounded the intrigue and left more mystery than answers. If it spoke the truth, this vampire had no intention of fighting Charon, but then why the subterfuge, concealment, and shadowy behavior? Why stalk him through Europe and then follow him to America? Maybe he meant to come on to Charon, but that made no sense, either, unless vampires engaged some courting ritual Charon never learned and Styx failed to mention. Too, though the guy utilized some powerful form of magic that Styx thought only the Vampire Council possessed, he never acted like a police agent or judge coming to sentence Charon to death for his crimes against their arbitrary laws. What did that leave? The answer to that, in a nutshell, left Charon the most confused. He ruled out every logical explanation.

Still, though the note brought a seeming peace offering, Charon would never take the bait, if for no other reason than out of an abundance of caution. Styx had provided him with the perfect vampire life, and any engagement with another vampire, whether friend or foe, and regardless of the circumstances, risked exposure. Because that other vampire most certainly would be on the Council's radar, and either he or someone watching him might wonder about Charon's freedom from Council authority. The note promised that this mystery guest in Charon's life would leave him alone for a while, so Charon decided to put it from his mind as best as possible. Then, when this one did appear again, as he alluded to doing, Charon would go into evasive action and avoid the idiot. And, at least for next time, Charon knew the dude's weakness: he would protect the innocent people around and thus let Charon escape.

Charon enjoyed another hour of sitting in the bar as the crowd swelled and the fury of dancing increased as the bar's closing rapidly approached. Coupling began in earnest, with people lowering their standards either because they feared leaving empty-handed for the night or because the beer goggles took over and average people became beautiful.

A number of men hit on Nate, who flirted and increased his tips but never so much as winked at the drooling men who wanted him.

Eventually the bar's lights illuminated the interior as if midday hit, and bouncers moved through the crowd to disperse them toward the exits. Most men calmly sauntered out, though a few fondled and kissed each other while a couple groups laughed and celebrated all the way to the doors. One drama queen screamed and yelled at his apparent partner, thinking he looked too long at someone or some such nonsense.

"Dude, let's go." A steroid monster with biceps ready to pop out of his skin motioned to Charon and twirled his finger.

Charon tilted his head and considered a retort when Nate rushed over. "Bry, he's with me."

Bry nodded and moved on, going to check the bathroom.

Nate smiled. "Just a minute."

About fifteen minutes later, Nate wiped his hands on a towel after finishing the dirty glasses and reorganizing the alcohol bottles. He said goodbye to the other bartender and hurried to Charon.

"Sorry. Thanks for waiting. It took a while tonight." He walked toward the door, so Charon followed, not knowing where they were headed. "It was crazy busy tonight. I mean, more than usual. I got way behind on keeping the glasses clean. Drives my boss nuts. He's anal. Can't handle the mess. At least he doesn't get too pissed. I mean, what else should I do? Either he hires another bartender, or I let the customers pile up while I wash away and they get angrier and angrier."

Outside, Nate reached in his pants and pulled out a set of car keys. He grinned. "Sorry. I'm babbling. Where to?"

"Do you mean, my place or yours?"

Nate smiled and cast his glance to the ground. "Uh, yeah."

Charon reached over and pinched Nate's cheek. "You're kinda shy here. I figured you were used to this."

Nate shook his head. "Yeah, you'd think so, right? That's the stereotype. Hot bartender in a gay bar, so lots of one-nighters and easy hookups. Well, it could be that. But that's not my style. Actually, I just got out of a relationship. Kind of a serial monogamist. Not intentionally. I'd rather that something stuck. Just hasn't worked out." Nate shrugged and smiled again at Charon.

"You aren't thinking this will develop into anything, I hope." Charon hated to dash his hopes before he at least tasted those luscious lips, but he also wanted to avoid some overwrought drama seeping into the night.

Nate laughed, a good sign. "Uh, no. You're from out of town. I knew that already. Actually." Now he turned bright red under the parking lot's glowing light. "Actually, I just lusted after you. I mean, I prefer a relationship, but between times, a one-nighter here and there never hurt anyone."

Charon stepped closer and planted a kiss firmly on Nate's moist lips. "So we're back to the question. Where to?"

Nate shrugged again. "My place, unless you want to go to your room or whatever. My roommate's gone for the weekend."

"As chance would have it, I never checked into my hotel. Your place sounds great."

Nate frowned. "Where's your bag?"

Oops. Sometimes Charon forgot the normal human things of life. He arrived on foot from Chicago, with nothing but the clothes on his back. "In my car. At the Marriott downtown." Luckily he lied easily, too. "I was so desperate for a drink that I rushed to the bar and assumed I could check in late. Now, though, I'd rather get somewhere fast and get you out of those clothes."

Nate nodded and grinned. "Wow. Um, yeah, let's do it."

A car ride with One Republic blaring from the speakers and Nate singing along took them about fifteen minutes away, to a modest apartment complex with outside entries. Nate led Charon up the stairs and opened the door to a small apartment with a cluttered living room, small kitchen, and two bedrooms with a bathroom between.

Nate leaned over to pet his cat and scratch her behind the ears, but she sped away when Charon walked in behind him.

"Weird. She usually loves people."

Charon grabbed Nate around the waist and pulled him close, licking at his ear and running one hand up his stomach before he pinched a nipple. "She knew I wanted you alone and couldn't bother with pleasantries for the evening."

Nate sighed and pressed his buttocks into Charon. He tilted his head back and strained to kiss Charon. It took all of Charon's willpower not to carry Nate into the bedroom with his vampire strength and ravage his body.

Instead he played human, pushing them along in a clumsy way as first shoes, then shirts, and then belts fell to the ground. He inched Nate toward one of the bedrooms, but Nate pushed him the other way.

"Wrong one," Nate whispered as for the first time he rubbed along Charon's crotch and then unzipped his pants. "His room has shit everywhere."

They entered a tidy room, but Charon hardly cared about his surroundings as he spun Nate around and led him to the bed, where he pushed him over and scrambled to yank his pants down to expose the bubble ass, deliciously shaved, now pointing up in the air as Nate wiggled it. Charon stuck his face right into the taint and his tongue probed as deeply as possible. Nate groaned and shoved his ass into Charon's face.

While tasting this scrumptious ass, Charon removed his own pants before he lurched up and shoved Nate onto the bed. He flipped him over and took his rock-hard penis deep into his mouth. The smooth, shaved skin about his shaft pressed into Charon's nose, smelling tantalizingly of a faint soapy scent mixed with earthy sweat from working all night.

"Ut-oh."

Charon wondered why Nate sputtered those words until he felt his hips press upward, his cock tip grow larger, and the warm sperm shoot down Charon's throat.

"Sorry," Nate stammered as he moved his hips back and forth and continued to eject his cum into Charon's mouth. "I didn't know."

Charon left the penis in his mouth as the last ejaculations seeped out of the tip and it gradually grew limper. He deliberately slurped it out of his mouth and swallowed what remained in it.

"Sorry." Nate glanced up.

"For what?" Charon cocked an eyebrow and grinned.

"Um, coming without a condom, or without warning you. Or maybe for coming so damn fast."

Charon played with Nate's semihard penis, then moved his fingers down to feel the still moist anal opening underneath.

"Not a problem on any front. Unless you're spent and don't want to help me." Charon stroked his hard dick, which like Nate's was ready to explode in just seconds.

Nate spread his legs, then reached down and grabbed his ankles, lifting his legs high into the air and again exposing that wonderful anus. "This is what I really wanted. Condom's in the drawer." Nate jerked his head toward the little nightstand.

To continue playing human, Charon took out the condom. He stood next to the bed and pulled Nate over, making him release his legs and then jamming his dick into Nate's mouth and thrusting back and forth. Near coming, he jerked it out and rapidly put the condom on.

He grabbed the bottle of lube from the drawer and smeared some of it onto Nate's butt, who moaned when Charon's finger slid inside, then rubbed it up and down his own dick. Nate again clutched his ankles and lifted his legs high in the air.

"Fuck me," he panted.

Charon obeyed. He gently pushed his head into the opening, waiting as Nate's anus grew wide to accept him. Nate closed his eyes and groaned and pushed for more of Charon to get inside.

Nice and tight, so wonderfully tight, Charon returned the favor of a too-fast orgasm when a few movements in and out, with Nate contracting his muscles and then gripping with his ass around Charon's shaft, and his own cum shot forth so fast and hard Charon wondered if he blasted right out of the condom.

He collapsed on top of Nate, licked at his neck, his eyelids and then kissed him deeply. Afterward, he lay tightly twisted in Nate's arms until the twinky college-boy bartender drifted to sleep.

Charon carefully removed himself from the bed, dressed quickly, and escaped the bedroom to find a place of rest for the approaching dawn. Thankfully, the salty taste of that boy's semen and the sensation of a tight ass engorging his penis commanded his attention as the sun drifted into the sky, instead of fears or even questions about that irritating vampire hunter. Even the uncomfortable crypt in which he concealed himself failed to detract from the physical pleasure with Nate.

Chapter Thirty-One: Summer's Ending

25 AUGUST 2014

Nederland, Colorado

Charon woke with a hunger in his belly like never before. He thought for a moment and scolded himself for going too long without feeding. One month ago he returned home from his wanderings in order to catch up on finances, admire his minions, and catch up on a few TV shows. But he never bothered to drink any blood after he returned. So tonight he felt as if he had starved himself almost to death.

Because of his superior strength and witchcraft, Charon could go a long time without blood, but not forever. Before Jordan rang for him or he smelled one of the young men's blood from afar, Charon hurried up the tunnel and out into the night, not even bothering to put anything on even though he slept naked.

The cool mountain breeze tickled his shaved balls and stirred his cock, so to avoid getting lost in a sexual fantasy or jacking off right there, he sped away and found himself in Greeley, a city near the Colorado plains, which seemed quaint enough but smelled of cow shit on this night because of the nearby meat-processing plant.

He concealed himself in Cottonwood Park, lest a naked buff guy cause alarm if someone spotted him, and waited patiently until two teenagers came hurrying into the park, glancing all around as if hunted by the FBI. Once underneath Charon's tree where he had perched himself up high, they fondled each other awkwardly, like the boy had never before felt a breast, and the girl had never before rubbed a penis. At first he intended to feed quickly and move along. Charon decided to watch instead, not because it gave him pleasure, although the guy was cute enough, but mostly because he thought it the right thing to do—to give them this moment of ecstasy before killing them.

"You finally turned eighteen," the young man whispered. "You promised you'd help me finish once it was legal."

"I will. I want it, too. I was just worried about my dad getting pissed since you're a year older."

The boy smashed his face into hers. "No more talking about it. Thinking of him won't help." He laughed slightly, then kissed her again.

The boy lifted the girl's shirt and grabbed at her small tits, almost like he honked two car horns instead of a woman's body parts. Charon stifled a laugh when the boy stopped, grunted, and the girl yanked her hand away from his still zipped-up jeans.

"Did you just come?" she asked, somewhat alarmed.

Panting, he just nodded.

"Can I get pregnant? What are we going to do?"

With their pleasure turned to her naïve, if not outright stupid, panic, Charon jumped down and cracked her neck while reaching with his other arm to ensnare the boy and drink his luscious blood. He slowed the crimson nectar passing over his tongue at one of the last scenes of the boy's life—earlier that afternoon as he sat naked in a bedroom with a hard-on, chatting on the phone.

"Dude. I gotta go. I gotta jack off so I don't come too fast tonight. I'll call and let you know how far she went when I get home." He'd hung up and stroked himself to completion in a matter of seconds.

Charon laughed at the fact his effort went for naught after he came in his own underwear moments ago.

Stupid teens, out after dark and alone in a park. They were asking for a random vampire to happen by and off them. Charon left the bodies under the tree and hurried home.

Sated, Charon hurried to his quarters and grabbed a pair of his favorite underwear and put them on, just because it felt odd to look at spreadsheets naked. With nothing but underwear was fine, though, which made Charon laugh out loud at the haphazard logic.

The intercom beeped, and Charon saw Jordan's alert light up. He pressed the button. "Yes, my dear?"

"Can I come see you? Alex has a question."

"Sure."

Moments later, as Charon sat in his bedroom, Jordan appeared. "Alex wants to see you. Up here. Alone."

Charon arched an eyebrow.

"I told him you'd look at me like that. Even imitated it." Jordan faked a masculine pose and did an exaggerated mime of Charon. "Like, suddenly the staff summons the boss? I think not, right?" Jordan sighed and returned to his own twink posture. "Still, he seemed so serious, I said I'd let you know when I came up to get our latest orders. But I know we don't have any, so then I figured I'd just pop you with it."

Charon thought about the waiting spreadsheets but wondered about Alex's request, then decided he really wanted nothing more than to chill for the night.

"I'm going to watch this movie"—Charon tapped at the latest adventure flick he stole from a home recently—"and then just hang."

"So can Alex see you or not? I just have to tell him."

Charon rolled his eyes. "You're sure this isn't going to piss me off? He doesn't want to leave, does he? That wouldn't be good."

Jordan grinned. "Right. Don't I know it." He motioned across his throat as if slitting it. "No worries there. I think it's his hormones. Though he just fucked my brains out this morning." Jordan spun around and raced down the hall toward the stairs at that last statement, leaving Charon to laugh to himself and wait.

A few minutes later, the burly football player walked into the room, seeming a little nervous with hesitant steps but still with a jock's confident posture.

"You wanted to see me?" Charon eyed Alex up and down. Alluring, if a bit buff for Charon's taste. "You seem even tighter than when you got here. Life at my castle must agree with you."

Alex flexed his bicep and grinned. "Yep. No problem there."

"So what is it?"

Alex let his arm fall to his side. "You know, I figure since we're slaves and all, but you treat us nice, well, maybe I could just let it fly. No worries, right?"

"It depends." Charon noticed Alex's growing excitement in his gym shorts as he stood looking at Charon.

"Well, you know I'm a top, right?"

Charon nodded. "I believe Jordan selected you for that attribute. If I was the only top around here, I'd either have to fuck a lot of boys all the time, or they'd have to be more versatile, and frankly I doubt a few of them could ever manage it. So you're one of my football tops."

As Charon spoke, Alex's dick poked straighter into the room. Charon, too, felt his loins stir, threatening to peek out of his briefs.

"Yeah, about that. Don't get me wrong. The sex here rocks. But, you know, sometimes the desire seeks something else. You know?"

"I do." Charon wondered at this game, letting his cock head spring from the elastic. "You still haven't gotten to your point."

Alex stared at the vampire's penis as he talked. "Yeah. That. I was just wondering if you ever switched. If you ever bottomed. Or wanted it." Alex reached into his pants and felt himself up.

Charon laughed slightly and closed the distance between the two men, who looked each other in the eye. He kissed Alex, caressed the hard biceps, and allowed Alex to reach around and clutch tightly at his ass.

They moved toward the bed as they kissed, and then Charon removed Alex's shorts and his own underwear. However, as Alex went to make his move, Charon embraced him in a tight hug.

"You sure that's why you're here?" He kissed Alex's cheek and reached his own hand down to play with Alex's hairy blond ass.

"What you mean?" Alex gasped, a throaty question, his eyes seeming to panic and then hope at the same time.

Charon pressed the tip of his forefinger into Alex's ass, which tightened in resistance. "*You* ever switch?"

"I'm a top."

Charon kissed him. "Being so macho all the time must exhaust you. The overused jokes about 'exit only.' The football dude stereotypes. You must long for something different sometimes, yeah?"

"I don't know."

Charon decided against more conversation and instead kissed Alex deeply. He pressed him onto the bed, continued petting and caressing, and Alex complied and even smashed their lips together more passionately when Charon's entire middle finger pushed all the way into his ass.

His virgin ass never completely relaxed even as Alex switched from crying out in a slight bit of pain to moving back and forth to the rhythm of Charon inside him. If possible, shooting this load felt more amazing than a typical orgasm, and Alex indicated his pleasure by shooting his load clear across the bed and onto the floor, screaming in ecstasy as he never did after fucking one of the other boys while Charon watched.

Finished, Alex jumped quickly to his feet. "That wasn't why I came."

"But you liked it."

Alex grinned, but his posture returned to Cool Football Player. "Good enough. Don't want it regularly."

"That's fine. But I'm glad I could be of service."

"You never answered my question."

"What question?"

"You know, if you ever switch hit?"

"Do I look like it? What do you think?"

Alex thought for a moment and shook his head. "Nah."

Charon smiled as he pushed himself off the bed. "And you must have known that on some level when you requested to come up here."

Alex squinted at Charon. "Maybe."

Charon stood inches from him. "And you liked it."

"Yeah," Alex whispered.

"Don't worry. You mean as much to me as the rest. No matter how you put out or enjoy sex."

Alex's cock began to stir again, so Charon took it in his palm and stroked back and forth. "Please clean this mess up before you leave." Charon kissed him softly on the lips and grabbed his movie on the way to the little theater on the second floor.

He made an announcement on the intercom about the movie, and a few minutes later, Travis, Brian, and Todd ambled into the room and took seats, chatting all the way.

"I wanted to see this when I saw the previews," Todd exclaimed. "But I had to go to Romania, and then I ended up here."

Brian whistled, and a few seconds later, his dog pounced into the room, wagging her tail, and curled up next to him in his recliner. "You never did explain what you were doing in Transylvania," he said to Todd. "Hunting for Dracula? You kind of found him." He pointed to Charon and they all laughed.

"I was in Bucharest, not Transylvania. Even if I did find a vampire."

Travis sat in the recliner next to Brian, while Charon took the remote and stretched out on the big leather couch to the side.

Todd stood in the middle of the room, surveying the remaining options and seeming to take this decision as seriously as if life and death depended on it.

"Over here." Charon motioned for Todd to come to the couch and allowed him to cuddle up into Charon's side.

Todd rustled around for a minute before getting comfortable as Charon hit play.

As the movie began, Charon petted Todd's hair and rested his chin on the boy's head. Watching the opening scene, where the buff action hero lay in bed with a hot bombshell and contemplated leaving her for the next dangerous assignment, Charon grew reflective about how first Bill and then Styx worried so much about him being alone.

He still thought it complete nonsense, because he had never desired monogamy and, even in his human existence, rebuffed the notion of settling down with one person for the rest of his life. How dreadfully mundane and boring. Besides, he'd found companionship with his gaggle of boys. He kissed Todd lightly on the head and then lost himself in the movie.

Only when the surprise twist materialized, when the main character's trusted friend betrayed him for his own protection, did Charon remember the vampire who hunted him.

Still, that fear that consumed him in Romania and then Chicago had faded completely by now, lost because of the reconciliation of the note and the fact that, true to his word, the vampire had left him alone once Charon reached Omaha. Still, Charon knew the vampire would return to monitoring him. Thus curiosity won the day, to the point that Charon wanted to seek him out and discover this gambit. Almost. Instead, he contented himself with remaining in his castle with the boys for a while longer and enjoying their company.

PART SEVEN: THE GAME INTENSIFIES

Chapter Thirty-Two: Testing the Hunter

11 SEPTEMBER 2014

Washington, DC

Curiosity got the better of Charon, more than any alarm. He'd worked diligently over the last couple days to eliminate his concern over the twinkle boots from the Oriental Theatre, regardless of his being a concealed vampire and witch. Charon was just as powerful. And Charon possessed the added protection of threatening the humans around them, which this stalker apparently disliked, since reports from Chicago claimed that a surprise fire broke out during the performance, unfortunately killing three people in the panic that followed, but no one else. Clever, actually, that he limited the chaos to three deaths and somehow wiped all traces of the supernatural from the scene and from people's memories, to the point it became an unfortunate conflagration and nothing more. At any rate, Charon could always pull a similar stunt to get away if needed. Threaten the innocent, and his stalker caved.

Happily without fear again in his life, Charon nonetheless was determined to operate with an abundance of caution. Thus he had planned this trip to the nation's capital, where he would begin a series of tests to determine the ability and scope of this one who wanted to meet with him. First, Charon needed to ascertain whether he operated at the behest of the Vampire Council, or if they somehow monitored Charon through him. All such tests after his transformation proved that the Council knew nothing about him, but the strangeness of this situation demanded a reanalysis.

Roaming along the National Mall, Charon admired the grandeur of the Washington Monument and paused atop the hill to glance at the White House, illuminated from afar. He smiled at the flag fluttering atop, indicating that the president would be in residence as Charon instigated a problem within his host city. To his back, the Capitol Dome glowed above him, and in front, he saw the Lincoln Memorial in the distance. He sauntered toward the World War II Memorial and turned, heading toward tidal basin in order to glimpse the Jefferson Memorial on its other bank.

He spied on the activity around it, limited at this late hour to a police car, a security guard, and one couple sauntering by, hand in hand. Charon kept his pace at human speed until he reached the other shore and sat on the monument's steps to admire the beauty from this perspective. With his vampiric vision, he contemplated the statement it made to see the Martin Luther King, Jr. Memorial across the way. Charon waited a few minutes, knowing that security cameras spied on him, and then walked away, as if continuing his nocturnal tour.

Concealed in a patch of dense trees nearby, he leapt into one in order to watch for a victim. He allowed pure chance to take over, with no thought to the individual his trap would ensnare. Whoever wandered by next would die.

When the ranting and raving homeless woman stormed into his vision, she yelled at her invisible tormentor and spit at the ground. Her torn sweater snagged on a branch, sending her into a harsher fit of hysteria, and then she spun around, seeming to search for a hidden succubus or perhaps a valuable possession.

No matter, because seconds later Charon swooped down and carried her high into another tree, clamping his teeth deep into her neck and draining her blood as he lifted her toward the heavens. But this was not about feeding, though Charon certainly enjoyed the blood. This had to do with his test. He quickly rushed to the steps of the monument and staged his kill by moving so fast that no human could see, too fast even for their advanced technology after they slowed it as much as possible to detect his presence. They would witness nothing but a blur and a deposited dead person.

The woman lay sapped completely of blood and arranged as if crucified before Jefferson's marble likeness. To humans, it would appear that a demented murderer orchestrated the scene, but any vampire would detect the telltale signs of a vampire's modus operandi.

After a night of sightseeing and a fitful sleep, the following night Charon repeated his deadly actions, leaving a jogging soldier splayed across the steps of the Lincoln Memorial.

Two murders in two nights led to headlines in the *Washington Post* of a serial killer on the loose. This fact led to an increased police presence, with officers roaming in pairs and fewer people out and about in the nation's capital because of this dangerous time. Still no sign of vampire law enforcement, however. No Council. No stalker.

With fewer victims from whom to choose, Charon fed off a Capitol police officer, which seemed fitting to display on the steps that looked toward the Supreme Court Building across the street.

Finally, with this third vampire kill, Charon got the desired result. He smelled vampires swarming into Washington, DC the next evening when he woke. He noted they hardly brought an army, just a few Nosferatu, but all reeked of some form of authority from the magic that Charon employed to detect them. The Vampire Council had arrived at last.

Charon hurried to the National Mall to watch and resisted a kill on this night, lest it prove too dangerous. From a perch atop the Museum of American History, concealed from the security guards and cameras but with a good view of the mall, he spied for signs of activity.

Sure enough, a couple vampires came into view, patrolling, watching, scanning the skies for signs of a recalcitrant vampire. Yet not once did they so much as glance toward Charon. Despite their advanced magic and a vampire's preternatural ability to perceive the fellow undead nearby, they seemed ignorant of Charon's presence.

To maintain the game, just before dawn Charon raced to the outskirts of town and ran the long and winding road toward Mount Vernon. He kidnapped a sleeping old man along the way, then decorated the hill behind George Washington's home that overlooked the Potomac River with the eviscerated body.

The next night, the same vampires roamed along the mall, making sure no humans saw them but nonetheless letting any vampire understand their presence, and thereby the threat of the Vampire Council. Charon sensed that more from the Council had arrived in the area now, too, patrolling as many of the nation's sacred spaces as possible. He spotted an African-American female vampire hiding in the shadows of the Pentagon and followed her all the way to the National Air and Space Museum near Dulles International Airport. She moved confidently, seemingly unafraid but unaware of his presence. She tilted her head in his direction one time, perhaps sensing something as he did with his stalker, but then moved along quickly enough.

Extending his reach, Charon finished that night with a body sprawled across the steps of Monticello in Virginia. He felt badly, at least a little, that two times he soiled the grounds of a place close to his favorite founding father, Thomas Jefferson, but at the same time recognized the impact of dead bodies in these places.

He laughed at the media reports he examined on the internet, as hysteria swept across the region about the brazen serial killer with the technological sophistication to skirt around all security systems at these sacred locations, and with the sadism to deplete the bodies of blood.

Thus, vampires lurked at every turn, all obviously from the Vampire Council from the way they hid from humans but made themselves known to vampires, with the bold confidence that nothing threatened them, even if a vampire defied their rules and risked exposure to humans in such an obvious way. This bravado, despite the fact they could not locate the perpetrator. Charon once again tested the Vampire Council and, to his satisfaction, confirmed their complete inability to find and punish him.

Ready to depart and find his next adventure, Charon decided to leave them one more present, just for fun. The White House, after all, needed a dead body, too. He snickered, imagining the ramped-up panic, the fear that would embrace the entire capital, and then the bafflement that, just like that, the murders stopped, the serial killer disappeared.

He drank from the young woman he found up late and studying alone in her dorm room, then carried her quickly to the White House steps, where he arranged her just like the others for the authorities to find. They would still be befuddled by the complete lack of clues to follow, this time despite the heavy Secret Service presence and state-of-the-art surveillance that protected the most powerful human in the world.

Laughing and wanting to admire his work, Charon perched himself atop the nearby Treasury Building for a good view. He almost stumbled over the edge at what he saw.

Right behind him, as quickly as he had worked and also too fast for humans to see, two vampires sped onto the White House grounds, one stealing the body and the other cleaning the crime scene. It took Charon mere seconds to stage the scene, and even less time for them to get rid of it. He paused a second to admire their beauty, the one a strongly built Greek god with long blond hair and bulging biceps. And, ah, the other one. Of course. His stalker, last seen at the Oriental Theatre in Chicago.

Somehow they were alerted to his crime tonight, yet never once did these vampires glance in his direction despite coming so quickly behind him. He could not tell whether or not they knew about his presence.

But the Greek god of the two frowned in concentration, raced away with the dead young woman and left his partner behind.

His stalker, mister long curly haired twink of a witch and vampire, then raced away from cleaning up the scene and suddenly walked right down the path, away from the White House and stopped in front of the Treasury Building. He pretended to admire the scenery and nodded at the Secret Service uniformed police officers as they patrolled and scrutinized him closely.

Unbelievable. Or completely confusing. Perhaps both. His stalker stood there below him. His stalker, acting on behalf of the Vampire Council, or perhaps part of the Vampire Council? Yet unlike previous times, he never indicated any knowledge of Charon's presence.

Charon thought himself perfectly concealed as that cute as hell bubble butt walked away. That beautiful vampire continued his nonchalant meandering, even pausing to push the pedestrian crossing button despite no cars driving around at this late hour. As he waited for the light to change, the same voice from the Oriental Theatre filled Charon's head.

Why are you hurting these people?

Charon swallowed the lump in his throat and smiled. He masked all thoughts, lest that vampire witch attempt to rummage around in his brain for answers, and jumped to the ground. He paused ten feet away and only continued when the walk signal lit up and the vampire stalker crossed the street.

Why so shy? You never act that way any other time. I told you that I'd leave you alone. You brought this meeting on, not me. I thought you finally wanted to talk.

Charon walked behind but refused to answer. His one burning question, however, demanded attention. "Are you with the Vampire Council?" he asked aloud, not wanting to give away all his magical secrets.

This time the vampire laughed. *That's complicated.* He came to a halt and spun around, his long brown hair whipping over his shoulder as he tilted his head and grinned. God, Charon wanted to have sex with him in the worst way, protecting himself be damned.

Before Charon could ponder a response or decide his next move, the vampire before him listened carefully and his eyes grew a bit wide. *Skedaddle. We'll chat another time.*

Charon sped away at the warning but felt the swish of air as Greek God ran past him the other way. He stopped and turned around to watch them. This vampire with the long blond hair returned without the body and screeched to a halt as he grabbed Charon's stalker around the waist and pulled him close, his fingers entangled in the curly hair.

"You okay?" Greek God whispered to the stalker, though Charon's vampire hearing allowed him to eavesdrop.

"Yep." Stalker vampire hugged Greek God back by wrapping his arms around his neck. With one hand, he waved a hand for Charon to leave, while winking at him at the same time.

"There's a vampire—"

Charon decided not to listen for the rest of that sentence as the stronger, taller vampire began to end the embrace. Charon ran with all his vampiric speed out of Washington, DC, away from Virginia, and to his next location for more testing of what the hell was happening with the Council and between his stalker and him.

Chapter Thirty-Three: Tests with No Answers

17 SEPTEMBER 2014

Nashville, Tennessee

His role as a Washington, DC serial killer proved, once and for all, that the Vampire Council possessed no means of detecting him, finding him, or otherwise affecting his perfect vampire life. He called them forth, managed to summon a gaggle of undead enforcers to the nation's capital when his killing spree threatened exposure of the vampires, but nothing whatsoever alerted them to his presence, even when he spied on them from nearby.

In short, nothing gave him away, not even the hot little stalker who tracked him through Europe, spied on him at the Oriental Theatre, and appeared in Washington, DC, despite the fact he knew Charon hid atop the Treasury Building. That one apparently even made out with a member of the Council but kept Charon hidden. Given the chance, he kept Charon's secret and only communicated with him when the other one left. He even helped Charon escape notice in the end. Fascinating.

So Charon stopped testing the Vampire Council but still needed to do something to try to learn his stalker's intentions. If anything, this intrigued him more than ever, but he determined to remain as careful as possible. Thus, he plotted his next move in the nation's country music capital, although first he desperately wanted to bang a cowboy.

Charon seldom listened to country music and rarely enjoyed the pop hits that everyone sang regardless of their typical musical tastes. He preferred something harsher, with strong bass and beating drums, and he detested the constant stories that the country genre insisted upon telling. It hurt his ears to wander the downtown streets of Nashville as old-school country music poured out of every bar doorway and window, while the street performers twanged away.

Except that allure of a young man with a big belt buckle, a cowboy hat, and those uncomfortable boots. The cowboy personified masculinity in American culture. Strong. Unafraid. Hyper jock, homophobic, and sexist. Detestable and delicious, all wrapped up in one.

Many of the men glanced suspiciously as Charon passed them, eyeing his tight jeans, comfortable tennis shoes, and casual long-sleeve T-shirt, as well as his hair, spiked and pretty, with no hat smashing it down. Nothing country about him; he looked as if he stepped right off the streets of New York City with his designer clothes and enormous watch. He could feel the ones who wanted to punch him in the face just for daring to saunter with such an effete nonchalance through their butch Southern realm.

Which, naturally, heightened the lust in Charon's loins when he stared back and winked, when he scanned their bodies, making them as uncomfortable as they made all those women with their lustful drooling. He loved pausing on their bulges, whether visible or not, just because they squirmed if they noticed and clenched their fists tightly at their sides.

Rather than seek the nearest gay bar to find the Southern out-and-proud cowboys who transformed the ultra-masculine cowboy get-up into the most pristine of outfits, Charon hunted for a closeted one in this macho environment.

Unfortunately, though he hoped to entertain himself with a drawn-out search for the perfect specimen, it took little effort to find his prey. But if he thought about it, the ease with which he located his mate for the night seemed painfully obvious. How many times in his human life had he ventured out with his straight frat boys to a sports bar, a club to slobber over the women, or just to dinner, and always found one like him at tables of similar guys. Sometimes he encountered a gay guy out with a group for whatever reason—work, a relative, just pals from before they came out—and they hooked up at the end of the evening once they each finished with their straight pals. Or, and Charon loved this scenario even more, he spotted a closeted guy desperately wanting to fit in with the rest of the jocks but incapable of controlling his wandering eyes or the way he flirted with the boys he admired by laughing too hard with them. That type of quest satisfied Charon all the more by the time he looked down to see their luscious red lips wrapped around his dick.

In a dueling pianos bar, with the awful country music blasting away from the mediocre singers who pounded on the keys like three-year-olds, Charon found a lovely cowboy of the closeted variety, pretending to chat with the woman beside him as his friends hit on her friends, all the while drinking his beer too fast and spying on the hot boys around him. Charon positioned himself nearby but not too close and dug out his phone, which he possessed as a prop and emergency communication system with Jordan. To feign that he waited for someone, he played Angry Birds while really casting a subtle glance from time to time at Mr. Gay Cowboy.

Their eyes met and the game began, Charon monitoring as this one struggled to pay attention to the babbling but too drunk woman next to him, all the while glancing at Charon about every ten seconds. Finally, he pulled himself away from her and walked toward the bathroom, making sure to pass right by Charon's table and staring him in the eyes the entire way.

Charon followed him to a hallway and reached out to grab his arm, pulling him farther into a corner just before he went into the bathroom.

"You don't really have to pee, do you?" Charon smiled when they stood in front of each other.

Cowboy glanced around, obviously afraid someone might see. "A little. But, I guess, no." He shifted nervously from one foot to the other.

"Want to go somewhere else?" Charon asked. "Someplace safer?"

Their eyes met again, and Cowboy licked his lips before he whispered the answer. "Yeah. But, I probably better stay."

"Why? So you can enjoy her beer breath tonight and hope against hope that she either passes out before it's time to go to your place, or that you get drunk enough to pretend she's me while she gives your limp dick a blow job?"

Cowboy laughed. "Something like that."

"Come on."

Charon pushed Cowboy along and toward the exit. Cowboy glanced back one time, but Charon had him outside before he could second-guess himself.

"Where we goin'?" he asked. "I should probably go back, actually."

Charon paused for a moment on the street to make the guy comfortable. "We'll just get a room right there." Charon pointed to the nearest chain hotel nearby. "My treat. And just text one of them. Tell them you got sick and didn't want to barf on her."

Cowboy laughed again. "I only had one beer."

"Then say you got the grievous shits from dinner."

He threw his head back and his eyes twinkled. "Got it. Got it." He reached into his pocket and pulled out his phone, furiously texting before looking at Charon again, tipping his cowboy hat up ever so slightly so their eyes could meet again.

In the typical-looking hotel room, with one picture of Nashville, two beds, and a TV, Charon wasted little time, and Cowboy responded in kind. Charon stripped off his flannel shirt, cupped his hand over the bulge in the jeans, and passionately kissed the cowboy, whose hat fell off in the process.

When he yanked the jeans down and grabbed the hard ass, Charon grinned. "I didn't know riding horses hardened an ass so deliciously."

Cowboy shook his head as he removed all of Charon's clothes, licking along Charon's shaft when his cock sprung forth from the underwear. "I don't ride horses. I'm a singer."

Charon stifled a laugh. How stereotypical. Masquerading as a tough cowboy and hanging out in straight bars, living the life of a closeted Southern boy by singing his heart out in a cowboy hat so no one could detect his sexual yearnings.

They kissed. They licked. They fondled one another. Cowboy proved one of few words, preferring to engage their mouths on various body parts instead of chatting away. In the middle of the bed, when Charon had him on his hands and knees, his ass cheeks begging for Charon to grab onto them, Charon put the cowboy hat back on his head. Then he mounted the cowboy, just like he might jump atop a raging bull for a round at the rodeo. The condom and lube slowed down the sensations that roared through Charon like electricity, heightening the anticipation, building closer and closer to climax but without the instant coming that occurred with Todd in Bucharest.

Charon reached around Cowboy as he purposefully pumped back and forth in his ass, clutching his dick and smearing the oozing precum over his tip and along his shaft, until he had a natural lubricant and jacked Cowboy to completion, his semen covering the comforter underneath and causing him to clutch his ass muscles around Charon's penis.

As Cowboy breathed heavily underneath him, Charon thrust away until he shot his load and pulled out. He collapsed on top of Cowboy and licked at his ear, then played more with his ass.

Sated, however, Cowboy turned back into the nervous boy of before. "You know, maybe I should go back?"

Charon grinned. "It's your life."

He reached over and began to dress rapidly. "What's that mean?"

"Nothing." Charon shrugged. "I'm good with a quickie. It's just, why don't you come out and get over it already?"

As he buttoned his shirt, Cowboy rolled his eyes. "Easy for you to say."

As quickly as they arrived, got naked, and fucked their brains out, Cowboy scurried out of the room without another word and ran away, much to Charon's amusement.

Charon remained naked a while longer, still thinking about the gorgeous ass that moments ago begged him for attention. He rented a gay porno on the television, jacked off, and then remembered why he came to Nashville.

He came for a reason other than to fuck a closeted cowboy. Not that he regretted the pleasant and extremely hot diversion. Or that he worked on any timetable. He just wanted to maintain the momentum that he had built in Washington, DC.

Charon dressed and continued to wander around Nashville, all the way until the bars closed and people streamed into the streets and toward their cars and hailing cabs. He saw Cowboy, leaving with his posse, the woman clinging to his arm, probably because she would otherwise fall on her ass.

True to his word, Stalker had left Charon alone until he showed up with the Vampire Council in Washington. What did his answer mean, that it was "complicated," when he addressed his association with the Council? While the Council hunted for Charon, this one assisted them but simultaneously concealed Charon from them.

Charon decided to figure this game out, but he still wanted to act cautiously, not giving away his home base or the full extent of his witchcraft.

But maybe a little of magic would help. Something to establish a communication channel. Charon used his power to bring forth a pen and paper to write a note. He asked the stalker to explain what he meant by a "complicated" relationship with the Council and to reveal the reason for his interest in Charon. Finished, Charon snapped his fingers and the note disappeared, along with the pen. He enchanted a spell to mail the letter but wondered if it would arrive at its destination because Charon only had the dude's beautiful face in his mind to use as a guiding address.

Charon walked through a wealthy suburb of Nashville, touring the area with no purpose, waiting for a response. He knocked the head off a yard gnome just because it looked at him the wrong way. A couple screwed their brains out in the kitchen, unaware that someone watched through their open window. Charon ripped down a Confederate flag and tore it to pieces.

Just when he pondered where to hide for the night, his letter appeared in his hand, an answer scrawled in purple ink underneath his questions.

> *I assumed you were smart enough to understand that "complicated" means I can hardly explain in a brief note. As for my interest in you, that's complicated, too. But stop thinking with your dick. It's not that.*

Charon laughed aloud and countered with another message of his own. He admitted to wanting to fuck his stalker, but then explained his disdain for childish games. Either they meet, or cut it out. The reply came more quickly this time.

> *Hello, Gorgeous. Fucking isn't in the cards, though the thought does bring a certain tingle to me. Anyway, there's a reason for me to play this cautiously. In time, you'll learn. Besides, isn't it clear by now that you're not in charge of this game? Go about your business and I'll come to you when it's time.*

A stalking tease. So he wanted to give Charon blue balls while he toyed with him. No doubt the refusal to even ponder sex stemmed from the blond hotty who hugged him in Washington. Still, what was with the flirting? And what could be so complicated that it caused him to reach out to Charon but refuse explanation?

Once inside a lair for the night, ironically hidden in the steeple of a Southern Baptist church, Charon thought about the curly-haired vampire and his game. Intriguing and odd. For the third time that night, Charon jerked off, this time at the thought of this one sucking him to completion.

Chapter Thirty-Four: Revenge

30 OCTOBER 2014

Albuquerque, New Mexico

The hunger consumed Charon. After feeding once in Nashville and returning to Colorado for a while, Charon starved himself in anticipation of this night.

As before, Vampire Stalker—the proper name that Charon now used to refer in his own mind to the twink-cum-witchy-vampire who spied on him—left him alone. Charon wrote no more magical correspondence, and Vampire Stalker sent nothing else and never appeared mysteriously in Charon's midst. As for his curiosity, it remained, but Charon realized that his demand for answers fell on deaf ears. Too, pushing the issue might bring unwanted attention to Charon. Thus, he returned to business as usual.

Contemplating his next move back at home, Charon realized that he had never sought revenge against his college nemesis. He slapped his head, astounded that he had forgotten the asshole so thoroughly. He panicked that the idiot had died before Charon got to him but located his Facebook page and discovered him retired in New Mexico, near his grandchildren.

At that point, Charon decided to stop eating because the deprivation would make him more desperate, more sadistic, more vile when he fed off the fiend at long last.

Not wanting to spoil Halloween because he'd promised Jordan a return hunting trip to Chicago, Charon decided to enact this deed that night. Charon hurried by the National Museum of Nuclear Science and History and into a modest area of homes and shops, finding the former professor's house easily enough.

Inside the boring bedroom, Charon sat on the edge of the bed next to the elderly man, sleeping peacefully. One would never guess his true nature. Or, at least, the hatred of which he was capable.

Charon reached over and shook the professor's shoulder. "Dr. Kellen? Dr. Kellen, wake up."

The old man started and gulped back a scream before he clutched the covers to himself.

Charon held up a hand to calm him. "Relax. You're safe for now. Remember me?"

The unkempt gray beard surprised Charon, because he remembered Dr. Kellen as always well groomed, the beard trimmed, the thick hair in perfect order.

"Who are you?" the man demanded, regaining some of the bravado Charon recalled.

"That's more like it." Charon smiled, reached down, and snapped one of the toes on Kellen's left foot. He screamed in agony and attempted to scramble away, but Charon caught him easily enough and made him stay on the bed as sweat burst out on his forehead. In his struggles, Dr. Kellen almost lost his pajama pants.

"You? What do you want?" Still making demands and acting in charge despite his poor little toe and predicament. At least he finally remembered Charon.

Charon nodded. "A fair question, given the circumstances. I'd ask the same thing if I were you. Not that you're in a position to insist upon anything. But I was counting on your shithead attitude to inspire me."

Again Dr. Kellen struggled as if to leave before Charon yanked him back to a sitting position next to him.

"Are you on drugs? What's wrong with you?"

Charon grinned. "You mean my strength? It's a long story. I don't want to bore you with it. Suffice it to say, I'm in control of the situation." Charon reached over and took one of Kellen's pinky fingers in his hand, threatening to break it. "Understood?"

Slowly, the old man nodded his ascent. "My wife will return soon, you know."

Charon laughed. "Nice try. You wouldn't want her to suffer, too, would you? Besides, according to your last Facebook post, she traveled to see her sister at the nursing home in Wyoming."

"I see you never stopped being an egotistical jerk." Kellen snarled.

Charon snatched the finger and this time broke it, enjoying the pompous ass's cry of agony.

"You see, that's just the thing we need to discuss. Let me get to the point. I want to reopen the conversation about my grade in your Philosophy class. I resent that your homophobic conservative ass detested my being openly gay. That you oh-so-cleverly jammed your conservative Christianity down everyone's throat, as if you knew Truth, and as if it wasn't dishonest to mask that holier-than-thou attitude in academic philosophy."

"I opened students' minds."

Charon frowned at Kellen. "Lying won't make this any better. How are your other fingers doing?"

"If you're going to kill me, just do it. But leave enough evidence so they can track your disgusting self down and throw you in jail to rot."

Charon shook his finger in the man's face. "Still so impatient. I thought people mellowed after they retired? Not you. Still a pig. Here's the thing. You can earn your life. All you need to do is comply with my will, and just for a little while. I warn you, though, to tell me the truth. Never lie. Do you understand?"

Dr. Kellen scowled next to Charon, holding his tender finger in a shaking hand, trembling but fighting for that self-confidence that always defined him. "You'll let me live?"

Charon smiled. "If you meet my expectations."

Kellen lifted a hand in the air and began to twirl a finger, a gesture Charon well remembered from his classroom behavior when he grew impatient with students who struggled for answers or to articulate their ideas. But he stopped when the pain from the broken finger shot down his arm.

"Get on with it," he spat through gritted teeth.

"I want to discuss my grade again."

Dr. Kellen jerked his head up to glare at Charon. "Haven't you moved on from that?"

Charon grinned and shrugged. "Apparently not."

"What about it?"

"What did I really earn?"

Dr. Kellen scrunched his brow and began to speak, but Charon reached over and placed his fingers on the old shithead's cracked lips.

"Remember, I'm in charge. So speak the truth."

"You pulled out a C minus."

"But you gave me an F? Is that ethical, oh wise philosopher?"

The knee on one leg bobbed up and down impatiently. This one despised the loss of control and the questioning of anything he ever did or believed. "By the letter of the law, I suppose you at least deserved a D. But by God, you never understood the philosophers. Always twisted them into your liberal beliefs. Your damnable situation ethics. Disgusting stuff, you. I thought about going lighter on you, and then I spotted you, enjoying that Kiss-in so much. You weren't even an activist. Just an opportunist. But there you sat in the student union, not only making out with the guy but with your hand on his crotch."

Charon laughed at the memory. "True. I didn't participate in the LGBT Alliance. Still, they needed hot frat guys to stick their tongues down twink throats for effect, don't you think? And when I noticed him grow hard, well, the impulse to fondle just took over. But that's beside the point. You admit that you flunked me out of spite?"

"Not exactly spite. On principle. You were smug. Got whatever you wanted with your charm, not hard work, despite a solid mind in there." He pointed to Charon's head. "You got frustrated because flirting with me failed. Because I demanded that you account for your sinful beliefs. Someone, at some time, had to put you in your place."

"Still," Charon scratched the bottom of his chin as if in deep thought, "throwing the Bible at me stretched credibility a bit far, didn't it? I mean, whether you liked me or not, that was wrong. Even if I was a jerk, as you so charmingly put it, you can't hurl things across the room at your students! And the Bible of all things, from such a pious man. Just wrong."

"So you know the truth. In points, you pulled out a C minus, though I have no evidence that you didn't cheat on that final exam."

"You don't have any evidence that I did, either. I liked Kant. I studied hard for that one."

"Then we're done. Leave me to these broken bones. We're even, if that's what you seek."

Charon patted Dr. Kellen on the back. "One more thing. One more thing. Do you remember that meeting, when you threw the Bible?"

"Vaguely."

"It was after the midterm. I was flunking—you claimed because I skipped class, failed to study, and disrupted the lessons when I did attend."

"All true."

"According to you. But then. But then, we met and I promised to work harder. And I did. I promised to attend class. Which I did. And I promised to debate more pleasantly, which I tried my best to do. Do you remember that conversation? And still you launched the Bible at my head when I refused to see it your way, when I refused to think that it condemned my homosexuality. Do you remember that?"

"Yes."

"Good." Charon patted him on the knee this time. "Then, do you remember our very last conversation? After the final, when we met to see if I pulled it off and passed your wretched course?"

"Get on with it." Again with the almost finger twirl. "As vaguely as the last one."

Annoyed, Charon simply slapped Kellen hard upside the head. He cried in pain but sat back up, trying again to show authority and hide his fear.

"Let me prompt that feeble brain of yours. Must be dementia. I sat there, appropriately cowed and respectful, as you added up the points and pondered your right as the almighty professor to determine my fate. Then you chuckled and grinned some awful smile at me. I can still hear your words. 'You flunked. Did you really think I was going to allow you to pass? I feigned it, just so you'd stay past the drop date and have to remain in my class.' Then you stood up, lording over me from behind your desk. 'I'm in charge. Not you.'" Charon grew angrier and angrier with each word, forcing himself to breathe deeply as the smell of blood consumed him, as the rage begged him to rip the man's head off and drink quickly to quench his thirst. "Do you remember?"

Dr. Kellen glanced nervously at Charon. "Again, only vaguely. But, yes, I remember the sentiment exactly."

"So you confess?"

Kellen frowned. "I wouldn't call it that. But we're on the same page regarding what took place."

Charon rose and stood before the trembling asshole in his little pajamas. "Did you really think I was going to let you live?"

Charon broke another finger, sending Dr. Kellen into a frenzy of activity to escape, but Charon held him tightly by both arms and stared into his eyes, his arms bruising from the force of the hold.

"I feigned it, just so you'd humor me with the truth." Charon allowed his fangs to descend and transformed into a vampire before the now-crying man. "I'm in charge. Not you."

Despite the thought making him want to vomit, Charon leaned over as if to kiss the man, but instead reached in and bit his tongue off. As he lay bleeding and shaking on the bed, Charon savored that small taste of blood. He fell on top of the professor, and bit off his ear. He controlled the rage and hunger, feeding himself over several hours of the night, allowing Kellen to pass out and then waking him again, almost sating his desire with the kill-drink but then bringing him back to life again. Finally, nearing dawn, Charon slapped the delirious man awake and launched his fangs deep into the man's neck, draining the last of his blood and giving into the hunger.

Finally, Charon got his revenge against the asshole lying bloodied before him. Whoever said 'forgive and forget' never experienced the sweet taste of revenge.

Content, smiling, and giddy, Charon started to leave when a note appeared in his hand.

Please stop. It would make things easier if you wouldn't kill the innocent.

Well, well. Look who materialized all of a sudden? Vampire Stalker. And, yet again, he revealed his weakness for humans? To respond, and still terribly ravenous because one human hardly made up for the long period of starvation, Charon burst into a neighbor's house and killed the couple sleeping in bed. He forwent the torture this time, however, out of sympathy for the innocent people who conveniently became dinner because they lived near an asshole.

Let that answer the pleas of Vampire Stalker. No one could manipulate Charon into behaving a certain way. No one had that power.

Yet another note appeared in his hand as he climbed into a cave to sleep for the day.

Please. Stop.

Charon thought that a rather lame response. He responded this time with a note of his own.

Apparently you're not as in charge of the game as you thought.

Chapter Thirty-Five: Priceless Treasures

29 NOVEMBER 2014

Hudsonville, Michigan

Strolling through an art gallery one evening during a special fundraising event in Denver, Charon stopped to admire an original Fabergé egg, for the first time in his life appreciating the intricate beauty and ornate decorating of the object. Before vampirism refined him, converting him into a wine enthusiast and appreciator of fine art, the eggs seemed foolish. After all, why put so much money into buying a mere egg, or why dedicate your artistic career to such an odd collection?

With life slowed down and time to contemplate the world around him, or in the current trend of being more mindful, Charon actually grasped what drew people to them. Returning to the palace that evening and finding an intense Xbox game of Madden playing out in the recreation room, in which the losers performed a dare for the pleasure, sometimes literally, of the victors, Charon realized that the large hallway connecting the living room to the formal dining room lacked artistic flare. Sure, the size of it and carved wood trim gave it a simple grandeur, but it needed an artifact in its center to draw your eye into the space instead of it being a mere transition from one room to the next.

What better than a glass-enclosed case with a Fabergé egg in it to transform the hallway completely?

Charon researched the possibility of purchasing or stealing one, but quickly became overwhelmed with all of the options. How could he choose a size, let alone the color or other details, and how would he know about its authenticity? Still, he slept through the next day and woke even more determined to add this piece to his collection.

First, he traveled to Evans, Colorado, where he had earlier located a fine craftsman and ordered the case in which he would display the egg. That proved easy enough.

A return trip to the computer in search of the ideal egg again began to overwhelm him when he hit upon an intriguing advertisement for fine art. The innocuous-seeming dealership called itself the Midnight Gallery and was located in the traditional Americana suburb of Hudsonville, Michigan, but closer inspection revealed something much more interesting.

The person posted for sale several fine paintings, a variety of sculptures, but specialized in Fabergé eggs. Nothing unusual there, except the gallery itself trumpeted the fact that it only opened in the evening and specialized in nocturnal exhibits. It claimed to do so as an avant-garde flourish, as a means to attract attention beyond the constraints of the traditional art world and expectations. To that end, it typically opened from 8:00 at night and closed at 1:00 in the morning, and special events started at 10:00 and ended with the chiming of the midnight hour.

More intriguing, the online reviews nicknamed it the Vampire Gallery. Everyone loved it and particularly adored its edgy mode of business. Some joked that surely the owner was an actual vampire. Funny, except everything else smacked to Charon of that being the reality.

Fascinated by the concept, Charon transported himself the next evening to Hudsonville and grew frustrated to find Midnight Gallery only opened to the public on Thursday, Friday, and Saturday. Charon explored nearby Grand Rapids for a couple nights, feeding off one wandering man, and then appeared at the gallery about one hour after it opened on Thursday. Predictably, given its unusual hours, Charon found it empty.

Except that a block away, Charon's senses tingled the alarm about a nearby vampire. The sensation intensified as Charon approached the gallery doors and flooded his system when he stepped inside.

Playing further with the nocturnal allure, Charon found himself inside a dimly lit space, with no furniture except a glass desk in one corner, in front of a door to the back room. The ceiling was a dark blue and purple, with tiny little lights illuminated upon it to mimic the stars shining down upon Earth. The walls, unlike other aspects of the architecture that implied night, were painted the more traditional white expected for displaying fine art, and each piece in the gallery had a spotlight specially assigned to it. Charon walked around and glanced at a Monet, and then some terrible mountainscape before he felt the vampire enter through the door behind the desk and turned around to greet him.

Because of his own magic and the spell Styx used to conceal Charon from the Council, the vampire seemed to have no clue as to Charon's true nature.

He smiled and said hello, acting human. "I don't get many people just wandering in without an appointment or specific interest. People usually wait for special events, so they can enjoy the atmosphere."

The dude with his fake grin annoyed Charon instantly. He stood just over six feet tall, with peppered gray hair and a mustache. He wore a pedestrian blue suit and tie, with shoes he must have purchased at Walmart. He was smug about his true nature as he acted the part of a human, assuming with a bold arrogance that no real human would ever suspect the truth. How did the Council allow this fool to act this way? Because he apparently behaved by feeding off the worthy and otherwise passing his time as a stupid gallery dealer, Charon guessed, instantly exasperated with the Council despite their having no control over him. Even more annoying to Charon, the gallery owner's opening salvo at Charon implied that, despite being open to the public, Charon's presence bothered him, or that in the least he wanted to size Charon up before giving him much time.

Charon smirked and clasped his hands behind his back, deliberately ignoring the outstretched hand in front of him. "I'm sorry. I was under the impression you held regular business hours."

Fake laugh and grin. Nauseating. Charon arrived with the hope of finding something interesting and different, but instead discovered nothing more than a narcissistic vampire toying with the humans, without the guts just to feed off them. He felt superior to those around him, when in reality he was nothing more than an insecure idiot.

"I'm Michael." He let his hand fall to the side when Charon continued to refuse the offer. "Welcome. I didn't mean to imply anything. It's just not customary, is all. How may I help you? Are you interested in a particular piece? Are you an art enthusiast?"

An innocuous question, sure, asked all the time in all sorts of situations, but context, tone, and expression spoke volumes about what the individual actually meant. In this case, Michael meant it dismissively. And what the fuck was an art enthusiast?

"Your website said that you specialize in Fabergé eggs. I was hoping to see them."

Michael smiled indulgently. "Of course, those are the more expensive items. You can imagine I have to display them in a more secure location. I don't really have the luxury of showcasing them except for special events or serious collectors."

Charon arched a brow. "More expensive than a Monet?" He pointed to the beautiful painting hanging at the center of the gallery.

"Well, that's a showcase item right now. I put a couple out, of course, for appearance. Here." Michael grabbed a brochure off the desk. "Maybe you'd be more comfortable coming to next week's festivities. I'm having a Christmas open house to kick off the holidays. Perhaps you've convinced me to display a couple of eggs on that occasion."

Charon tilted his head and squinted at the asshole. "What made you decide that I shouldn't be here? Certainly not the clothes? I'm wearing jeans, but they're designer. Was it the sweatshirt? I just like wearing professional sports logos. I enjoy the orange and blue of this old Cleveland Cavaliers shirt. Again, it wasn't cheap. Just fashioned to look old. But why would you strictly go by appearances? You've no idea what I'm capable of buying."

Michael leaned against his desk and folded his arms in front of his chest. "Yes, these are very expensive items. Certainly you can understand my need for caution? Besides, even when one has the money, one must appreciate fine art to be here. Nothing about you spoke of such. Was I wrong? I'm so sorry. Perhaps we should start over."

"You've no idea, do you?"

"I don't understand your meaning."

Charon nodded. "Fascinating. Even with me standing here and interacting, you've no clue. I'm a vampire, too." He descended his fangs to prove the point, but put them away right after.

Michael pushed himself off the desk and stood in a defensive posture. "What's the meaning of this?" Michael lost the fake sophisticate voice and sounded like any mundane male you might pass on the street.

"That's better. You can desist with your bad acting job. I was just intrigued by your advertisement. I'm quite serious about searching for a Fabergé egg. I ran into your website and suspected you were a vampire and wanted to check it out. Interesting ploy, to place yourself in a more conservative area of the country. True, you'd make a splash in New York or London, but middle of nowhere America, that gives it a special flare. You're like an attention whore of some off variety, but you pull it off well enough. Still, the affect is a bit over the top."

Michael glared at Charon. "Did you come here just to insult me? That's why I avoid most vampires."

Charon mocked a frown at Michael. "Ah, Michael doesn't like the truth. But relax, my friend." Charon walked over and patted Michael's shoulder, then straightened the thin blue tie around his neck. "I just want to buy an egg. Maybe you could give me the vampire discount."

Michael regained his composure and smiled, though thankfully he spoke with his normal cadence and not the put on of a high-end snotty gallery owner. "I never mated like other vampires because I really don't enjoy our kind. I like humans better. I'm sorry, but you're no exception. If you wanted a new vampire friend, you came to the wrong place. But if you want an egg, I'll sell you one and you can be on your way." Michael clicked his tongue inside his mouth. "What, now you don't like the truth?"

"Oh, I already knew it. Let's have a look at the eggs, and I'll be off."

Michael guided Charon to the back of the gallery, where he unlocked a set of double doors and pushed them open into a smaller room, decorated in much the same way as the first one. But instead of paintings, Charon viewed about nine Fabergé eggs, carefully displayed, each on their own pedestal with a light above shining down upon them.

Michael moved into the room. "I'll allow you to choose and we can make restitution via email."

He paused, waiting for Charon to respond, shifting from one foot to the other. No doubt he failed to detect the threat because he assumed the Vampire Council and its rules protected him.

"You know," Charon said as he walked into the new space, "I had no idea I was going to kill a vampire when I began this evening. I honestly came simply because I was fascinated by what you offered here. I wanted to see it for myself. And I really am in the market for an egg. But killing a fellow vampire? Never entered my mind until I met you."

Michael grinned a derisive smile. "You wouldn't risk the Council taking your life just because we don't get along. You know what? I don't even want to indulge you with a sale. Just go."

"Michael, Michael, Michael." Charon walked toward Michael and grabbed him by both shoulders. He next chanted a spell under his breath and incapacitated the vampire. It would only last a few seconds, but Michael sensed the danger too late. He flinched, moved to protect himself, but stood frozen in place.

Charon shoved him against the wall and latched onto Michael's neck, breaking through the skin as Michael screamed in anger. By the time the spell wore off, Michael had lost too much blood and only struggled a little before Charon chanted a spell to light his body on fire. As his dying corpse smoldered, Charon flung it onto the ground and wiped off his mouth.

The world was freed of one more insufferable idiot.

Charon took his time perusing the merchandise, analyzing each egg, picking it up and checking it out in different light, and then comparing and contrasting different color combinations. He picked three, no longer satisfied with one, and sauntered casually out of the gallery.

As he concealed himself for the night, he wondered what Stalker Vampire would say about a dead vampire instead of innocent humans.

Chapter Thirty-Six: A Time Out

24 DECEMBER 2014

Zelienople, Pennsylvania

Charon stood admiring how perfectly the Fabergé eggs accented the grand hallway, just as he anticipated when he first sought them. It particularly pleased him that he switched from one egg to three, which he placed closely enough to each other that the beauty complemented each egg, but separated enough that they each held their own, too. One crimson, one yellow, and one a deep blue, all with golden accents and clasps.

He closed the case of the last one and decided to get on his way. After all, he'd instigated a Christmas Eve tradition and hardly wanted to disappoint Americans with the belief that the Christmas Eve serial killer failed to strike this year. He had even sought out the ideal victim.

Yet playing with his eggs before leaving reminded him of the tension between himself and the Vampire Stalker that erupted after he had killed that ridiculous vampire-cum-gallery-owner.

Stalker twink had sent another note, this one with such a moral superiority it made Charon rip it up and refuse to respond. Vampire Stalker claimed he wanted to cooperate with Charon on a matter of the gravest importance, but his actions against a fellow vampire made it almost impossible. Still, he sought a meeting in order to seek a truce between himself and Charon, because the issue he faced could also doom Charon.

After a couple days, he sent a second note, directly threatening Charon. He called Charon a coward for the latest vampire killing and stated that he could easily notify the Vampire Council about Charon's existence, despite their not currently knowing a thing. He promised not to do so immediately, however, because of the danger that Charon could assist him in facing.

The threat pissed Charon off even more than the ethical superiority of the first correspondence. If he could sic the Council on Charon, why not just do it? And if he needed him for something, why this silly game instead of coming out and explaining the situation? Enough. Charon burned the next missive with his mind before even reading it. That completed their interaction to Charon's satisfaction because he had heard nothing else from Vampire Stalker until the previous night.

He almost destroyed this one, too, but Vampire Stalker apparently knew Charon well. To entice him to read it, he put a shirtless picture of himself on the cover. Charon actually smiled when he read the first line.

I knew that sexual enticement would get you back, even though we both know I have no intention of following through with any offer. Perhaps you can just jack off to a picture of my nipples.

After laughing, Charon spoke a response and sent it magically at once. "Send a picture of your shaved anus and we may have a deal. I'd reciprocate with a dazzling image of my cock."

You must win all the boys over with your subtle charm and lovely way with words. Of course, you will never know about the status of my anus, shaved or otherwise. I got you intrigued again, at least. I desperately want to speak with you, to explain the situation, but you must desist with the indiscriminate killing. At least humor me for a bit.

He went from moral authority to threatening to expose Charon to the Council to desperate lover. True, Charon had decided a while ago that he wanted to learn the truth behind this matter, eventually, but not at the expense of losing himself and his carefree life. Not at the expense of becoming just another vampire in the mix. And certainly not at the expense of obeying this one, let alone of being placed under the authority of that irritating Vampire Council.

In a classic move to avoid making a decision, Charon delayed answering this request and instead proceeded with his original plans for the day. Charon raced across the nation, stopping in Zelienople, Pennsylvania, for the third and final time that week.

He stood outside the tiny red brick church, one pulled right from the book of Americana classic churches, with the white farm-style house sitting on the grounds nearby for the pastor. A sign standing nearby labeled it as the parsonage.

Rather than the drawn-out and elaborate torture of previous years, which built to the Christmas Eve kill, Charon cut to the chase this year. After all, his torturing of the victims and attempts to reform them never made it to the media or public consciousness, only Charon knew about that aspect of the murders. His admiring serial killer fans merely needed a dead clergyman. And so many other matters consumed his attention this year, not least of which was gathering all the elaborate supplies requested by the boys this time around for their holiday celebration.

Charon glanced toward the center of town, decorated for the season with wreaths, red bows, and twinkling lights wrapped around seemingly every post. Americans, he pondered, confounded him. They would protest this latest Christmas Eve kill, lament how it soiled the sacred holiday, yet all would gather around the television to hear the latest news about it. Admiring fans would post on Twitter and Facebook about the killer's latest exploit. They would denounce it as evil and authorities would declare their intention to find the culprit. Still, the entire episode would launch the Christmas Eve Killer into even greater fame. As much as they wanted him caught, people longed for him to get away, to continue the thrill and story for them, so they could comfortably sit in their living rooms and ponder their much more fortunate lives, simply because their pastor was not crucified on this holy day.

Which brought him to poor Pastor Doberman, sitting with his family at dinner right now and finishing up his last bite of pie before heading to his little Lutheran Church for the evening's two worship services. Charon turned around and spied into the white frame house, with the perfect little family gathered around the table. *Herr* Pastor got up, kissed his wife goodbye, and hugged his children, then grabbed his coat, headed out the parsonage door, and walked across the well-manicured lawn, by the hideous plastic manger scene with the colors chipping off and Baby Jesus turning a sickly shade of yellow, and into his office at the church.

Charon ran behind before he could close the door and sat quietly on the couch in the pastor's tidy office. He crossed his legs and waited patiently.

Frank Doberman walked into the room, flipped on the light switch, and tilted his head slightly when he saw Charon sitting there. He made no move to run away and gave no gasp of surprise.

"Funny, I wondered if you might target me. I fit the profile. I knew I did. I even thought about alerting the authorities, but to what end? I had no proof. Just a hunch." Frank crossed the room and sat in an armchair opposite Charon, as casually as if he met a parishioner for a scheduled meeting.

"Who do you think I am?" Charon asked.

Frank laughed. "Don't patronize me. The Christmas Eve Killer, come to take his toll. If I thought I had any prayer of escape or getting help, I'd try. But I'm a realist, perhaps too much of one." He grinned. "My wife always warned me about that. I'm at peace with my maker. I guess a bit of dignity at the end means something to me, at least."

Charon squinted across the room in awe at this one's deportment. So calm. Strange, for someone meeting their death. "Are you going to try to convince me to spare you in some other way, then? Try to appeal to my humanity? To some Christian sentiment?"

Frank smiled, still acting the calm part of a pastor. "Would it do any good?"

Charon simply looked back.

"I thought not. So why bother?" Frank crossed his legs and sat back in his chair. "Perhaps you'd indulge me in one thing." He paused for a response, but Charon merely stared coldly back at him. He nodded. "Why? Am I permitted to understand your motives, before you take my life? It seems more than just a serial killer out and about, doing his broken thing. You're calculated. Particular. Why?"

Charon grinned. "I don't have to tell you anything."

"Of course not." Frank nodded his agreement.

"Your approach to this death fascinates me. I suppose for this bit of entertainment, I'll satisfy your curiosity. I kill because I must in order to survive. As a vampire, I have little choice." Charon paused to allow that information to sink into Frank's understanding.

Frank continued to provide no sign as to his reaction or mental state. "I've no idea if you mean that literally or figuratively. Or if you really believe it."

Charon shrugged. "Regardless, I spoke the truth. As for my victims, you seek an answer for why I target pastors on Christmas Eve. First, you must know that this is just a game I play on this particular night of the year. Other times, it's more random. Or calculated, but with different prey in mind. This is just a little Christmas tradition I started, really by mistake more than anything. Now, Americans expect it. Demand it, really."

Frank folded his hands calmly in his lap. "But it's not just pastors that you target. You seek conservative ones in small-town churches."

"See?" Charon pointed at him. "You're just like everyone else. You feign indignity at the prospect of a serial killer offing good Christian men, but you bothered to learn all about it, down to details about the choice of people to die, specific enough to know that you fit the profile."

"I'm not immune to pop culture."

"You don't have a clue why I target conservative assholes?"

Frank smiled. "I appreciate your candor. But no, I don't."

"I despise your hatred of gay and lesbian people. I wish I could rid the world of all of you."

"I don't des—"

Charon waved his finger in the air. "Don't even start with me. I don't want to hear your insipid justifications, or that bullshit about loving the sinner but hating the sin."

"Well enough." Still calm. Still no inflection in the voice. "So I'm not allowed to have a contrary point of view? Is that really worthy of death?"

"I'm not interested in a conversation about your free speech rights. Freedom and democracy are human contrivances that have no effect on me any longer. And I don't want some long drawn-out philosophical ruminations on the matter. You seem quite intelligent. You can guess my response."

Frank nodded. "About what I do to those who struggle with that issue. About my attempts to block laws that sanctify your unholy relationships. Probably."

"Good. Then how would you like to die?"

"I don't get a chance to repent or plead my case?"

"No." Charon stood up. "Because any repentance would be for show, not real. And this isn't a courtroom, with a law that we follow, and judge and jury. This is my form of justice. This is my decision to purge the world of a least one hatemonger."

"But what if I'm right, and you end up in hell because you ignored the Bible's injunction against lying with another man?"

Charon laughed. "That would be the least of my worries."

Still, Frank amused him more than most victims. Charon admired his quiet dignity and continued self-assurance, even when faced with certain death. No groveling on the floor, begging for a second chance. No admission that he only did what he did to make a buck. Wrong though he was, at least he legitimately believed his homophobia.

So Charon moved swiftly across the room and drank the pastor's blood until he died, peacefully in Charon's arms. He staged the body as if sitting in his chair, reviewing his sermon for that night. Charon surveyed the small office, unsure if the authorities or media would even pick up on this year's Christmas Eve killing. It would appear like a heart attack or stroke, something quite natural. But Frank earned that dignity, too, even if it meant no one learned the truth.

"I know the truth."

Charon jumped so high his head almost went through the church ceiling. He spun around to find Vampire Stalker staring at him, with almost the same complacent but sad face Frank carried throughout their conversation.

"Why didn't you stop me?" Charon regained his composure and stood defiantly in front of him.

"To show you that I'm not the Council. I don't necessarily love all of their rules, either. I don't approve of this"—Stalker pointed to the victim—"but I'm not a judge sent to impose my will upon you, either."

Charon walked out of the church at a human pace with his little friend following quietly alongside. "Are you going to explain this game finally?"

"Maybe."

Charon rolled his eyes and mocked the whiny voice. "Maybe." He sighed. "What the fuck does that mean? Maybe. Either do, or don't. This gets tiring."

"Do, or do not. There is no try." Stalker deadpanned Yoda's voice.

Despite himself and his annoyance, Charon laughed. This one, much as he accused Charon of it, knew the art of seduction far better.

Vampire Stalker stopped so Charon did, too. He glanced around and then patted his leg. "Come." That dog, the one Charon suspected of being a vampire, came sprinting over and sat beside him. "I'm tired of keeping it from you, too. But until I know that I can convince you, I have to wait."

Before Charon could react with either his vampire speed or magic, Vampire Stalker and his dog completely disappeared.

PART EIGHT: REVELATIONS

Chapter Thirty-Seven: New Year's Eve

31 DECEMBER 2014

Nederland, Colorado

Charon grinned at the bombshell sitting across from him as the man squinted in confusion. Not the brightest bulb in the box, but boy, was he easy on the eyes. Tall, blond, with piercing blue eyes that stared back at Charon as Kevin fidgeted with the zipper on his jacket. He carried the lean muscular-but-athletic build of a basketball player, and his beard appeared to be trimmed carefully.

"I mean, I know I agreed to it and all, but I thought you kidded me. Like, who really has a hidden castle and could run that fast, carrying me? I expected a game for the night. Something fun. Not for it to be true. Actually, you know, I don't even do these things very often. Too scared, I guess."

Charon nodded. "I understand your confusion. It sounds fanciful to my ears, too, if I think about how I'd react in your situation. Still, now that you've had time to process it, the offer stands. No more worrying about playing it straight. No more concern about your basketball teammates catching onto your true identity. It will certainly cause a scandal that you vanished into thin air, never to be seen again, but really, isn't that what you want? Exactly what you pled for when we went up to my room?"

Earlier that evening, Charon had pretended Kevin and he accidentally met in the hotel bar, though in truth the vampire had stalked this one throughout the night after first seeing him. Alone. Lustfully glancing about, but afraid. Charon even pricked his arm to taste the blood and saw more deeply into Kevin's soul, about his wish to make out with guys and leave the ultra-straight jock life behind. Despite his outward confidence, he lacked any courage to carry through with it.

Armed with that intimate knowledge, Charon had seduced Kevin and, in the afterglow of sex, offered to bring him on board as another one of the boys. A tad older than the rest, probably in his late twenties, but not in terms of maturity. And emotionally, he appeared far behind most of them. Besides, Charon had promised the gaggle of young men in his employ a present for New Year's Eve. They would never believe it came in the form of a hot athlete.

It ended with a love-crossed Kevin agreeing to the conditions of employment, the same all the boys agreed to before coming here, but now Kevin had to cope with the truth of the whole thing. Because he had acted alone this time, Charon had forgotten how Jordan prepared each one in advance for the truth, to avoid dealing with the shock that Kevin manifested. Charon saw that he had pressed the issue too hard in the hotel room, that he'd hurried the situation along, but Kevin had been set to depart the next morning and Charon had wanted to meet his own promise to bring the boys a gift. It all required a haphazard negotiation. Lesson learned, Charon decided—never again attempt to bring a new one on board without Jordan's involvement. He'd just been lucky with Todd.

Kevin jumped off the couch in Charon's bedroom and paced back and forth. Charon stood up, too, and grabbed the man by both shoulders, pulling him into a hug.

He kissed his neck and caressed his back. "Relax."

"It's just a lot."

"I know." Charon moved his hand up and down his back. "But, as we also discussed, once you got here, once you agreed to the conditions and I brought you to the castle, there's no way to reverse the decision."

Kevin stepped away, but a wry grin spread across his lips. "It is liberating. I mean, right, it's what I wanted?" He ran his hands through his hair. "Still. Wow. But, like, you carried me here easily. I guess you also meant that you'd kill me if I decided to back out. It's either join your harem or die."

Charon laughed. "I never called it a harem."

"Yeah, well, it kinda sounds that way."

"I also explained that you'd be a leader here. Other than Jordan, who remains in charge, they'll look up to you. You're the only celebrity they'll ever meet."

Kevin blushed. "Then I'd rather not, you know, take it up the ass."

Charon roared a laugh. "That, my friend, is up to you. Like earlier with me, you could merely exist on blow jobs the rest of your life. No rape is allowed here. True, you're imprisoned. But in a strange way, it comes with the ultimate freedom. Few obligations. No public to taunt you. No worry about coming out to the world."

Kevin smiled. "Got it." He glanced around the room. "So, like, you're going to present me like you brought them a new puppy? Can I at least clean up first?"

"By all means." Charon motioned toward the bathroom. "Towels and everything you need are in there. I'll wait here."

As he waited, Charon flopped onto the couch and grabbed the formal invitation that sat on the coffee table. In addition to being a first-rate seductress, Vampire Stalker showed a sense of humor. After disappearing on Christmas Eve, he wrote to Charon that they should wait until after the holidays to resume their tête-à-tête. He had left Charon alone until this morning when the invitation appeared in Charon's hand through magic.

On heavy stock paper, as if inviting him to a royal wedding, Vampire Stalker offered the following:

My Dearest Fiend,

Now that I know you a bit better, I imagine that this invitation will require a good deal of negotiating. I understand how you operate, and I think you gained a sense for the same in me. Thus the quite formal invitation to enter this back and forth about when, where, and how to meet. I am inviting Your Majesty to sit down with me, and only the most formal of announcements will do.

The reason for my seeking your assistance—or perhaps more accurately, cooperation—grows more urgent, though not yet at a panic level.

Thus, if you would be so kind, state your terms and conditions. I will start by promising to meet you alone, without my friends from the Vampire Council. I do request a public setting, not so that you can injure and maim the innocent, but for my own protection. Respond at your leisure. As agreed upon when last we chatted, I think this can wait until after the holidays. Perhaps in the spring?

Charon tossed the invitation aside. He decided that he would, indeed, agree to terms and conditions and then meet Vampire Stalker to hear his story. For some reason, which perhaps defied logic or disregarded his own safety too easily, Charon trusted him not to involve the Council, not to attack, or in any way threaten Charon. After playing the game for this long, more than anything, Charon wanted to learn the madness behind the flirtation.

Kevin emerged from the bathroom with nothing but a towel wrapped around his waist. "What do you want me to wear?"

"I don't mind you that way." Charon grinned.

Kevin smiled back. "Yeah, but, uh, I'm not real comfortable meeting a bunch of guys this way."

"I thought you hung out with guys that way all the time?"

"Yeah, well, the locker room is hardly erotic, and no one's checking me out."

"No one that you know of."

Kevin laughed slightly. "Right. So, I have to go this way?"

Charon shook his head. "I was messing with you. Around here, you can wear whatever you want. I'll warn you that they keep the temperature of the palace roaring hot, like a desert, as if we lived right on the equator."

"Why do they do that?" Kevin scratched his head.

"Because they prefer to wear as little as possible. Most gallivant about in their underwear. Some go naked half the time. Occasionally, they decide to wear designer clothes, but that has nothing to do with modesty and everything to do with vanity. Anyway, what do you want to wear? You can also make a list of what you want on a permanent basis, and I'll bring it to you tomorrow. I completely forgot to get you anything. You're by far the tallest one around here, so I'm not sure what will fit you."

"Gym shorts or something? And a T-shirt? That's all I really need."

Charon walked over to his dresser and opened a drawer. "That, I can accommodate." He threw a plain light blue T-shirt across the room, followed by a pair of red shorts.

Kevin dropped his towel right in front of Charon, not in an enticing way, but just like he did a million times in the locker room in front of guys. He snapped the elastic band around his waist to indicate the completion of getting dressed, then held his arms out and displayed himself to Charon.

"Well, how does the new puppy look?"

"Ravishing. Let's go."

Charon led Kevin out of his quarters, down the stairs, and headed toward Jordan's room. They found Jordan, uncharacteristically sitting by himself in bed and reading a novel. As usual, he wore nothing but a very tight and very seductive pair of hot pink underwear. Jordan spied over the top of his novel after they walked in, then dropped his book and sat up when he saw Charon and Kevin.

"Boss man! You should have warned me of your approach. I would've done something more appropriate, like start to jack off or something." He spoke to Charon but looked Kevin up and down the entire time. "And who, pray tell, is this delish boy toy you brought to me? Ginormous. Look what he's doing to me!" Jordan pointed to his underwear, where the tip of his now-hardened cock peeked out at them.

Charon grinned but shook his head. "I'm afraid that living here and being in charge has made a barbarian of you. Would you not intimidate the poor boy before he even gets used to this place?" He walked over and pinched the tip of the pink member as it stuck out.

"Ouch! Warn me before we do S&M."

"Get up. This is Kevin. He's our newest addition. You'll have to acclimate him to the place, show him around, give him the rules and regulations, blah, blah, blah. But not tonight, okay? Spare him tonight."

"What's up with tonight, then?" Jordan bounced out of bed and walked around Kevin, continuing to check him out. Still rock hard.

Kevin, the poor dear, stood paralyzed. He glanced around, smiled at Jordan's antics, but otherwise looked as if Charon had brought a statue into the room.

"The New Year's Eve present I promised." Charon motioned to Kevin, who squirmed at the attention.

Jordan whistled. "Cray-cray. Like, I got ready for a chill-tastic TV or gaming system. Maybe new underwear." He licked his lips. "But this. Wicked."

"Wicked indeed. Now stop making him uncomfortable."

"Does he talk?" Jordan leaned against Kevin, attempting to discreetly check out his package but failing miserably at the discretion part.

"Yeah, I talk. When I feel like it. Just not sure, you know, in this situation."

"Nice to meet you." Jordan snapped out of whore behavior and into pleasant host mode, even sticking out his hand to shake Kevin's.

As they shook hands, Jordan pulled Kevin closer, staring into his eyes and causing his penis to spring out the top of the pink thong. Now able to observe their interaction more closely because Jordan took over, it pleased Charon to see the evidence of Kevin's returned interest in Jordan. No doubt these two would fuck their brains out eventually. Or now.

"Would you two like a moment alone before we go to the others?"

Kevin's cheeks turned bright red, while Jordan just snickered.

"Sure." Jordan shrugged. "What do you think?" he asked Kevin.

"Sure."

"Such enthusiasm." Charon rolled his eyes. "I'll go gather the boys. Don't take long."

"Dude"—Jordan pushed Charon toward the door—"this one will make me shoot in like two seconds. No worries." He closed the door once Charon stood in the hall.

The evening proceeded delightfully after Jordan emerged with Kevin. They introduced him to everyone, again causing Kevin to turn bright red at all the attention. And then they partied 2014 out of existence and ushered in 2015. Most of them wore party hats and diapers, to honor the New Year's Baby, and nothing else. Naturally, it devolved into a complete bacchanal, which Charon enjoyed immensely before retiring when his body signaled the approaching sun.

Chapter Thirty-Eight: The Agreement

3 JANUARY 2015

Nederland, Colorado

After exchanging a couple of magical notes, Charon grew annoyed with how long it might take for Vampire Stalker and him to agree on a meeting time, place, and the other conditions if they must write back and forth, even with the element of enchantment. He therefore proposed they take the interaction to a new level of tricks. Both agreed to project themselves into the room of the other in order to hold a proper conversation.

A few seconds later, Vampire Stalker appeared in Charon's study as an apparition, standing before him as if he'd just walked into the room. He looked like a ghost, because Charon could see through him, while at the same time make out his exact features and see his facial expressions. Charon assumed that he materialized in much the same way on the other end.

When Vampire Stalker stared into Charon's eyes, he giggled, then hunched over and grew serious, pointing at Charon, who sat casually in a chair.

"Lord Vader, rise," he deadpanned in the voice of the Emperor.

Despite the childish reference, Charon laughed loudly. "You look more like a ghost or something come to haunt me."

"Nah, Star Wars is way more cool."

"Yeah, well, I'm not afraid of the Emperor. And I won't convert to goodness at the end, like Darth Vader. And I certainly won't do your bidding. Though you do a good Yoda, too."

"Star Wars taught me everything I need to know in life." Vampire Stalker laughed and shook his head. "Anyway, you're defensive a lot."

Charon shrugged, a bit stung by the accusation. Vampire Stalker had a way about him, as if he saw into Charon's soul or attempted to know him in some intimate way that unnerved Charon. It struck him at that moment that he acted like Bill, allowing Charon his space but always seeming to peer more deeply into his psyche. Or into his very soul. And, as with Bill throughout college and right up until the moment he'd left those millions for Bill and allowed him his ministry in Bay City, Michigan, Charon reacted by dismissing the thought from his mind. Unfortunately, a part of him began to accept the truth of it, which he hated even more.

"Can you sit down?" Charon asked, irritated. "We need to be on equal footing, or we're already done with this negotiation."

Vampire Stalker grinned but obeyed, somehow pulling a chair over and sitting right in front of Charon, so that their knees practically touched in the vision.

"Better?" he asked.

"Better."

"Sorry I hit a nerve."

"You can just leave if you came as my psychologist."

Again Vampire Stalker laughed. "I'm done. To business, then." He sat up straight in the chair and mocked tightening a tie around his neck, despite the fact he wore a nice sweater and tight pair of jeans.

Charon laughed. This one entertained him even as he annoyed the shit out of him. "So what is this about?"

Vampire Stalker shook a finger at Charon. "That's for when we meet. I'd be more comfortable going over that face to face. Today, we set up the terms and conditions."

"This sounds like a diplomatic negotiation between countries."

"Well, it is complicated. We're not just two blokes out to chat or hook up. We're both vampires. And extremely powerful ones with magic. Right? And, we're meeting for a specific purpose, each with a threat against the other. I could expose you to the Council, even if it created a vampire war. And you could maraud around and kill innocent people, more than you already do, which would kill me inside. So, in a sense, it *is* a diplomatic negotiation."

"Point taken." Charon nodded. "So how do we proceed? I'm not necessarily a student of international relations."

"Let's start with the nuts and bolts. How about this: are you available to meet at ten on January 30th? p.m. obviously. In New York City?"

"Let me ask my secretary." They both laughed. "I think I can manage that."

"Great!"

"Where, specifically?"

"The Brooklyn Bridge. It's beautiful, with great views. Public, for the safety of each other. Yet anonymous enough, especially at this time of year, because most people will hurry across or run out and take a picture, then head to some warm place. Only fools, or perhaps vampires, would linger on it and risk freezing their asses off."

"Vampires don't get cold."

"I believe that was part of my point."

"Okay. Cool."

"Okay. Cool." Vampire Stalker mimicked Charon but smiled, then laughed a little.

"What's that about?"

He shrugged. "Just that sometimes, for a gay guy, you act like a frat boy jock. Maybe trying too hard for cool and casual? Or maybe that's just you."

"There you go again, trying to be my therapist."

Vampire Stalker held up his hands. "Relax. I think it's hot. We're cool."

God, this one so enticed Charon. He infuriated him but at the same time called to him. He wanted to choke him. And then Charon wanted to pull him into the most passionate kiss he could imagine.

"So, uh, that's good. We already ended our negotiations. Time, place, all set." Charon acted to end the conversation by beginning to stand up.

"Not so fast. We have a couple other items."

Charon rested back into his chair. "Like?"

Vampire Stalker sighed. "We just both need to understand the situation. On the one hand, I want to solicit your services, which brought me to you in the first place. However, I won't pretend that you have total authority. I just want to get that straight from the beginning. You're not all-powerful to me."

"Yeah, you're a warlock." Charon smirked. "Got it. Me, too. All even."

He shook his head. "That's only part of the point, isn't it? Both vampires. Both know powerful magic. So it puts us on a level playing field. Except you're willing to attack the innocent, and I can't abide that. So in your mind, you have the upper hand."

Charon smiled in agreement.

"But don't forget, I have the Vampire Council." Vampire Stalker let those words sink in as he stared across at Charon. "To this point, I kept you secret from them because I believe with all my heart that we need you, and that you'll be willing to help, once you hear about the danger. But I do have limits. I can find you. And I therefore could lead them to you. It wouldn't be hard for them to discover what you've done. That you exist off their radar. Do you understand?"

Charon lost the smile on his face. This one played a coy game and shrewdly calculated at every turn. He was all business now, and Charon detested being put in his place by anyone. "Fine."

"Before you start pouting or want to run away and not meet me, can we talk about one more thing?"

"You're getting on my nerves." Charon felt like a caged and threatened tiger.

"Because you're not in control. And it makes you feel vulnerable and exposed." Again Vampire Stalker sounded so much like Bill. "Do you know how I discovered you?"

Charon shrugged. "Magic, I assume."

"Kind of, but not really. It was actually by chance. I felt your presence in Michigan. Last spring. I was there and watched you make a kill, fascinated that you were a vampire but gave off no vampire vibe. Nothing to alert me to your presence, like I should have felt from any other vampire. I was totally awed by the fact that you existed outside of the Vampire Council. You're right, I detected a strong magic somewhere. I was actually about twenty miles away, and just felt your presence. So I went to investigate, and imagine my surprise to find a vampire at the other end. I may have left it at that. I may or may not have told the Council anything, but then I saw you give that man all that money. A friend of yours, I assume."

Bill. Even though Charon left him securely in the past and with a fortune to accomplish all his dreams and help people, he haunted Charon. Perhaps Bill possessed a power of his own, without even knowing it.

"So you're a spy, as well as a witch and vampire. Congratulations." Charon stood up to end the conversation once again.

Vampire Stalker did not move. "I monitored you for a few days after, then followed you to Romania. That's when I began stalking you, as you so charmingly put it. I did it partially because of the danger we face and the help you could give us. That's where your power comes into the equation. But I also felt kind of bad for you."

Charon laughed. "For me? Why on earth would you feel that way about me? You've no cause for concern in that regard, I assure you."

"Of course that's what you want everyone to think. But Bill was right. You're lonely. Not alone. You mingle with people. Fuck the boys left and right. Still, there's more to you, if you'd dig into that loneliness."

Charon smiled. "I'm afraid you read that incorrectly. Besides, I now have my boys with me. I can go to them whenever I want. I'm hardly alone."

Just like Bill, Vampire Stalker smiled indulgently, clearly disagreeing but not pushing the issue further. Good. Time for him to go.

"Are you done now? I thought we established that you're not my psychologist."

He grinned. "And I'm not. So I'll see you on the 30th?"

"On the Brooklyn Bridge, where we'll pretend to freeze our asses off like humans, just to maintain the secrecy. Got it."

"Good. Thanks."

Charon moved toward the apparition who now stood. Mere inches from Vampire Stalker, close enough that if they actually stood in the same room they would feel each other's body heat and perhaps get aroused by the proximity, Charon whispered to him.

"Two can play at that game. Because you like me. You don't want me to know it, and you don't like to admit it to yourself. But part of what prompted you to follow me is your attraction to me. I know it. You want me." He blew him a kiss.

"Good night." The corner of Vampire Stalker's lip curled up, almost ready to smile, and with that, he vanished.

Chapter Thirty-Nine: His Boys

17 January 2015

Nederland, Colorado

Charon looked around his living room, at all the boys laughing and playing games, and smiled to himself. How absurd for Vampire Stalker, who only watched him from afar and hardly knew him, to think Charon lived a lonely life.

Bill, too, just never understood. He made deep connections with the people around him, wanted to know their inner feelings and become as intimate as possible with everyone he met. That was his personality. That motivated him. He always assumed that everyone needed that, and then projected onto Charon how he would feel if he lived like Charon.

Charon surrounded himself with people when needed, but he did not care the same way about their deepest emotion and secret dreams. He enjoyed moving from one group to the other, having fun, having sex, relishing life and moving on. Being free of attachments liberated him. It freed him to explore the world and his own lusts and passions. He could pick up and move at a moment's notice.

And it allowed him to get people out of the way who no longer served a purpose or who might block what he wanted.

Besides, now as a vampire, with the world at his fingertips, he glanced at the lovely specimens before him. They gave him company. They became his latest fraternity, if you will. He loved their energy and passion. Their constant hormones in complete overdrive, and even just their simple tastes or desires that he met with what he brought them and with the world he created inside his palace.

He hardly felt alone with them around and at his disposal at any moment.

"Come on," Joe landed on Charon's lap, with his long dreadlocks tickling Charon's chest, his soft skin enticing. "Play with us. It's fun."

"Why would we need to play bowling on the Wii and force the loser to take off an article of clothing, when we could all just strip down and get at it? Besides, everyone's wearing nothing but a swimsuit because this is your beach party, so it'd take one loss to get to the nudity. Might as well just rip 'em off." Charon snapped the elastic on his swimsuit and wound Joe's hair around one of his fingers.

Joe smiled and then pinched Charon on the cheek. "You don't get it. Arousal. Heighten the anticipation. Besides, yeah, the swimsuit comes off quickly enough, but then if you lose again, it's like truth or dare, only without the truth. Just the dare. So lose a second time, and bend over, baby, I'm going to fuck you up the ass." That made Joe laugh really hard.

Charon held him down and tickled him until he cried out to be let go. Joe rolled away from Charon, then launched back at him and kissed him. "At least watch us play."

"Okay. I'll referee."

Charon enjoyed watching them play their silly game, particularly the dare part, and laughed as everyone had a good time in the palace. "Whoa!" he screamed out. "Penalty!"

Everyone turned to him, wondering what was up, some almost fearing that Charon was actually angry.

"Benjamin, come here."

Benjamin reluctantly put down his controller and walked his slight body over to Charon. His brown eyes grew wider and wider as he got closer. Instead of relaxing all of them, Charon heightened the tension with a quiet and steady gaze. Benjamin bowed his head.

"What did you do wrong?" Charon asked.

Benjamin only shrugged in answer. But when his hands began to tremble, Charon took pity on him. "You intentionally missed that last shot. As referee, I know who plays that game the best. I know the one of you who never misses. And I also know who was getting frustrated that everyone else lost their swimsuit and moved on to wonderful dares, while that hot little cock in your shorts was bursting to get out. You cheated. So I get to punish you."

By the end of the monologue, most of the others smiled and started laughing, followed by Benjamin who looked up with a twinkle in his eye. "You can't prove it."

"I don't need proof. As a penalty, you have to do five dares in a row, but you must keep your swimsuit on for the rest of the game."

Everyone laughed hard except Benjamin, who screamed, "No! That's cruel and unusual punishment!"

But he obeyed, and everyone enjoyed the challenge of coming up with tasks for poor cheating Benjamin that also forced him to remain in his trunks.

The rest of the night passed in much the same way, with their beach party in full swing, and Charon either watching or participating, depending on his whim. Sometimes it almost acted like an old-school bacchanal, with nothing more than alcohol and sex fueling the festivities. But just as quickly they reverted to childhood, at one point all playing board games on the floor.

As Charon sat, watching big burly Alex teach little missionary Todd how to play chess, a wave of melancholy hit Charon. He worried little about sickness, since they lived a completely quarantined life down here. And none apparently brought any serious virus or disease with them. But he looked at Kevin, the oldest of them, and saw the ever-so-slight signs of aging on his late-twenties face, more a man than the cherubic others, regardless of their build and background. What would become of them, as the years went by?

And what did Charon intend to do about it? Replace them at some point? Set up a retirement ward on one of the floors? Would they die off and leave him alone?

Damn Bill and Vampire Stalker. They planted this seed of doubt in his mind. They ruined his night of pure revelry with their hints about Charon being alone and longing for something. He refuted them, quite honestly, with the number of people and ways that he surrounded himself with what he wanted, including his harem of fine boys. Until he accidentally glimpsed into the future just now and started to wonder about their fates.

Charon left the room and went to the wine cellar, picking one of the most expensive bottles of the lot, one he had stolen from the owner of a professional football team one night after the guy snubbed a fan because the poor little girl wanted an autograph. It'd pissed Charon off, so he had followed him home and robbed him of a number of precious items. He'd just tossed the Super Bowl ring in the river.

He uncorked it, smelled the delicious aroma, and swished it in his glass. The first taste, just a tad bitter, promised a wonderful and full Meritage once it breathed for a bit. He took the bottle and his glass back to the living room to continue his contemplations.

Melancholy gave way to a plan, or at least an idea, about what he might want to do. The obvious answer hit Charon before he even went to get his wine bottle. Convert them. Turn them all into vampires. Freeze those lovely faces and bodies at this very moment, and never worry about needing to replace them or watch them grow old or get sick.

Yet that obvious answer presented just as many problems. Sure, it would free them from death, and liberate Charon from watching them age. But it might also, quite literally, liberate them. He could avoid teaching them magic, but even just turning them into vampires would allow them to escape. And, with whatever blood or alchemy converted them into the undead, the Vampire Council could suddenly sniff them out. Suddenly, instead of autonomy from the damn Council and just having to worry about whatever the fuck Stalker wanted, Charon would have eleven minions running around, all capable of ratting him out, whether wittingly or by mistake. It risked too much.

Unless...

Charon grabbed his wine, kissed each of the boys good night, and hurried to his private quarters. He locked all the doors and went into his office, removed the life-size painting of a beautiful naked man from the wall, and entered the code to unlock the door to his secret lab. Not even Jordan knew this room existed, only Charon, because in here he practiced his magic and worked to invent any new potions or powers that he might desire.

Yes, he would convert them, but with a twist. First, he would figure out whatever magic Styx developed over all those decades that kept the conversion of Charon a secret from the Vampire Council. That way, he would have no concern about the Council finding out about all of them, and thus finding out about Charon. He also decided to change it from a potion that the person drank to a simpler spell that Charon could enchant. No more strange orange liquid that glowed. Then, once he secured that part of it, he would need to create his own spell, his own tweaking of the enchantment, to make sure he controlled all of them.

Charon went to work immediately. As with their coming to his underground palace in the first place, Charon would offer them a choice, of course. They could either remain as they were, human, living there and enjoying anything they wanted, and live out their lives in service to him as humans and never leaving. Or, he would offer to make them into vampires, but under the condition that they submit to his will, continue to live under his absolute authority.

Once transformed, they could leave the palace, perhaps with or without him. They could live forever. And the Vampire Council need never discover them or Charon. But he could determine when and how they left, what they did, and call them back to him whenever he wanted.

An army of sorts. Charon snickered at the idea of possessing his own army of twink vampires. Perhaps he would even call them the Twink Brigade, which made him laugh even harder.

He finished out that night with his experiment, getting close but not quite mastering it. He awoke the next evening and took the entire night doing the same. He recreated the liquid potion and then set to work on making it a spell instead. He got close. Very close. He knew because he could analyze his blood, not as some human scientist in a lab, but by a combination of lab experiment and magical analysis. In that way, he could actually see the spell. To make sure, he snuck down and with vampiric speed and took a couple of samples from two of the boys without their knowing. He could compare their human blood to his vampire blood. Then he mixed part of his blood with human blood and yelled in excitement.

That created vampire blood, but without the spell. Thus, he could magically see the difference between his concealed blood and the blood of an average vampire.

By the end of the third night, he perfected the ability to create a vampire that the Vampire Council would never detect, all with nothing more than saying the words in the right way as he called forth the magical elements around him.

Drinking the last glass of the beautiful wine that he had started at the beginning of this plot, he scoffed at Styx. Charon wondered about that one, again remembering the bouts of seeming insanity, such as the time he claimed butterflies flew out of his ass. How on earth had it taken Styx centuries to figure out the potion, despite his powers of witchcraft and hatred of the Council? Charon isolated it in a matter of days and then transformed it even further.

True, he looked for something that already existed in his own blood, but still. Too easy. Styx proved more and more a goof than anything. A sadistic one. A sad one, given the loss of his true love. But a complete goof nonetheless.

Over the next few nights, Charon backed off some of his judgments about Styx because of his own failures in attaching new magic to the formula that concealed him from the Council. He tested a few versions on victims, whom he converted into vampires but failed to control, and thus killed them. Some middle-aged man in Greeley. An elderly woman in Estes Park. A homeless person in Longmont. He came close on the last one, who came to him, but it only lasted a minute before he tried to flee and forced Charon to exterminate him.

Close. Oh so close. Charon wanted nothing more than to perfect his experiment without interruption, especially because he would bet all his Bitcoin that he knew exactly how to fix it, but alas the calendar turned to January 29th, and he had a rendezvous the following evening.

To amuse himself, especially in the event that Vampire Stalker annoyed him, he also continued his plot to steal *The Starry Night* from the Museum of Modern Art in New York City. Might as well take advantage of being there to finish off that charade.

Walking through the streets of that vibrant city before going to rest for the day, Charon thought nothing about feeding, nor did any of the hot men tempt him into sex, because he focused on nothing more than his potion. Converting his boys now consumed him.

Indeed, he wanted nothing more than to wake that evening, have his meeting on the Brooklyn Bridge with Vampire Stalker, and then hurry back to Colorado to complete his mission. He smiled to himself, for just before the sun's light rose high above Charon, who hid in his own secret underground New York shelter, the enchantment came to him. The exact words that he was sure could accomplish his goal.

Chapter Forty: Rendezvous on the Brooklyn Bridge

30 JANUARY 2015

New York City, New York

Charon woke in his New York lair excited when he remembered the enchantment that came to him as he fell asleep that morning. The magical principles formed before his eyes, and he knew without even testing it that he had figured out the solution to his problem. He wanted nothing more than to hurry to demonstrate it, especially with all the worthy subjects running around this city upon which to experiment.

He stopped, however, when he remembered why he had come to New York in the first place. His meeting with Vampire Stalker. And as much as he wanted to assess the validity of his spell, he wondered if that little magical twink would watch him from afar and scold him, if his actions would somehow impinge upon this meeting at the Brooklyn Bridge.

Because as much as he wanted to see if he'd figured out how to convert his boys by concealing them from the Vampire Council but still beholding them to himself, he also wanted to at last find out what so fascinated Stalker about him.

He woke a few hours earlier than the planned rendezvous, so Charon walked at a human pace through the streets of New York, taking in the people, the scenery, the bustling energy. He enjoyed a good visit to this great place, though truth be told, he could only take a few days of it before the solitude and quiet life of Colorado called to him. The bustle of energy excited him, sucked him in, until all at once it overwhelmed him and forced him to flee to solitude. He swore that even deep underground the city's cacophony of noises flooded his senses.

Everyone hurried along tonight, with the chill wind cutting them to the bone. Charon forgot his coat and so snatched one from a coat rack when he walked past a high-end restaurant, using his supernatural speed to avoid detection. He hardly needed protection from the cold but looked too conspicuous meandering about in nothing but a sweater when everyone else froze their nuts off.

Every restaurant looked packed with smiling and laughing people. A romantic couple sat in a window, chatting away. Next to them, an elderly gay couple toasted. As he moved into a warehouse district, fewer people bustled by, but trucks still drove around and a few workers finished their jobs.

At a little before the appointed hour, Charon arrived below the Brooklyn Bridge and peered up at its majesty. So solid. It soared out over the river, seeming to defy gravity. The brick appeared solid, as if nothing could take it down. He wished for more time to sit and admire its beauty, its old charm and charisma. He loved that they constructed it with flare, that it functioned as art as well as for transportation. Too many things today went up simply to function, like a concrete mass that transported vehicles from one side of a river to the next without making a statement.

But there, standing as if anyone might do such a thing on this night, he spotted Vampire Stalker, looking out over the river at the skyline, seeming very human in his deep contemplation. His curly hair blew back in the wind. Like Charon, he wore a winter coat but, so typical of a vampire lost in his own world, wore no hat or gloves. Come to mention it, neither did Charon. Vampire Stalker was so hot. So alluring.

Their magical worlds suddenly collided as Charon thought about him, because he jerked his head over and stared directly at Charon. Charon waved slightly, and Vampire Stalker tilted his head and smiled.

Charon determined at least one thing that needed to come from this meeting. Stalker must have a real name, and since he knew so much about Charon already, Charon wanted to learn that much about him.

When Charon stood on the bridge next to him seconds later, they smiled awkwardly at one another and shifted back and forth. Gay friends might hug, straight dudes and acquaintances fist bump or shake hands. Neither seemed appropriate. So instead they nodded and began nonchalantly walking across the bridge, as if two guys just out for the night.

"I thought you might back out," Vampire Stalker said.

Charon laughed. "I'm too intrigued. I want to know what this is all about. But I'm going to set down the first condition of our meeting."

Stalker grinned. "What's that?"

"I want to know your name. In my mind, I call you Vampire Stalker. But that doesn't seem appropriate anymore."

"Vampire Stalker?" He laughed really hard. "Yeah, I'd rather you just call me Jaret. This isn't some twisted love scene, or some vampire serial killer episode."

"Jaret?" Charon asked. "That's your name? Or did you make that up to heighten the mystery?"

Again he laughed. "Jaret's my name. Given by my mother. You're the one who likes mystery in your name. Would you prefer that I call you Charon or Blade Haden?"

Charon stopped at the sound of his actual name. At first he wanted to lash out, but then he shook his head and smiled. "See. That's why I needed to know your name. You know everything about me, it seems. Calling you Jaret feels like it levels the playing field. Even though you're otherwise a complete mystery."

"I like it that way." Jaret grinned, almost like an evil villain. "Anything else before we get started?"

Charon shrugged. "Not that I can think of."

"We agreed on a few things. We're both vampires." Jaret walked over to the edge of the walkway, pausing to look at the New York skyline. "And magically, I think we match up pretty well. So really, we're on equal footing. That's important here."

"Not totally equal." Charon leaned toward Jaret, so their shoulders touched, just to test how much flirting he could get away with. "You have the threat of exposing me to the Vampire Council. That gives you one up. It's one of the reasons I kept my distance."

Jaret shook his head. "I get what you mean, but think of it this way. First, I'm asking a favor of you. That's the whole point of our meeting." Charon took note that he answered without moving away, if anything pressing back into Charon. "Threatening you might push you away. And then there's the matter of what you might do to innocent people to get away or stop me. I don't want you to go on some rampage because you're afraid of me. I like you. So don't worry."

"That reminds me. I have one more thing before I hear about this favor you want. It's not so much a condition as a curiosity."

"What's that?" Jaret tilted his head toward Charon as he asked the question and smiled.

"Why do you always look at me that way? This sometimes feels more like a seduction than a business deal, despite your protests to the contrary."

Jaret grinned widely. "I think you're totally hot. Incredibly so. I go for strong bad boys. In control. So, yeah, I enjoy flirting with you. Like I said, though, it's not going anywhere because I'd never betray my hubby. Still, as my best friend says, you can be on a diet and still read the menu."

This time Charon roared with laughter. "You may give me the worst case of blue balls ever."

"I doubt you ever go to bed unsatisfied. Any number of boys around here would swallow your load in two seconds. What's your other condition?"

"Curiosity. Not condition." Charon held a finger in the air to emphasize the correction. "What's your association with the Vampire Council?"

Jaret nodded. "It's complicated. Like I said, I'm not on it." Jaret began walking again when a couple people went rushing by, bundled up against the harsh wind. "But my husband is."

"The blond bombshell I saw you with in Washington?"

"Yep." Jaret turned and wiggled his eyebrows at Charon. "Hot, isn't he?"

"Yeah." Charon rolled his eyes. "And most certainly a top, so not compatible with me."

"Right. But that helps us get along." Jaret leaned into Charon, then placed his head on Charon's arm as they continued to walk.

Charon gritted his teeth. "You're an asshole."

"What?"

"Blue balls."

Again Jaret laughed. "Okay. I'll stop." He straightened up. "Also, my best friends, at least most of them, they're on the Council. But here's the thing. Sometimes I agree with them. Sometimes I don't. Kind of like with you." Again he leaned into Charon. "Sometimes I like you. Sometimes I think you're a raging prick. Sometimes you're just evil. Actually, that's kinda how I see the Council."

They walked in silence a bit farther.

Charon finally reached out and grabbed Jaret's arm to stop them. "So, what's this about? If it's not about you just teasing me until I go mad, what?"

"Should we go somewhere else to talk?"

"I don't suppose you'd come to my lair? I won't rape you."

Jaret laughed. "First, you wouldn't be able to before I ripped your head off. Don't underestimate the incredibly strong blood that converted me. Second, I might enjoy it so don't even tempt me." He held out his hand. "Lead the way."

Safely in his underground bunker, Charon rethought having so easily given up his secret location. But as he poured wine, one of his best bottles, he figured Jaret could have found him anyway.

Comfortably sitting across from each other in fashionable chairs, Charon lifted his glass in the air. "To your proposal."

Jaret clinked their glasses together and sat back. "This is good shit."

Charon, once again, laughed at him. "Sometimes you act and sound ancient. Other times no older than me."

"The ancient part comes from the dudes I hang with. They *are* ancient. You and me? We're probably about the same age."

"Since you'll escape before the sun rises, you'd better make your pitch."

"Let's cut to the chase. The Vampire Council has a secret from everyone. I mean from all the vampires. It started a few years ago, but it came to their close attention about a year ago. They've kept the whole thing hush-hush. They don't want a bunch of panicked fucking vampires running around. That would not be good. Second, they need to devise a plan of attack, and would rather surprise the enemy than give away what they already know. See, a war's brewing. Between vampires and a force that could actually bring us down. Whacked, fucking crazy Christians. The conservative ones. But get this, they have magic. And we think, a vampire on their side. So there's a war coming. A vicious one."

Charon took a moment to let that sink in.

"Sounds nuts, right?" Jaret grinned. "I mean, a possible supernatural war between vampires and right-wing Christians, with a renegade vampire on their side?"

"Batshit crazy. But I believe you." Charon refilled their glasses. As he poured into Jaret's glass, he asked, "And what does this war have to do with me?"

Jaret sipped his wine. "You're threatened, too. But that's not why I stalked you. Which, by the way, it was more trailing you, like a detective, than stalking. Anyway, I'm seeking your assistance, and it has to be on the down low, because I don't entirely agree with the Council's approach to this coming fight. Too careful. Too restrictive. This is war, and we need everything we can get to fight it. Including you. If you'll agree to help, I'll coordinate things with you but not tell them. You survive by helping make sure vampires win, but the Council won't be any the wiser." Jaret paused. He cleared his throat. "Finally, you'll need your boys converted to being vampires. Your spell works." Jaret stood and straightened his pants. "I gotta go. So Anthony won't get suspicious."

"Anthony? That's your man?"

Jaret smiled. "Yep. Why aren't you freaking out?"

"About the war? Because it's not completely real to me yet. We'll get to that eventually."

Jaret shook his head. "Not that. About the fact I knew about your plans with your harem?"

"It's because you're a fucking witch. And I'm kind of used to that with you." Charon stood and walked with Jaret toward the exit. "I assume we'll have to meet, when this gets going? For you to tell me more about it, fill me in on the Council's plan, and then explain what in the hell I can do with my army?" Charon did feel a little odd that he so completely and quickly believed everything Jaret just told him. He trusted this one, which was rare in his life.

"Yep. We'll talk. We've got a couple months. Oh, and, uh, if you don't mind my saying. The other thing about you bringing over the boys is, well, that's a good move for you. Maybe figuring yourself out some more."

Charon rolled his eyes. Not this again. He handed Jaret his coat. "I'm willing to consider assisting, under the terms you outlined that keep my identity a secret. Even from your lover."

"Especially him. Believe me." Jaret rolled his eyes.

Again they stood awkwardly at the tunnel leading to the real world above, their strange relationship making the appropriate farewell ambiguous at best.

To Charon's surprise, Jaret took control of the situation. He leaned forward, stood on his tiptoes, and planted a light but sensuous kiss right on Charon's lips. Without another word, he pulled away, winked at Charon, and sped away as he laughed.

Charon touched his fingers to his lips, as if trying to keep the essence of Jaret with him. Strange, the effect that one had on him. It almost made him want to obey the Council so they could become friends.

Fuck that. Instead, Charon vowed to complete his plan to steal *The Starry Night* before he left New York. He'd been working on his scheme for months, especially flirting with Tricia and mapping out the building, just like an elaborate plot from a movie. Instead of using his vampiric speed, he staged this as if a common criminal did it, even used his real name, since otherwise Blade Haden was dead. All this just to enjoy himself, but now he wanted to complete the project just to spite Vampire Stalker. Besides, he needed a present for the boys when he announced their invitation to transform into vampires.

Chapter Forty-One: From Harem to Brigade

1 FEBRUARY 2015

Nederland, Colorado

Charon studied *The Starry Night*, which lay propped against the side of his bed, admiring the absolute beauty of the masterpiece. He practically swirled himself into the picture as the colors and lines and dimensions spun him into the darkened sky it portrayed. All his now. Lost to the world. He almost regretted taking such a famous and inspiring painting from human eyes. Almost. Except that he wanted it as the centerpiece of his living room. Besides, humanity loved a mystery. Americans craved a conspiracy theory. In that regard, Charon provided a service to them, as with his being the Christmas Eve serial killer. They could marvel for the rest of history at the brazen theft and awe at the fact that the masterminds behind it concealed themselves from all cameras, despite the incredibly tight security at MOMA and the urban atmosphere surrounding it. Too, they would wonder at the use of a dead person's identity. The killing would revolt them at the same time that it enticed them and pulled them further into the grip of the story. The news channels should actually pay Charon for the pleasure of covering the story, because without a terrorist attack, natural disaster, or other such calamity, no one turned to their constant cycle through mundane news. Now everyone would watch for a few days, anyway, to see if new clues emerged.

He could stare all night at Van Gogh's creation, but instead he got up and entered his secret laboratory. One more time he tested the blood, and it worked. He therefore shot from the lab, raced into his rooms and up his secret tunnel, and finally out into the bitterly cold Colorado night. The snow fell all around him, with few people venturing anywhere in the canyon because of the late hour and treacherous conditions. The wind nearly blew him over before he concentrated on planting himself in one spot. A perfect night, really, to conduct his last test.

Charon eventually found himself in Glen Haven on a narrow one-lane road up the side of a mountain and next to a creek. He followed it until he came upon a modest cabin that looked as if it might slide right onto the frozen water and rush down the slope. Peering into the window, he saw a solitary man watching television, wrapped tightly in a blanket. Middle-aged. By himself.

Charon walked around the dwelling and entered through the front door, as if he lived there. He made no attempt to conceal himself, even stomped the snow out of the bottom of his shoe to announce his arrival. He took in the cramped surroundings, with hunting gear, fishing poles, and half-finished projects lying on the floor. One table tilted to its left, missing a leg. Passing through the kitchen, he noticed its cleanliness but still with the counters full of notes and tchotchkes.

He stared right at the man as he finally went into the little sitting room, but the guy never moved a muscle until Charon stood directly in front of him. Even then, he lifted his head slightly, just enough so that his eyes went from staring at the television to looking at Charon.

"I always hoped someone would come to take me away."

Charon tilted his head and lowered his brow.

The man grinned—ironically, Charon assumed—and nodded his head. "I sensed you outside. Come for me. Good. Let's be done with this shit." He waved his hand to indicate his surroundings, as if that explained everything. "I don't mind your testing on me before you do it."

"How did you know all of that?" Charon finally spoke in a whisper.

He shrugged. "A curse. My whole life, I hear what people think. See shit. Can't escape it. Tinfoil over all the windows never worked. Then, tried to take care of it myself a few times, but I'm a total coward and backed out every time. Hell, I may have succeeded this time, who knows. Because either chance brought you here, or all my attempts to call evil finally worked."

He unwrapped the blanket and stood up. From the window, he had appeared a lot older than the man in about his forties standing before Charon. His sunken eyes with dark circles told the tale even better than his words.

"I ain't interested in telling you my whole story. I'd rather just be done with it."

Charon smiled. "I'm not that interested in your life, either. I'd like to hurry, too."

He yanked down the collar of his T-shirt to further expose his neck. "Then just do it."

Charon obeyed. He lunged forward, took hold of the man, and sunk his fangs deep inside the main artery. Just before death, however, he pushed him away, bit into his own wrist, and his vampire blood dripped onto the floor. Before the wound healed itself, Charon enchanted the spell and pressed his arm against the man's lips, who drank involuntarily, his mind wanting to die but his evolutionary instincts fighting to survive.

He transformed into a somewhat handsome man of average height, perhaps in his mid-twenties, slight of build with short brown hair. He looked at himself and nodded, but his eyes remained unchanged pools of dread. They still looked vacantly at Charon. They continued to plead for death.

"You need me to try to get away." As he finished the sentence and with the speed of a newborn vampire, he spun around, smashed through the window, and began to sprint up the mountainside.

Charon remained in the room and just thought the command. *Halt.* Out the window, the man lurched to a stop and stood frozen on the hillside. *Return.*

He walked casually back down the mountain, climbed through the window, and once again stood in front of Charon.

"Worked. Now finish me off."

"You tried to get away?"

He nodded. "Yeah. I was running my ass off, not knowing where to go, really, thinking maybe you'd chase after me or something, but instead, even though I kept telling my legs to fuckin' run, they planted themselves right there like a tree. Then they spun me around, and I was commanding my body to come back right here."

"Fascinating." Charon smiled, unable to contain his excitement at the success of his spell.

To end the man's misery, and perhaps as a thank-you for assisting him so pleasantly, Charon immolated him with a spell in a matter of seconds. Once outside, he watched for a few minutes as the cabin, too, went up in flames.

A short time later, Charon found himself back in his underground palace, carrying *The Starry Night* from his room and down to the living room, where he covered it with a cloth. He summoned Jordan on the intercom, and seconds later, he sashayed into the room, wearing a light green swimsuit, as if enjoying a day at the beach.

"Boss man!" He grinned and winked. "What's up?"

"I need you to gather everyone into the room at once. I have a gift for all of you and an important announcement. Or perhaps I should say, offer."

Jordan tilted his head slightly, the smile disappearing. "Sounds serious."

"It is. But nothing to worry about. Good news all around."

Jordan smiled again. "Swag. You had me worrying for a minute."

"You'll find this rather wicked, actually."

Jordan beamed. "Wicked? Really! Next you'll be using chill-tastic, just like me. I'll round 'em up. Any special attire for the day?"

"Whatever. Nothing specific required."

Charon waited for the boys to congregate, standing in the living room and admiring the grandeur of the space. He still often marveled that he had built this palace with his own hands. His mind drifted to the future, where soon he would command a brigade of vampires instead of a human harem. Eventually he must reveal to them what Jaret explained, that a war was coming, one in which their services were required for the greater good of vampires. Charon must convince even himself of the necessity of participating in such a thing, when all his life he had worked against conformity or worrying about the welfare of the masses over himself.

But he trusted Jaret. For whatever reason, they developed a connection, an intimacy, and it lured Charon into believing what he said, and knowing that his army must assist in this endeavor. Charon would create this defense force, and then use it in this impending battle against those Christians. A shadow force that he commanded, and that only Jaret otherwise knew existed.

As his boys trickled into the room, however, Charon determined to wait for another day to tell them about combat and their role in it. Tonight, they must celebrate.

To heighten the anticipation and excitement, he greeted each of them with a long, lingering kiss as they came into the room. When everyone assembled, Jordan winked at Charon and plopped down on the floor, right at his feet.

"Tonight is a very special night, for all of us. You'd never guess what I'm about to offer you. First, though, a gift. Because I love all of you. Your obedience is important to me. I appreciate it. Your lust for life inspires me. Well, your lust in general does that." All of them snickered and laughed. "I'm not one for giving speeches or wasting time, so here goes."

Charon whipped off the sheet that covered the painting. A few of the boys tilted their heads, appreciating the painting but with no clue as to its story. Most seemed to recognize it as famous, but again nothing seemed to register. Except for Alex, the burly white football player from Detroit, who spent most of his time pretending to be straight, or straight-acting, despite liking to suck cock as much as the rest of them. He even adopted a somewhat dim-witted persona to go with the jock act, which he threatened to expose as false with his reaction to the painting.

He whistled. "Wow. Van Gogh. Intense."

"You know the painting?" Charon asked Alex.

"*The Starry Night*. Who doesn't know that?"

Charon laughed. "In this room, everyone but you."

"Oh! Right! I remember that from Art History class!" Todd chimed in with his Nashville Southern drawl. "Now I do."

A few others lit with recognition, and they took turns coming up to admire the painting. Together, the assembly took down the mundane print of a Pride Festival in Sydney, Australia, that hung over the fake fireplace and replaced it with *The Starry Night*. They admired it some more before Charon returned them to the business at hand.

"That was a gift to all of you." Charon pointed toward the painting. "A symbol of what you mean to me. But, despite its value, it's really the least important part of the night. I mean, I got it partially just because I wanted it." They laughed at him.

Kiki's shot his arm into the air, powered by his enormous bicep, smiling slightly with luscious lips, and his brown eyes twinkling with curiosity. "So what's up?"

"Yeah! Tell us!" Phil bounced up and down on the couch as he yelled.

Soon everyone chimed in and pleaded for information, until Charon held up his hand and asked for quiet.

"I have another offer for each of you. If you'll recall, before we brought you into my legion"— Charon swept his hand over the crowd to indicate all of them, giggling a bit at calling them a legion—"you agreed to do so for life. To remain trapped in my palace, but with all the amenities you could imagine. My proposal significantly changes that reality. As before, you may accept or decline. That's up to you."

"What is it?" Phil again, bouncing around with excitement.

Joe jumped out of his chair, his dreadlocks whipping around as he fell into Charon and clung to his waist while dropping to his knees. "The anticipation is killing us!" Everyone in the room cackled at the dramatic antics, thus helping Joe with his need for an audience from time to time.

Charon lifted him to his feet and pinched his butt. "Sit that cute ass down, and we'll get to it a lot faster."

Even Jordan fidgeted in front of Charon. Of course, because of the skimpy swimsuit and Jordan's general demeanor, the anticipation made him hard enough that the tip of his penis winked at Charon.

"You'll have two choices." Charon stared at each one of them in turn. "First, you may remain as you are. Nothing, really, to explain on that front. You'll stay in the palace, fully provided for, maintain it, but play, enjoy yourself, and nothing will change from your current situation. Except that gradually you'll grow old. At some point in the future, you'll die."

The boys started glancing at one another. More of them twitched around nervously, and they looked at Charon as if daring themselves to believe what he might next offer. Hoping, but trying desperately to quash it, lest it be something else completely.

"Or—" Charon paused. "Or, you'll still be beholden to me, completely. You'll still obey my commands. Your freedom will continue to be at my behest. So you'll have greater opportunities to venture out of the palace. To go places. But always at my will. And always with the provision that I could call you to me at a moment's notice. You won't be able to defy me. Understood?"

They all nodded, though still confused as to the actual offer on the table.

"I created a potion. As you know, I'm a vampire."

They laughed at the ridiculous comment.

"Of course you knew that. But also a witch. You understood that, too. I can convert all of you into vampires. I *want* to give you eternal life. Your age will freeze at some ideal point. Your power will increase. You'll be able to accomplish everything you do at incredible speeds. Yes, you'll become vampires, just like me." As the boys began chatting away and growing in excitement, Charon clapped and brought their attention back to him. "But!" he yelled. "But—" His voice returned to normal. "The spell which will accompany the conversion will keep you beholden to me. There's no option in this. Either you remain human and in my palace, or you convert under these restrictions.

"I'll be able to call you to me at any time. I'll still control you. Oh, like me, you'll be hidden from the authorities who govern vampires, the Vampire Council. So we won't have their rules to follow. Just mine. You'll still maintain my palace. We'll still spend most time here. But you won't age. You won't get sick. It just adds a delightful new dimension to our existence together."

Jordan jumped to his feet, tilted his neck, and held his arms out to Charon. "Take me first. Right now." Everyone laughed at him. He straightened his posture and smiled widely. "So life continues like now except I won't get wrinkles, I live forever, and can fuck more forcefully. What's not to like? I'm all in. De-lish."

As Charon anticipated, it took little time for everyone to agree. Even Kevin, his older more-contemplative basketball player, wanted this alteration.

"Then let's begin. I'll take you in my quarters. Wait here and come up one at a time."

As Charon headed for the stairs, Jordan raced to follow him. "Me first!" he declared.

Charon stopped and grinned. "Actually, you last. Trust me."

Jordan mock frowned but returned to the room. Surprisingly, timid Todd, his little missionary from Romania, ran forward. "Can I be first?" he whispered to Charon.

Charon picked him up and rushed up the stairs, whispering into his ear as they went. "Of course, my little angel."

One by one, he converted them in the most sensual act ever performed with his little harem. They kissed and caressed him before engaging in a sexual act, different for each of his boys, until he bit into them just as they came, followed by forcing his blood into their mouth and chanting the spell that kept them under his control. He kicked them out immediately after finishing so he could move to the next one, until at long last Jordan raced into the room, completely naked and his cock engorged with blood.

"Come here, hot stuff." Charon grabbed him into a kiss and rubbed the precum over Jordan's penis, stunned to see his favorite minion struggling to keep from coming at this slight touch.

Jordan giggled and whispered into Charon's ear, "You've no idea how many times I fantasized about this moment. Do me. Please."

Despite fucking a few of the other boys, while some sucked his cock, and though each and every one of them came at the moment of transformation, Charon saved his own orgasm for Jordan. Sure, his vampire strength would allow full completion in one night with each and every one of them, a gay guy's dream of endless ejaculating, but he wanted this last conversion to be extra special and so had saved himself.

He spit on Jordan's ass, after the young man launched on the bed and wiggled it doggy style at him, then lustfully inserted his penis into the tight hole. As he pumped away, controlling his own desire to shoot immediately, he reached around and grabbed hold of Jordan's slight but lovely dick. It hardly took a minute before semen shot across the bed and Charon's muscles spasmed with his own orgasm.

Before the entire sensation of orgasm left them, he pushed Jordan flat onto his stomach and shoved his legs apart. With fangs descended, he licked at Jordan's ass and then bit into his taint, concentrating to pull enough blood out of this intimate area in order to kill his victim.

As life passed out of Jordan, Charon pushed himself up, rolled Jordan over, and propped him up with a hand, then forced his own still solid penis into Jordan's mouth after cutting it open with a fingernail.

Jordan sucked greedily at the blood as it transformed him, too, into a vampire. Charon continued to thrust in and out of Jordan's mouth, even after his penis healed and Jordan joined the undead, all the way until once again a thrill shot through his body and cum shot down Jordan's throat.

"Vampire sex rocks." Jordan smiled widely. "Fucking cray-cray. Delish cum, boss. Whoa."

"And you get to do that for an eternity."

Jordan rolled into Charon's arms and kissed him deeply.

After a moment of making out, Charon kissed Jordan's cheek. "We better get back to them."

Charon and Jordan hurried down the stairs and back to the living room, where the others sat talking about and experimenting with their new vampire powers.

To test his potion, Charon ordered them all to sit in front of him for instruction by doing nothing more than thinking the command and willing it into action. They complied within seconds, each staring eagerly into their master's eyes.

"Gents, you've a lot to learn about being a vampire. Over the next few nights, I'll instruct you. But—" Charon held up a finger and paused. "—not tonight. For your first night as vampires, we party!"

And party hard they did, with drinks, sex, games, and all the revelry one might expect from a group of horny and powerful young gay men with nothing to worry their little heads.

Charon participated and watched with amused fascination, excited and proud of his creation. Yet in the back of his mind lurked concern about how he also destined this White Party to become a Vampire Brigade in an impending war.

About the Author

Damian Serbu lives in the Chicago area with his husband and two dogs, Akasha and Chewbacca. The dogs control his life, tell him what to write, and threaten to eat him in the middle of the night if he disobeys. He previously authored several novels now out of print, and is excited to reignite his writing with Ninestar Press! Coming this fall, his latest vampire novel: *The Vampire's Protégé*.

Email: DamianSerbu@aol.com

Facebook: www.facebook.com/Damian-Serbu-267169761008/

Twitter: @DamianSerbu

Website: www.DamianSerbu.com

Coming Soon from Damian Serbu

The Vampire's Angel

Set during the French Revolution, *The Vampire's Angel* traces the lives of three characters: a Parisian priest (Xavier), his noble sister (Catherine), and a vampire from America (Thomas). The priest and vampire fall in love, but hardship ensues as they struggle with separate demons. Thomas resists his impatience and temper, while hiding his undead nature from the man he loves. Xavier combats a devotion to the church and societal obligation, both of which speak against following his heart. As France crumbles around them, Catherine fights to maintain the family's fortune, even as she falls prey to the schemes of a witch doctor who casts a spell upon her. Will the death, danger, and catastrophes of a revolution doom these three, or will they find solace from one another and ultimate harmony? Find out in *The Vampire's Angel*.

Also Available from NineStar Press

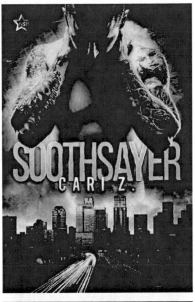

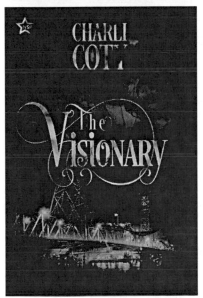

www.ninestarpress.com

CPSIA information can be obtained
at www.ICGtesting.com
Printed in the USA
LVOW11s2028210817
545870LV00001B/17/P